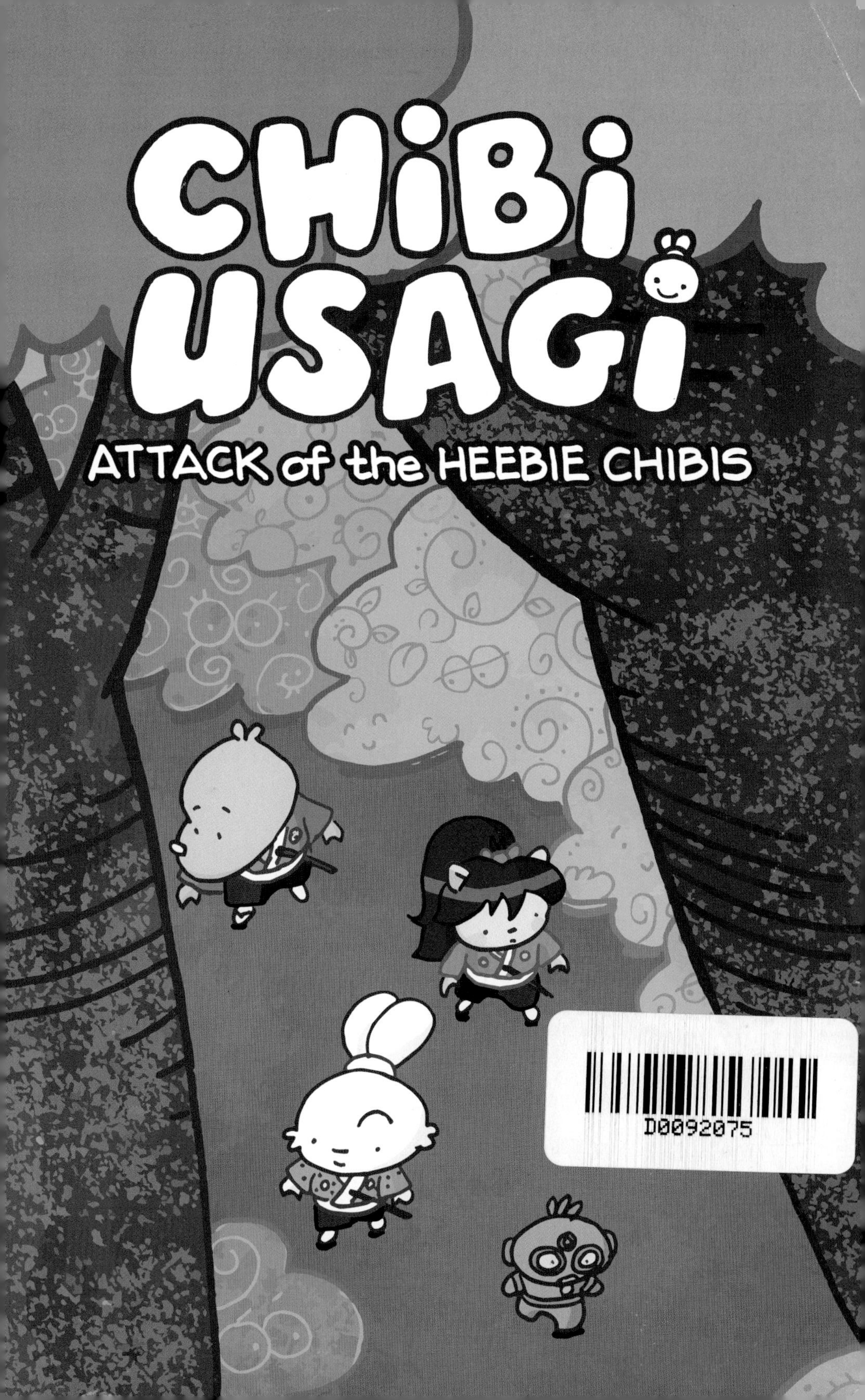
CHIBI USAGI
ATTACK of the HEEBIE CHIBIS

Cover Artist
Julie Fujii Sakai

Cover Colorist
Emi Fujii

Editor
Bobby Curnow

Collection Editors
Alonzo Simon
& Zac Boone

Collection Designer
Jessica Gonzalez

ISBN: 978-1-68405-790-0   24 23 22 21   1 2 3 4

Nachie Marsham, Publisher
Rebekah Cahalin, EVP of Operations
Blake Kobashigawa, VP of Sales
John Barber, Editor-in-Chief
Justin Eisinger, Editorial Director, Graphic Novels and Collections
Scott Dunbier, Director, Special Projects
Anna Morrow, Sr. Marketing Director
Tara McCrillis, Director of Design & Production
Shauna Monteforte, Sr. Director of Manufacturing Operations

Ted Adams and Robbie Robbins, IDW Founders

Facebook: **facebook.com/idwpublishing**
Twitter: **@idwpublishing**
YouTube: **youtube.com/idwpublishing**
Instagram: **@idwpublishing**

STORY BY

JULIE AND **STAN SAKAI**

ART BY

JULIE AND **STAN SAKAI**

COLORS BY

EMI FUJII

LETTERS BY

JULIE SAKAI

This project was a collaboration of our family

Daniel negotiated the contract, Emi did
the beautiful coloring and design work,
Julie and Stan wrote and did the art. This
could not have happened without the
love, encouragement, and respect we
have for one another.

We dedicate this book to you, our readers,
with much thankfulness and gratitude.
May this book inspire you to collaborate,
connect, and create.

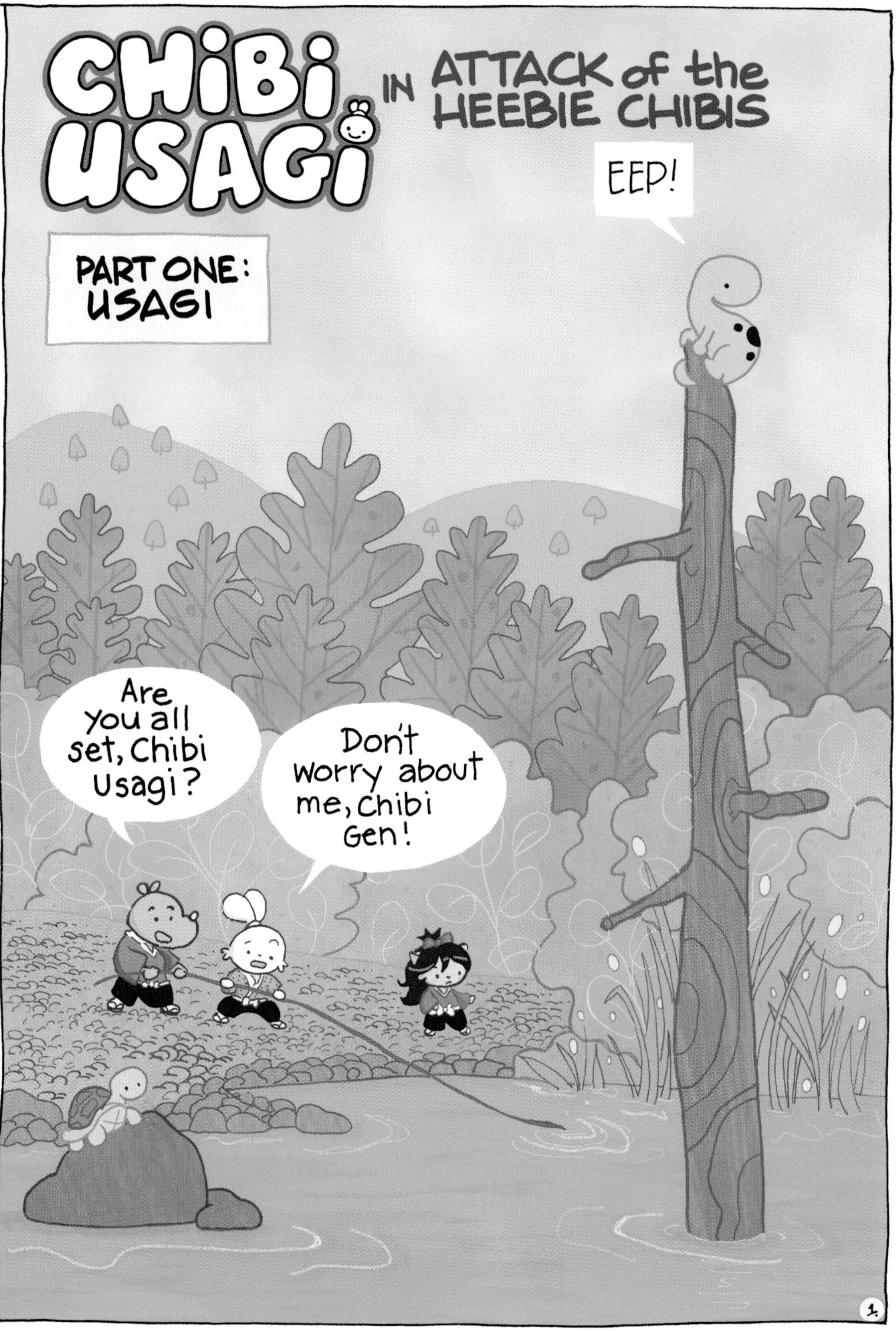
CHIBI USAGI
IN ATTACK of the HEEBIE CHIBIS
PART ONE: USAGI
EEP!
Are you all set, Chibi Usagi?
Don't worry about me, Chibi Gen!

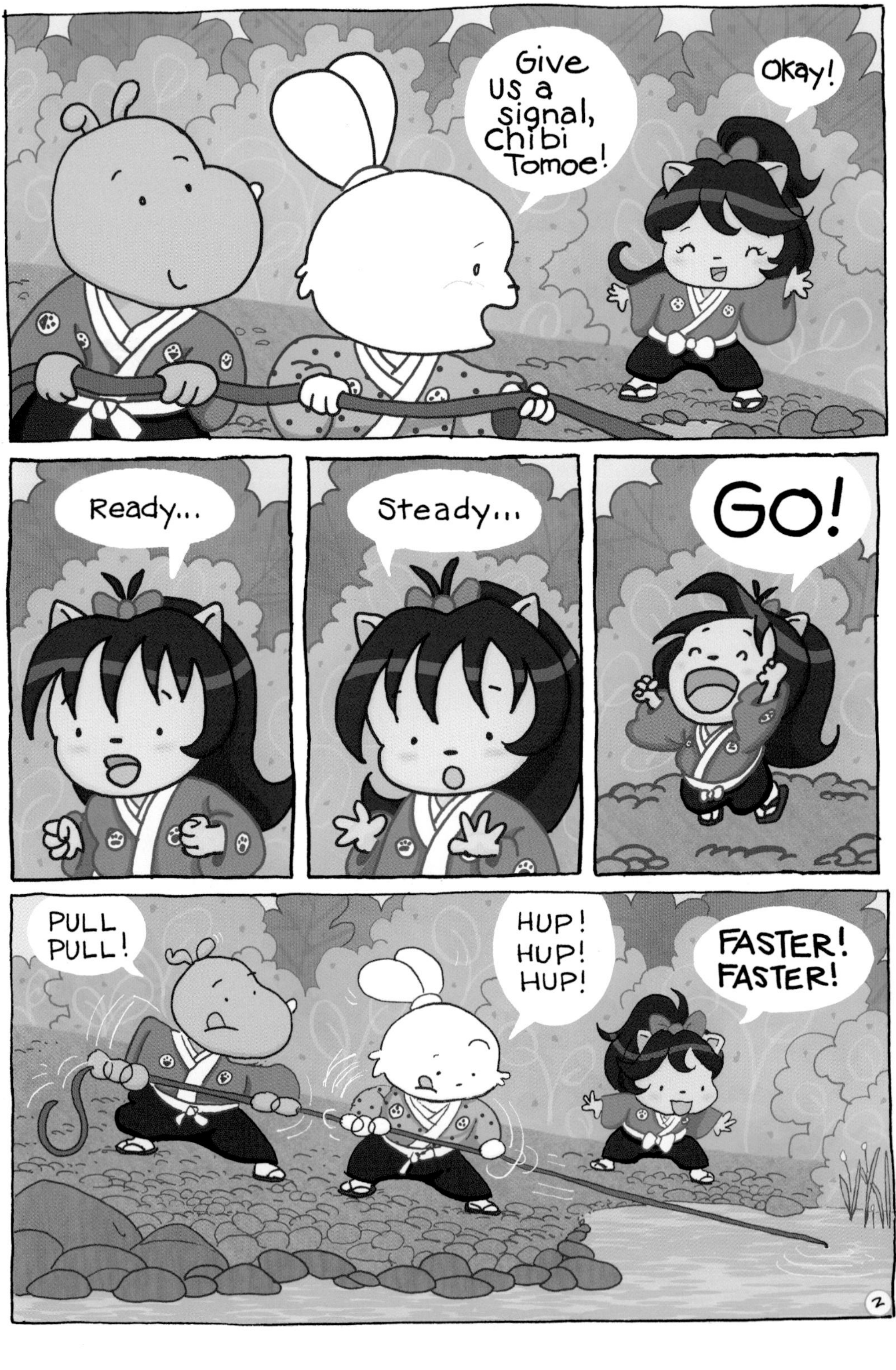
Give us a signal, Chibi Tomoe!
Okay!
Ready...
Steady...
GO!
PULL PULL!
HUP! HUP! HUP!
FASTER! FASTER!

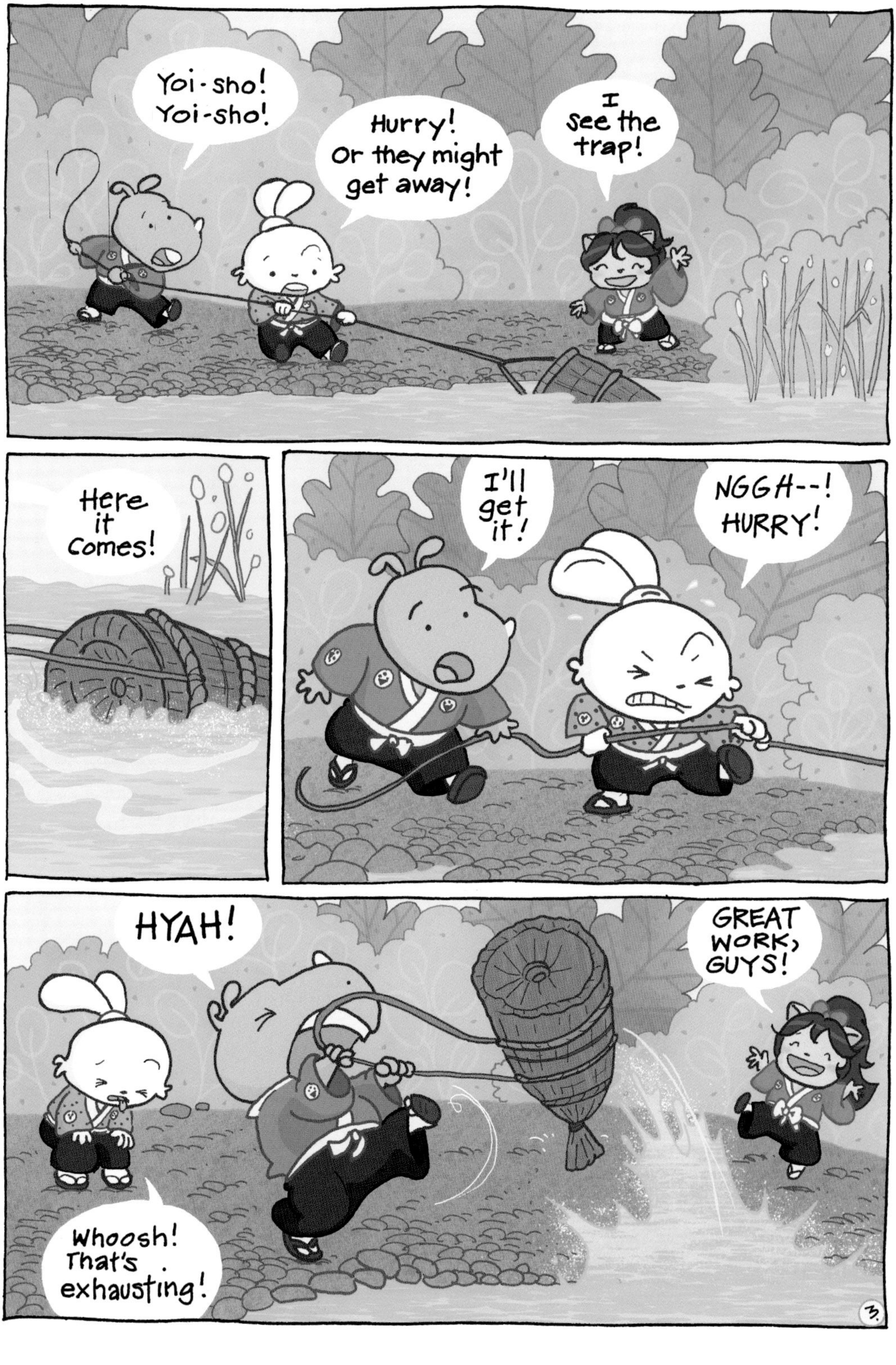
Yoi-sho! Yoi-sho!
Hurry! Or they might get away!
I see the trap!
Here it comes!
I'll get it!
NGGH--! HURRY!
HYAH!
GREAT WORK, GUYS!
Whoosh! That's exhausting!

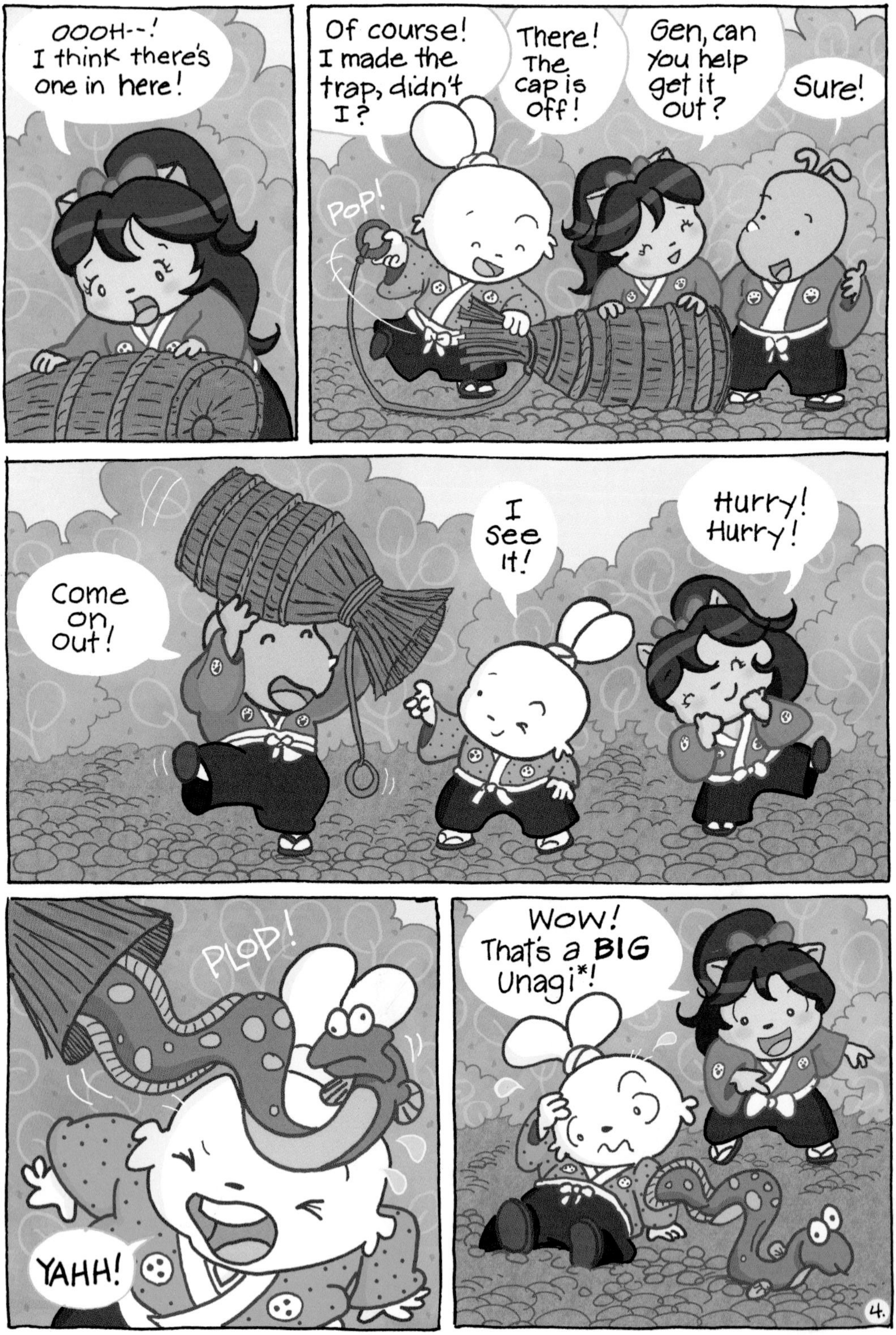
OOOH--! I think there's one in here!
Of course! I made the trap, didn't I?
POP!
There! The cap is off!
Gen, can you help get it out?
Sure!
Come on out!
I see it!
Hurry! Hurry!
PLOP!
YAHH!
WOW! That's a BIG Unagi*!
4.

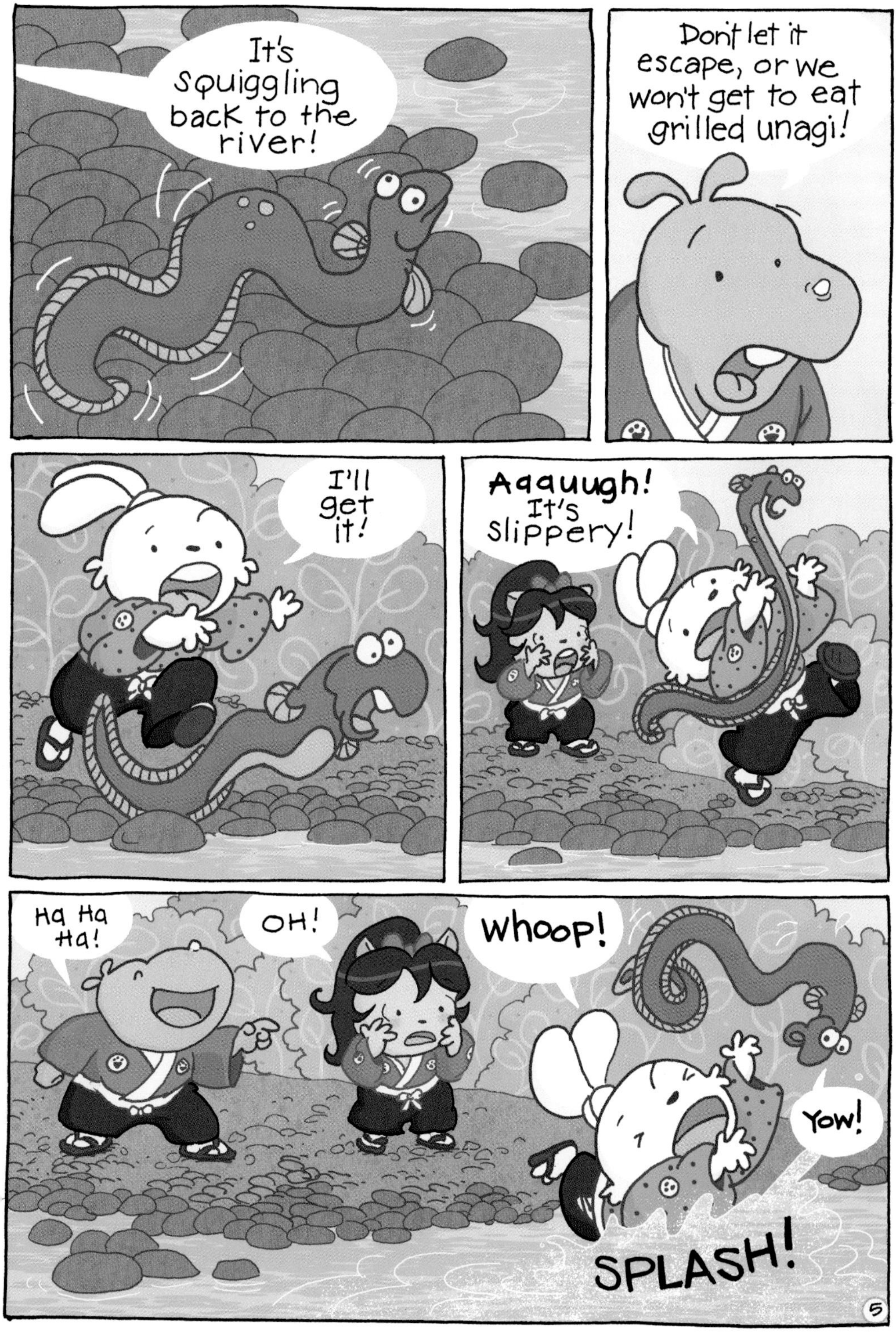
It's squiggling back to the river!
Don't let it escape, or we won't get to eat grilled unagi!
I'll get it!
Aaauugh! It's slippery!
Ha Ha Ha!
OH!
Whoop!
Yow!
SPLASH!

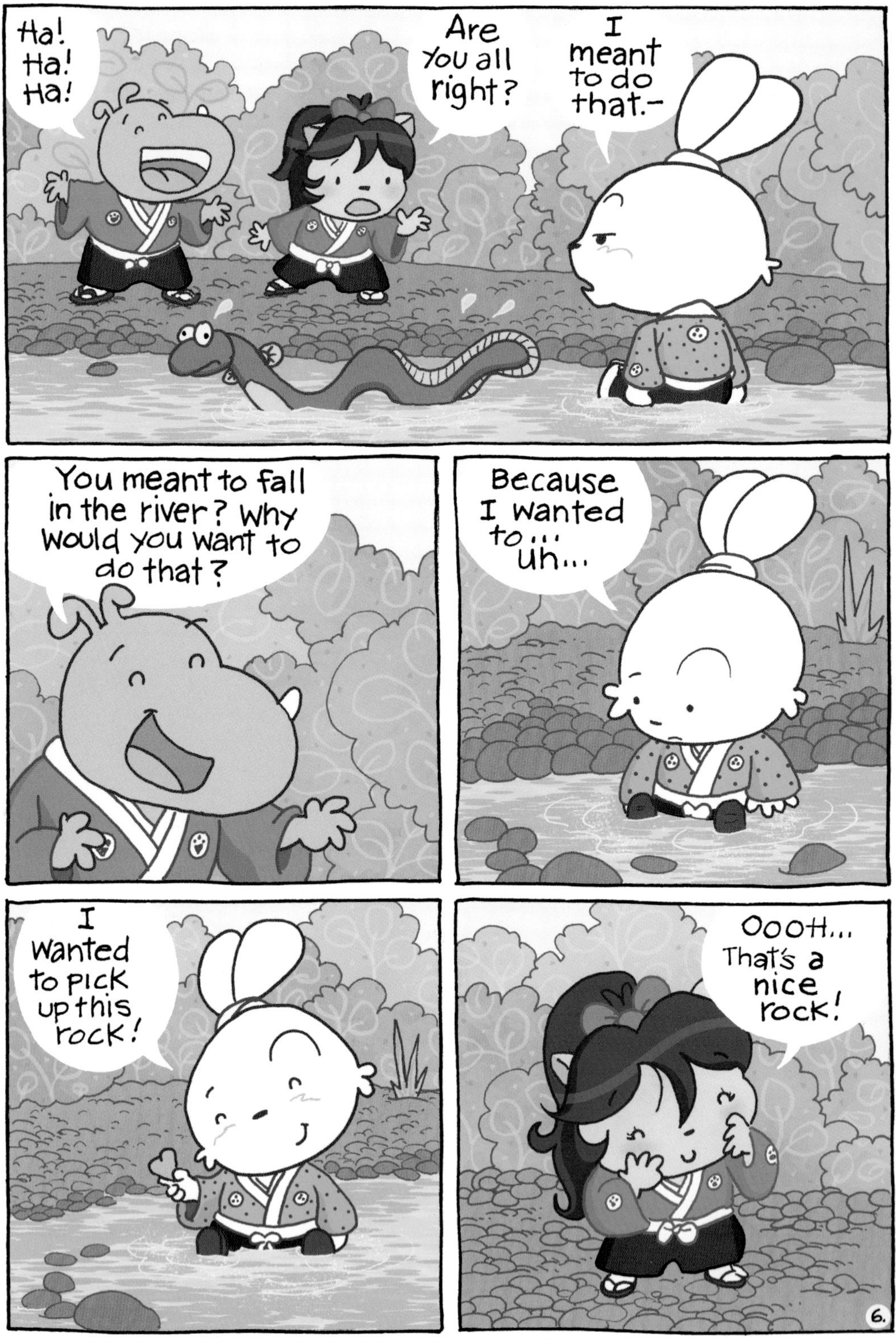
Ha! Ha! Ha!
Are you all right?
I meant to do that.–
You meant to fall in the river? Why would you want to do that?
Because I wanted to... uh...
I wanted to pick up this rock!
OOOH... That's a nice rock!

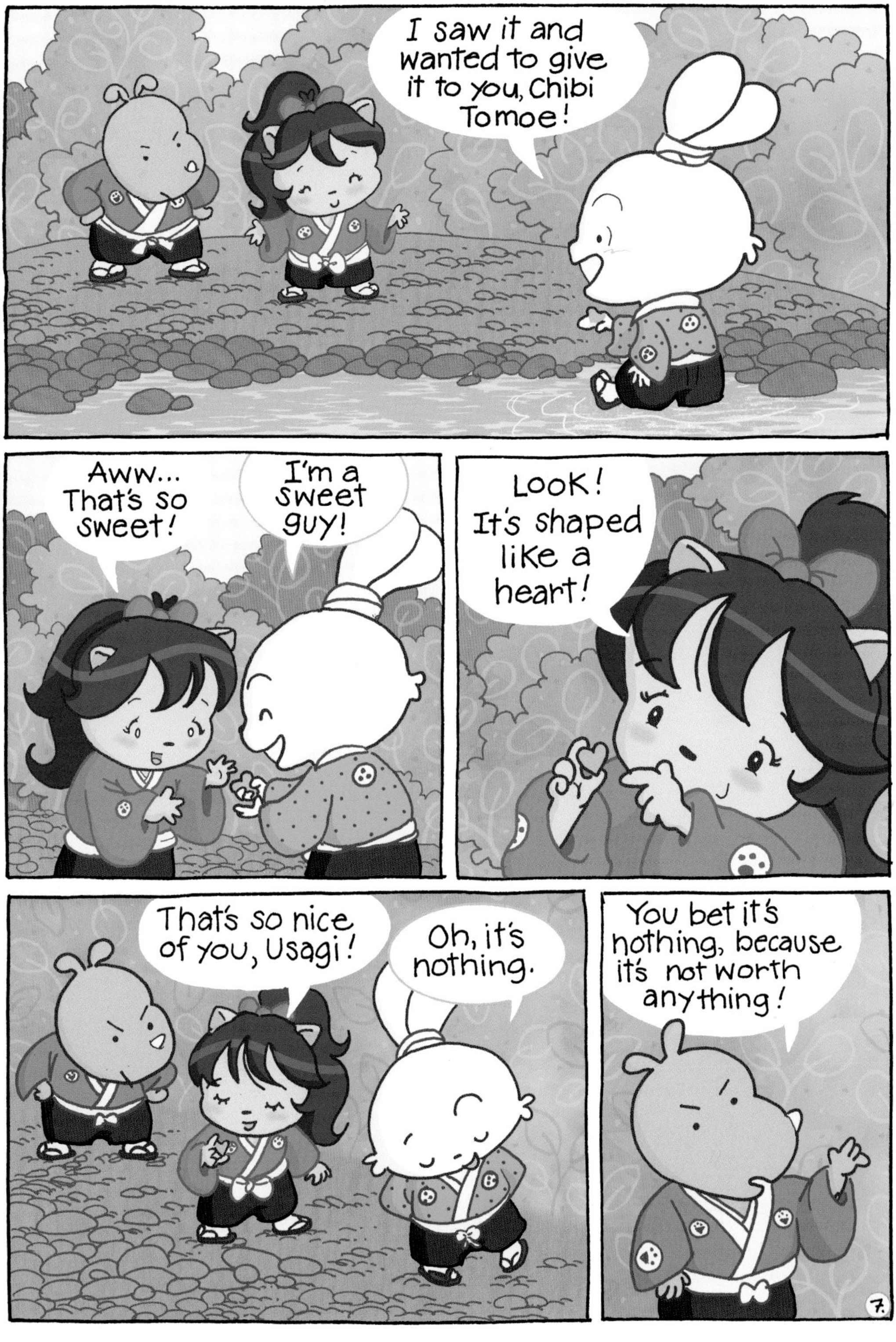
I saw it and wanted to give it to you, Chibi Tomoe!
Aww... That's so sweet!
I'm a sweet guy!
Look! It's shaped like a heart!
That's so nice of you, Usagi!
Oh, it's nothing.
You bet it's nothing, because it's not worth anything!
7.

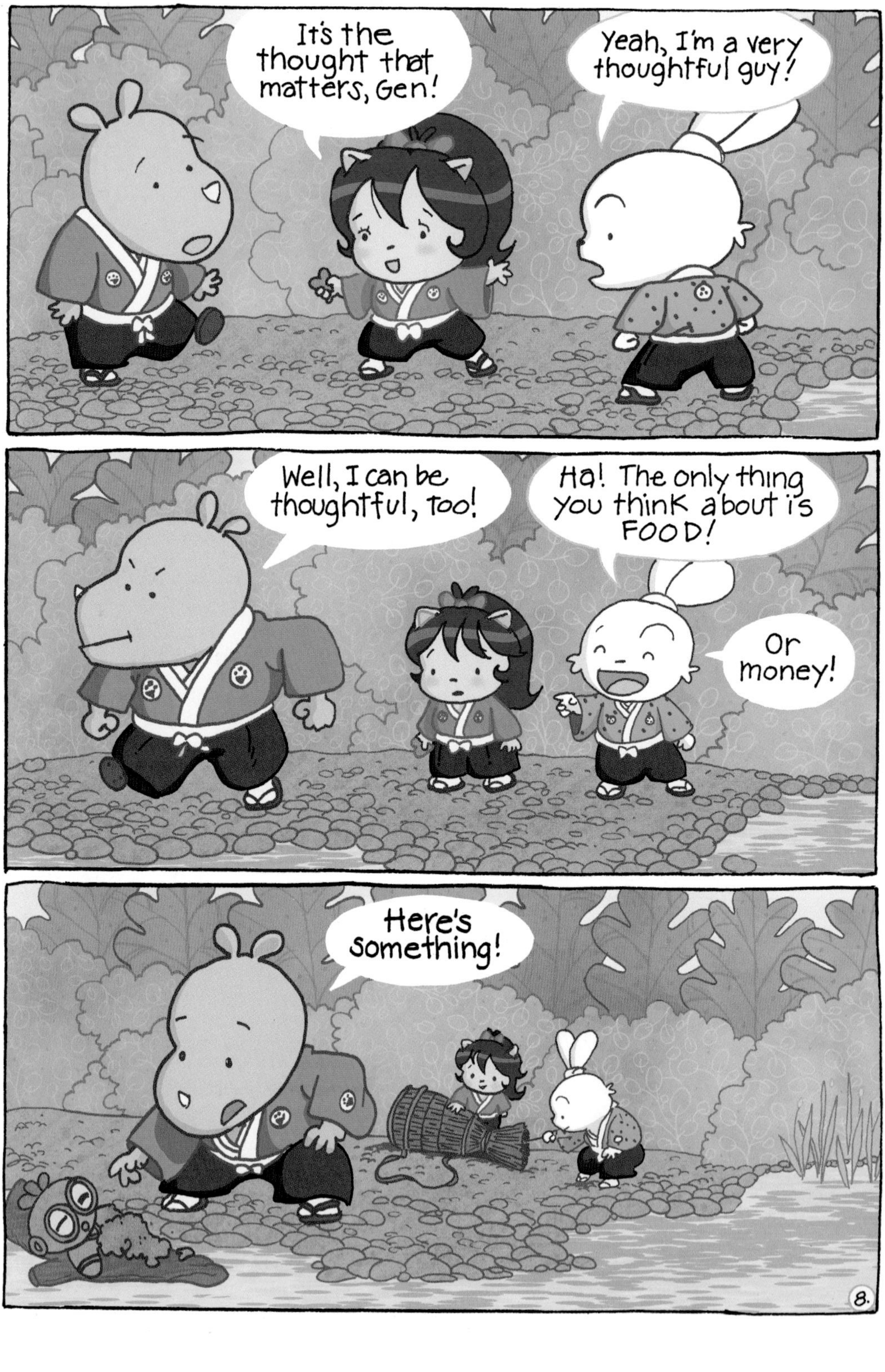

It's the thought that matters, Gen!
Yeah, I'm a very thoughtful guy!
Well, I can be thoughtful, too!
Ha! The only thing you think about is FOOD!
Or money!
Here's something!

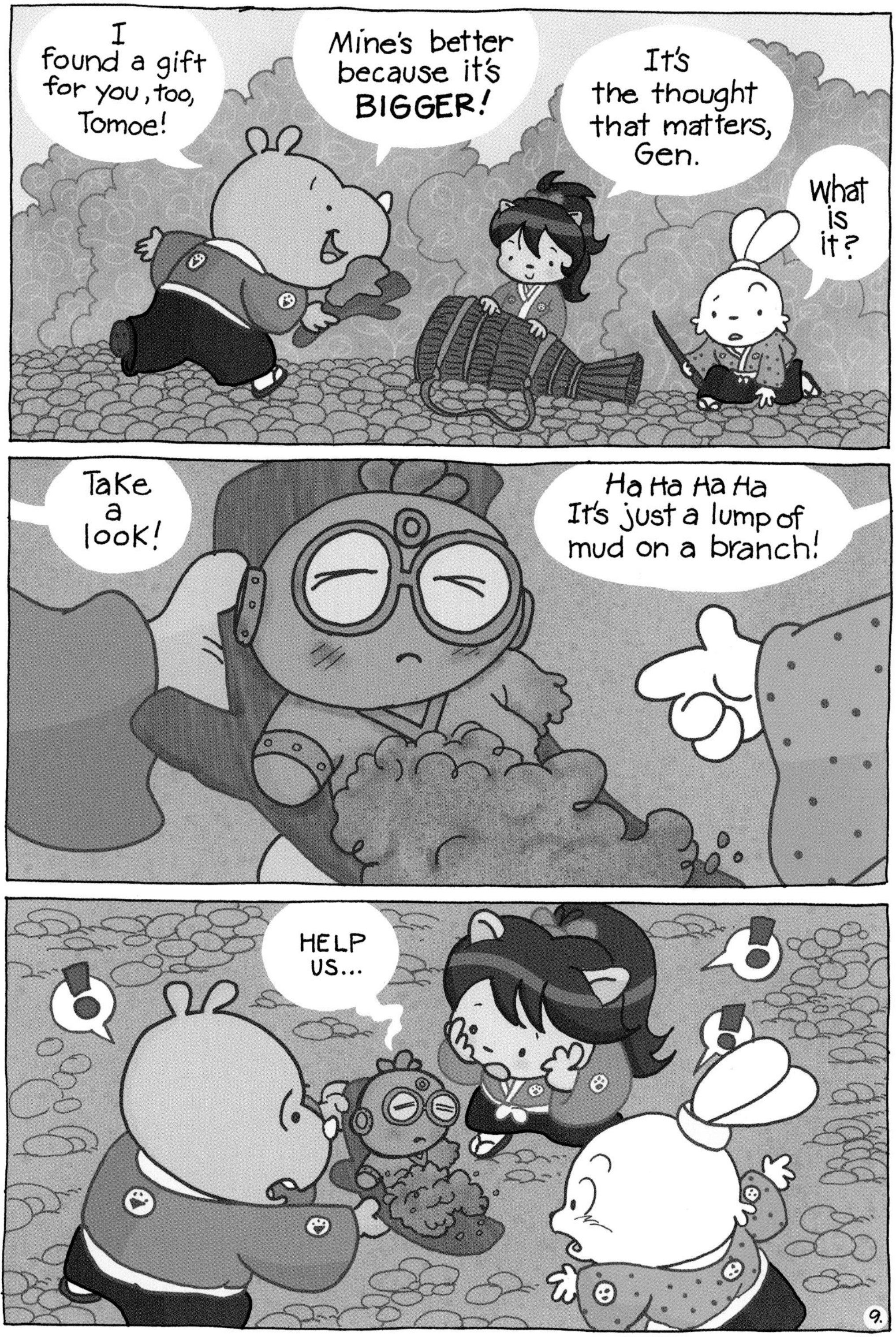
I found a gift for you, too, Tomoe!
Mine's better because it's BIGGER!
It's the thought that matters, Gen.
What is it?
Take a look!
Ha Ha Ha Ha
It's just a lump of mud on a branch!
HELP US...
!
!
!

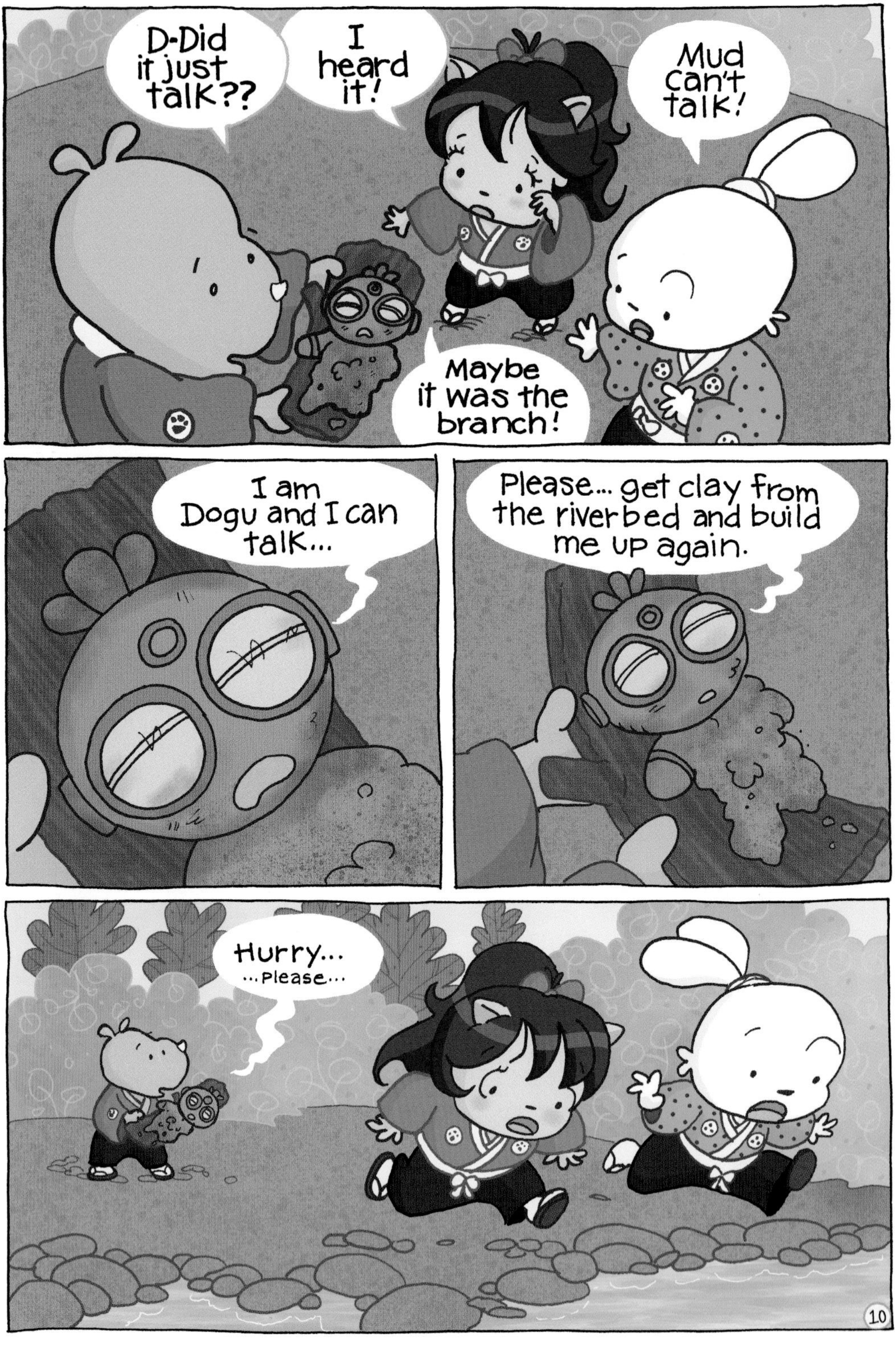
D-Did it just talk??
I heard it!
Mud can't talk!
Maybe it was the branch!
I am Dogu and I can talk...
Please... get clay from the riverbed and build me up again.
Hurry... ...please...

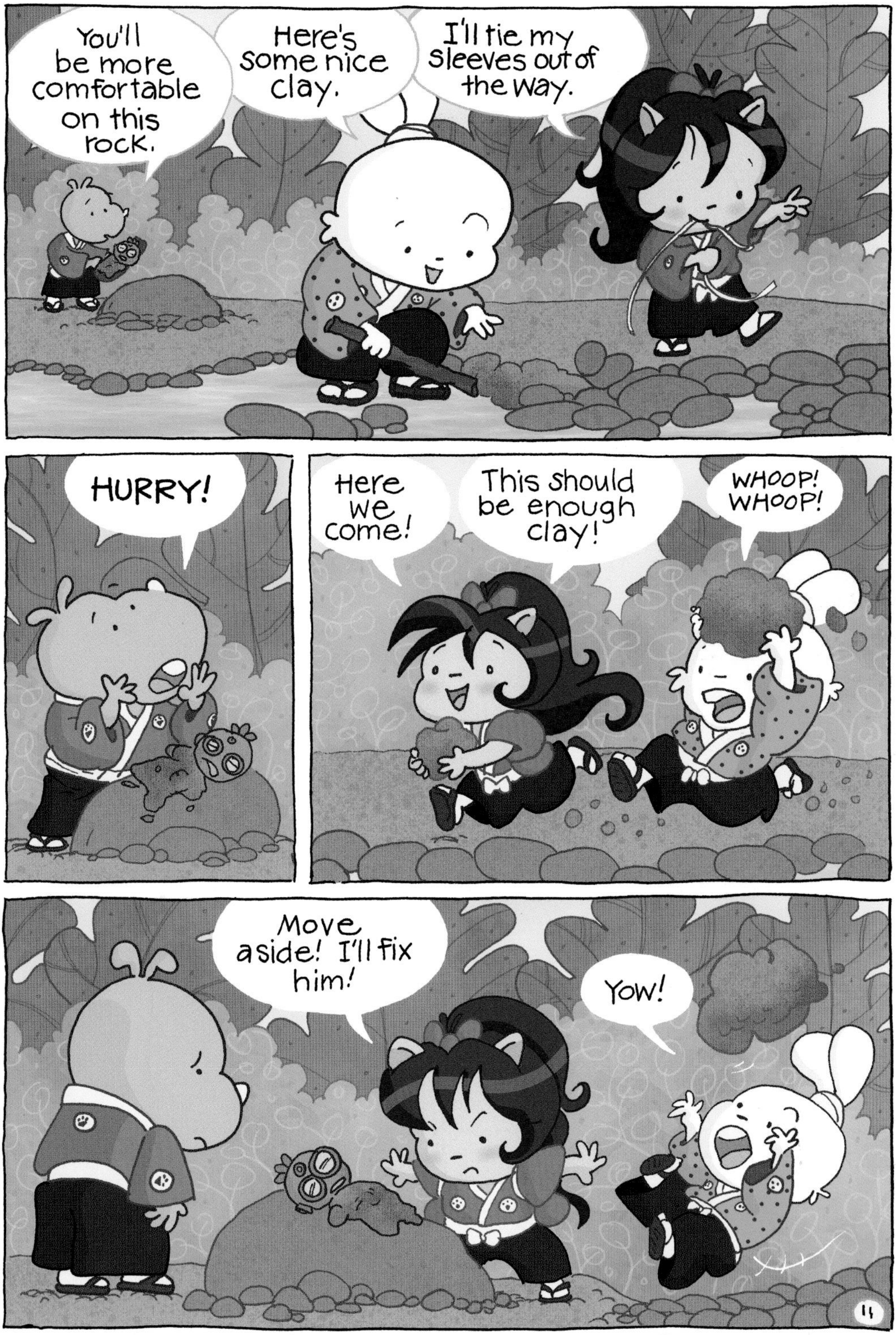
You'll be more comfortable on this rock.
Here's some nice clay.
I'll tie my sleeves out of the way.
HURRY!
Here we come!
This should be enough clay!
WHOOP! WHOOP!
Move aside! I'll fix him!
YOW!

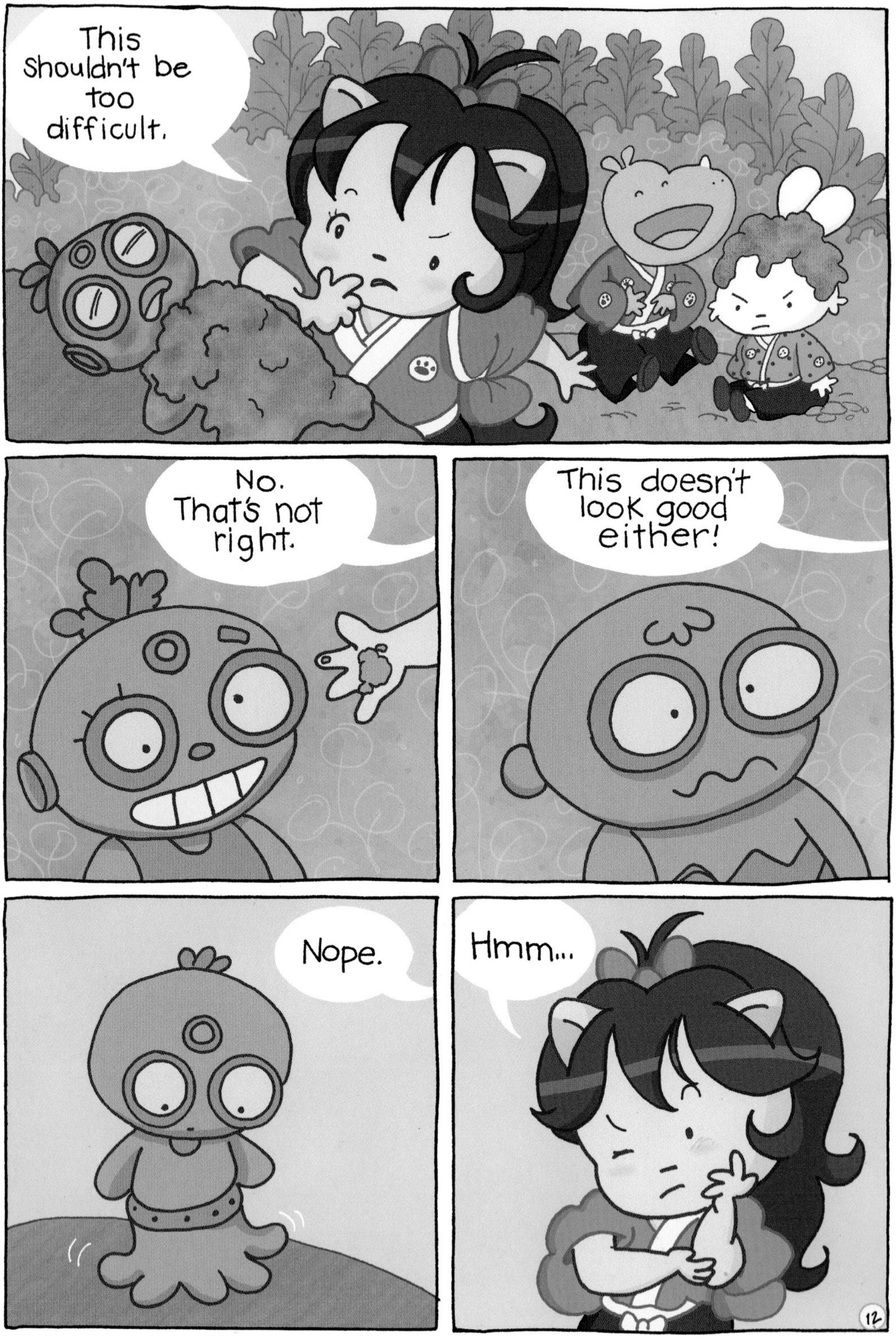
This shouldn't be too difficult.
No. That's not right.
This doesn't look good either!
Nope.
Hmm...
12

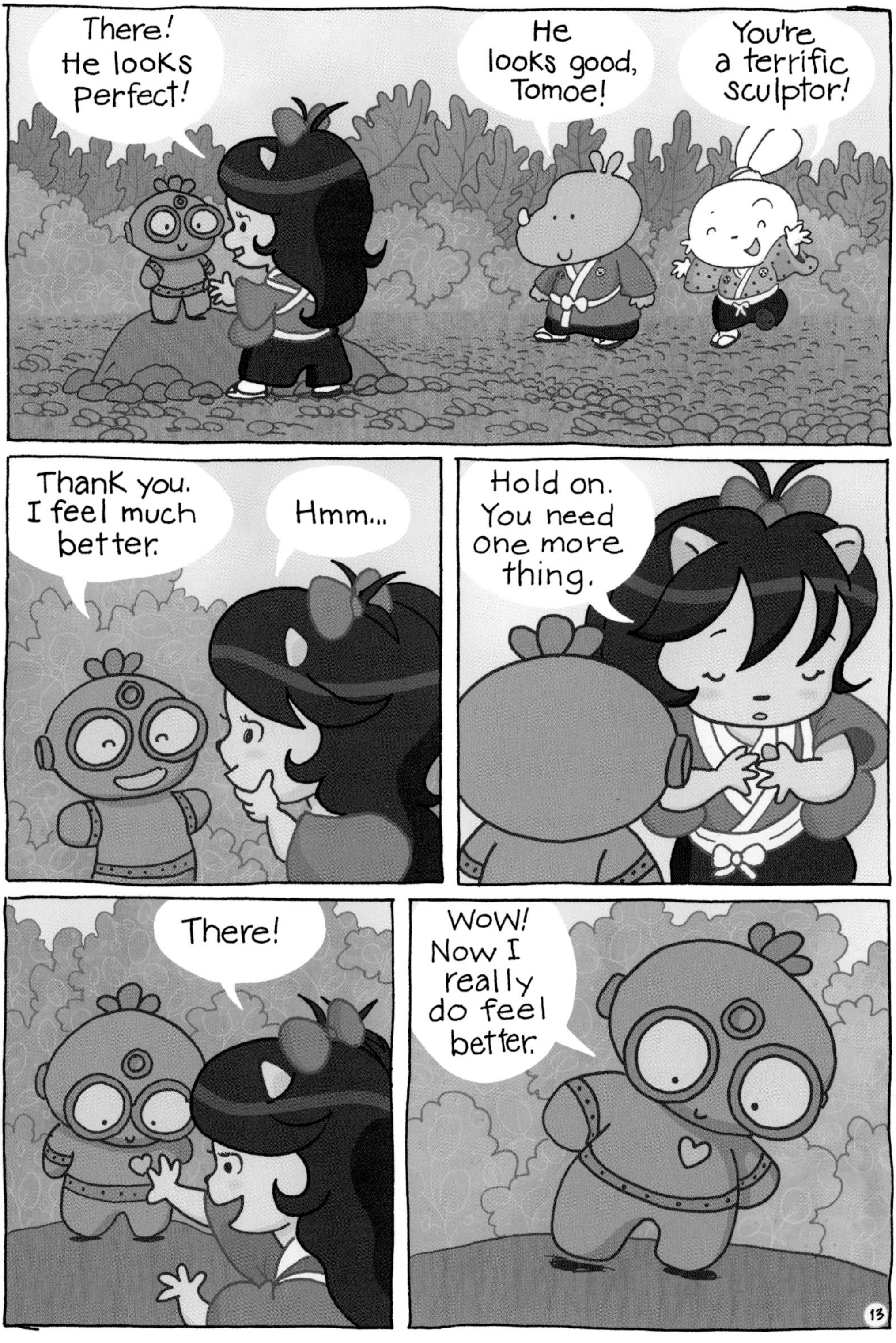
There! He looks perfect!
He looks good, Tomoe!
You're a terrific sculptor!
Thank you. I feel much better.
Hmm...
Hold on. You need one more thing.
There!
WOW! Now I really do feel better.

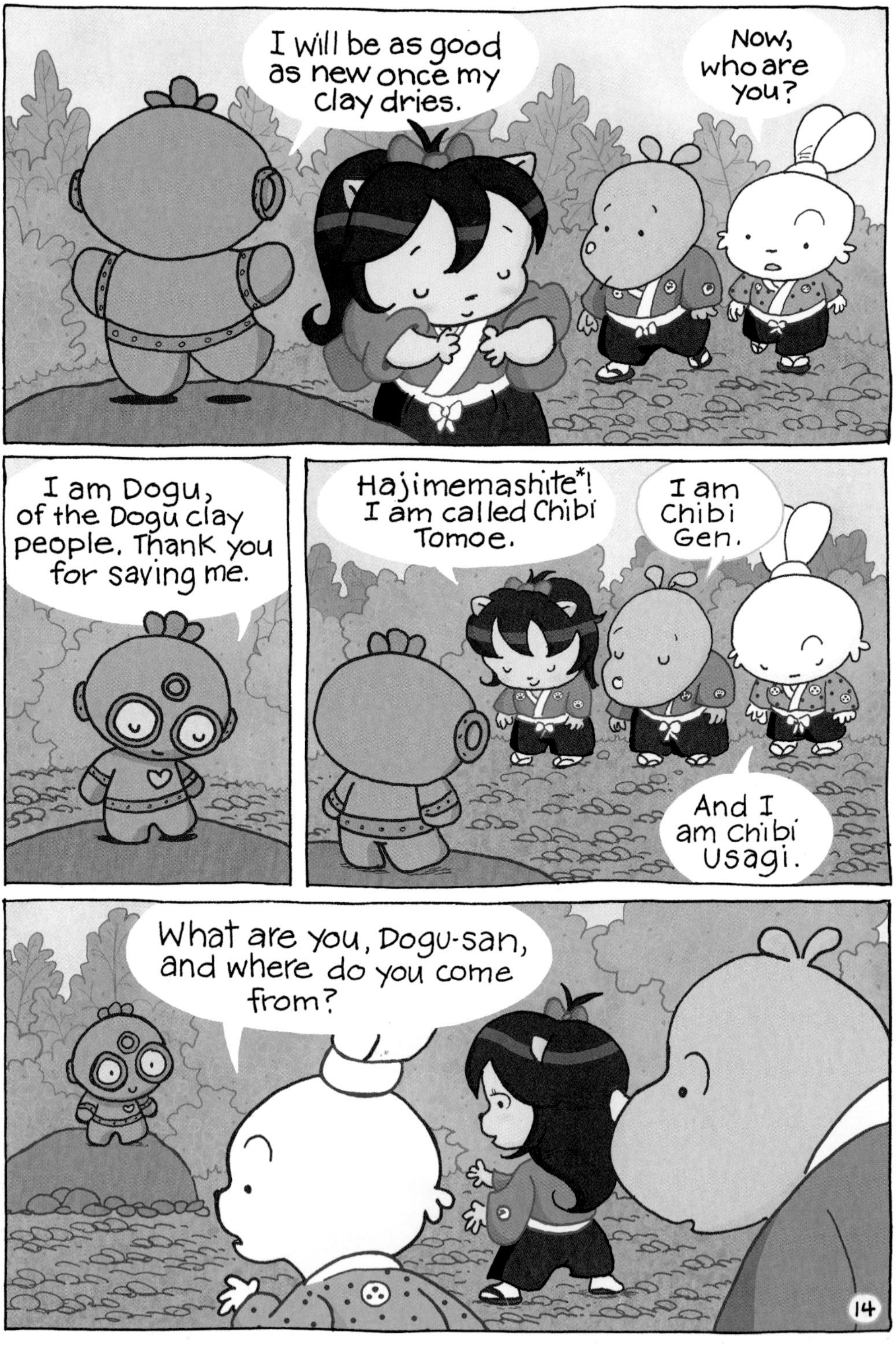
I will be as good as new once my clay dries.
Now, who are you?
I am Dogu, of the Dogu clay people. Thank you for saving me.
Hajimemashite*! I am called Chibi Tomoe.
I am Chibi Gen.
And I am Chibi Usagi.
What are you, Dogu-san, and where do you come from?

*"Nice to meet you for

PART TWO: DOGU'S STORY

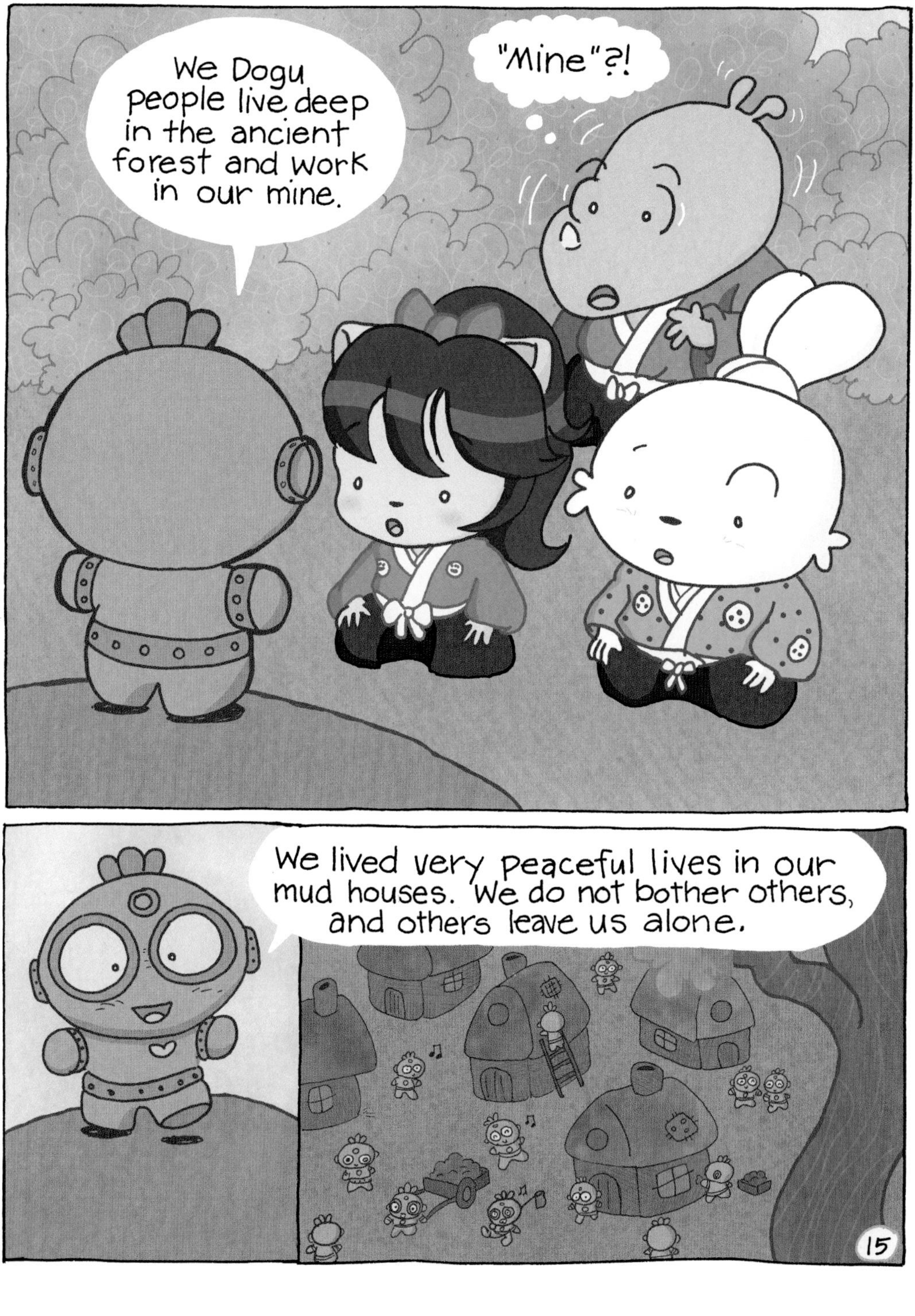
We Dogu people live deep in the ancient forest and work in our mine.
"Mine"?!
We lived very peaceful lives in our mud houses. We do not bother others, and others leave us alone.

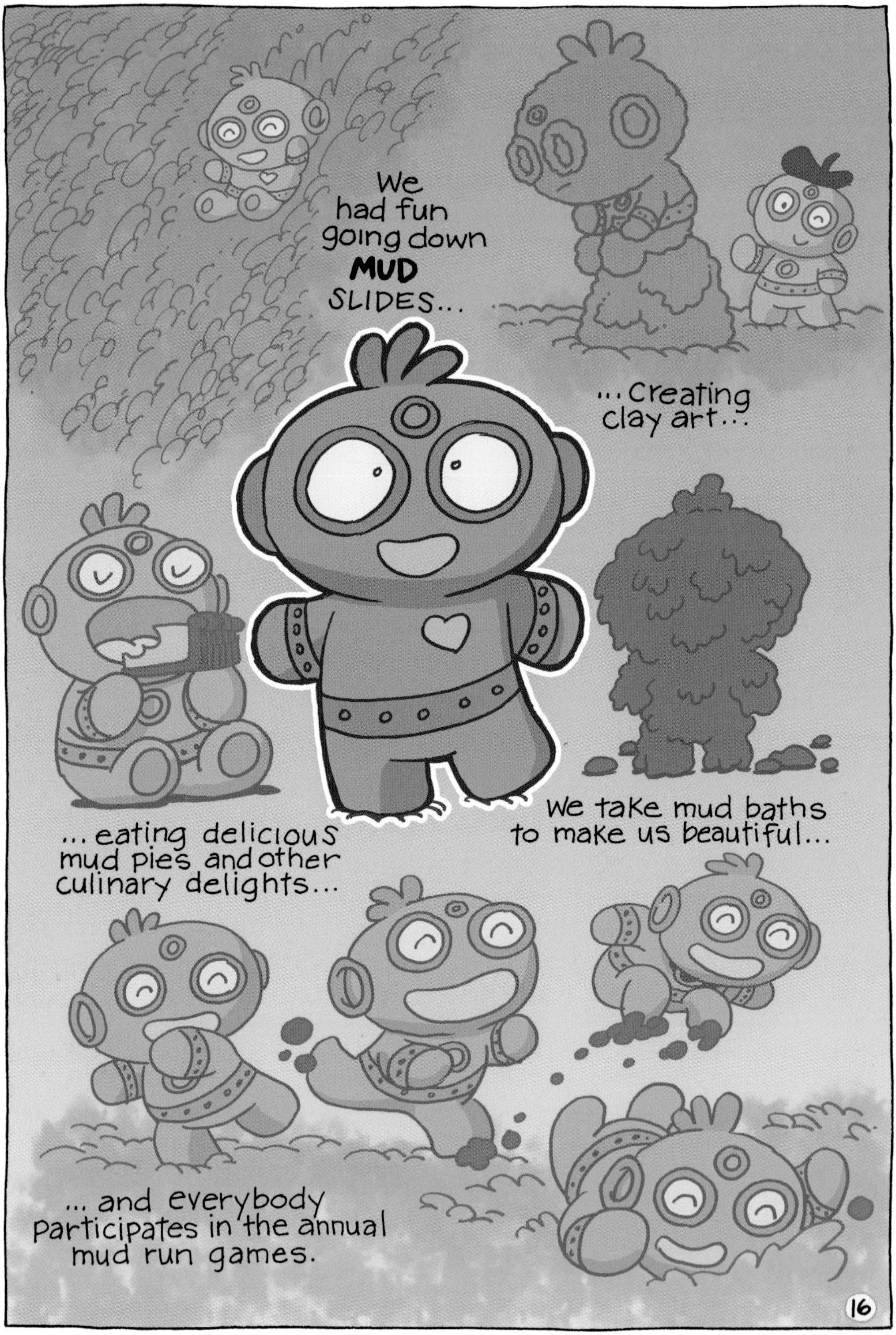
We had fun going down MUD SLIDES...
...creating clay art...
...eating delicious mud pies and other culinary delights...
We take mud baths to make us beautiful...
... and everybody participates in the annual mud run games.

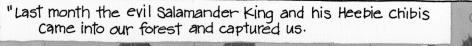
"Last month the evil Salamander King and his Heebie chibis came into our forest and captured us.

"We Dogus are forced to work as slaves in our own mine!

"He keeps us in line by threatening us with water that will dissolve us..."

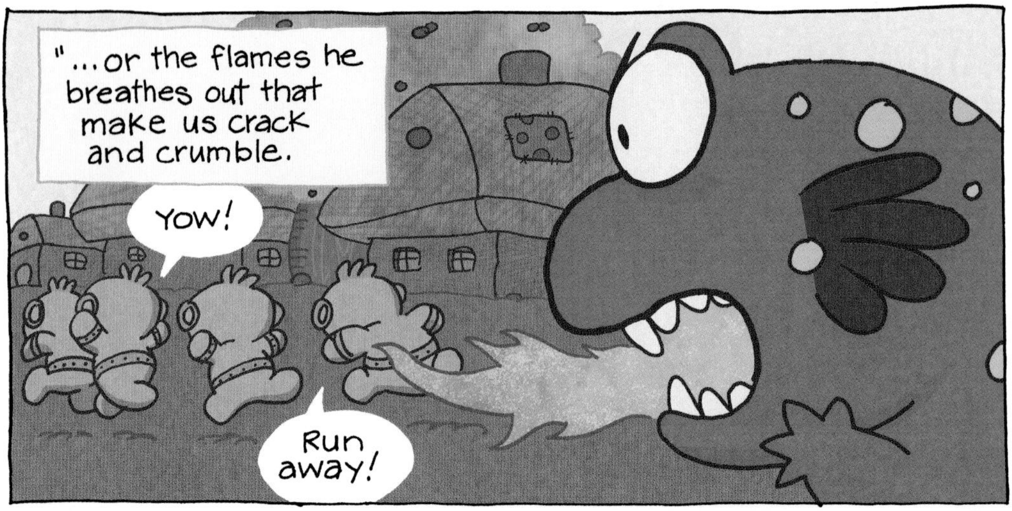
"...or the flames he breathes out that make us crack and crumble.
YOW!
Run away!

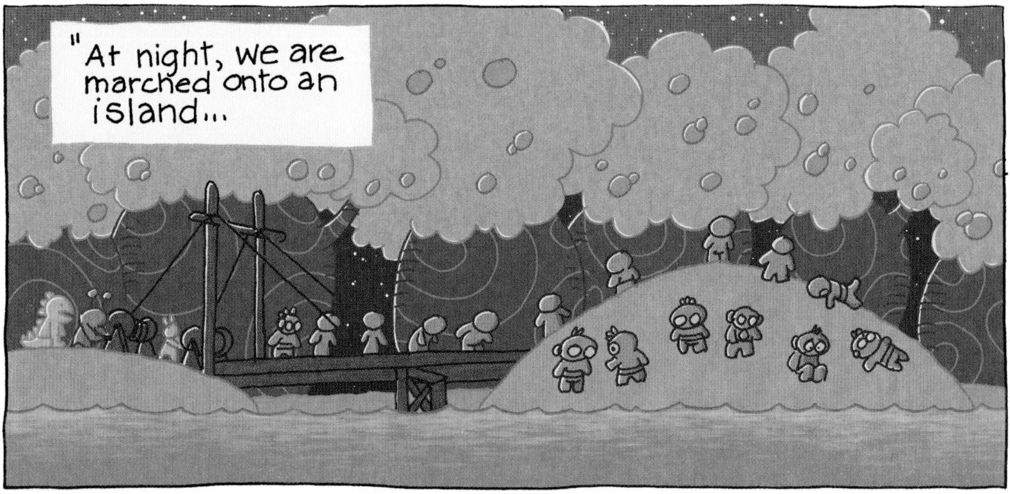
"At night, we are marched onto an island...

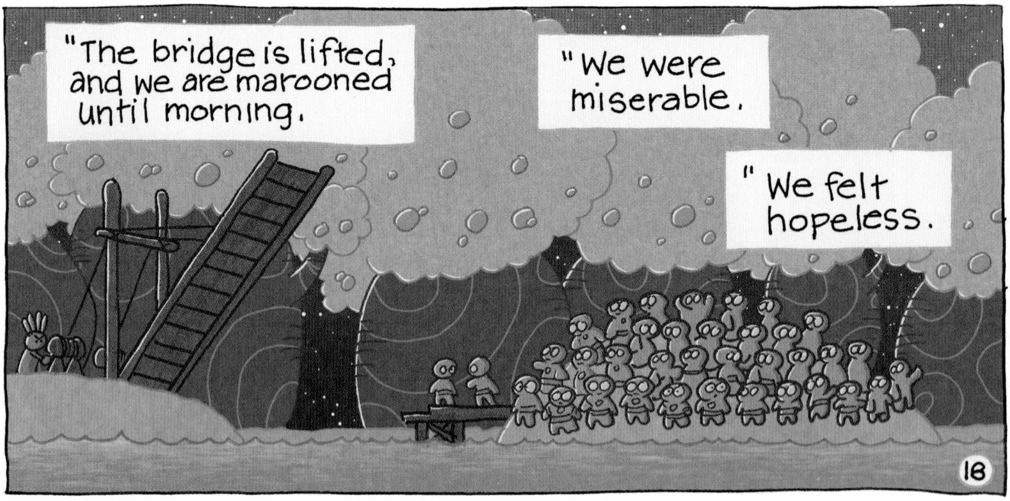
"The bridge is lifted, and we are marooned until morning.
"We were miserable.
"We felt hopeless.

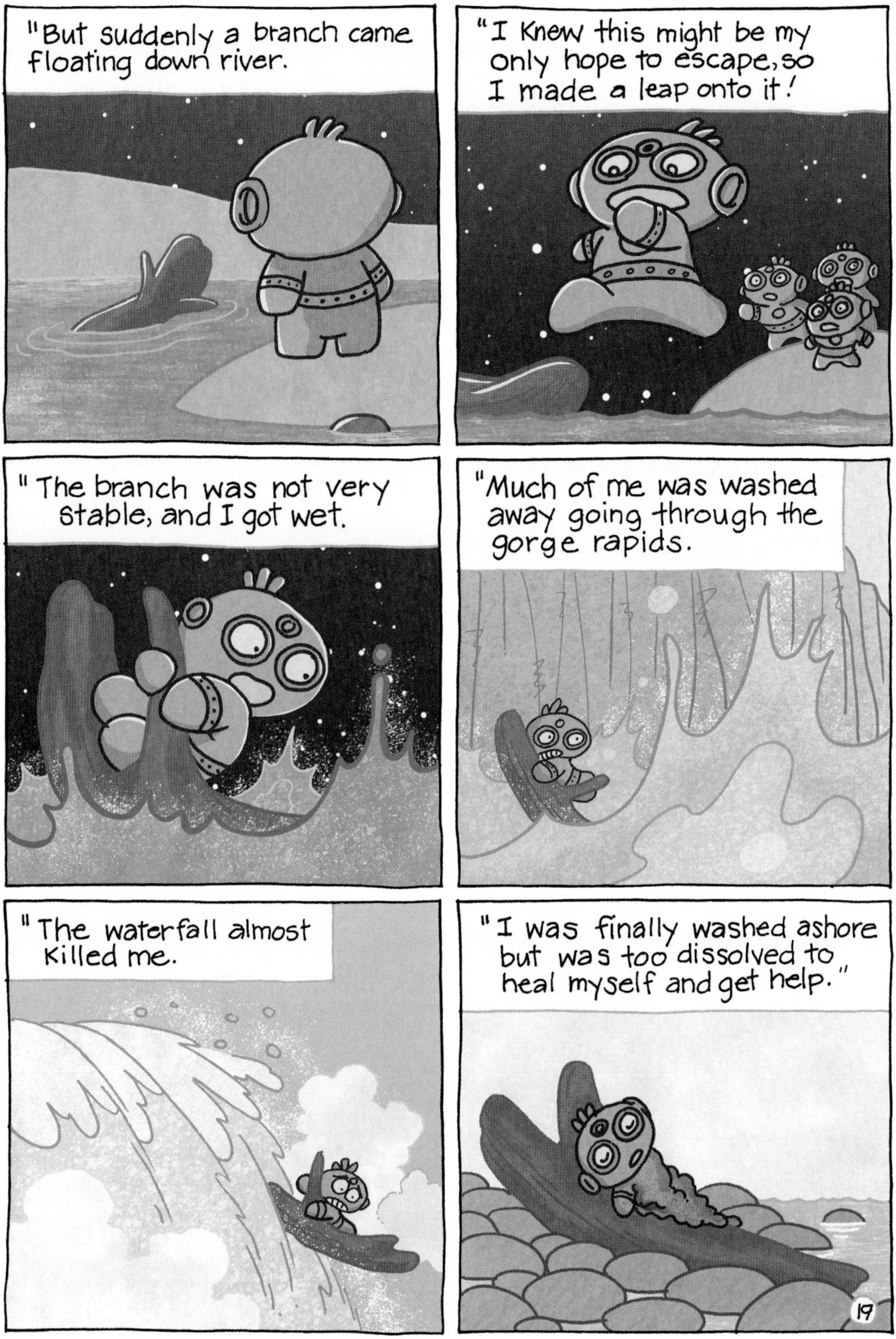
"But suddenly a branch came floating down river.
"I knew this might be my only hope to escape, so I made a leap onto it!
"The branch was not very stable, and I got wet.
"Much of me was washed away going through the gorge rapids.
"The waterfall almost killed me.
"I was finally washed ashore but was too dissolved to heal myself and get help."
19

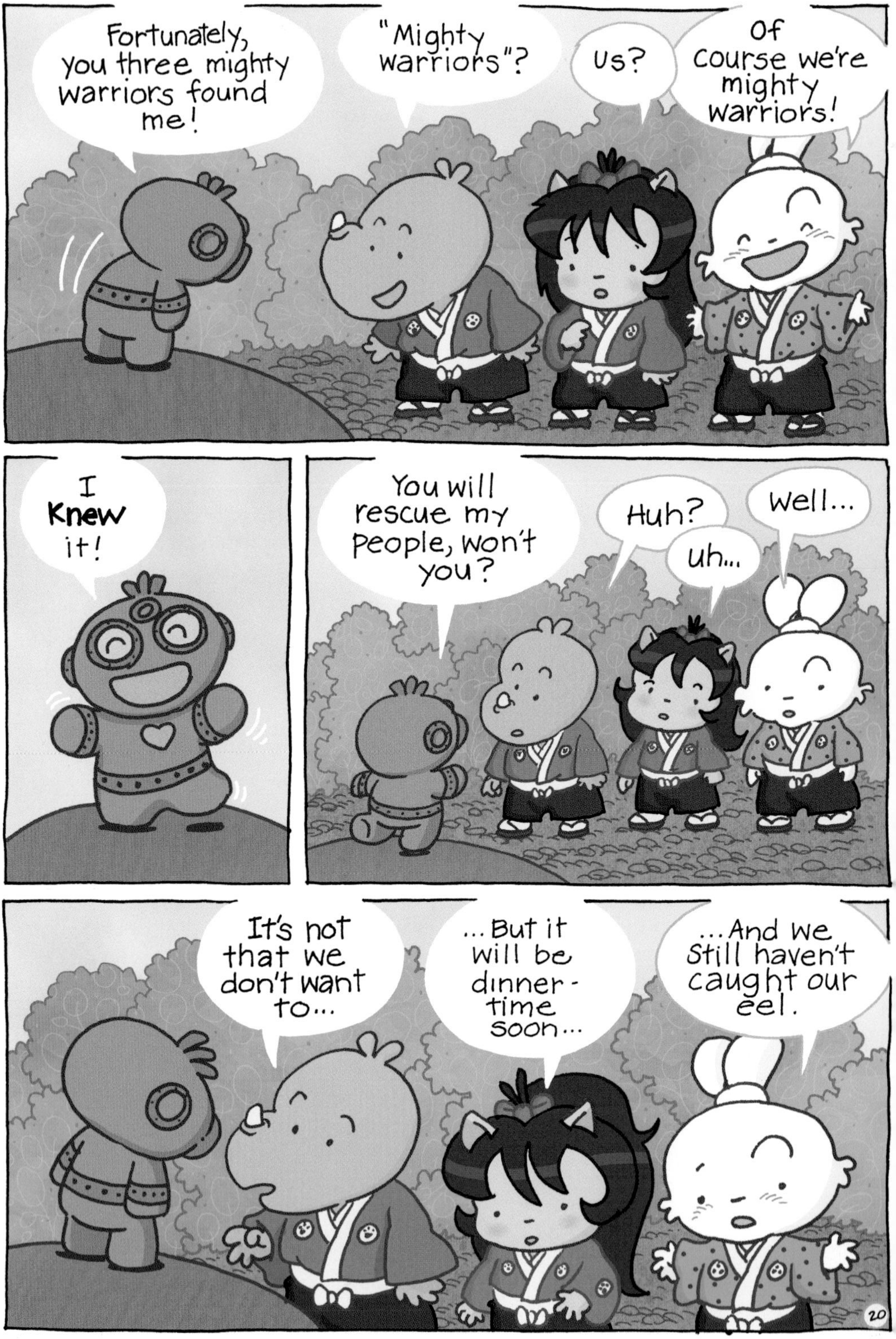
Fortunately, you three mighty warriors found me!
"Mighty warriors"?
Us?
Of course we're mighty warriors!
I Knew it!
You will rescue my people, won't you?
Huh?
Uh...
Well...
It's not that we don't want to...
...But it will be dinner-time soon...
...And we still haven't caught our eel.

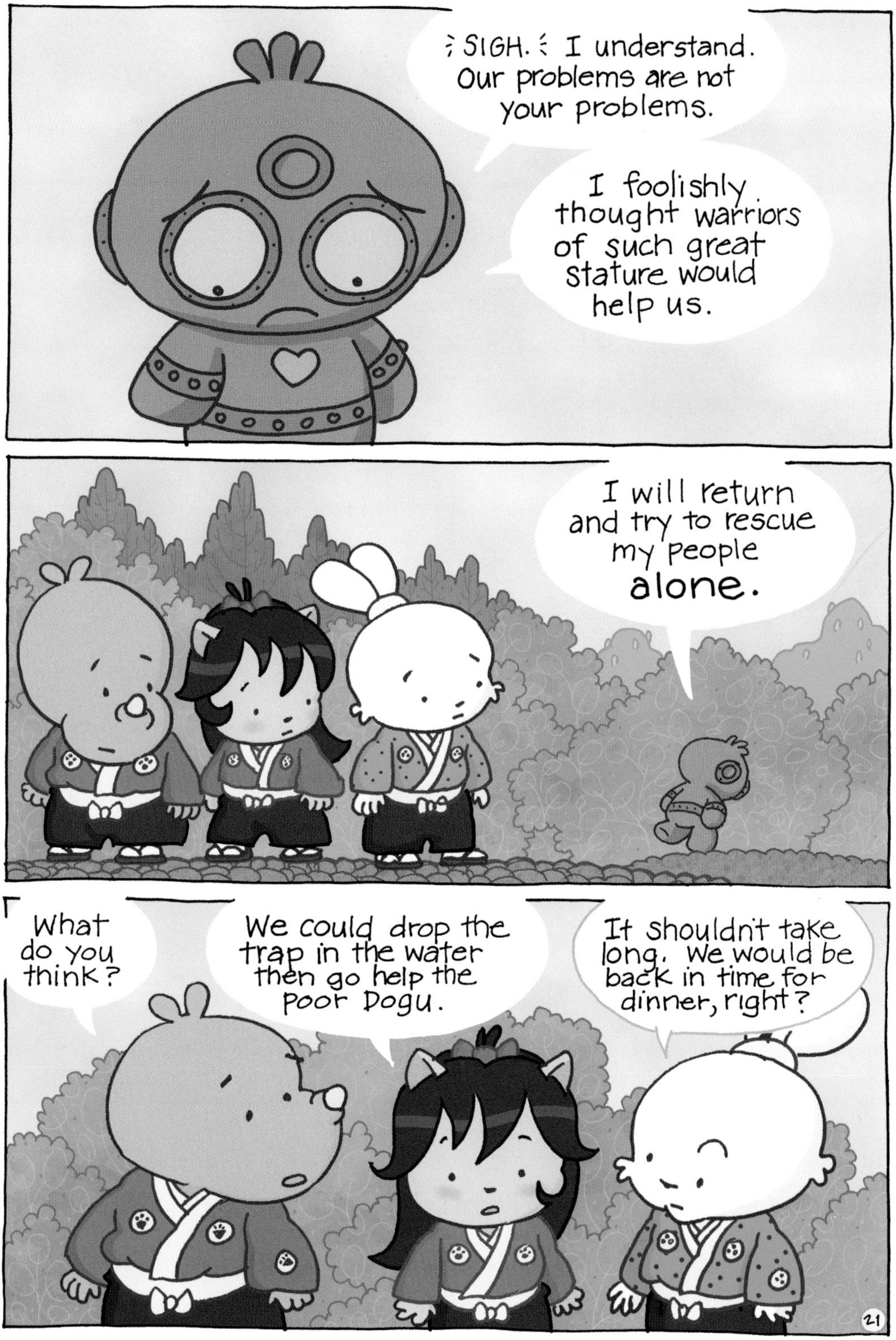

SIGH. I understand. Our problems are not your problems.
I foolishly thought warriors of such great stature would help us.
I will return and try to rescue my people alone.
What do you think?
We could drop the trap in the water then go help the poor Dogu.
It shouldn't take long. We would be back in time for dinner, right?

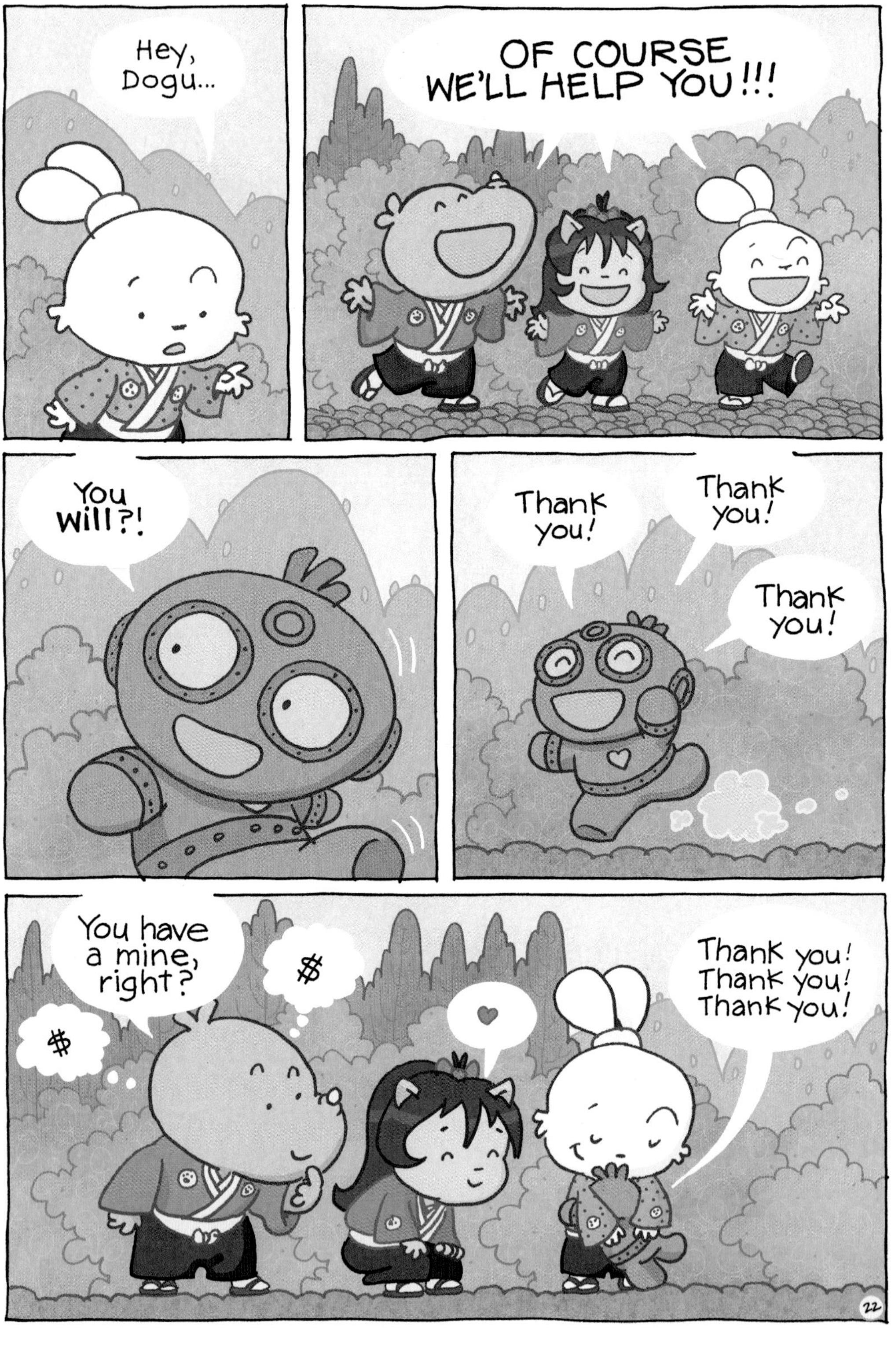
Hey, Dogu...
OF COURSE WE'LL HELP YOU!!!
You will?!
Thank you!
Thank you!
Thank you!
You have a mine, right?
$
$
Thank you! Thank you! Thank you!

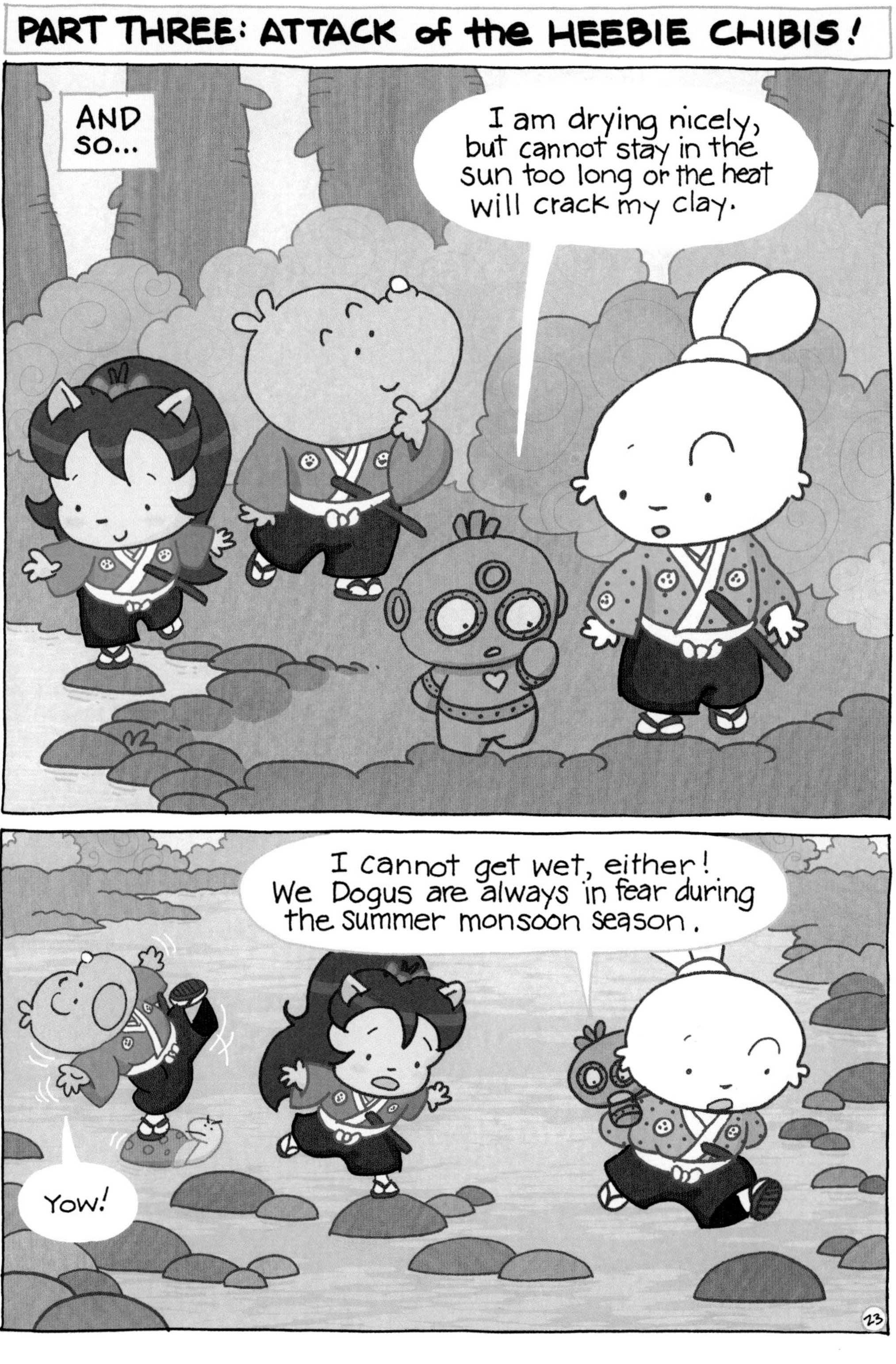
PART THREE: ATTACK of the HEEBIE CHIBIS!
AND SO...
I am drying nicely, but cannot stay in the sun too long or the heat will crack my clay.
I cannot get wet, either! We Dogus are always in fear during the summer monsoon season.
YOW!

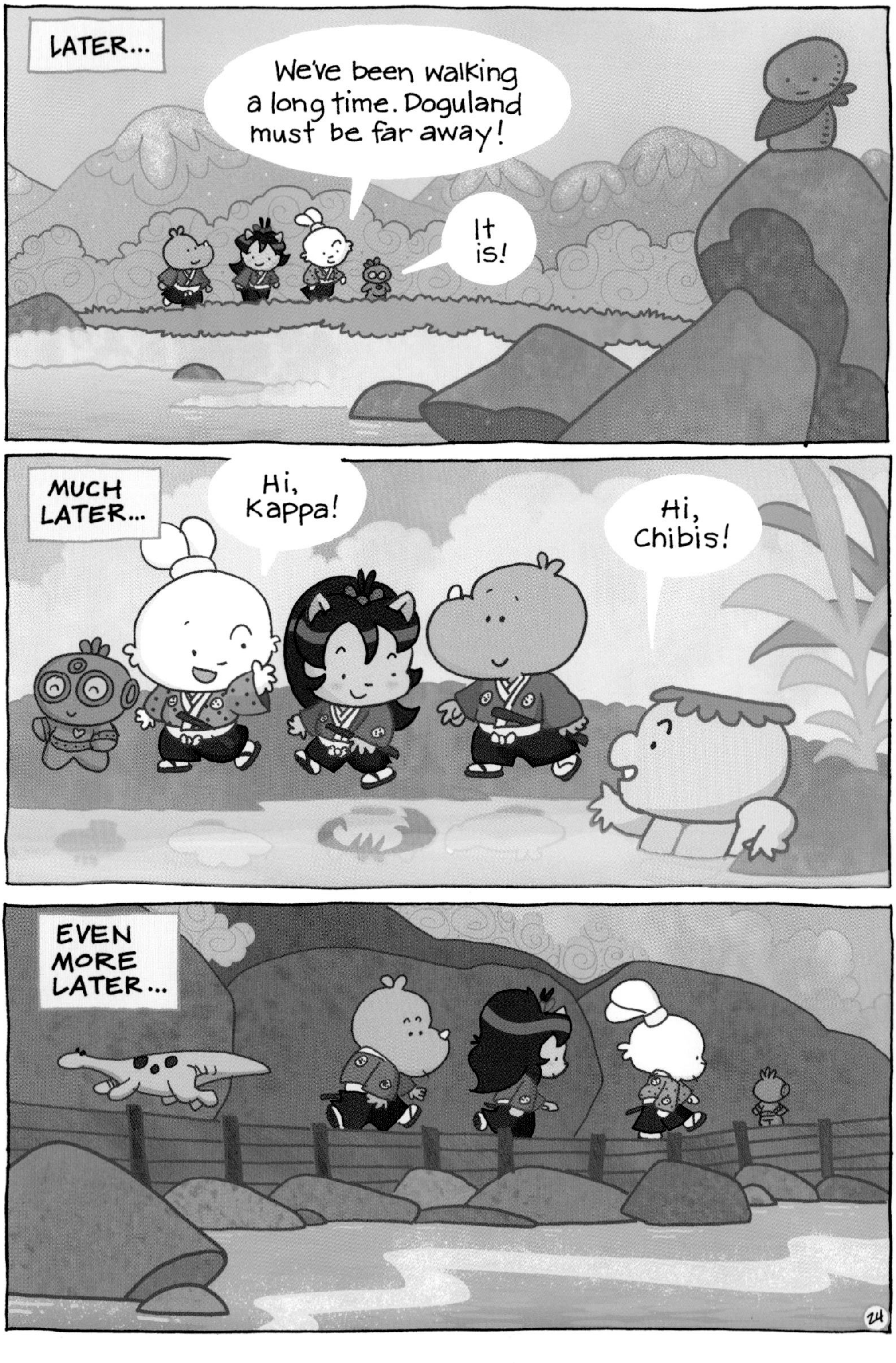
LATER...
We've been walking a long time. Doguland must be far away!
It is!
MUCH LATER...
Hi, Kappa!
Hi, Chibis!
EVEN MORE LATER...

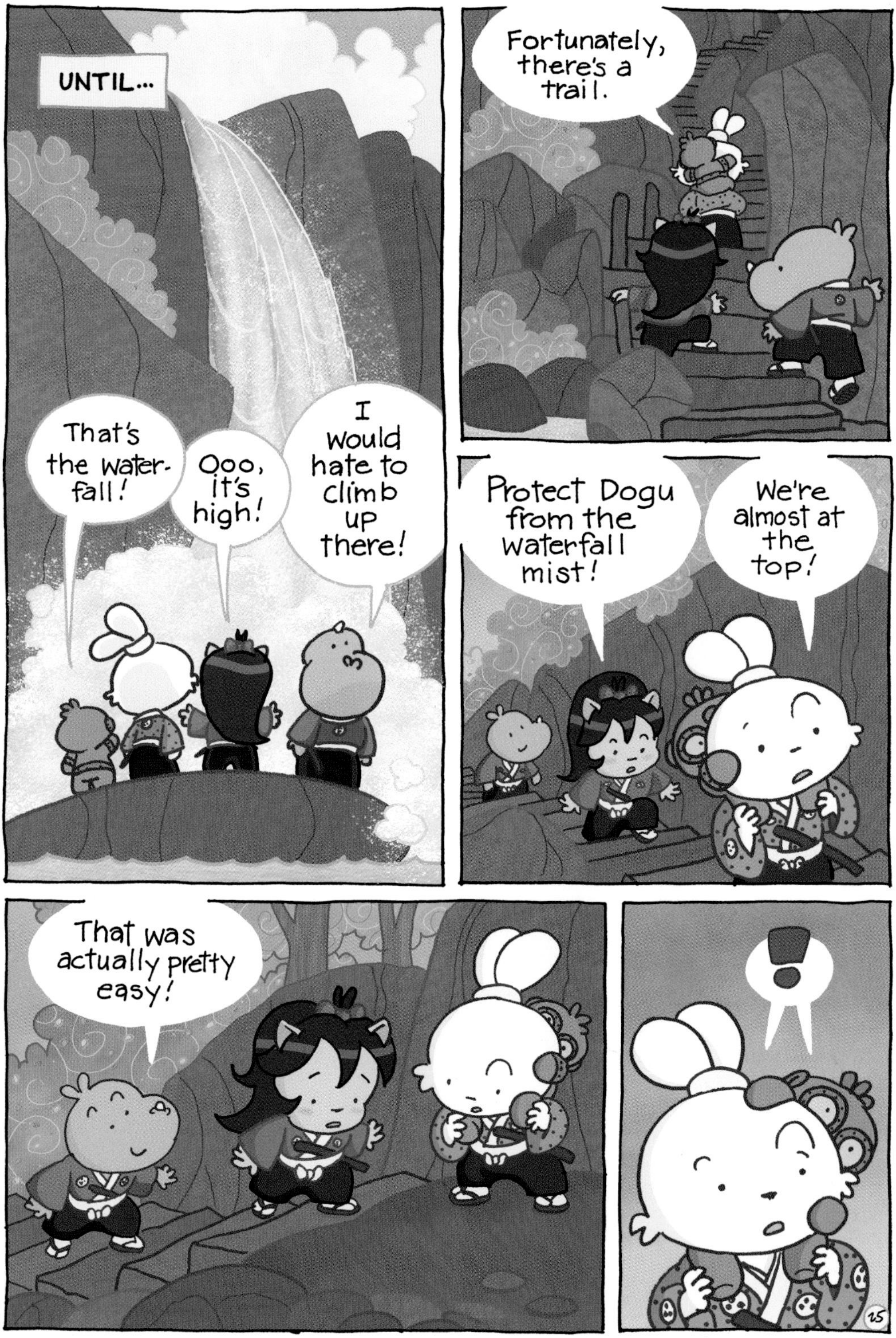
UNTIL...
That's the water-fall!
Ooo, it's high!
I would hate to climb up there!
Fortunately, there's a trail.
Protect Dogu from the waterfall mist!
We're almost at the top!
That was actually pretty easy!
!

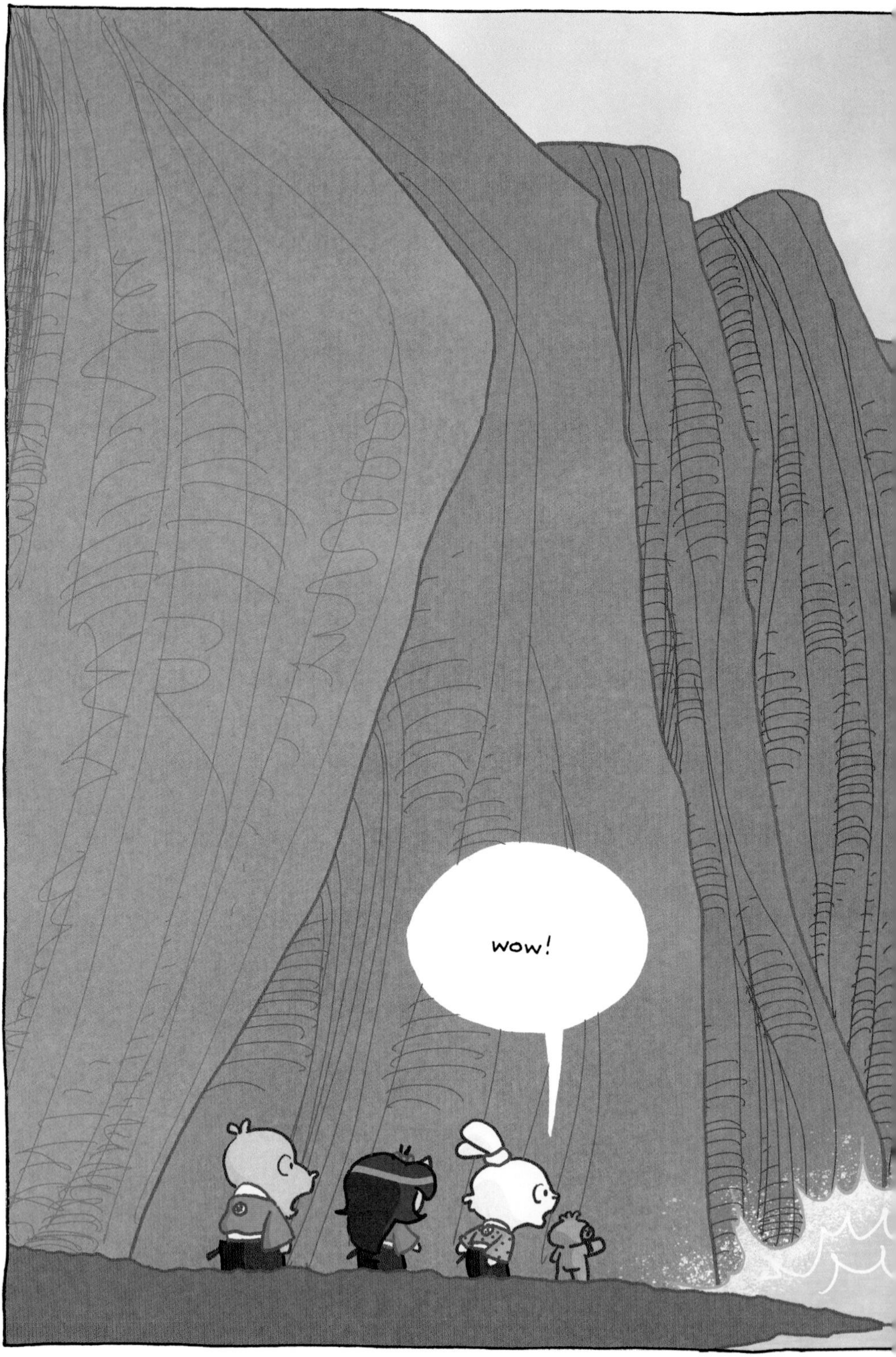
WOW!

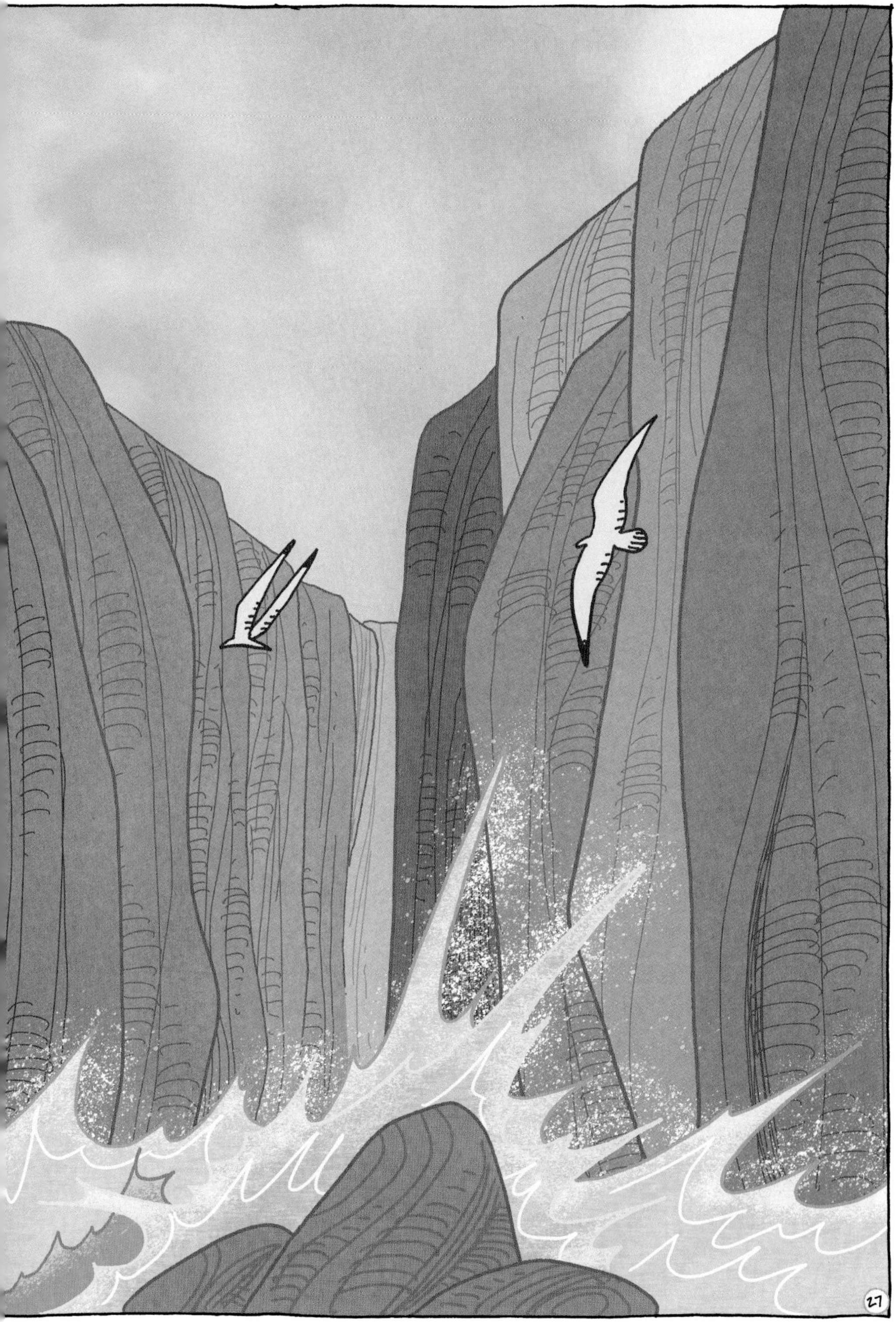

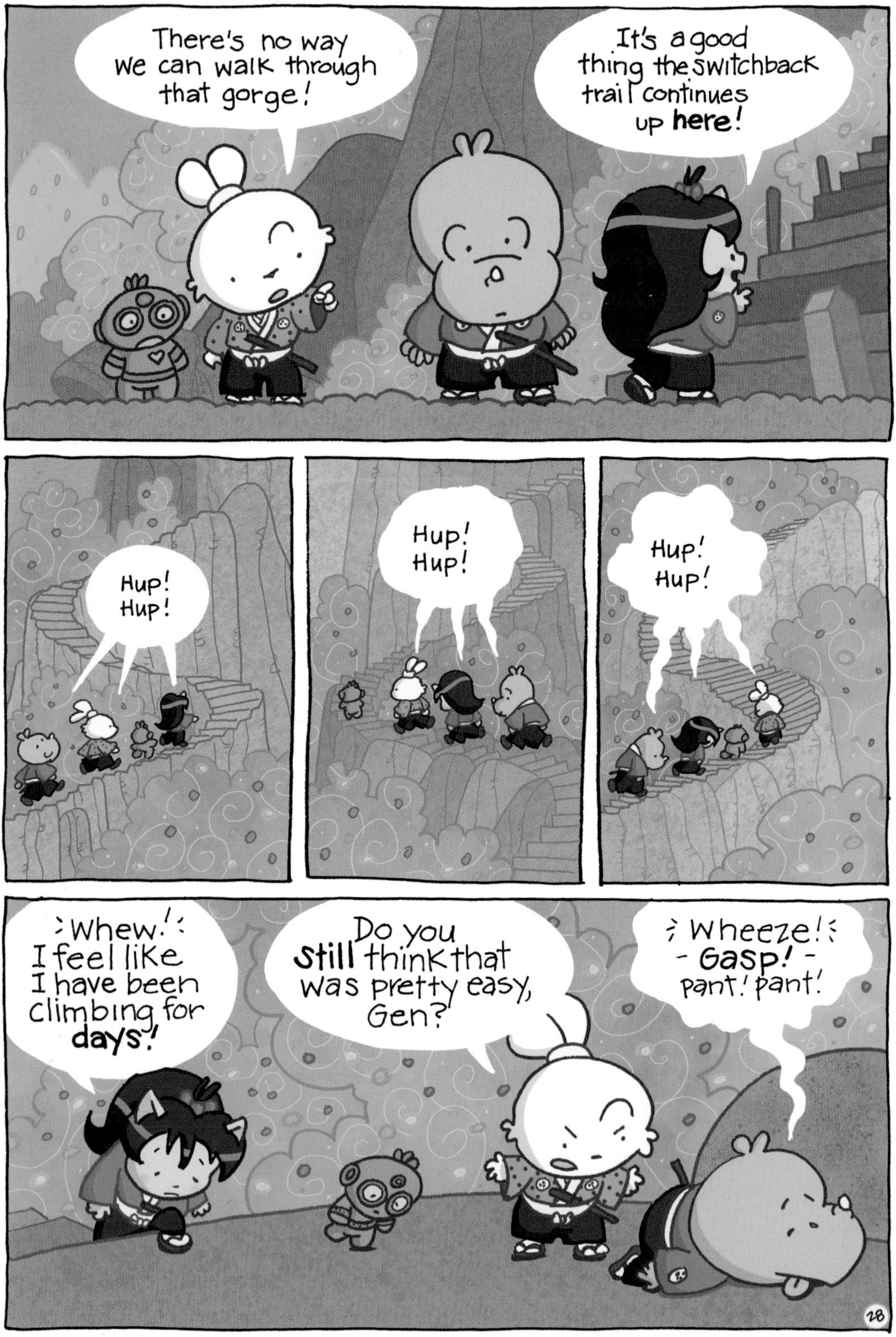
There's no way we can walk through that gorge!
It's a good thing the switchback trail continues up **here**!
Hup! Hup!
Hup! Hup!
Hup! Hup!
Whew! I feel like I have been climbing for **days**!
Do you **still** think that was pretty easy, Gen?
Wheeze! - **Gasp!** - pant! pant!

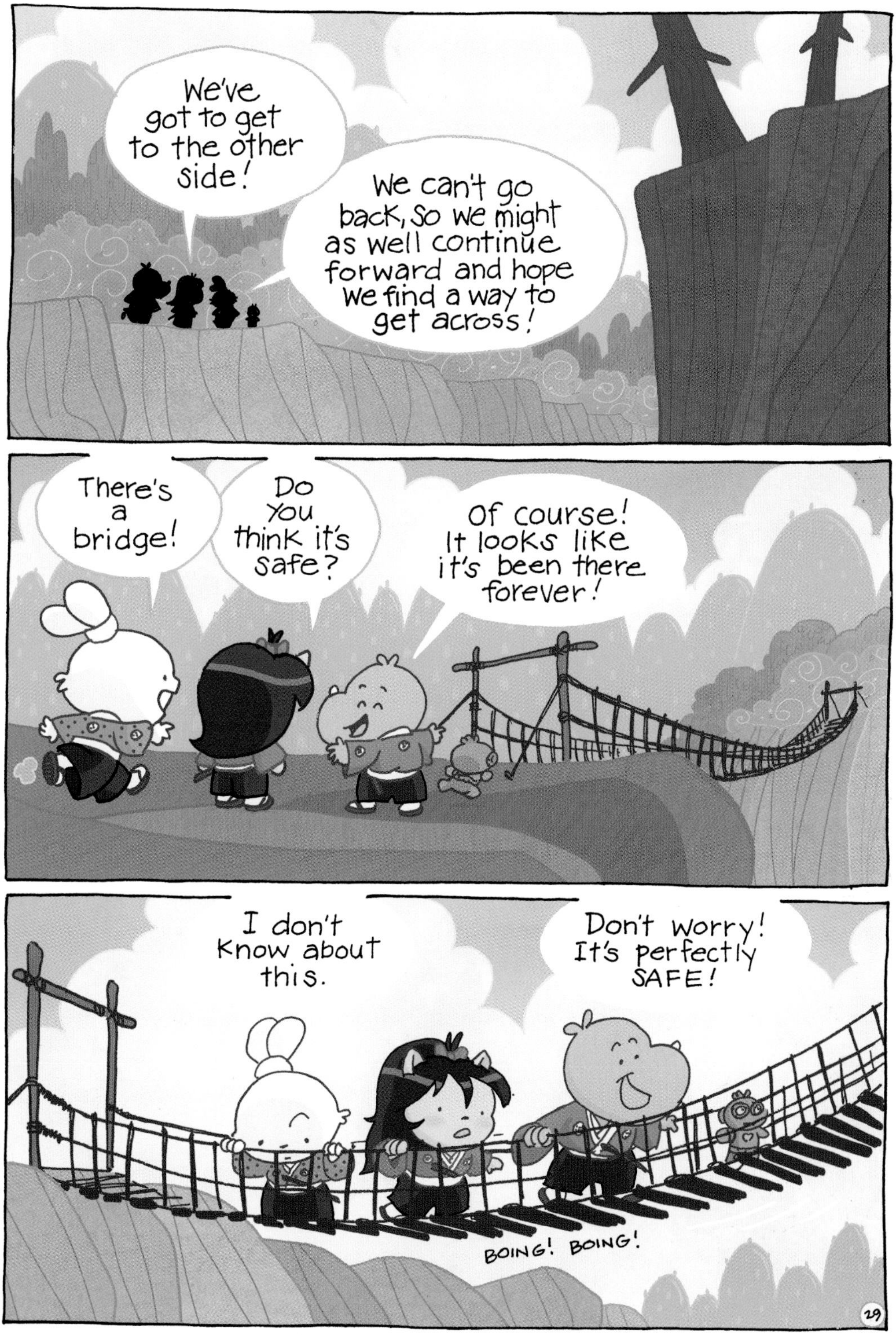
We've got to get to the other side!
We can't go back, so we might as well continue forward and hope we find a way to get across!
There's a bridge!
Do you think it's safe?
Of course! It looks like it's been there forever!
I don't know about this.
Don't worry! It's perfectly SAFE!
BOING! BOING!

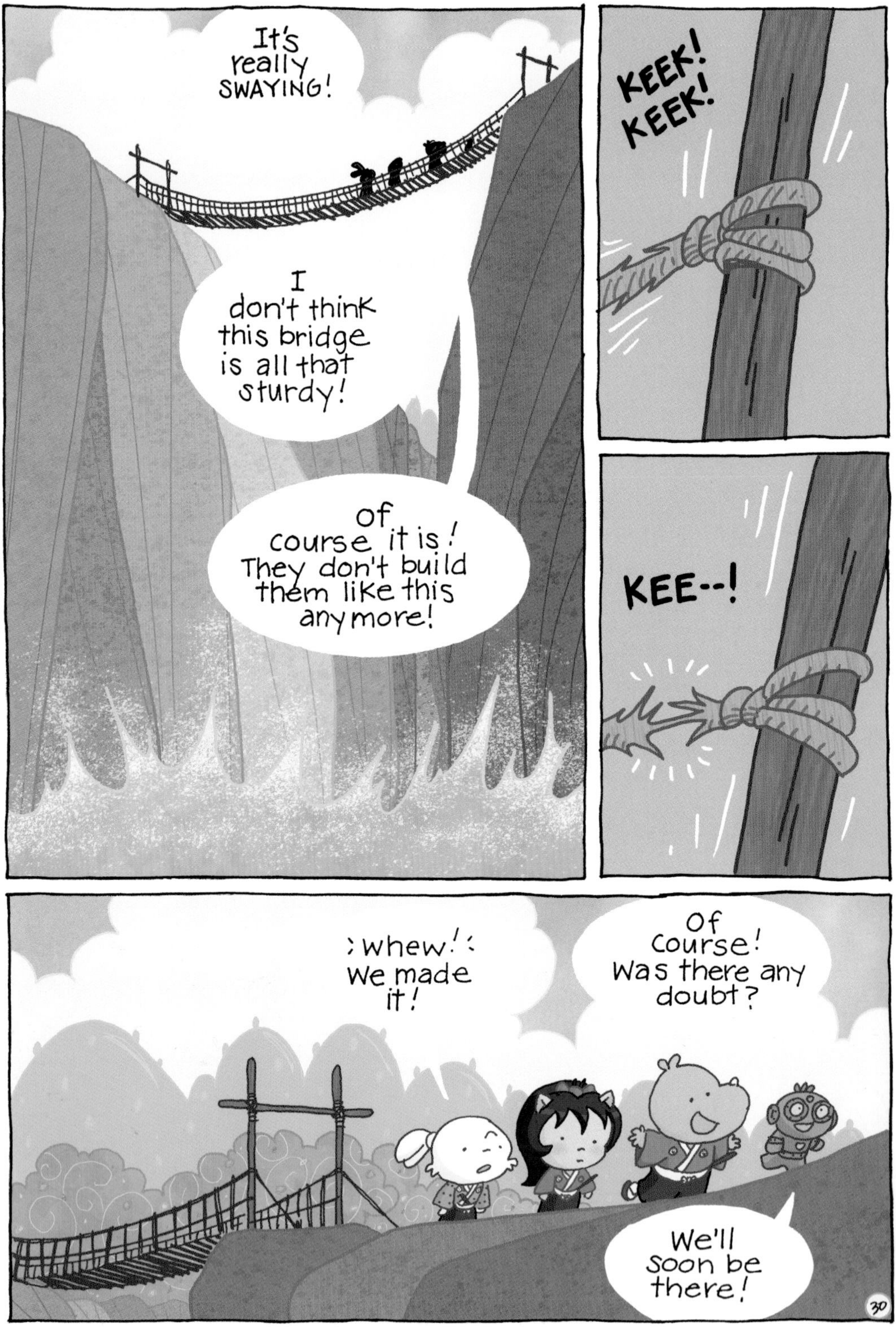
It's really SWAYING!
I don't think this bridge is all that sturdy!
Of course it is! They don't build them like this anymore!
KEEK! KEEK!
KEE--!
whew! We made it!
Of course! Was there any doubt?
We'll soon be there!
30

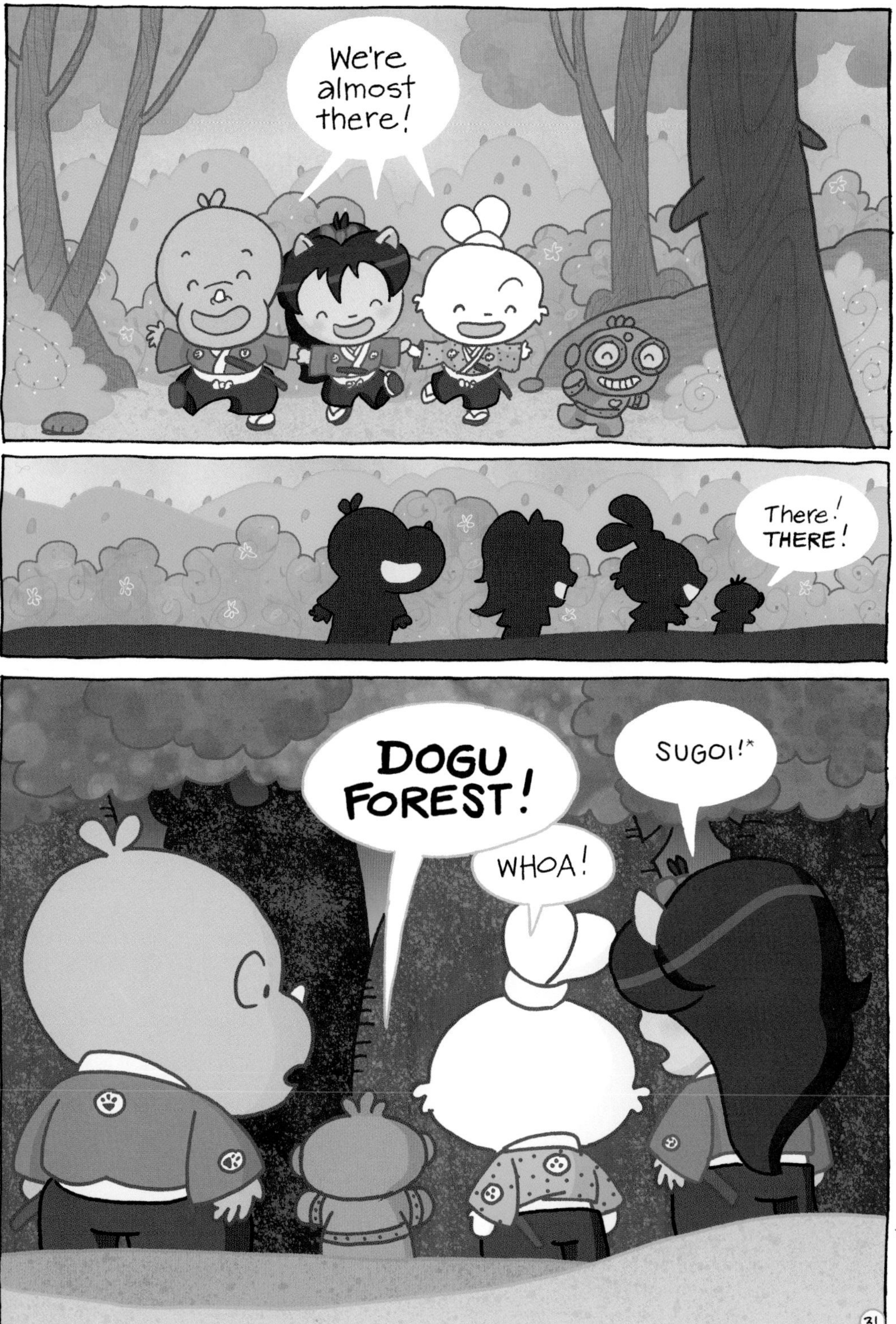
We're almost there!
There! THERE!
DOGU FOREST!
SUGOI!*
WHOA!

*Amazing!

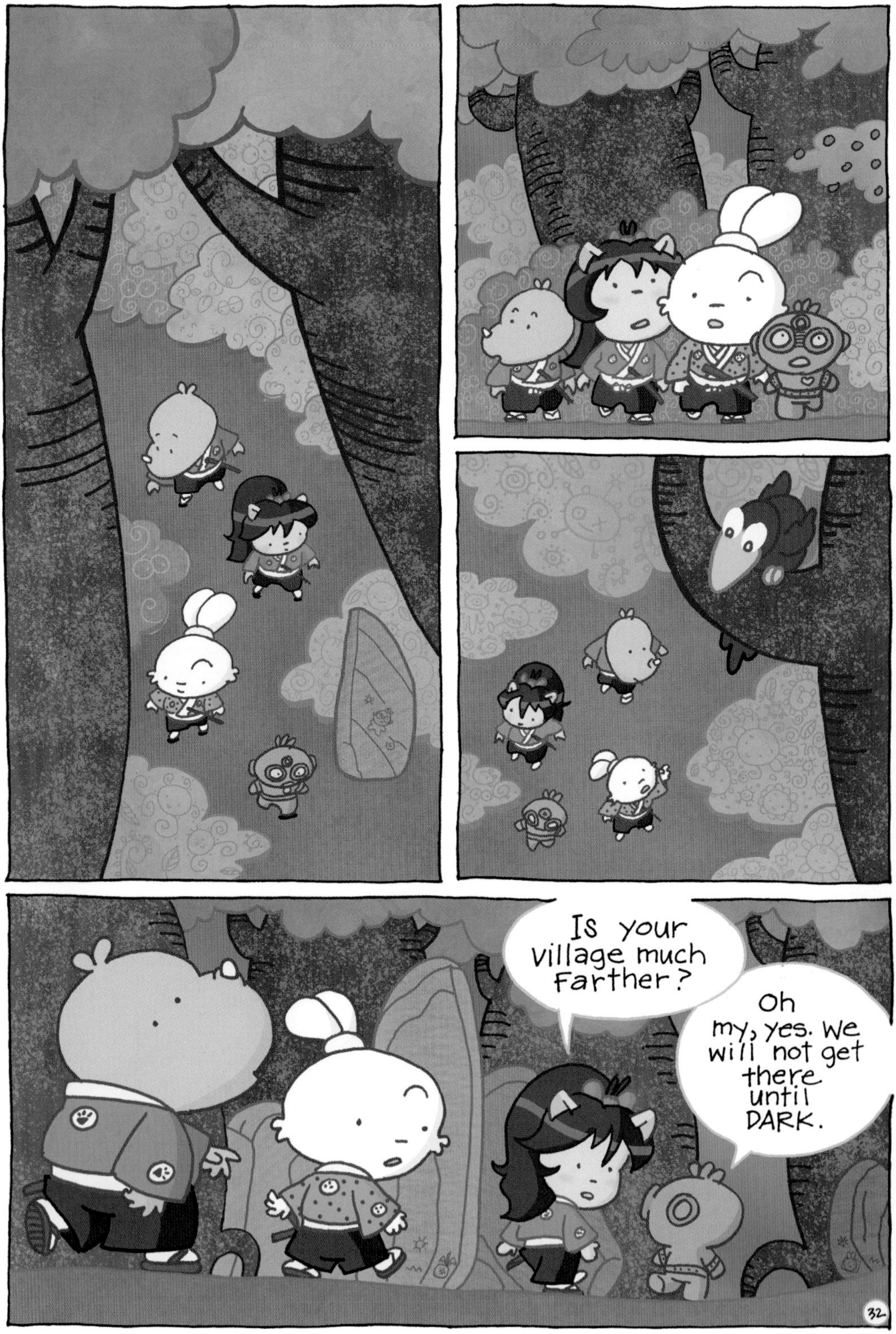
Is your village much Farther?
Oh my, yes. We will not get there until DARK.

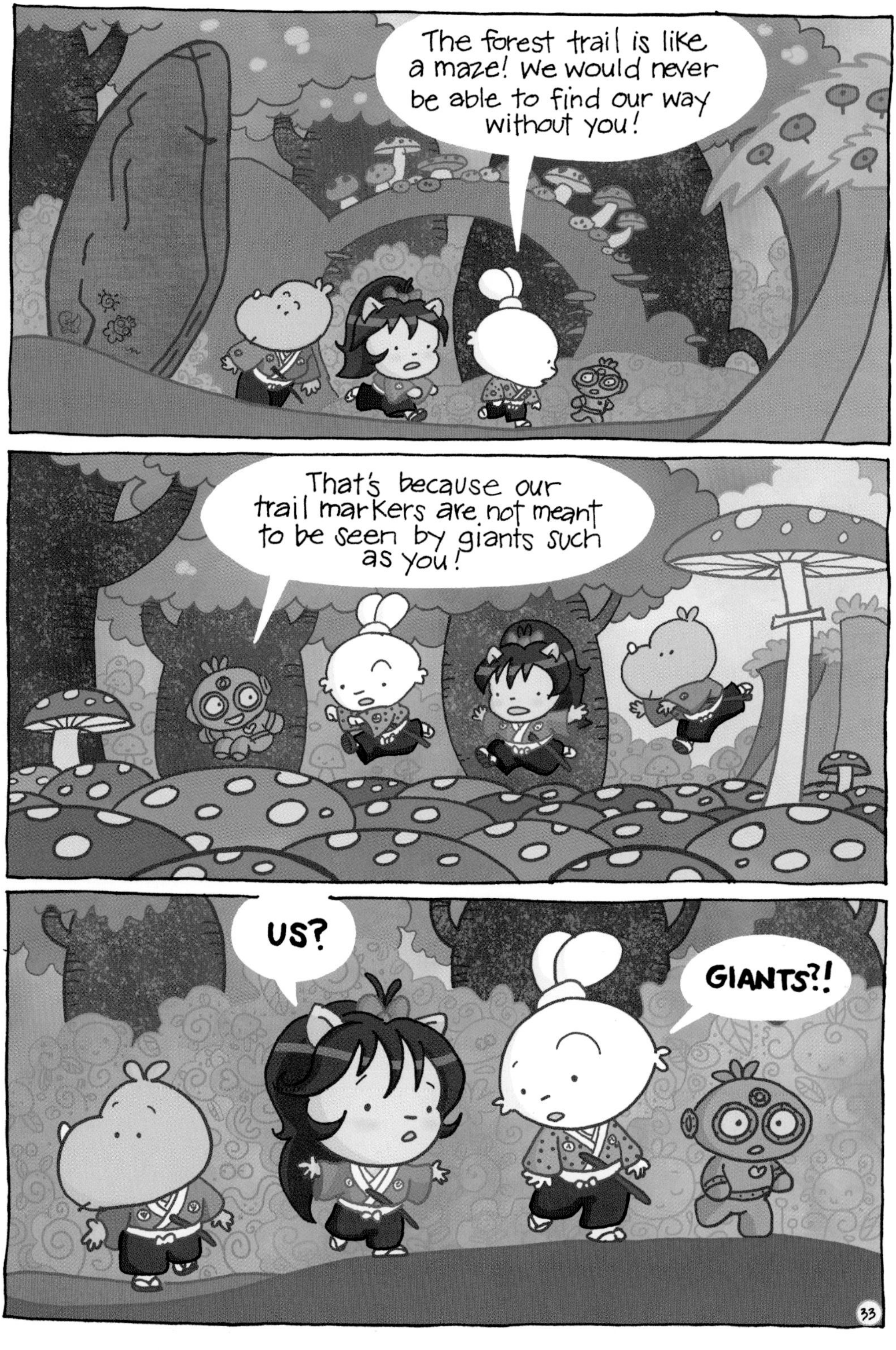
The forest trail is like a maze! We would never be able to find our way without you!
That's because our trail markers are not meant to be seen by giants such as you!
US?
GIANTS?!

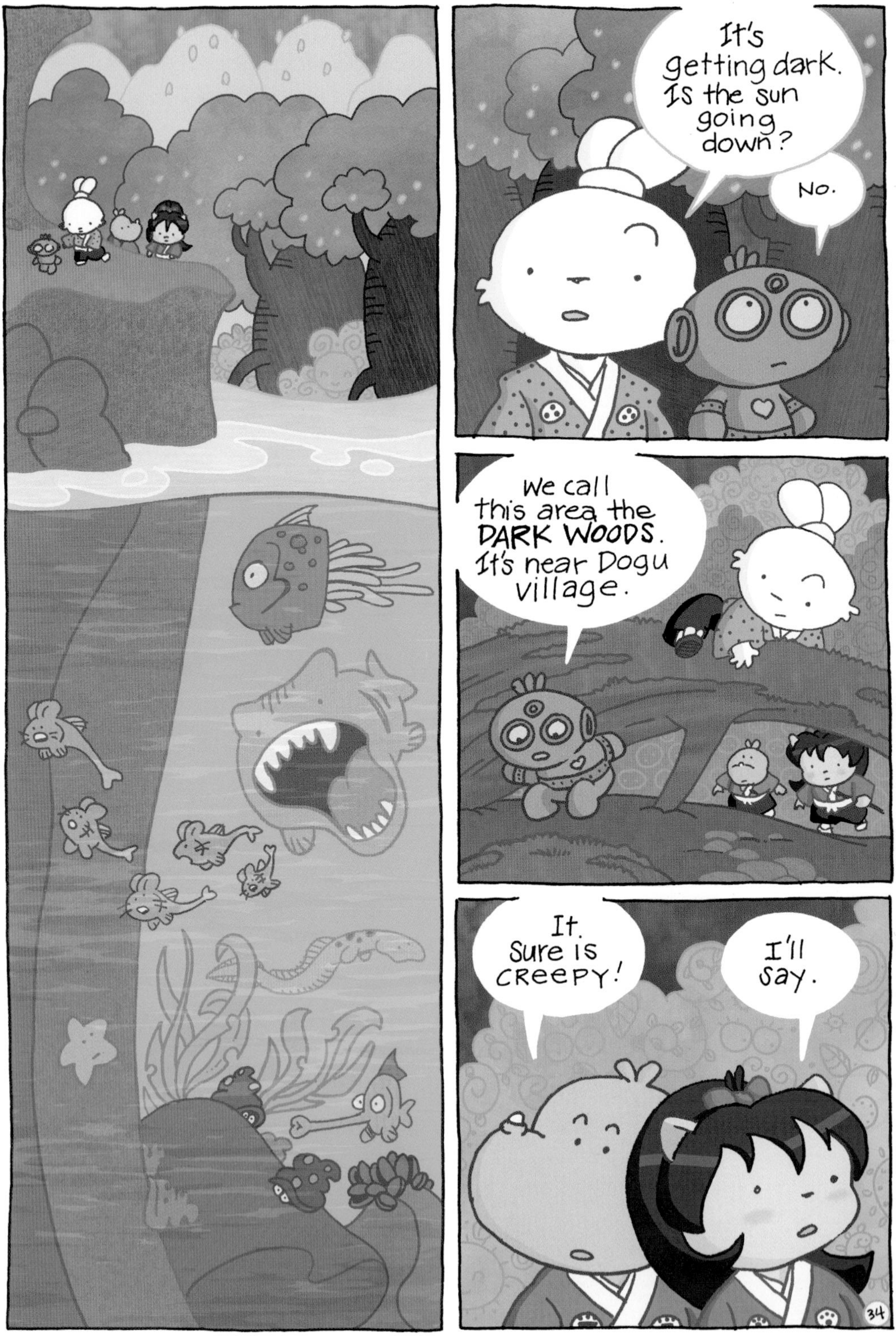
It's getting dark. Is the sun going down?
No.
We call this area the DARK WOODS. It's near Dogu village.
It. Sure is creepy!
I'll say.

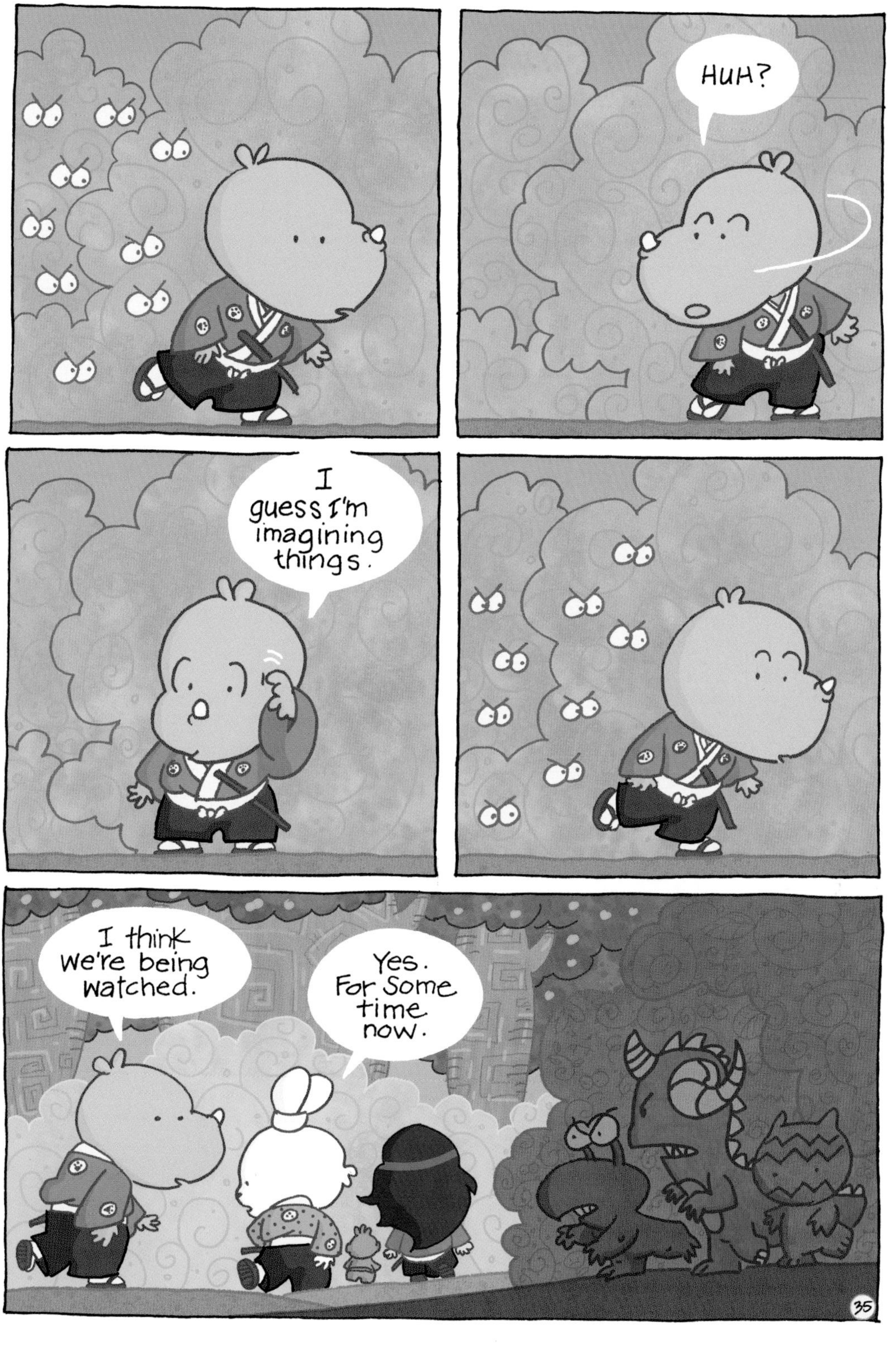
HUH?
I guess I'm imagining things.
I think we're being watched.
Yes. For some time now.

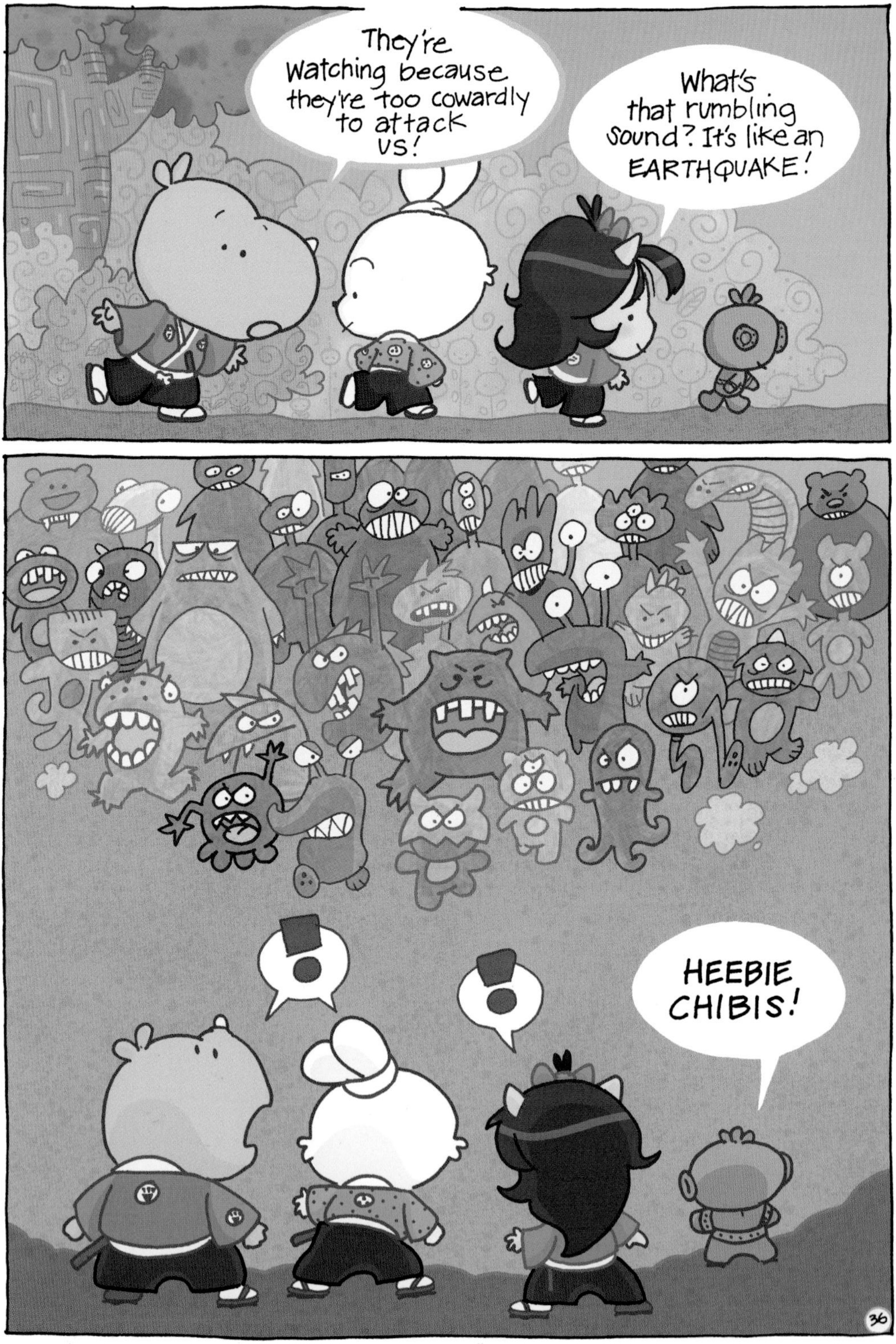
They're watching because they're too cowardly to attack us!
What's that rumbling sound? It's like an EARTHQUAKE!
HEEBIE CHIBIS!

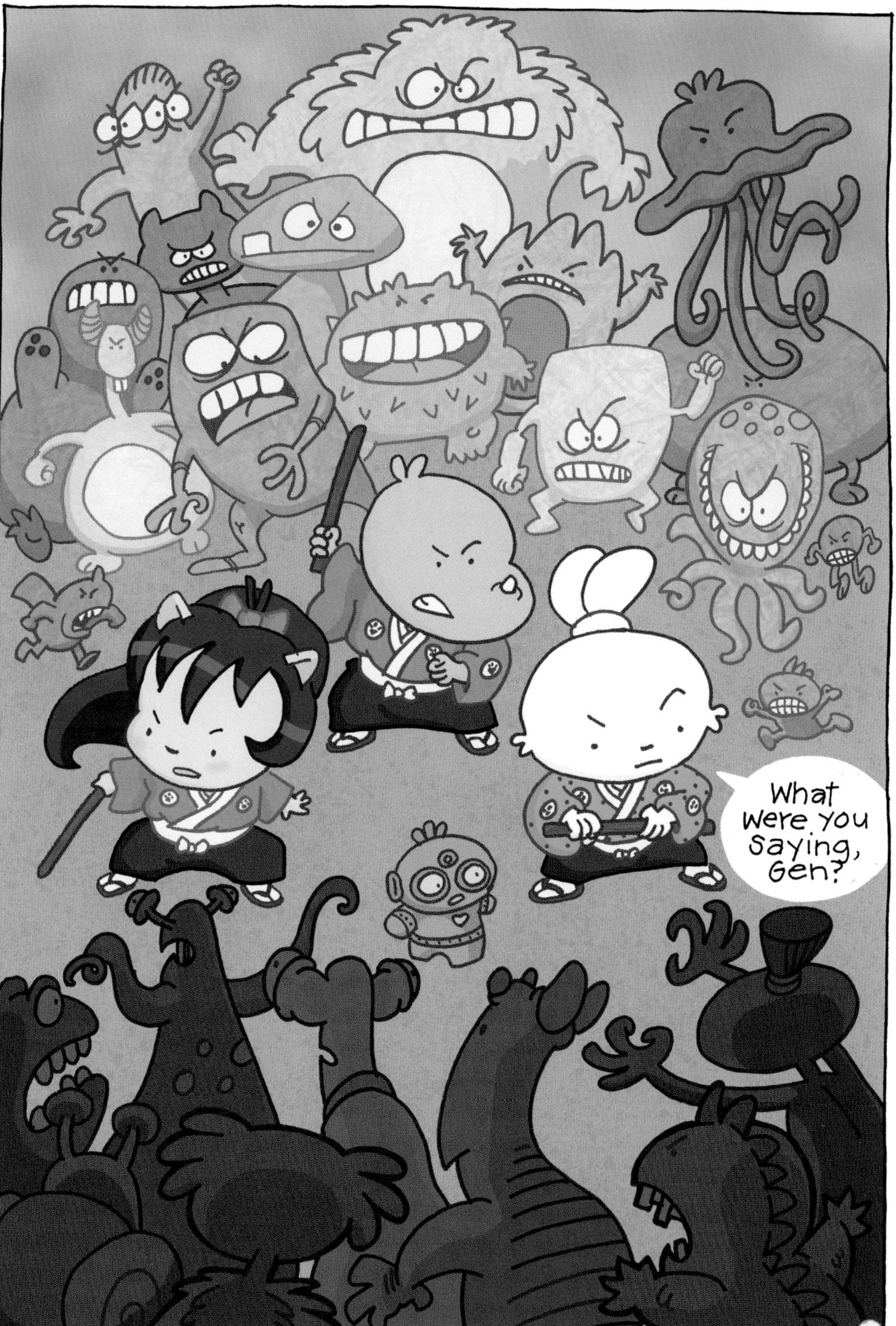
What were you saying, Gen?

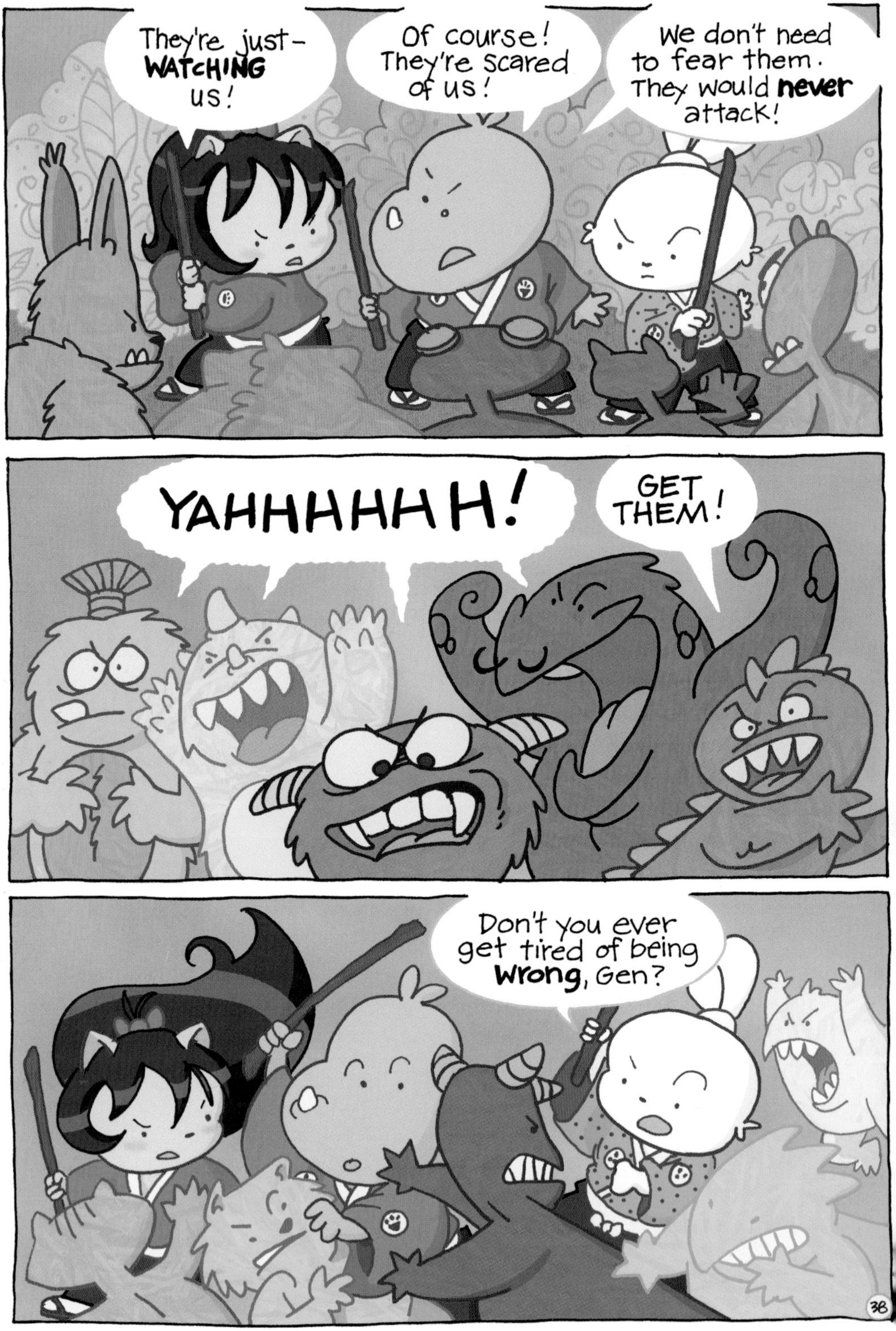

They're just-
WATCHING
us!
Of course!
They're scared
of us!
We don't need
to fear them.
They would **never**
attack!
YAHHHHHH!
GET
THEM!
Don't you ever
get tired of being
Wrong, Gen?

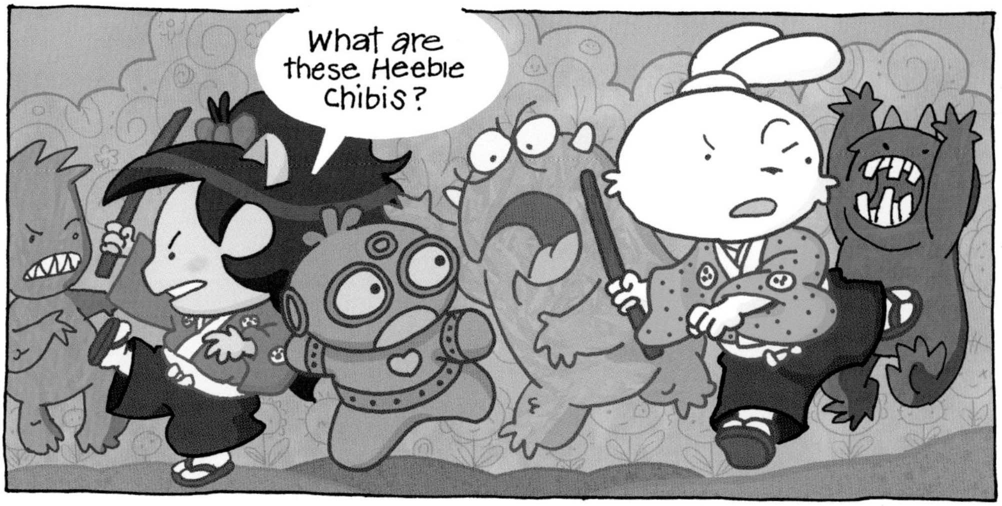
What are these Heebie Chibis?

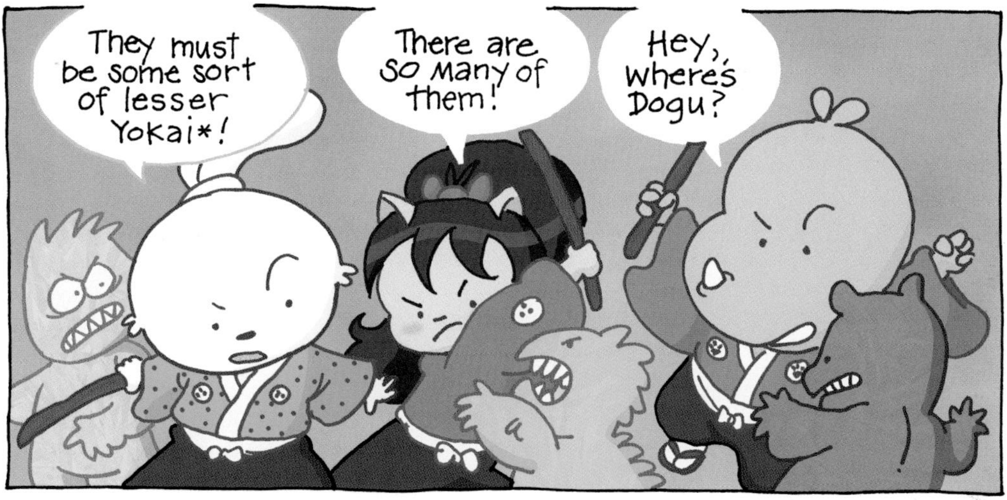
They must be some sort of lesser Yokai*!
There are so many of them!
Hey, where's Dogu?

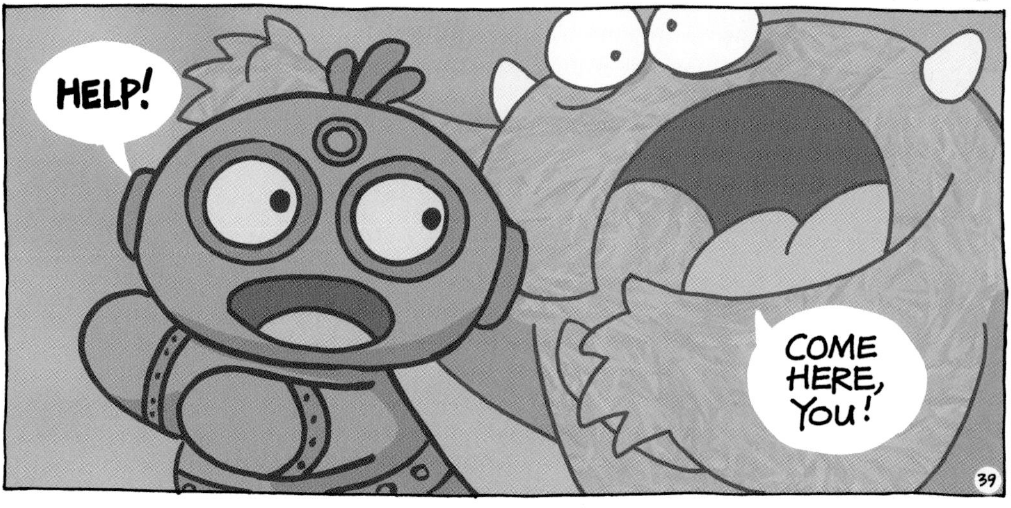
HELP!
COME HERE, YOU!

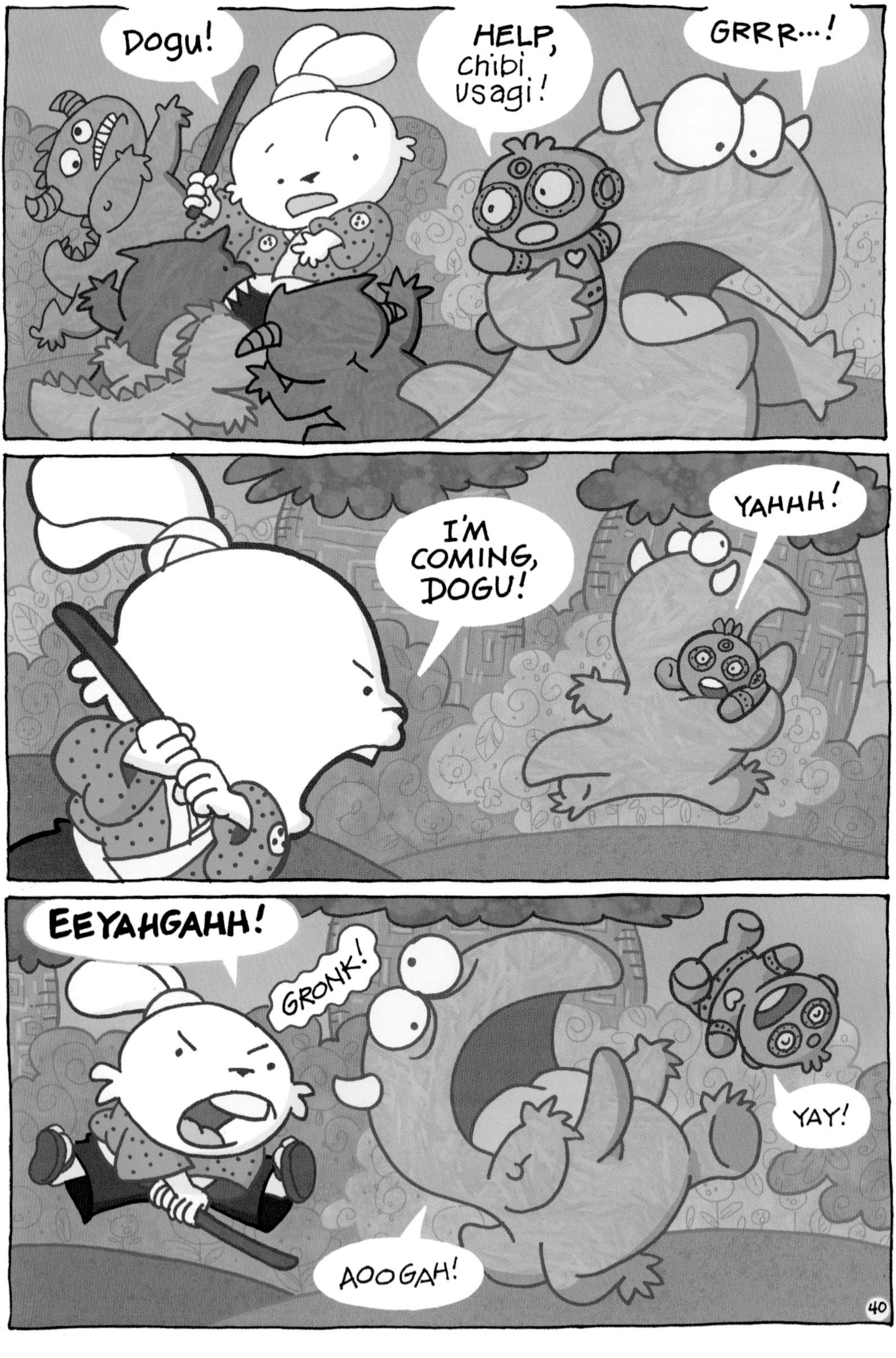
Dogu!
HELP, chibi usagi!
GRRR...!
I'M COMING, DOGU!
YAHHH!
EEYAHGAHH!
GRONK!
YAY!
AOOGAH!

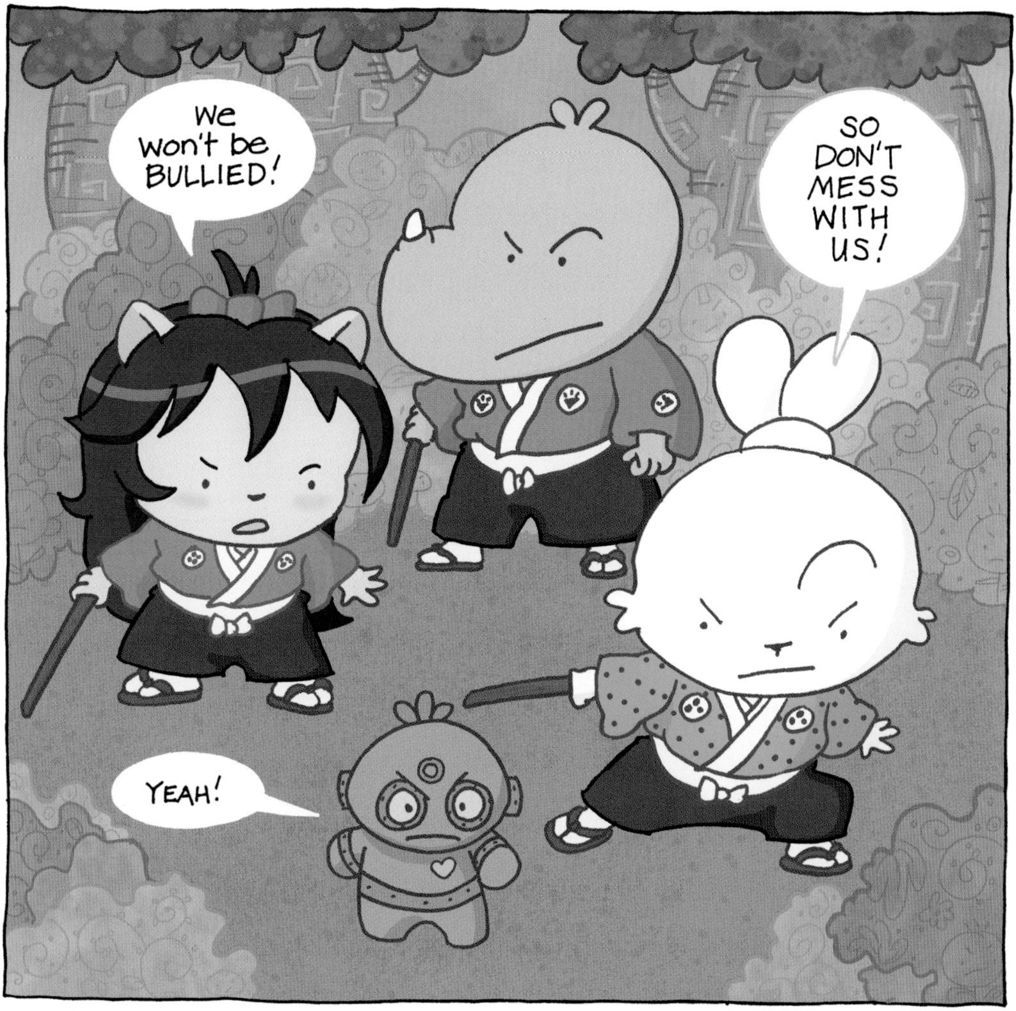
We won't be BULLIED!
SO DON'T MESS WITH US!
YEAH!

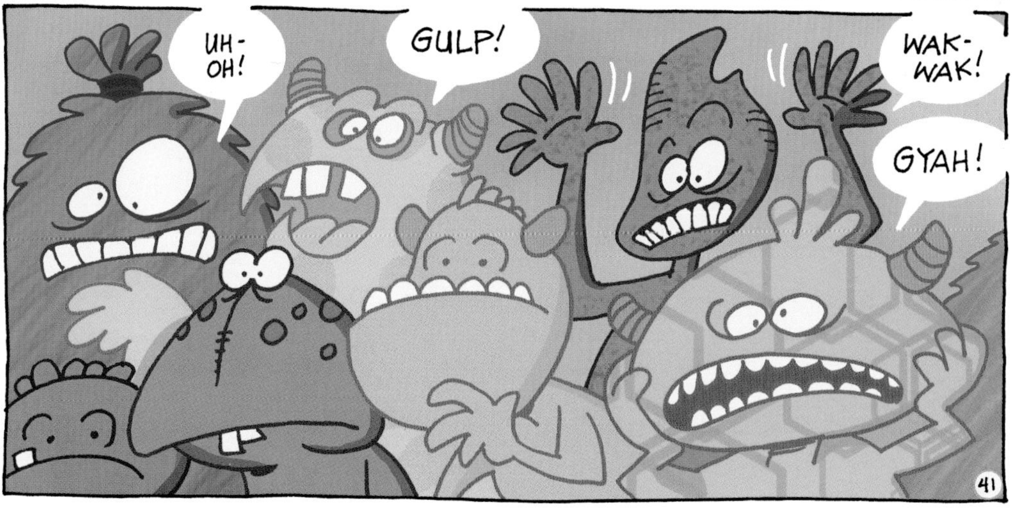
UH-OH!
GULP!
WAK-WAK!
GYAH!

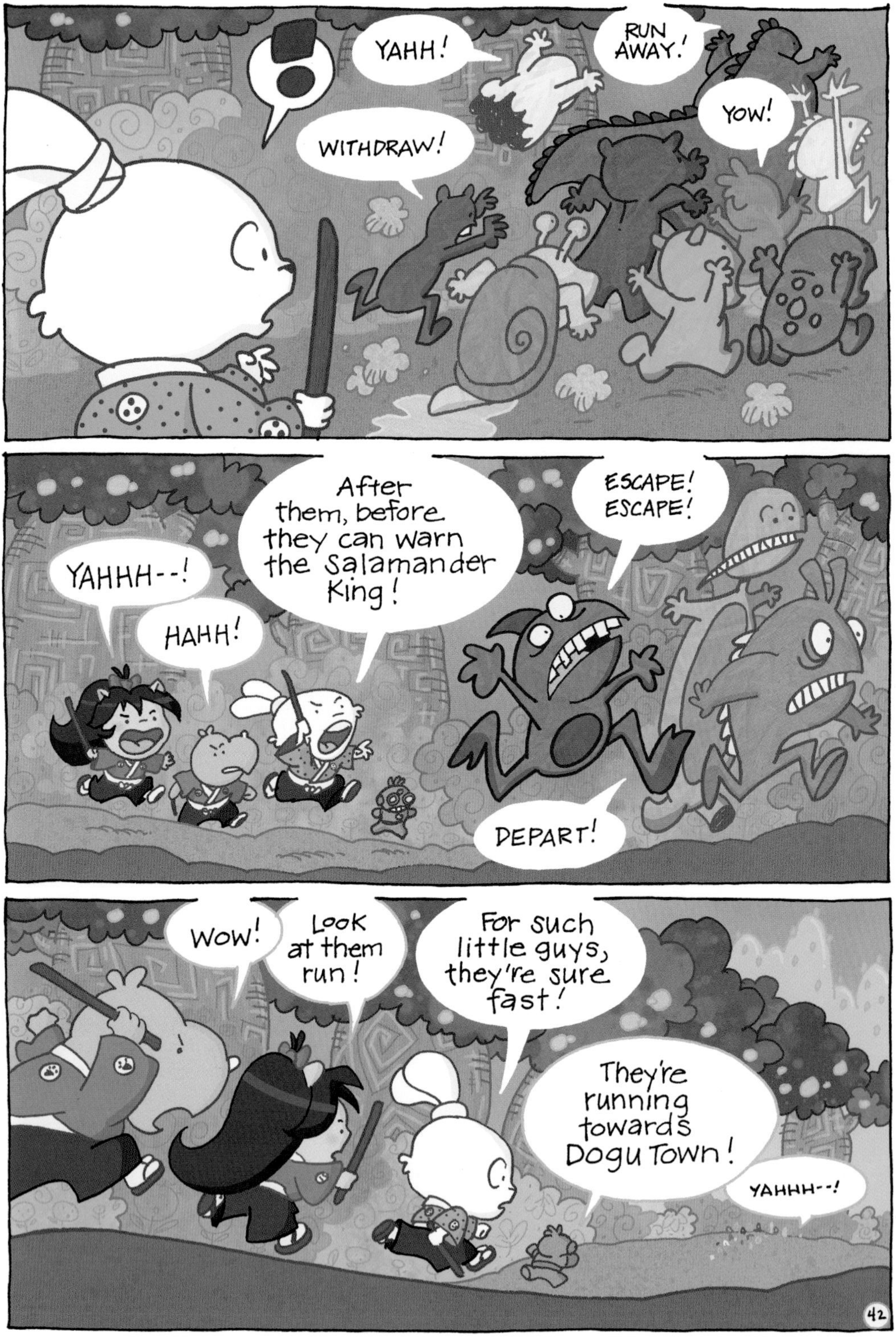

YAHH!
RUN AWAY!
WITHDRAW!
YOW!
YAHHH--!
HAHH!
After them, before they can warn the Salamander King!
ESCAPE! ESCAPE!
DEPART!
WOW!
Look at them run!
For such little guys, they're sure fast!
They're running towards Dogu Town!
YAHHH--!

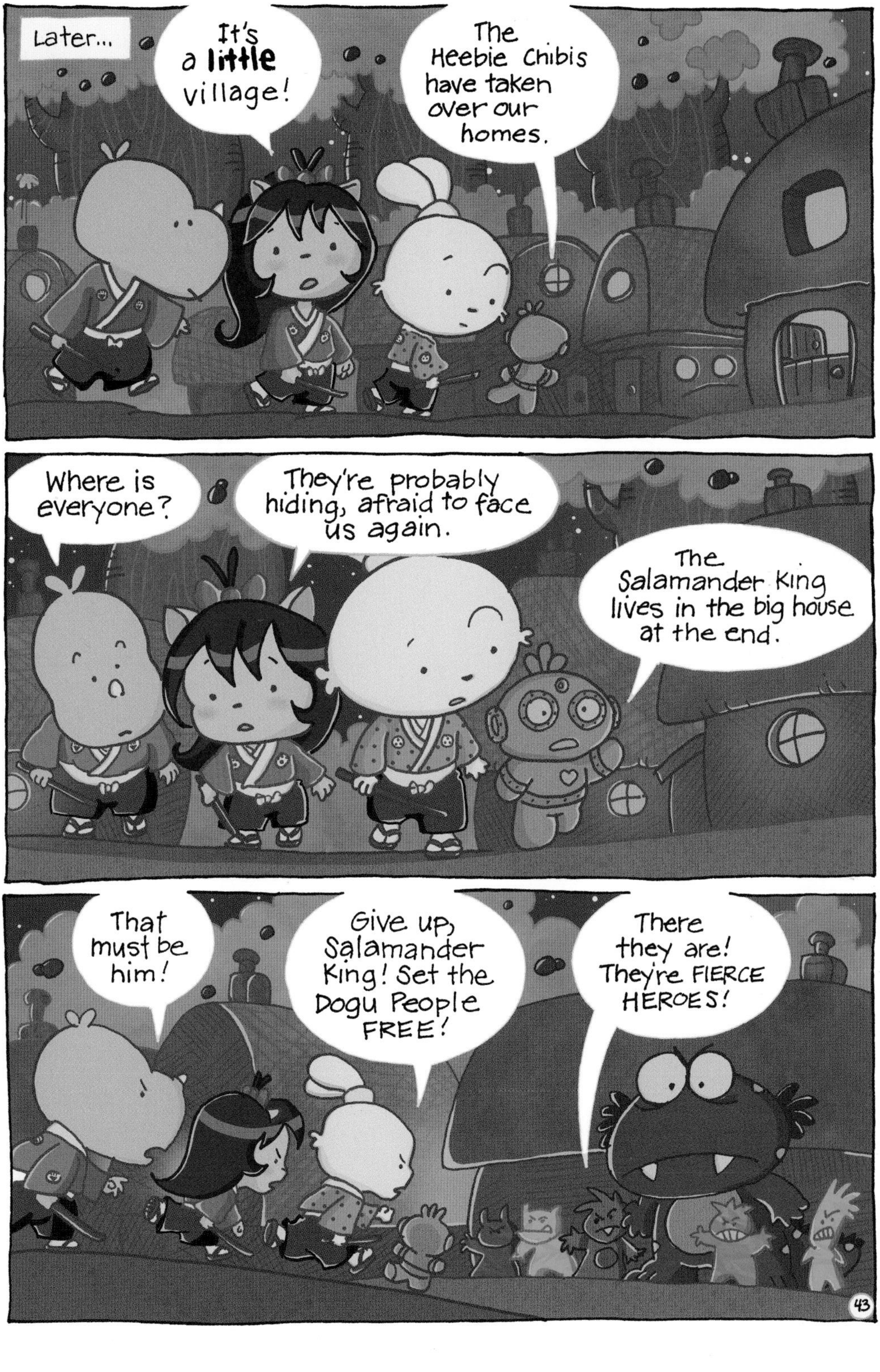
Later...
It's a little village!
The Heebie Chibis have taken over our homes.
Where is everyone?
They're probably hiding, afraid to face us again.
The Salamander King lives in the big house at the end.
That must be him!
Give up, Salamander King! Set the Dogu People FREE!
There they are! They're FIERCE HEROES!

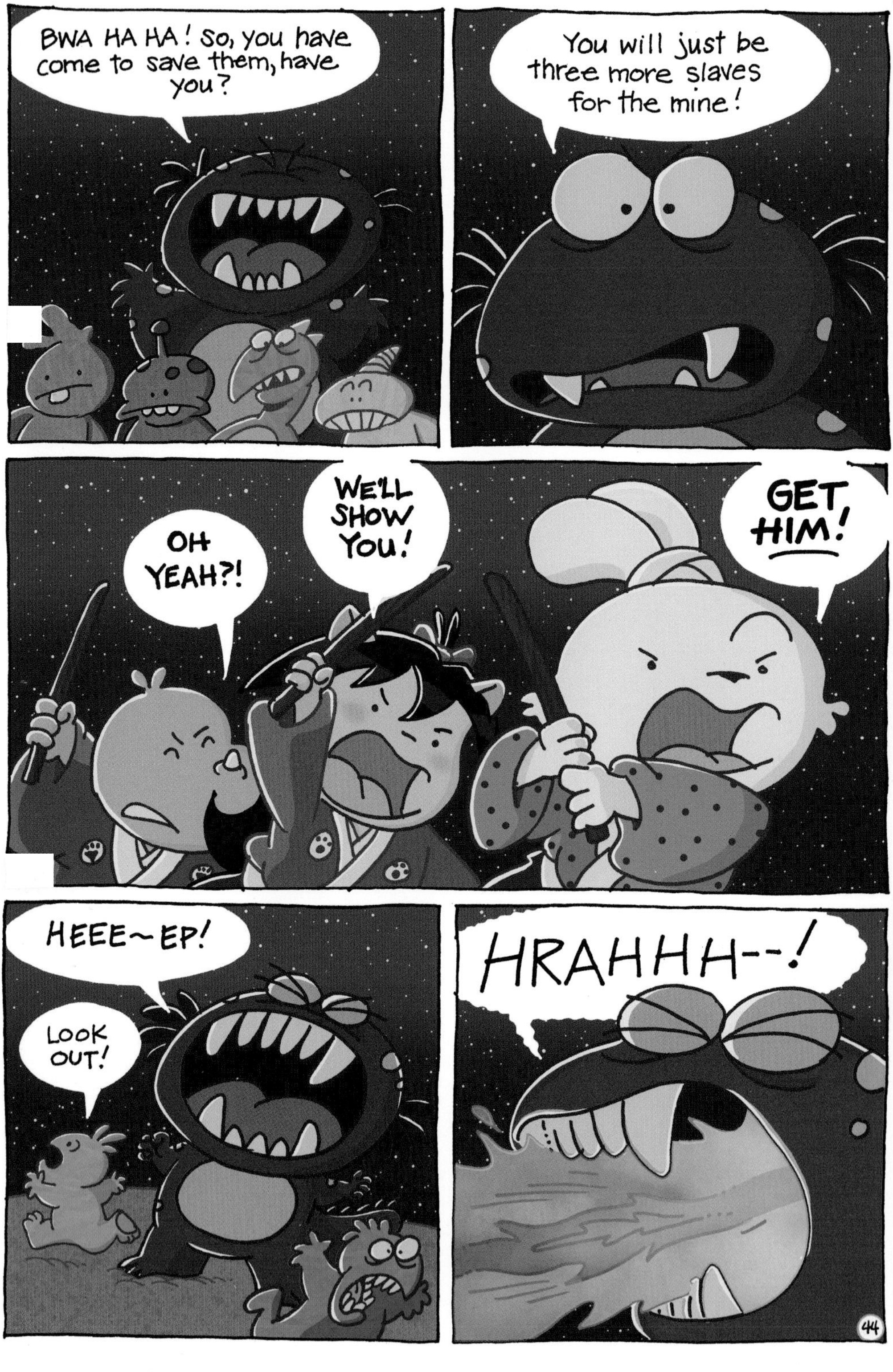
BWA HA HA! So, you have come to save them, have you?
You will just be three more slaves for the mine!
OH YEAH?!
WE'LL SHOW YOU!
GET HIM!
HEEE~EP!
LOOK OUT!
HRAHHH--!

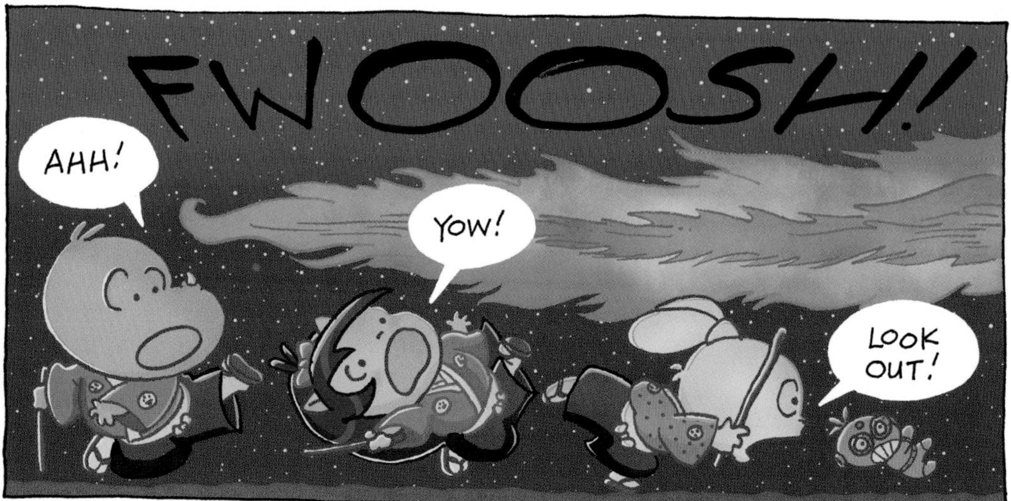
FWOOSH!!
AHH!
YOW!
LOOK OUT!

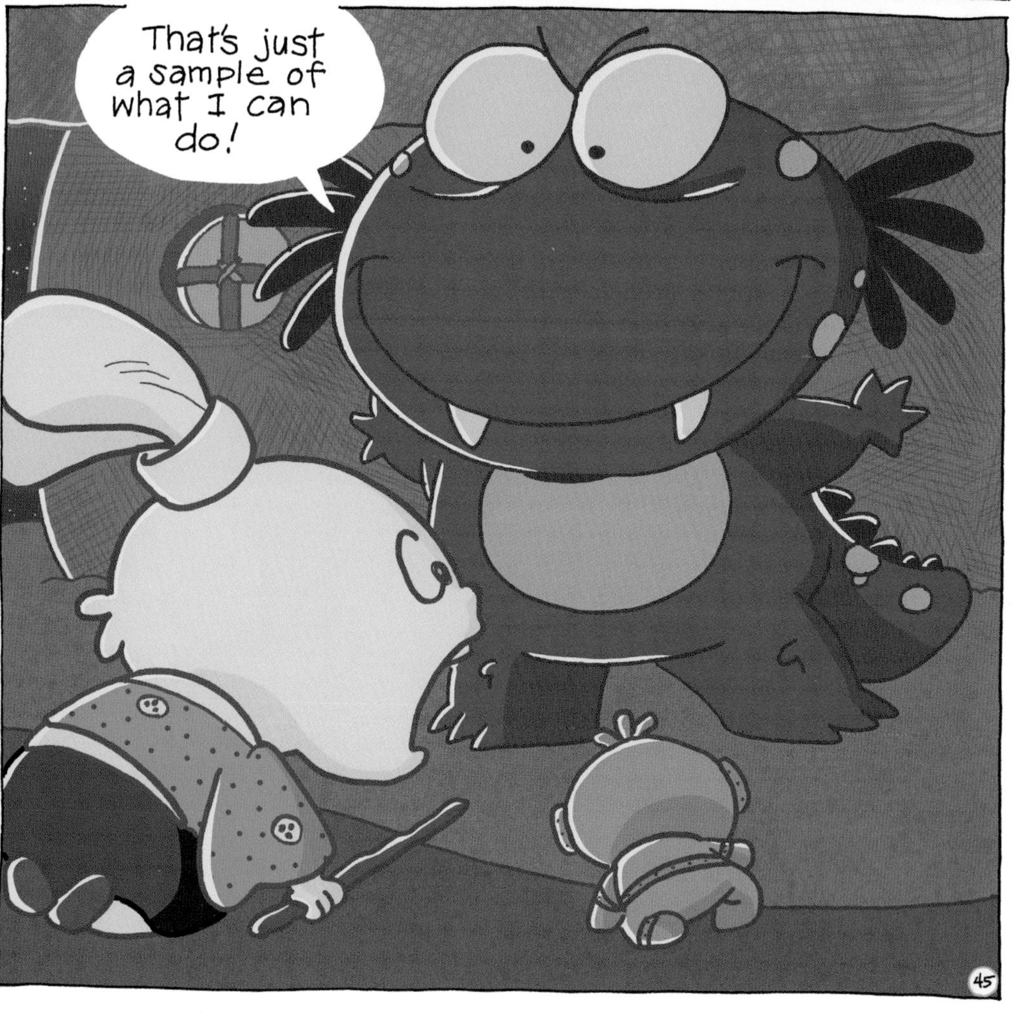
That's just a sample of what I can do!

PART FOUR: PRISONERS of the SALAMANDER KING

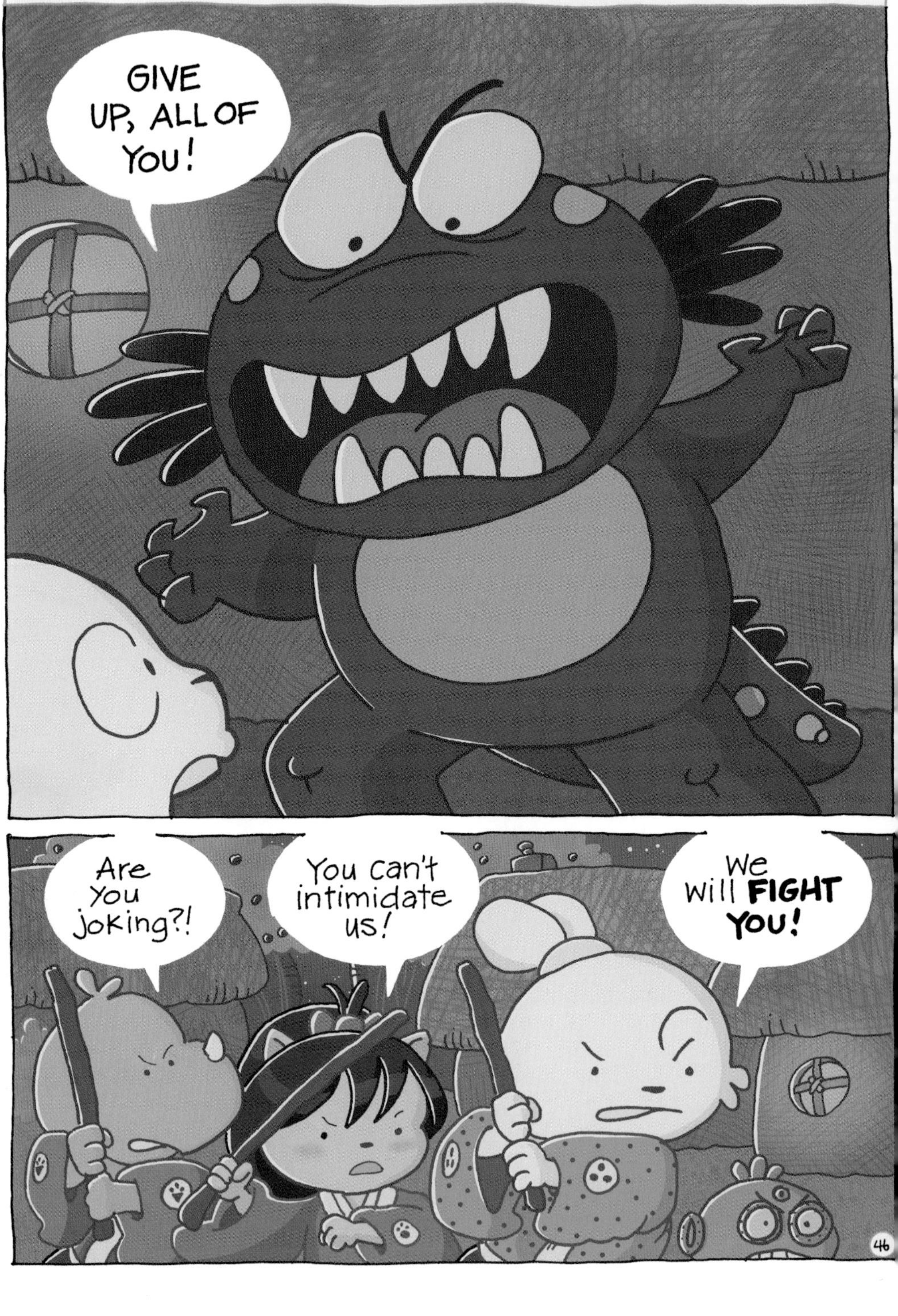
GIVE UP, ALL OF YOU!
Are You joking?!
You can't intimidate us!
We will **FIGHT YOU!**

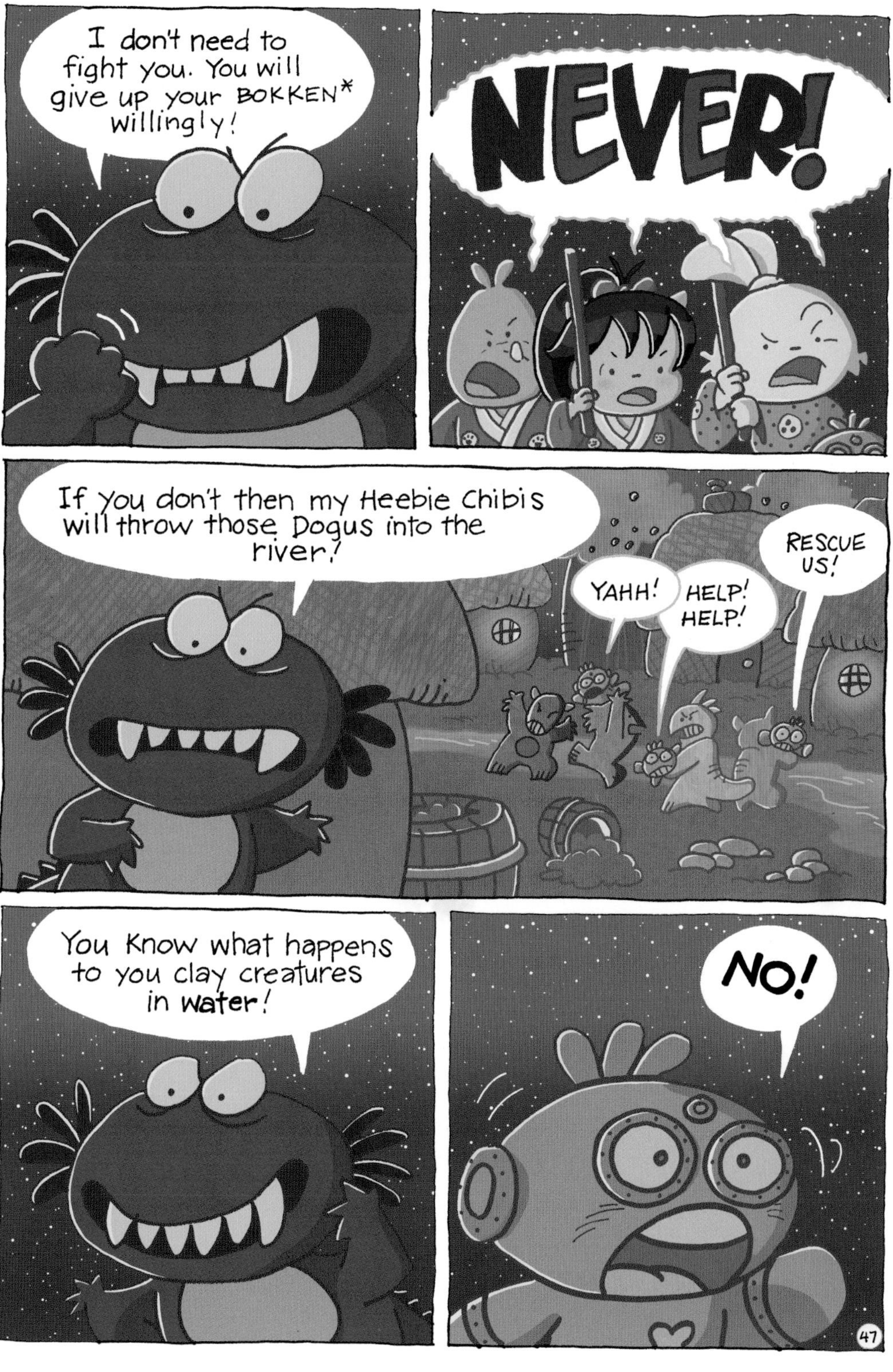
I don't need to fight you. You will give up your BOKKEN* willingly!
NEVER!
If you don't then my Heebie Chibis will throw those Dogus into the river!
YAHH!
HELP! HELP!
RESCUE US!
You know what happens to you clay creatures in water!
NO!

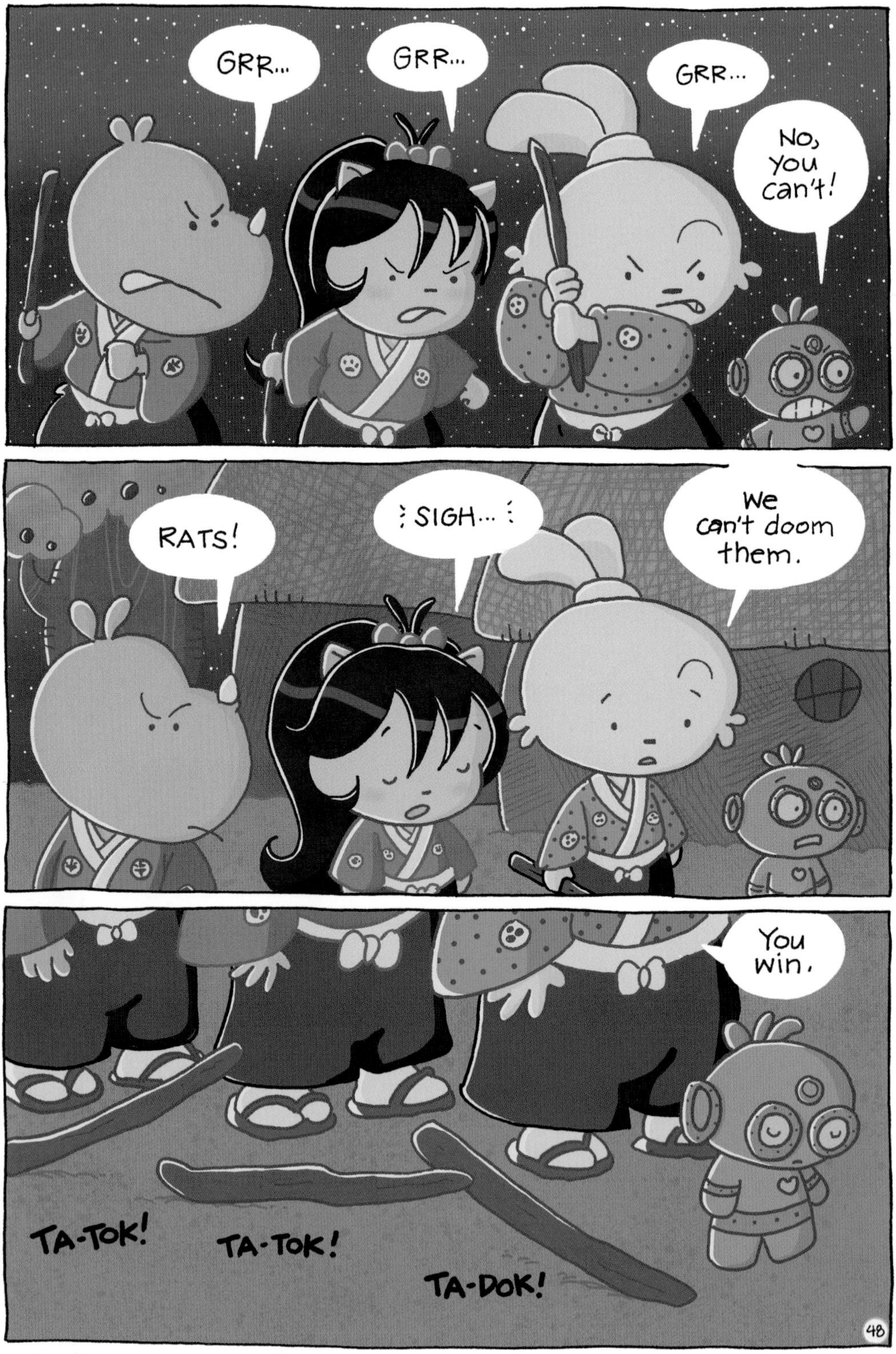
GRR...
GRR...
GRR...
No, you can't!
RATS!
SIGH...
We can't doom them.
You win.
TA-TOK!
TA-TOK!
TA-DOK!

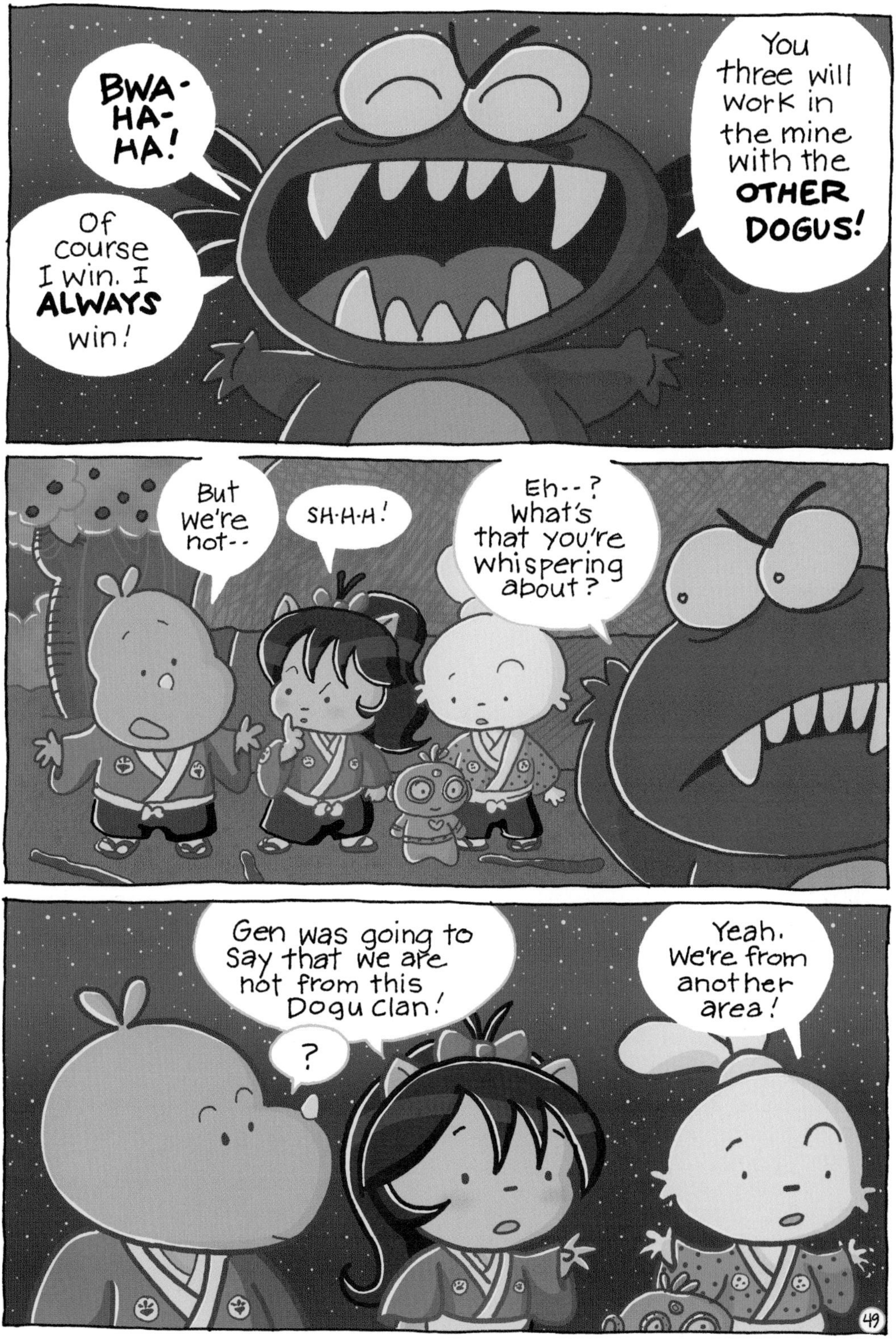
BWA-HA-HA!
Of course I win. I ALWAYS win!
You three will work in the mine with the OTHER DOGUS!
But we're not--
SH-H-H!
Eh--? What's that you're whispering about?
Gen was going to say that we are not from this Dogu clan!
?
Yeah. We're from another area!

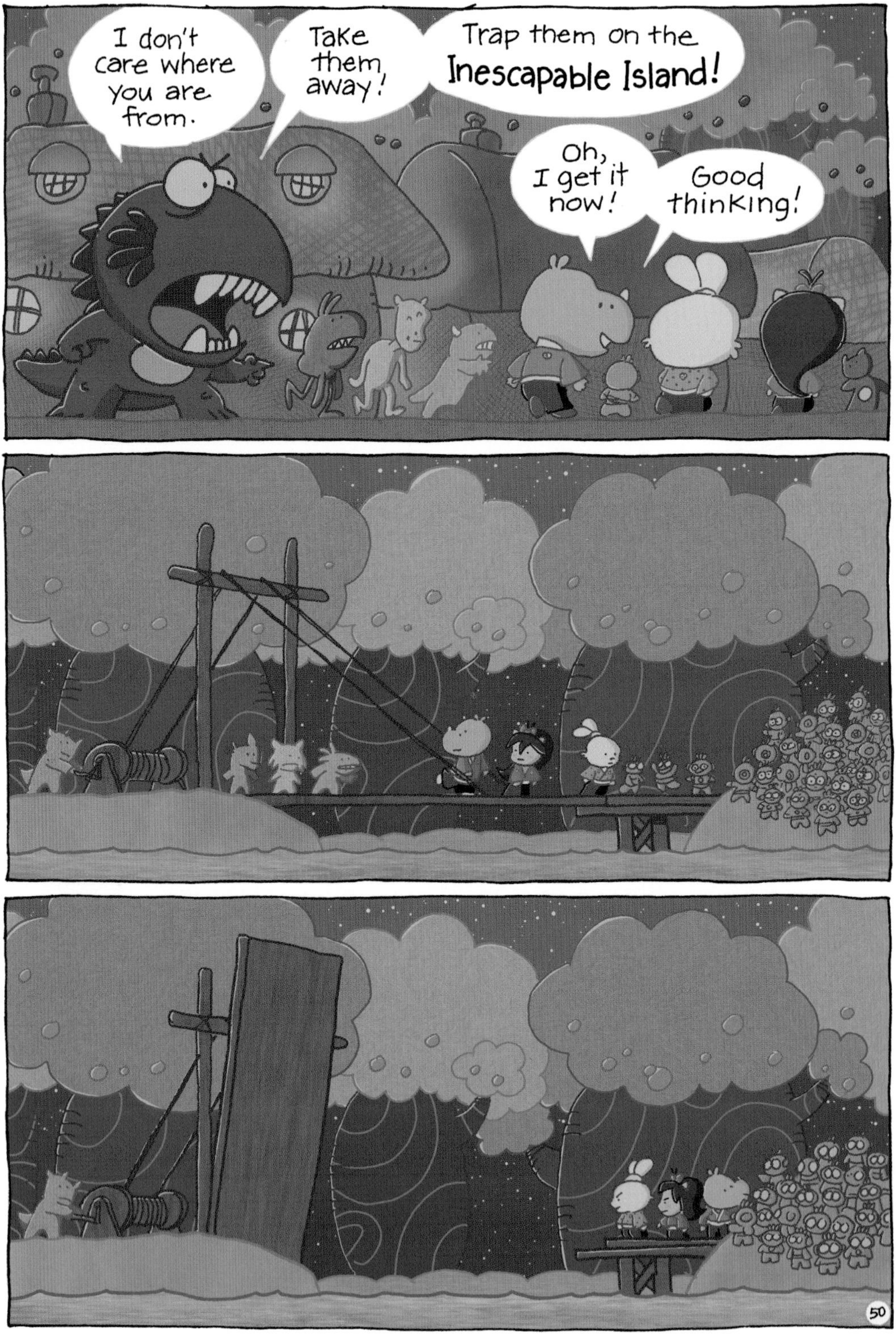
I don't care where you are from.
Take them away!
Trap them on the Inescapable Island!
Oh, I get it now!
Good thinking!

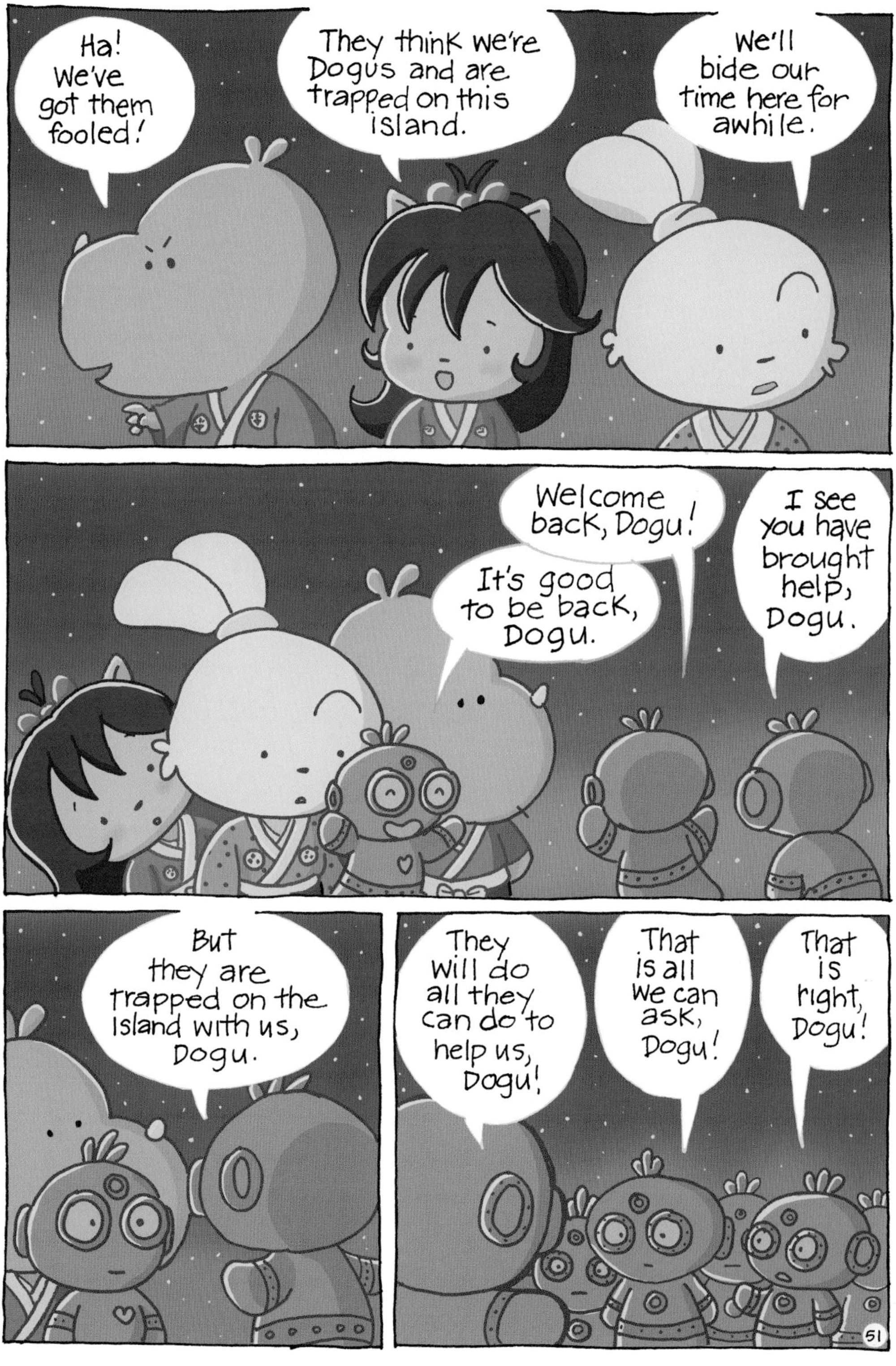
Ha! We've got them fooled!
They think we're Dogus and are trapped on this island.
We'll bide our time here for awhile.
Welcome back, Dogu!
It's good to be back, Dogu.
I see you have brought help, Dogu.
But they are trapped on the Island with us, Dogu.
They will do all they can do to help us, Dogu!
That is all we can ask, Dogu!
That is right, Dogu!

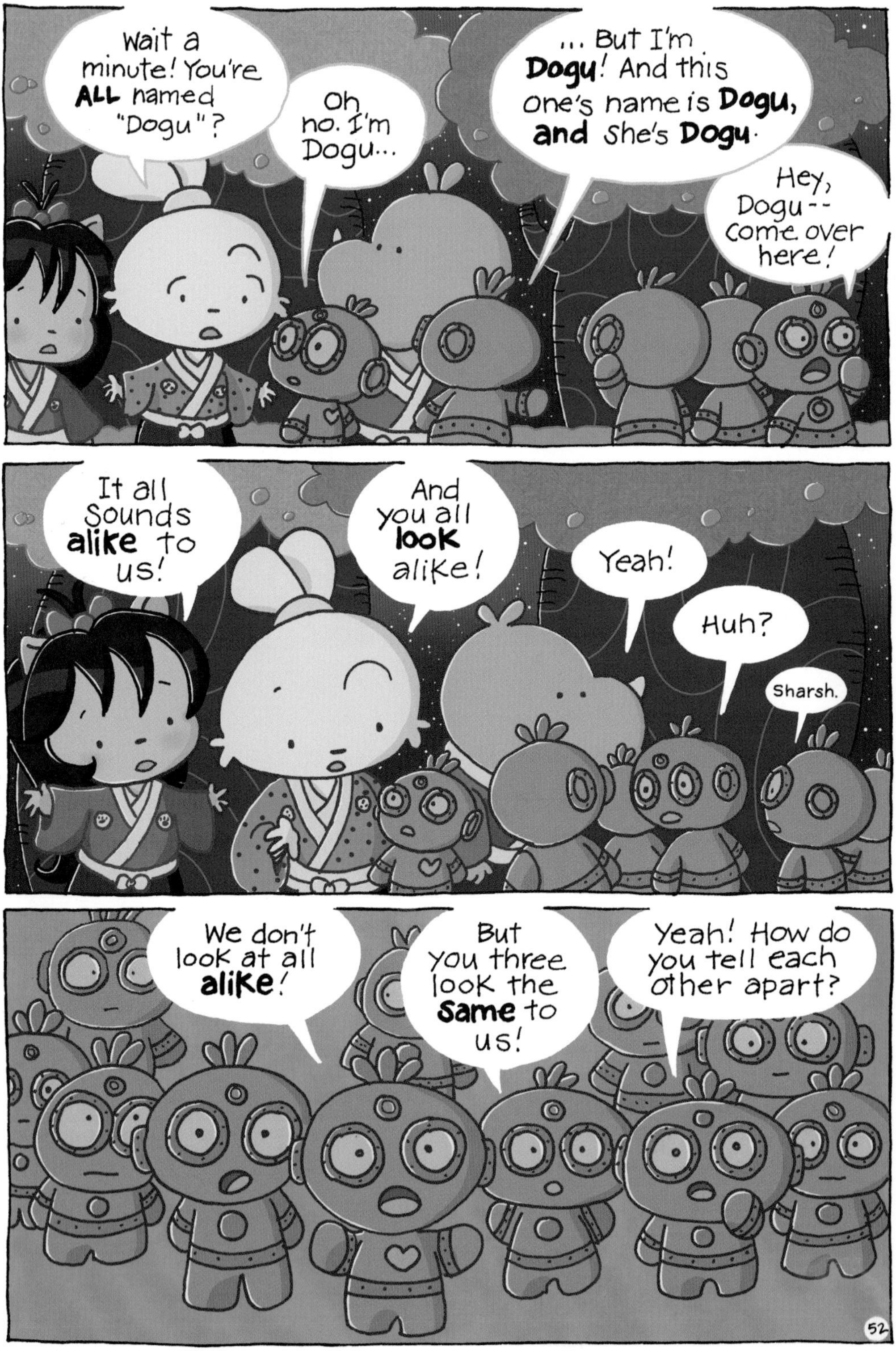
Wait a minute! You're ALL named "Dogu"?
Oh no. I'm Dogu...
... But I'm Dogu! And this one's name is Dogu, and she's Dogu.
Hey, Dogu-- come over here!
It all sounds alike to us!
And you all look alike!
Yeah!
Huh?
Sharsh.
We don't look at all alike!
But you three look the same to us!
Yeah! How do you tell each other apart?

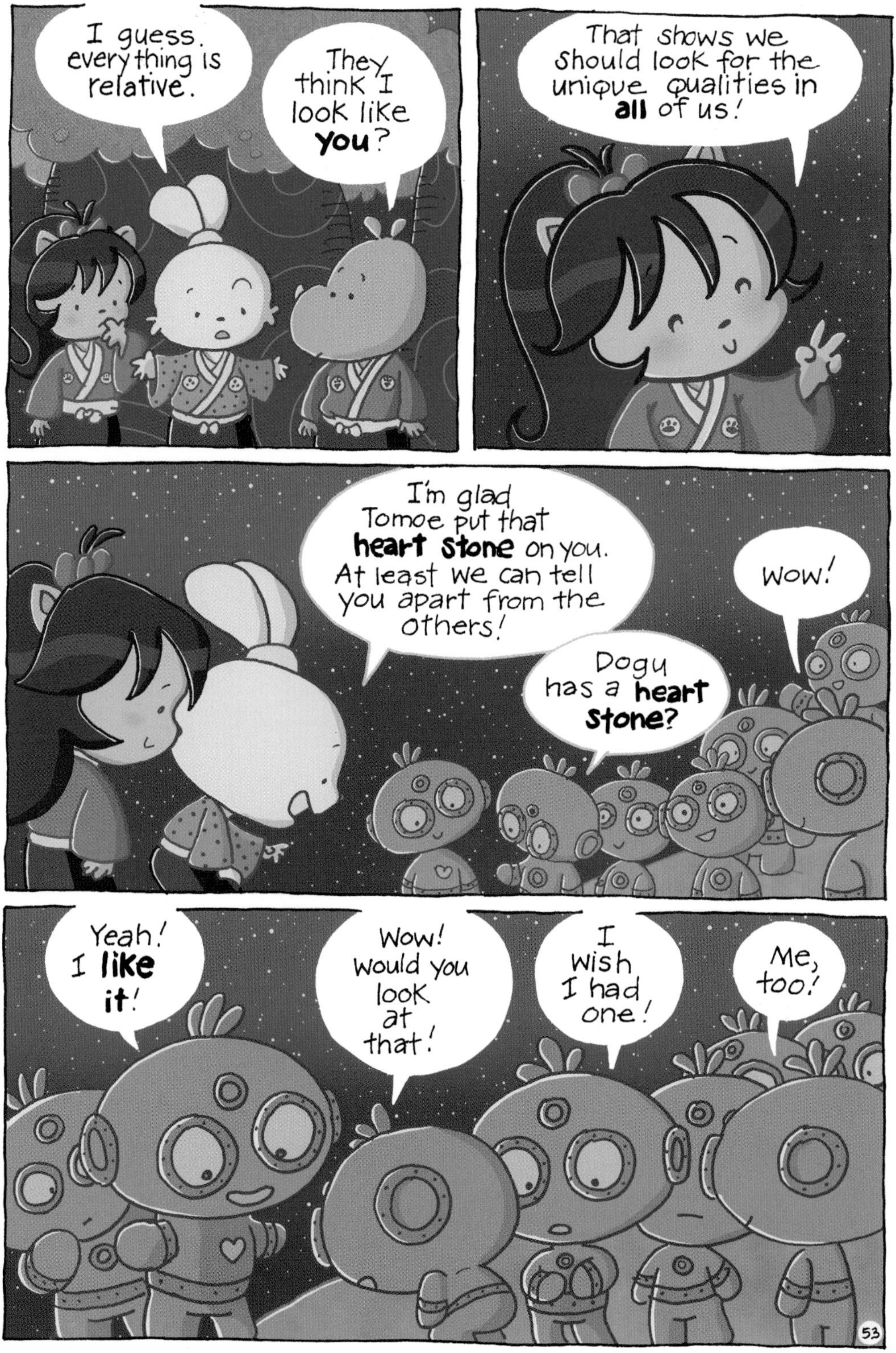
I guess. everything is relative.
They think I look like **you**?
That shows we should look for the unique qualities in **all** of us!
I'm glad Tomoe put that **heart stone** on you. At least we can tell you apart from the others!
Wow!
Dogu has a **heart stone?**
Yeah! I **like it**!
Wow! Would you look at that!
I wish I had one!
Me, too!

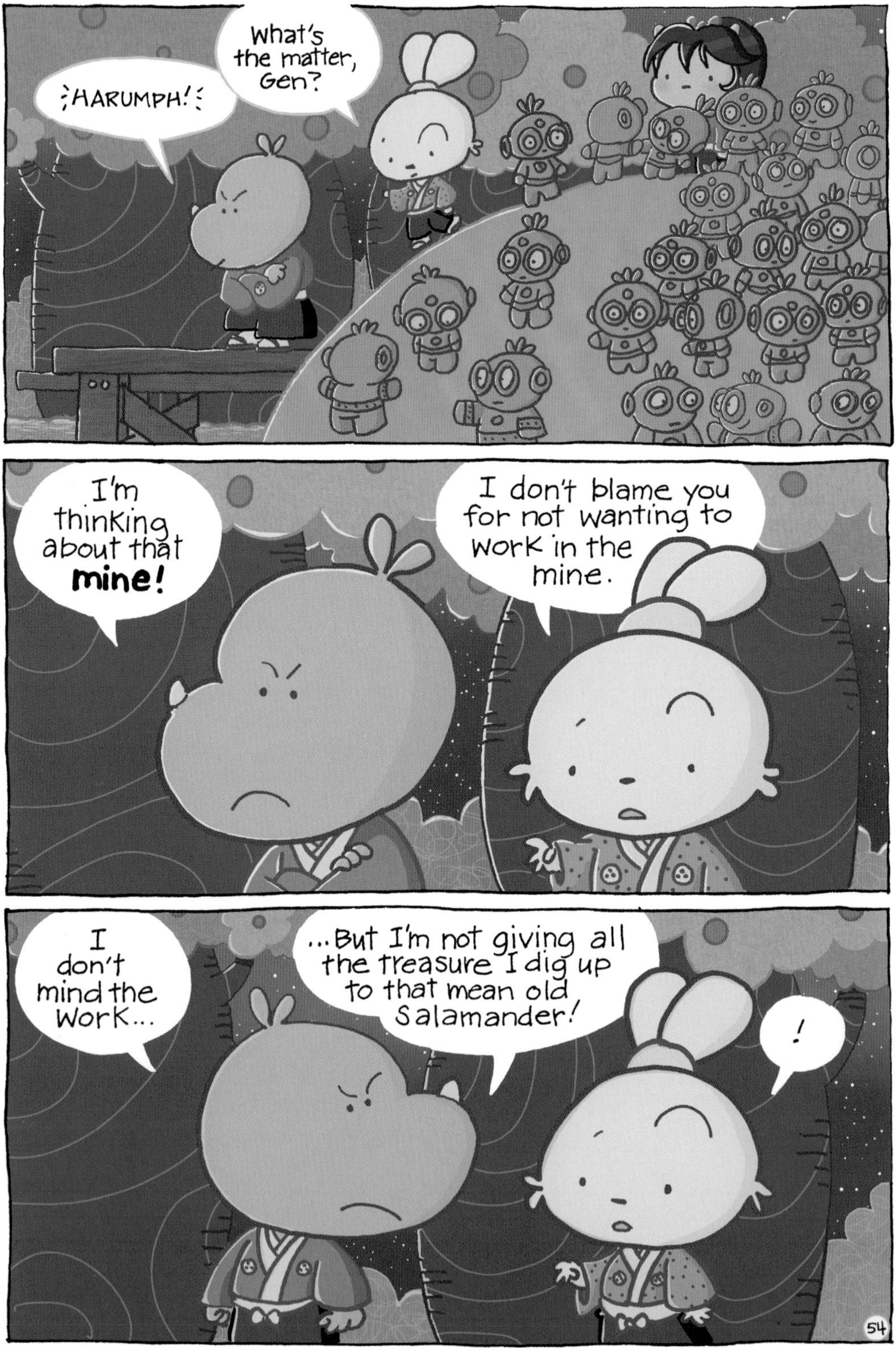
What's the matter, Gen?
HARUMPH!
I'm thinking about that **mine!**
I don't blame you for not wanting to work in the mine.
I don't mind the work...
...But I'm not giving all the treasure I dig up to that mean old Salamander!
!

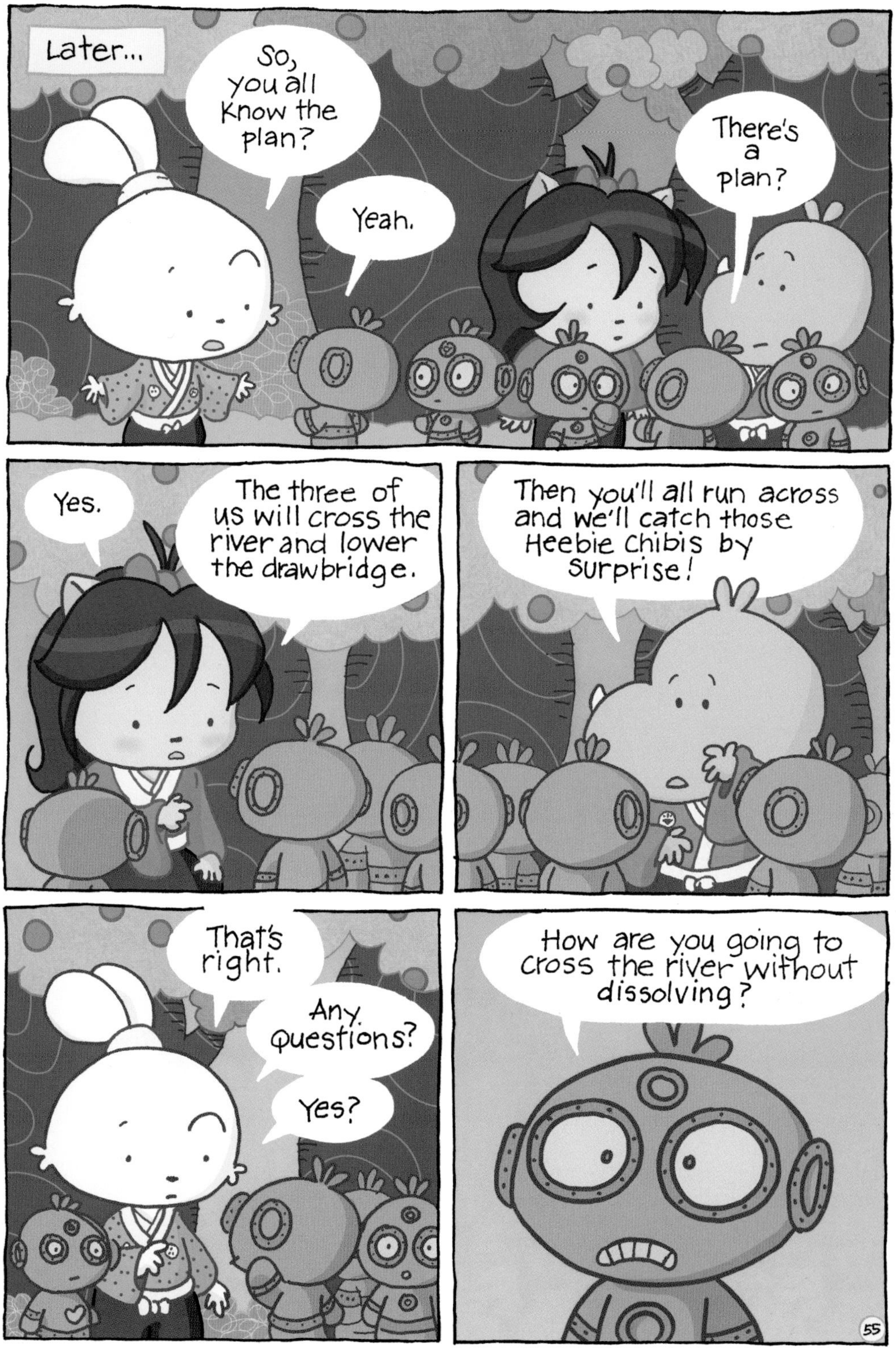

Later...
So, you all Know the plan?
Yeah.
There's a plan?
Yes.
The three of us will cross the river and lower the drawbridge.
Then you'll all run across and we'll catch those Heebie Chibis by surprise!
That's right.
Any questions?
Yes?
How are you going to cross the river without dissolving?

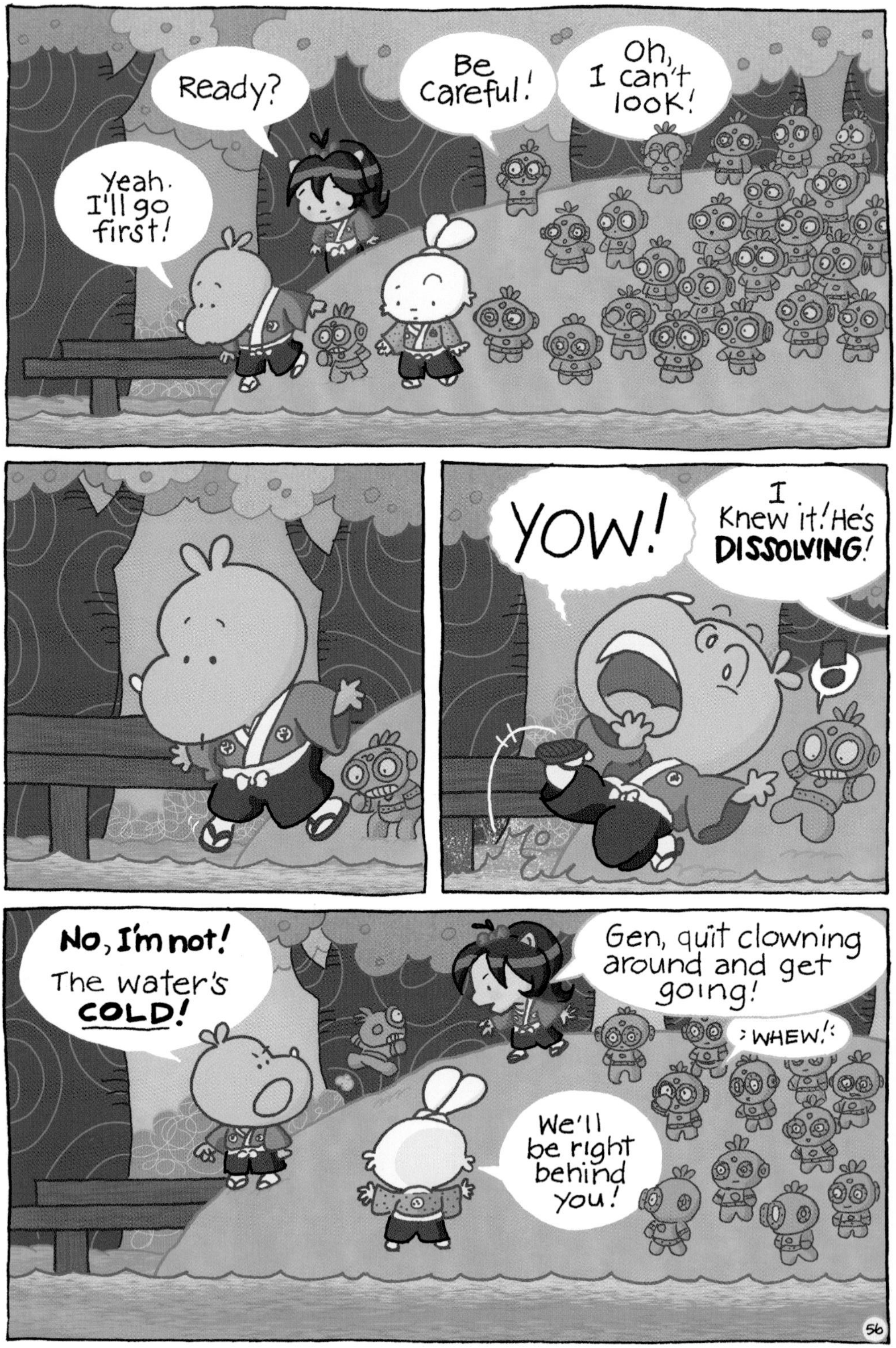
Yeah. I'll go first!
Ready?
Be careful!
Oh, I can't look!
YOW!
I. Knew it! He's DISSOLVING!
No, I'm not! The water's COLD!
Gen, quit clowning around and get going!
WHEW!
We'll be right behind you!

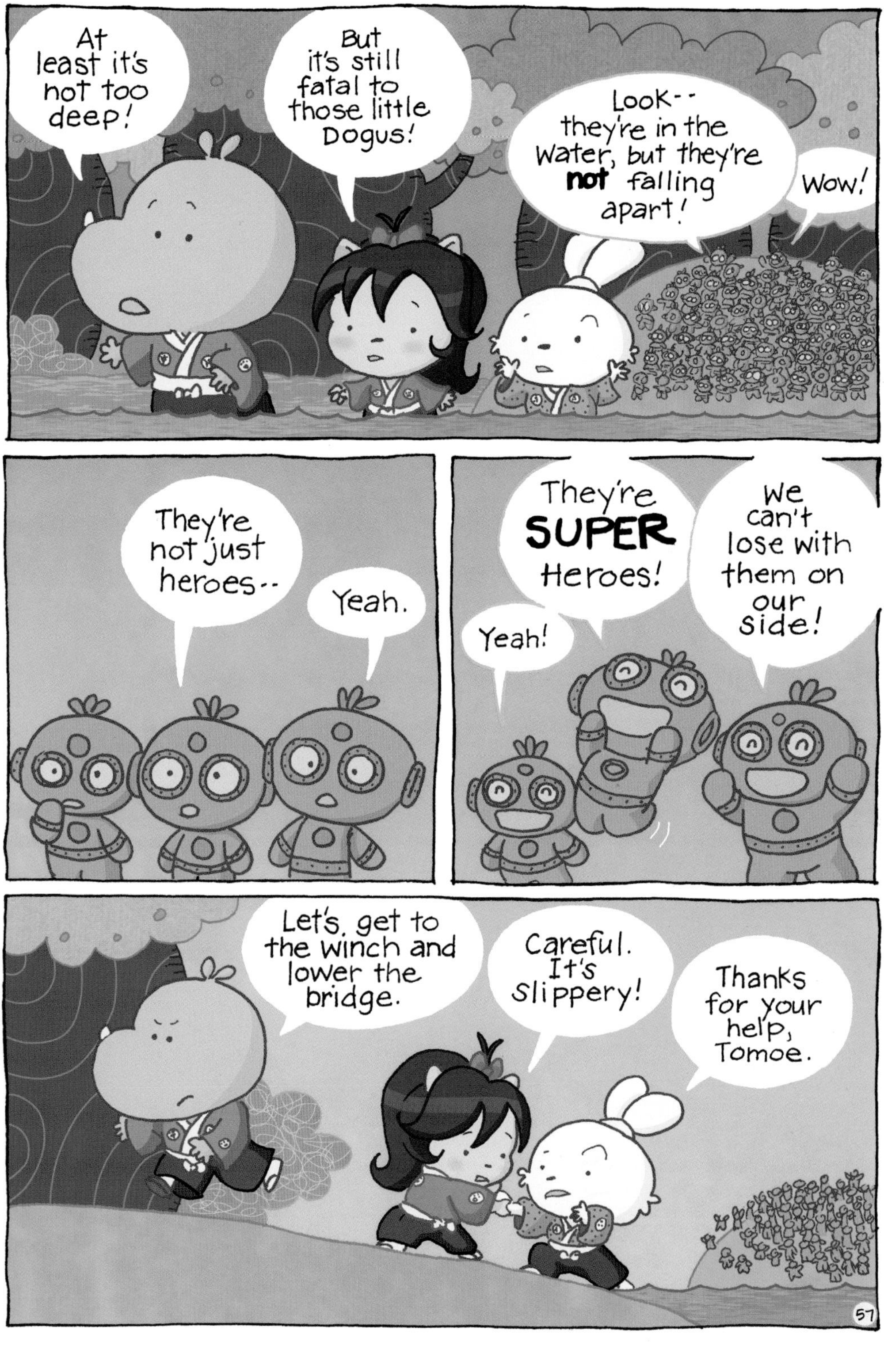
At least it's not too deep!
But it's still fatal to those little Dogus!
Look-- they're in the water, but they're **not** falling apart!
Wow!
They're not just heroes--
Yeah.
They're SUPER Heroes!
Yeah!
We can't lose with them on our side!
Let's get to the winch and lower the bridge.
Careful. It's slippery!
Thanks for your help, Tomoe.

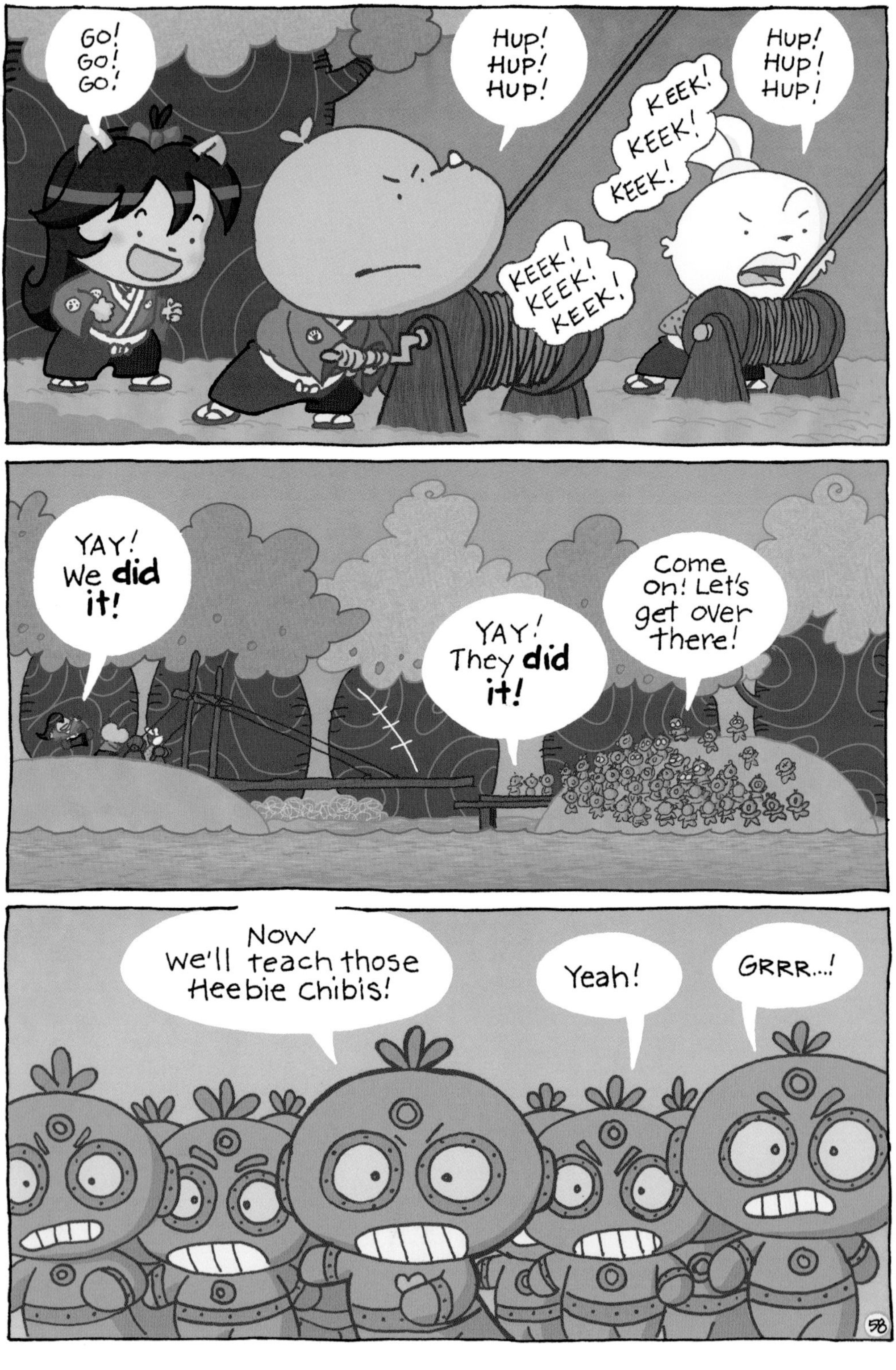
GO! GO! GO!
HUP! HUP! HUP!
KEEK! KEEK! KEEK!
HUP! HUP! HUP!
KEEK! KEEK! KEEK!
YAY! We did it!
YAY! They did it!
Come on! Let's get over there!
Now we'll teach those Heebie Chibis!
Yeah!
GRRR...!

PART FIVE: THE PRISONERS ARE REVOLTING!

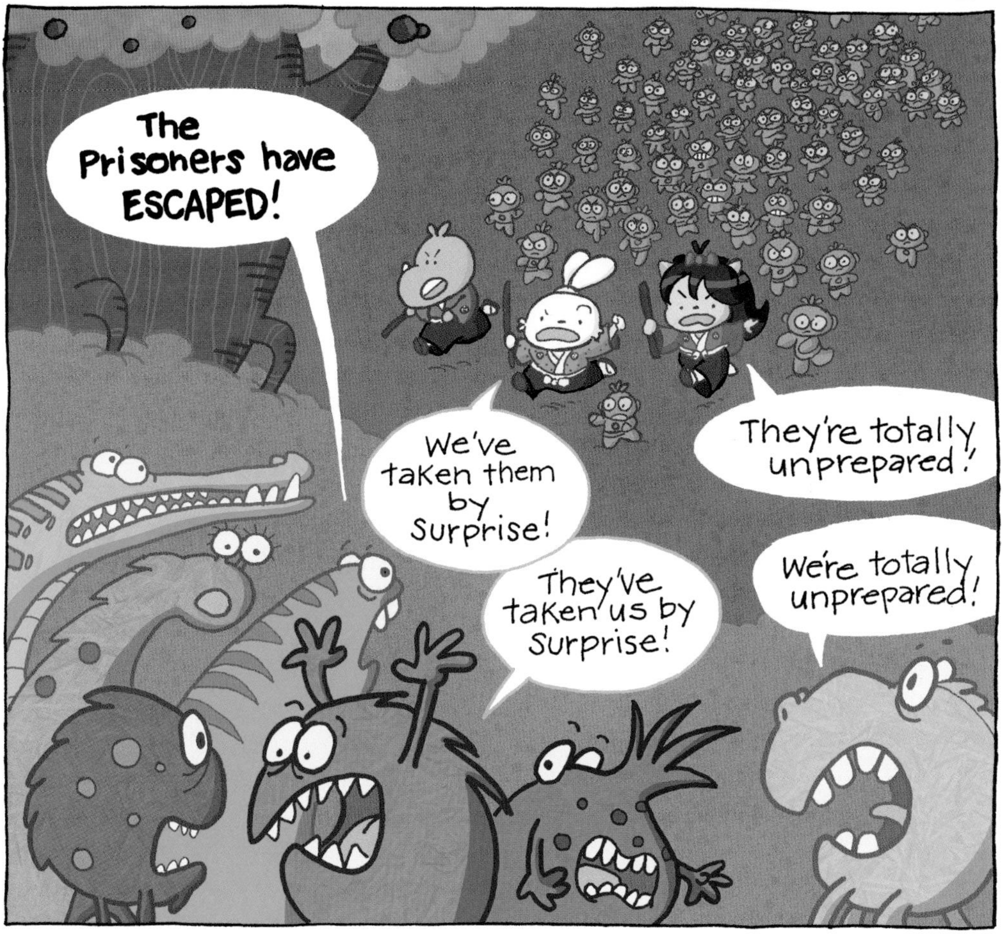
The Prisoners have ESCAPED!
We've taken them by Surprise!
They're totally unprepared!
They've taken us by Surprise!
We're totally unprepared!

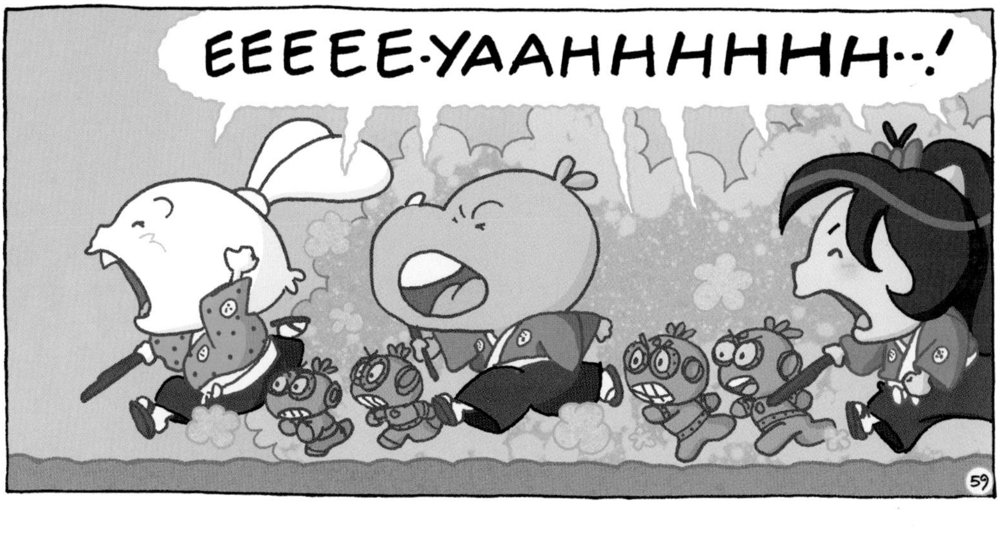
EEEEE-YAAHHHHHH..!

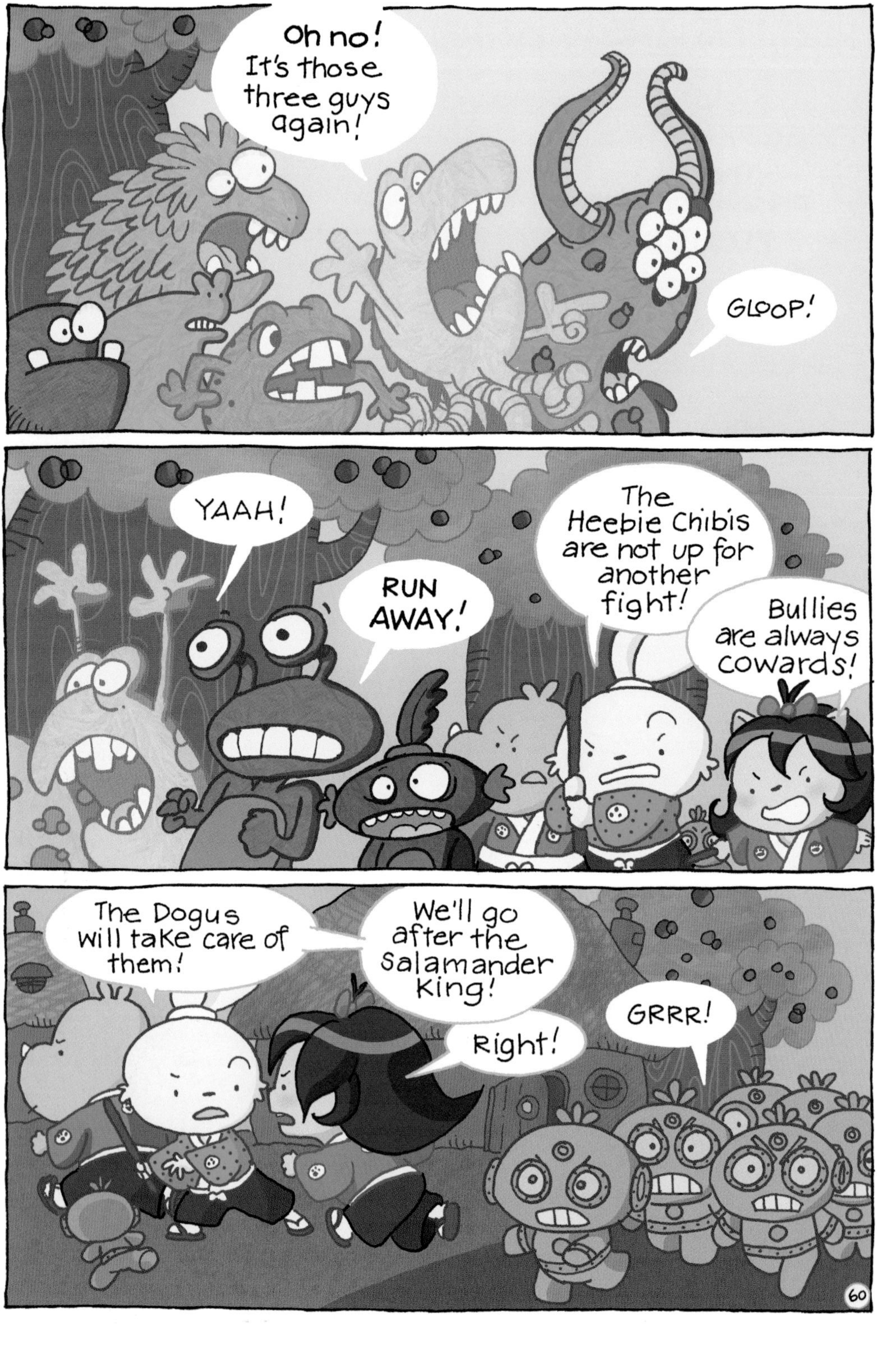
Oh no! It's those three guys again!
GLOOP!
YAAH!
RUN AWAY!
The Heebie Chibis are not up for another fight!
Bullies are always cowards!
The Dogus will take care of them!
We'll go after the Salamander King!
Right!
GRRR!
60

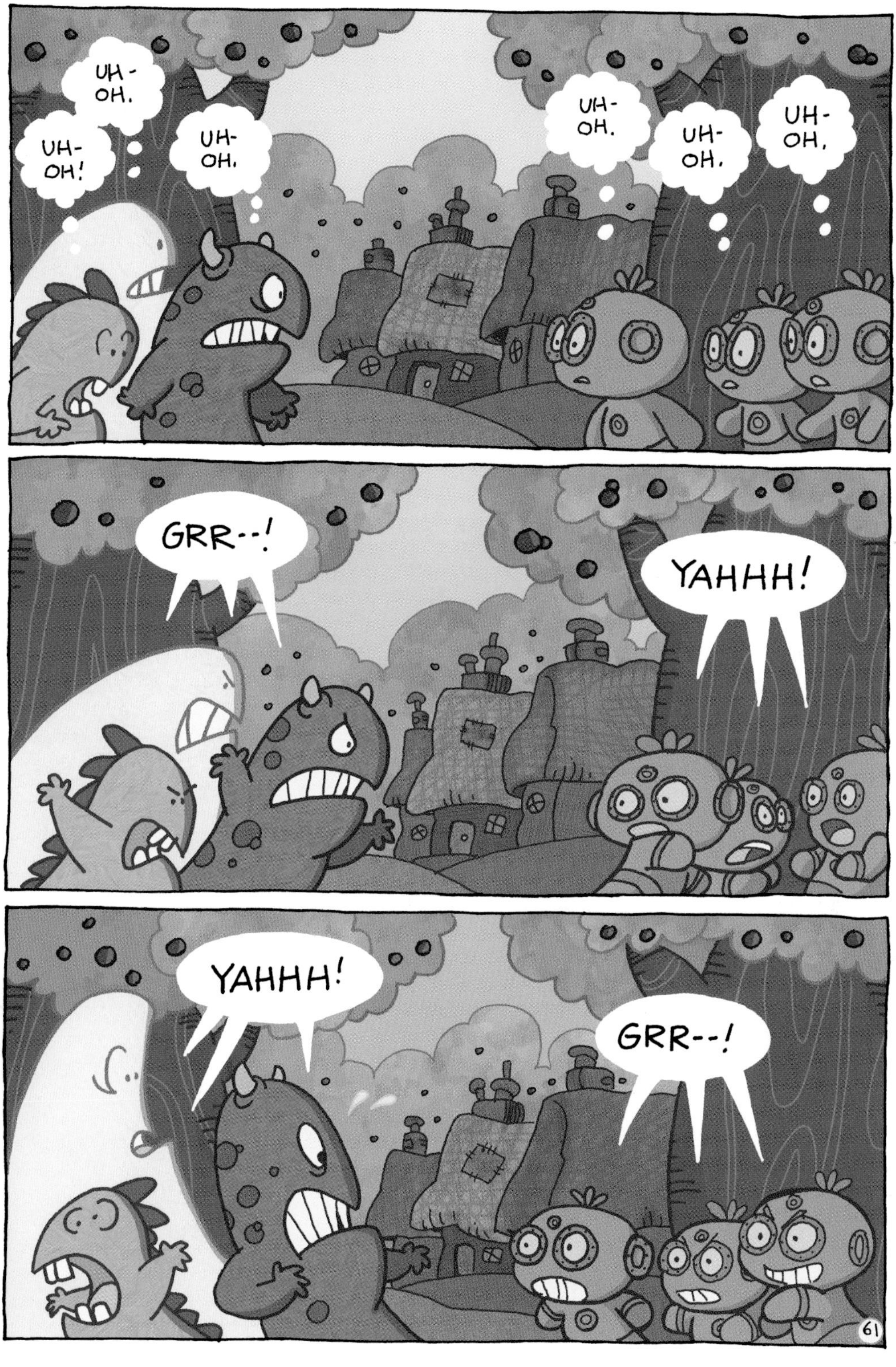
UH-OH!
UH-OH.
UH-OH.
UH-OH.
UH-OH.
UH-OH.
GRR--!
YAHHH!
YAHHH!
GRR--!

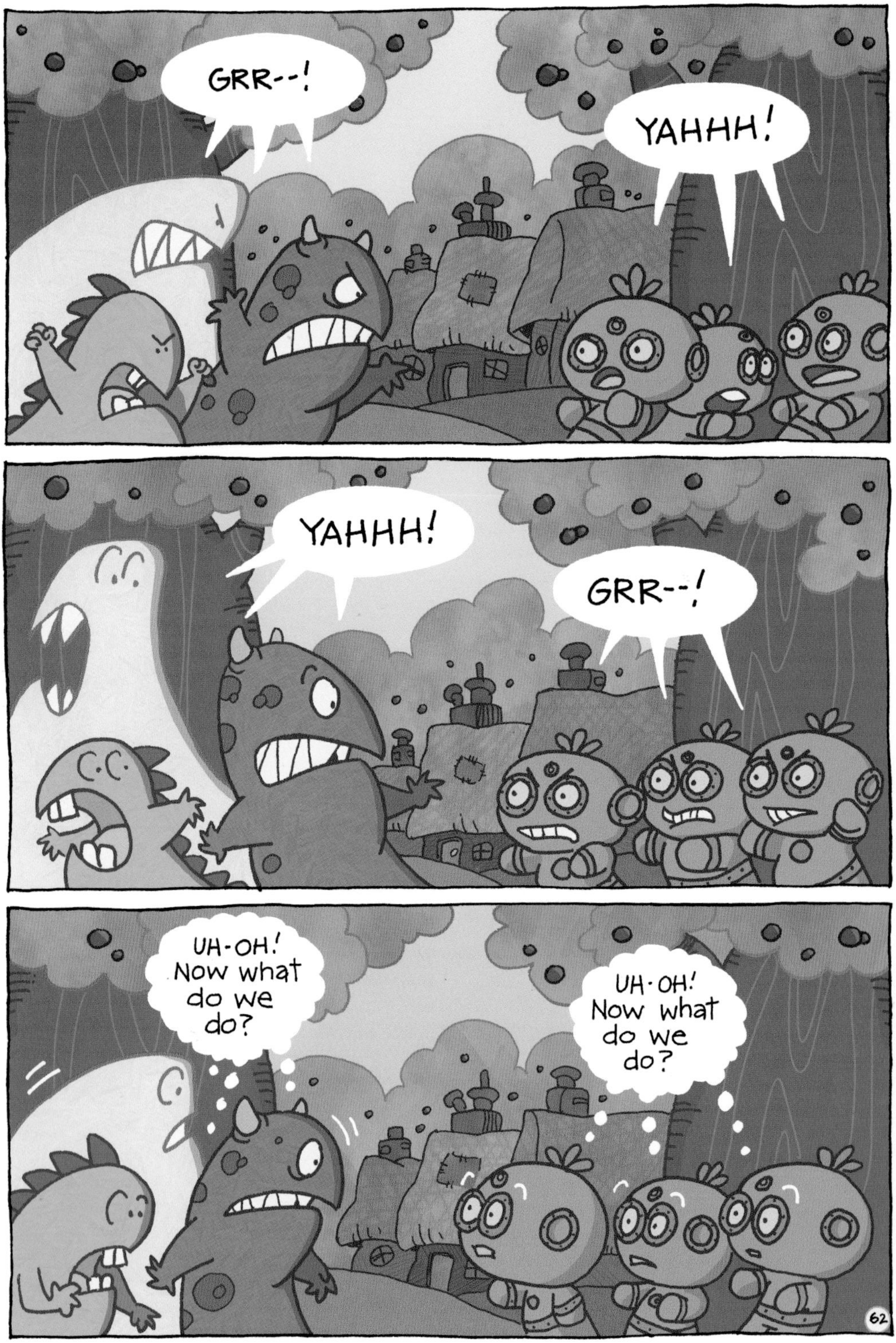
GRR--!
YAHHH!
YAHHH!
GRR--!
UH-OH! Now what do we do?
UH-OH! Now what do we do?

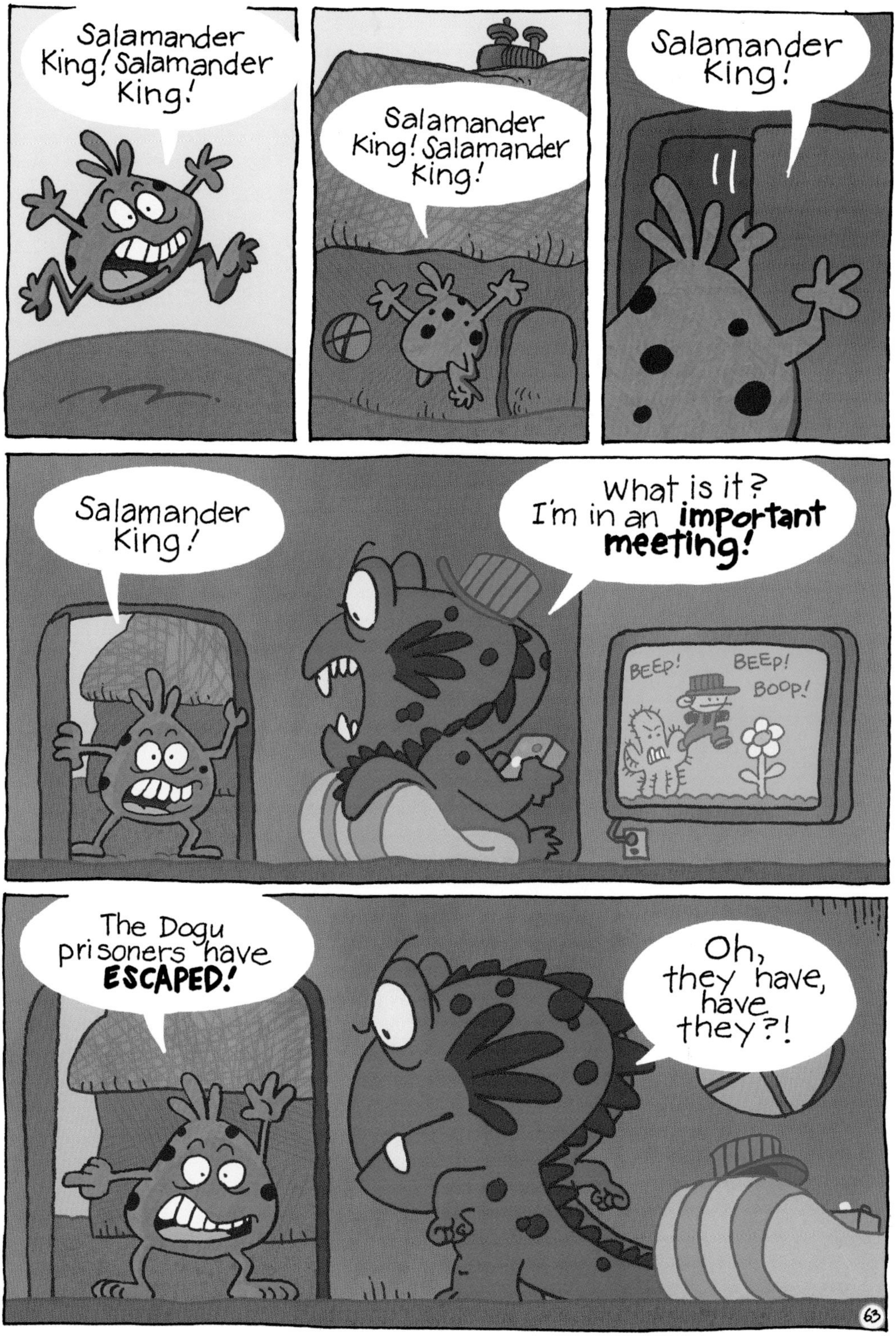
Salamander King! Salamander King!
Salamander King! Salamander King!
Salamander King!
Salamander King!
What is it? I'm in an **important meeting!**
BEEP! BEEP! BOOP!
The Dogu prisoners have **ESCAPED!**
Oh, they have, have they?!

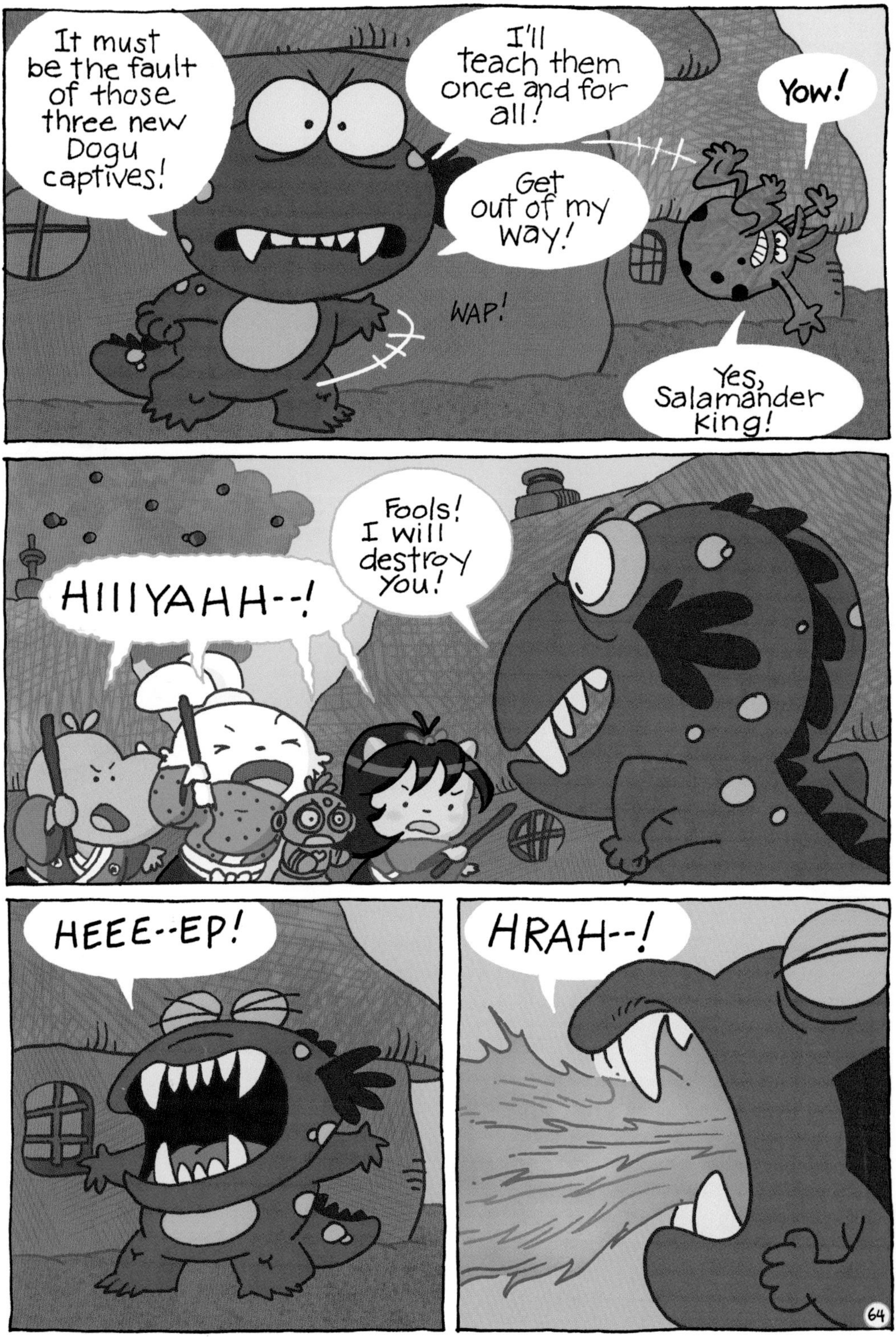
It must be the fault of those three new Dogu captives!
I'll teach them once and for all!
Get out of my way!
WAP!
Yow!
Yes, Salamander King!
HIIIYAHH--!
Fools! I will destroy you!
HEEE--EP!
HRAH--!

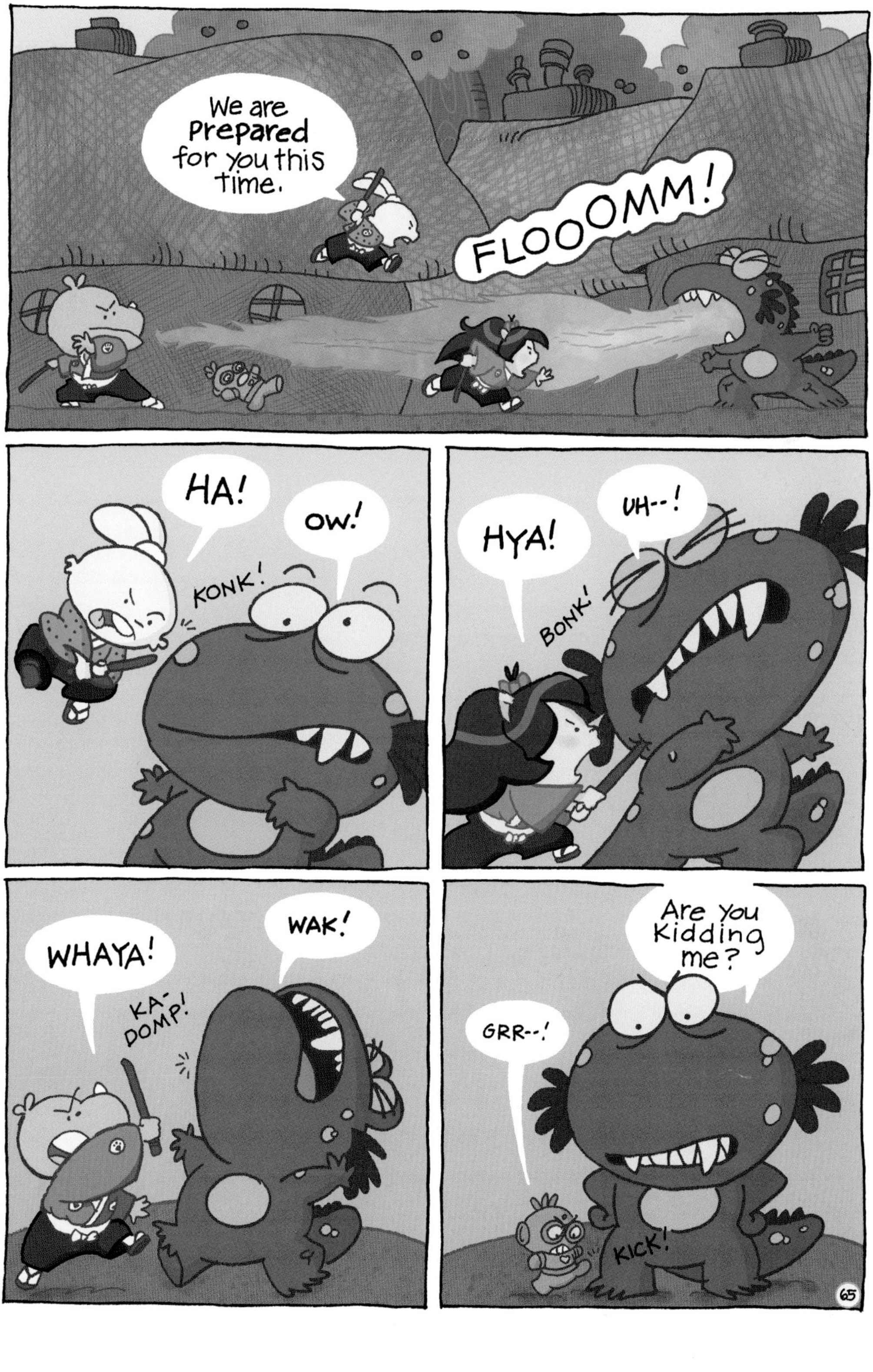
We are Prepared for you this time.
FLOOOMM!
HA!
OW!
KONK!
HYA!
UH--!
BONK!
WHAYA!
WAK!
KA-DOMP!
Are you kidding me?
GRR--!
KICK!

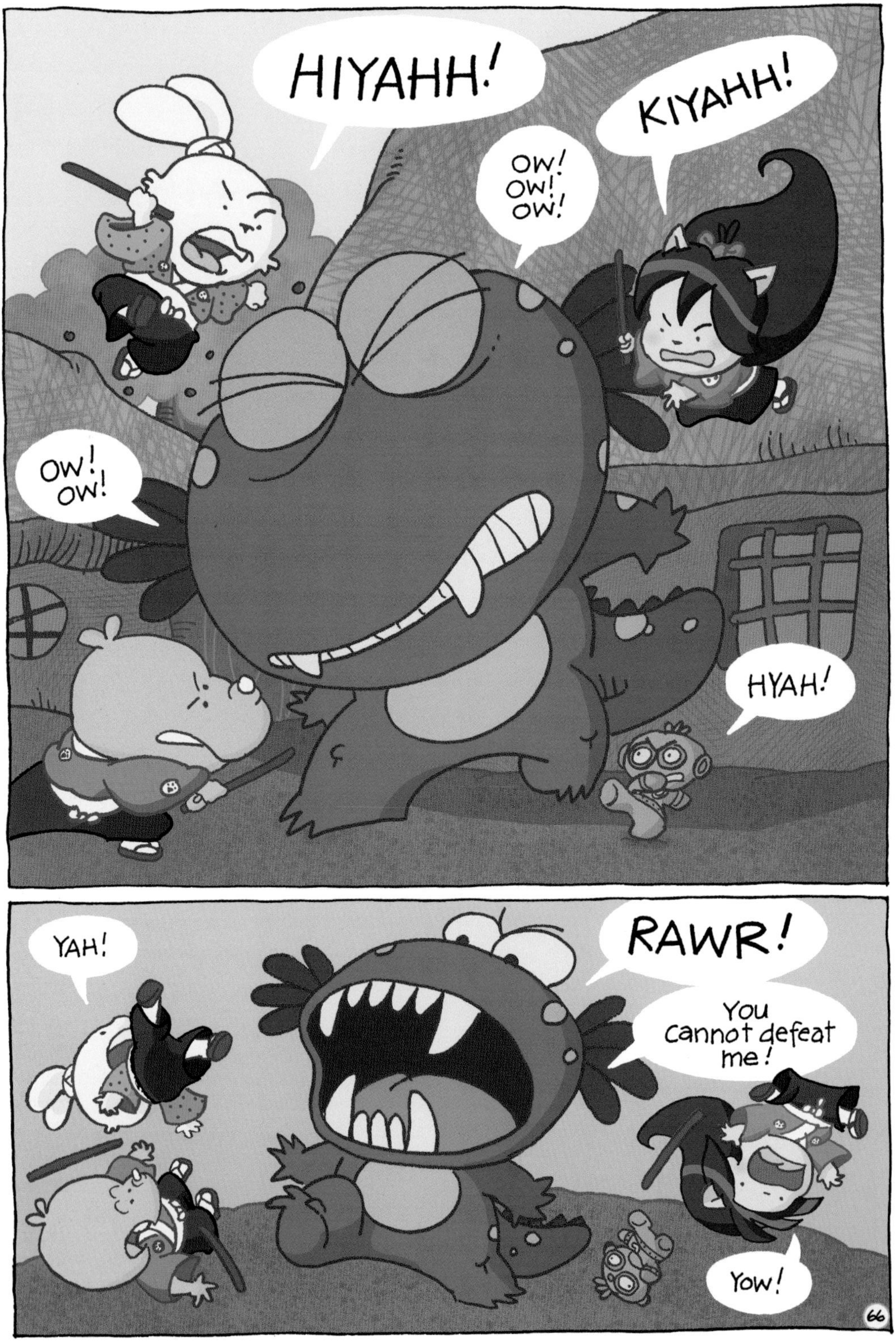
HIYAHH!
KIYAHH!
OW! OW! OW!
OW! OW!
HYAH!
YAH!
RAWR!
You cannot defeat me!
YOW!

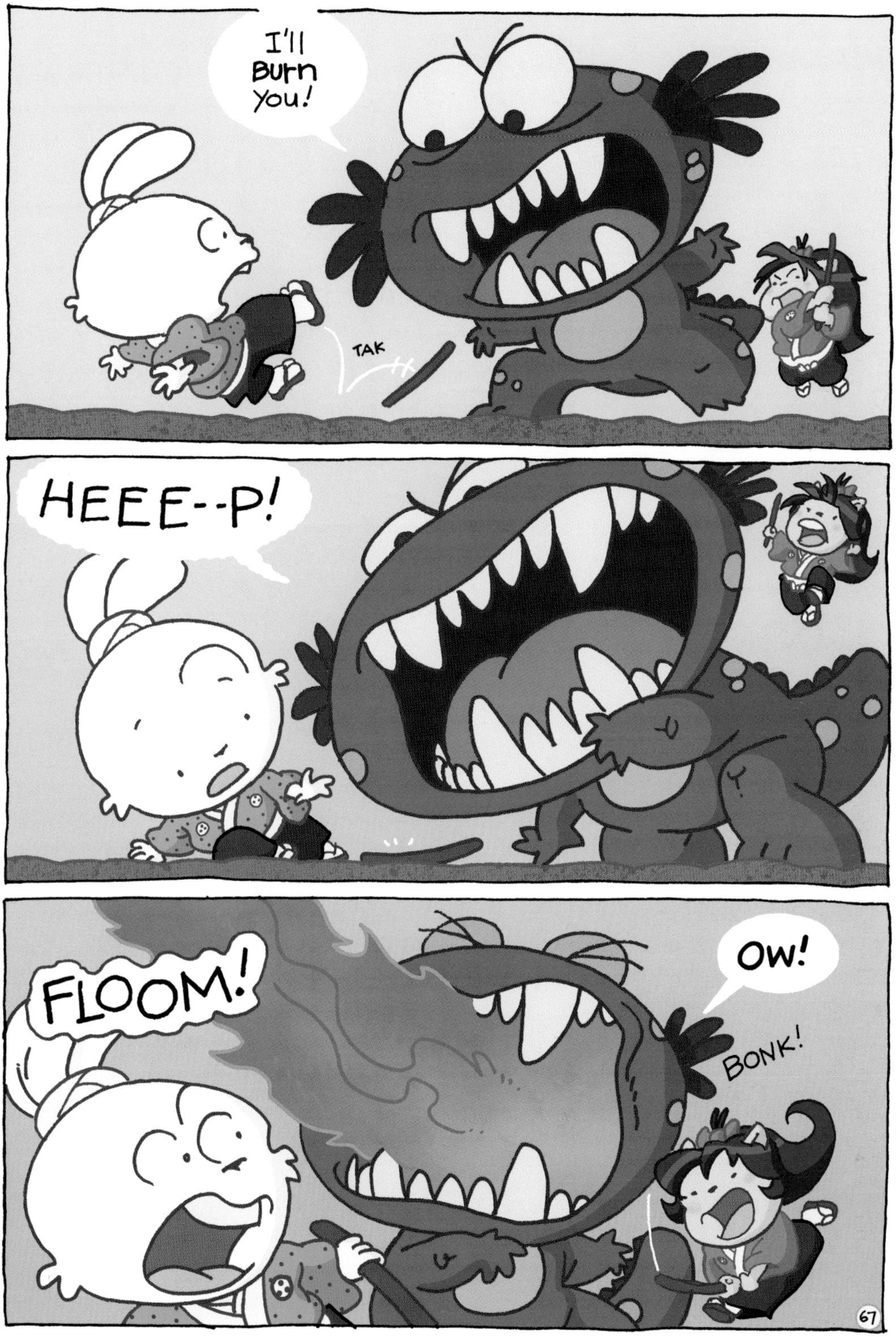
I'll Burn You!
TAK
HEEEE--P!
FLOOM!
OW!
BONK!

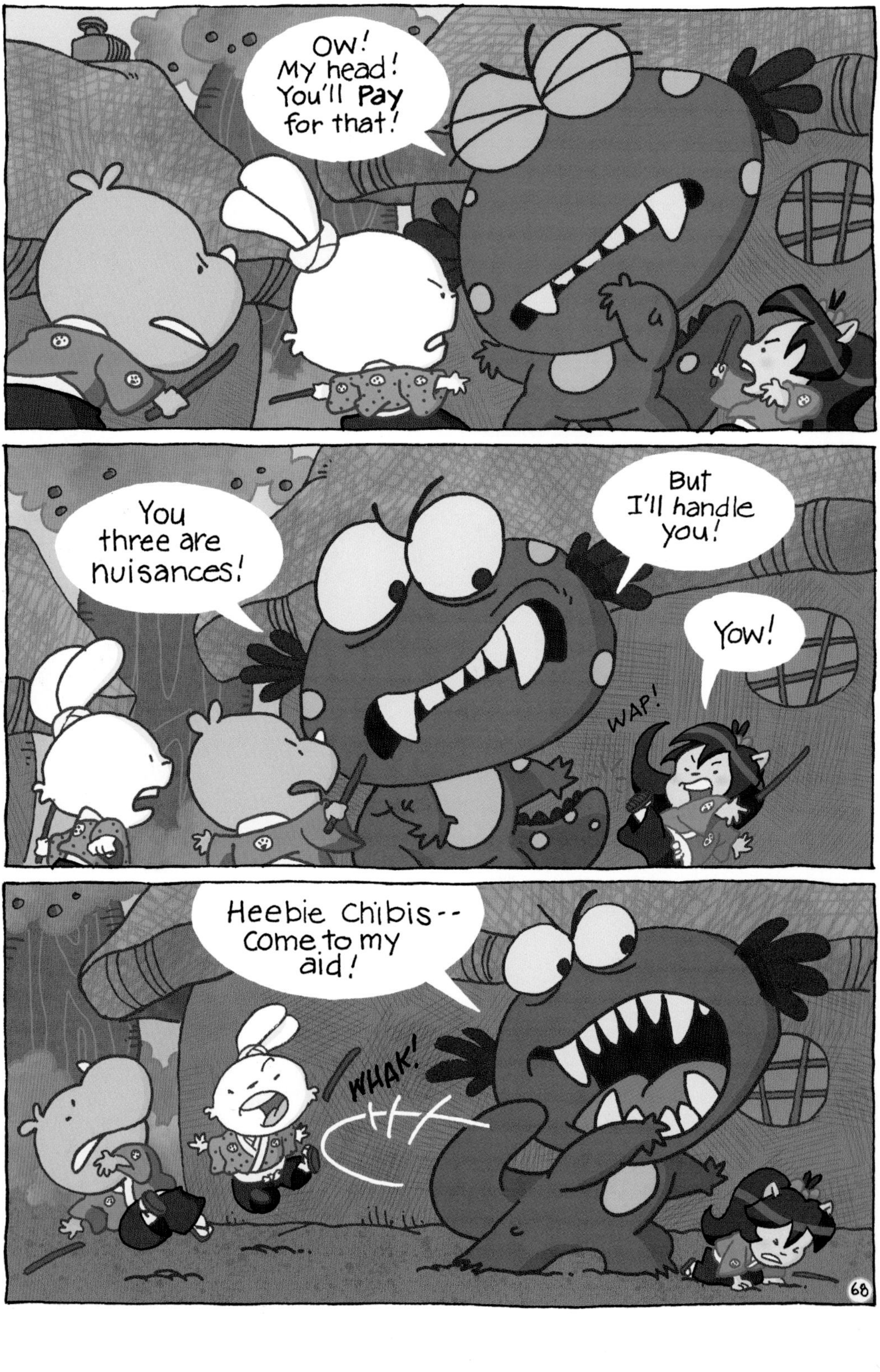

Ow! My head! You'll Pay for that!
You three are nuisances!
But I'll handle you!
WAP!
Yow!
Heebie Chibis-- Come to my aid!
WHAK!

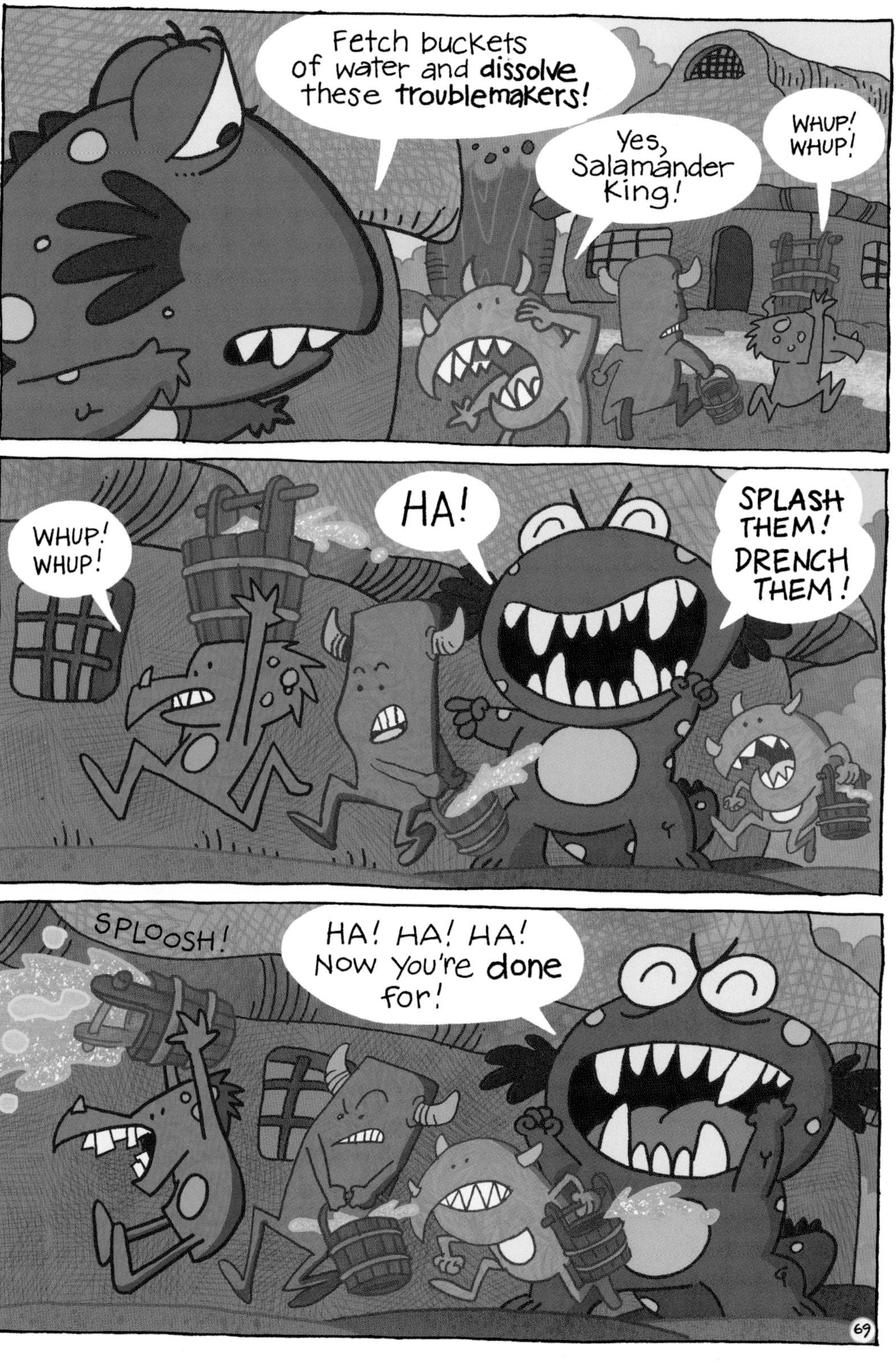
Fetch buckets of water and dissolve these troublemakers!
Yes, Salamander King!
WHUP! WHUP!
WHUP! WHUP!
HA!
SPLASH THEM! DRENCH THEM!
SPLOOSH!
HA! HA! HA! Now you're done for!

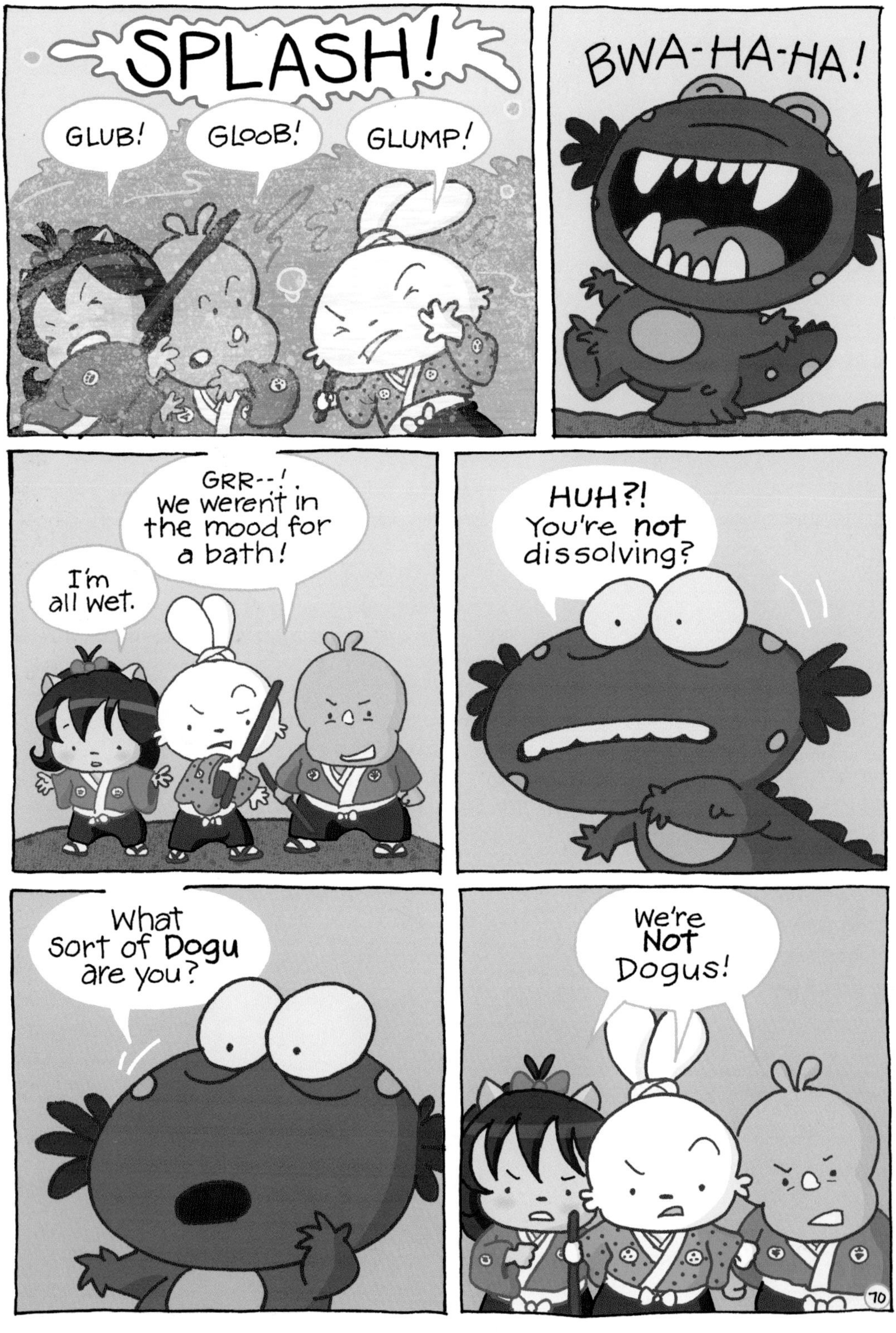
SPLASH!
GLUB!
GLOOB!
GLUMP!
BWA-HA-HA!
GRR--! We weren't in the mood for a bath!
I'm all wet.
HUH?! You're not dissolving?
What sort of Dogu are you?
We're NOT Dogus!
70

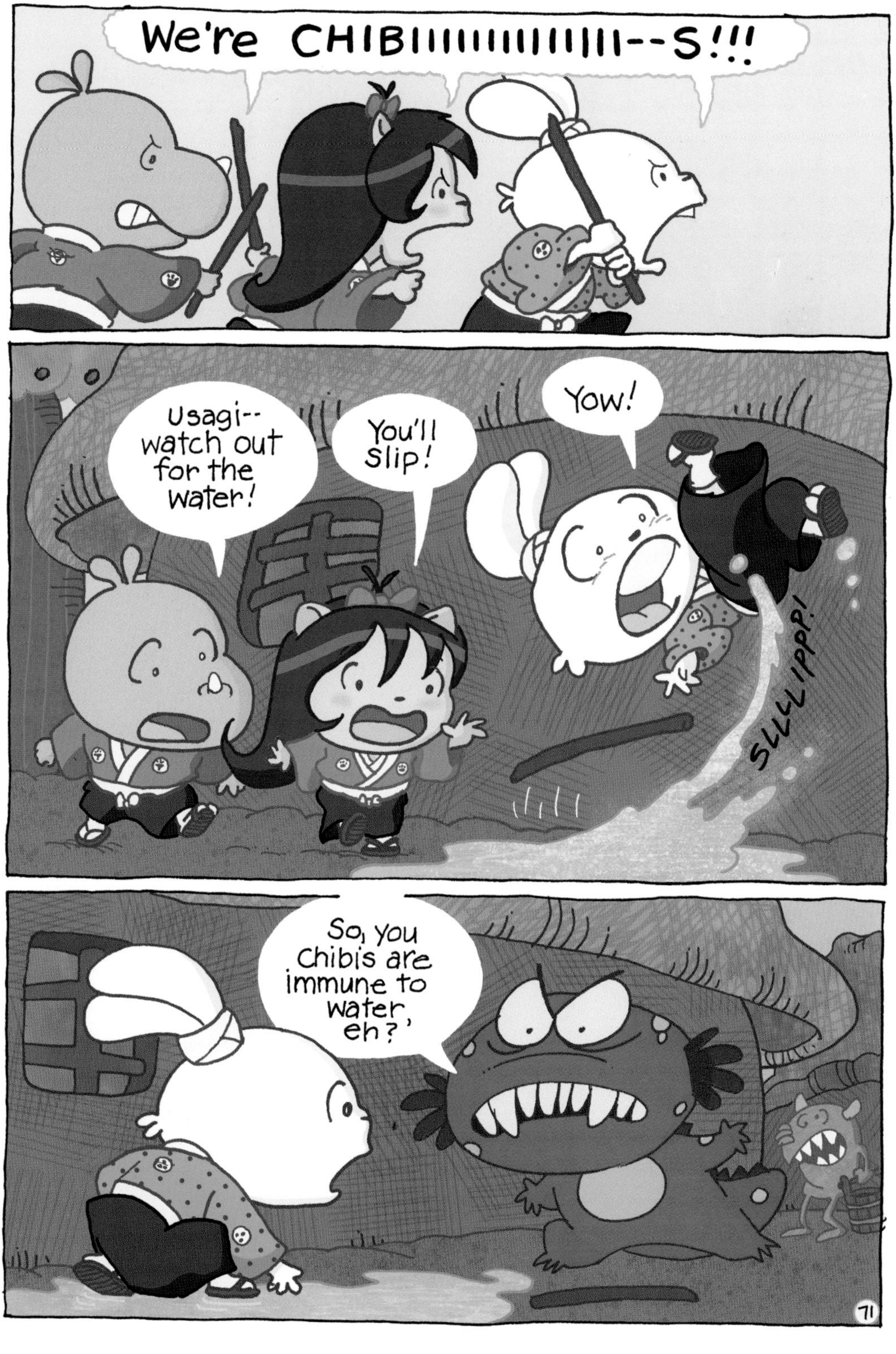

We're CHIBIIIIIIIIIIIIII--S!!!
Usagi--watch out for the water!
You'll slip!
Yow!
SLLLIPPP!
So, you chibis are immune to water, eh?

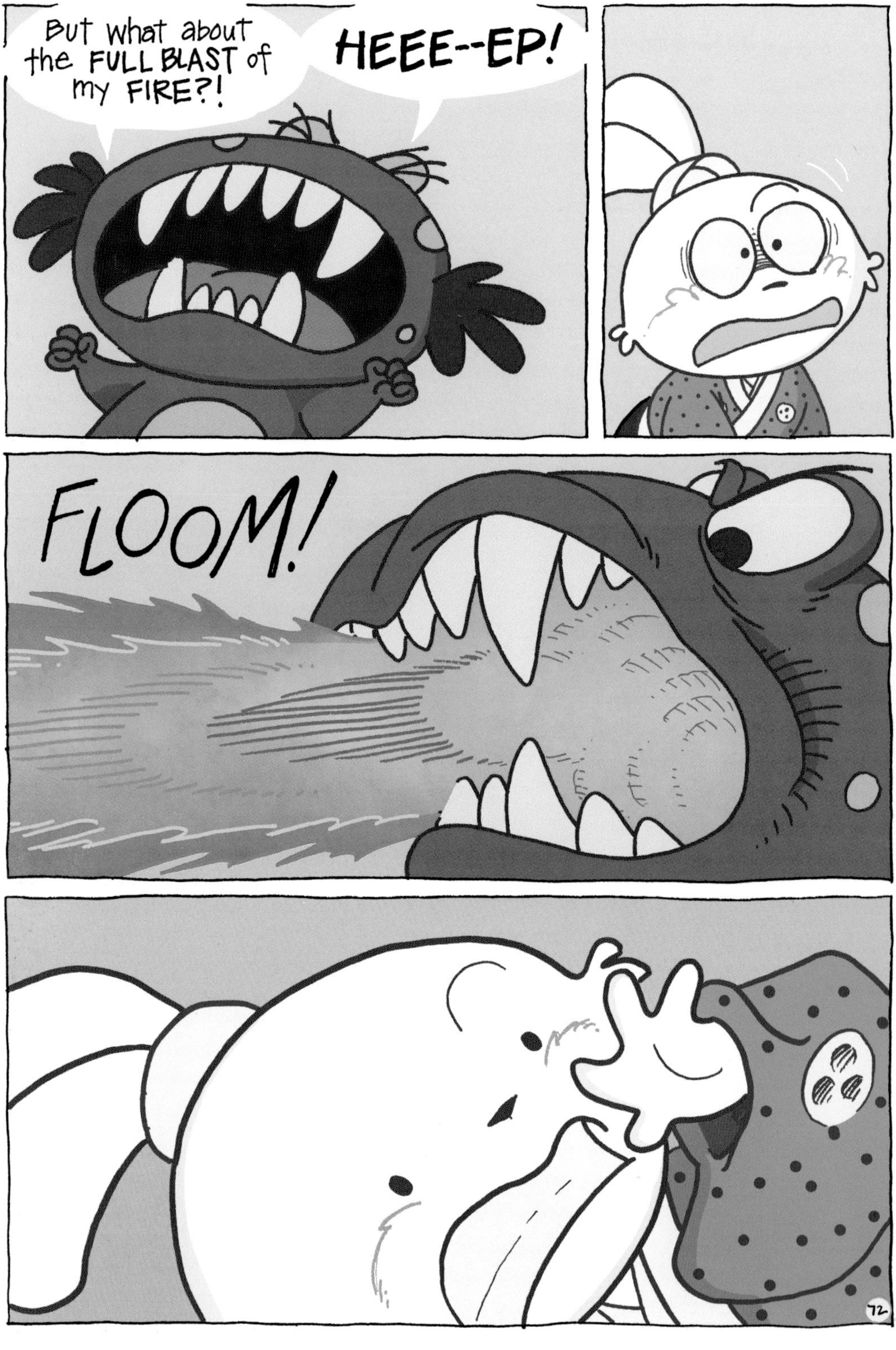

But what about the FULL BLAST of my FIRE?!
HEEE--EP!
FLOOM!
72

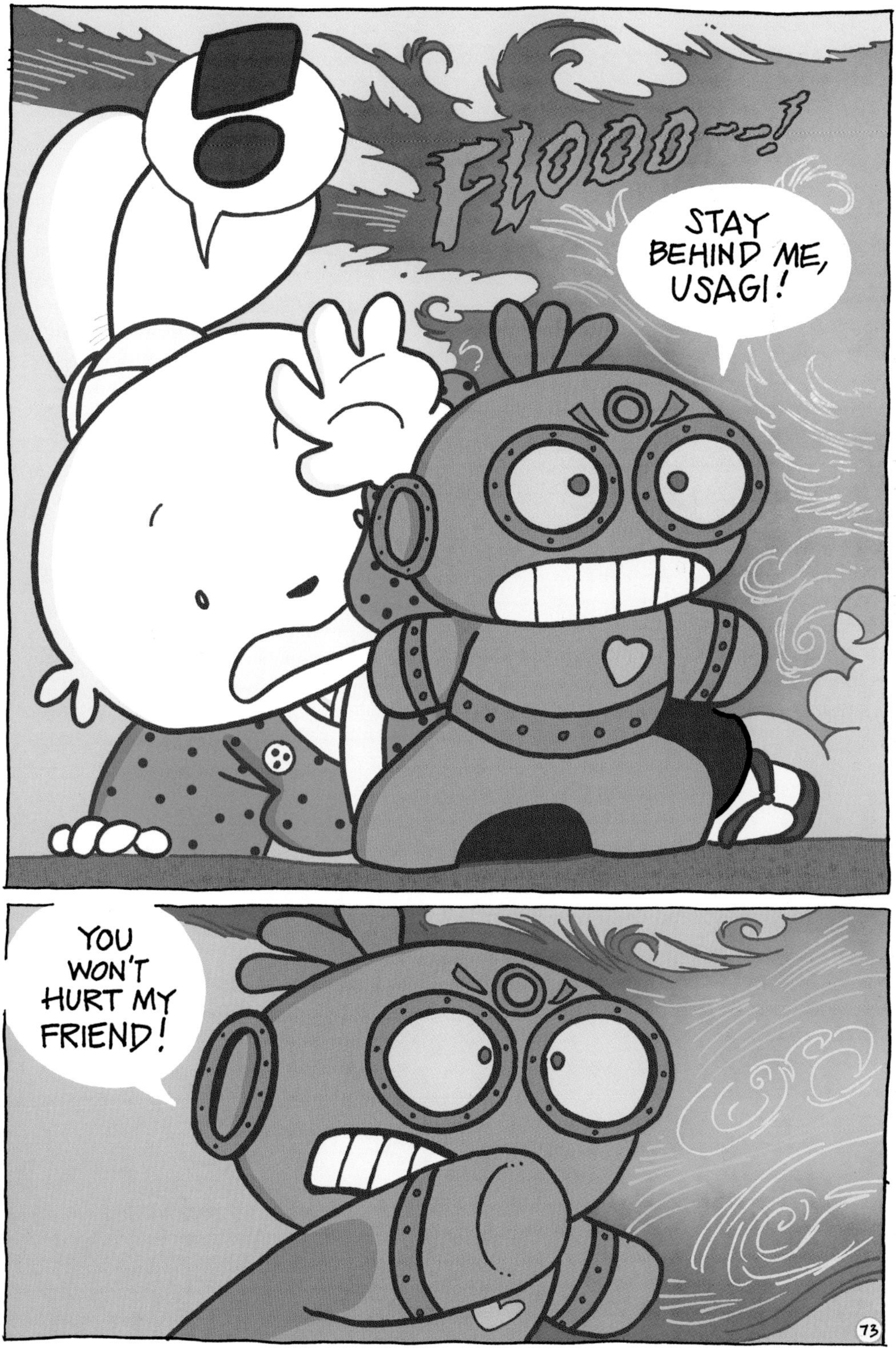
FLOOO--!
STAY BEHIND ME, USAGI!
YOU WON'T HURT MY FRIEND!

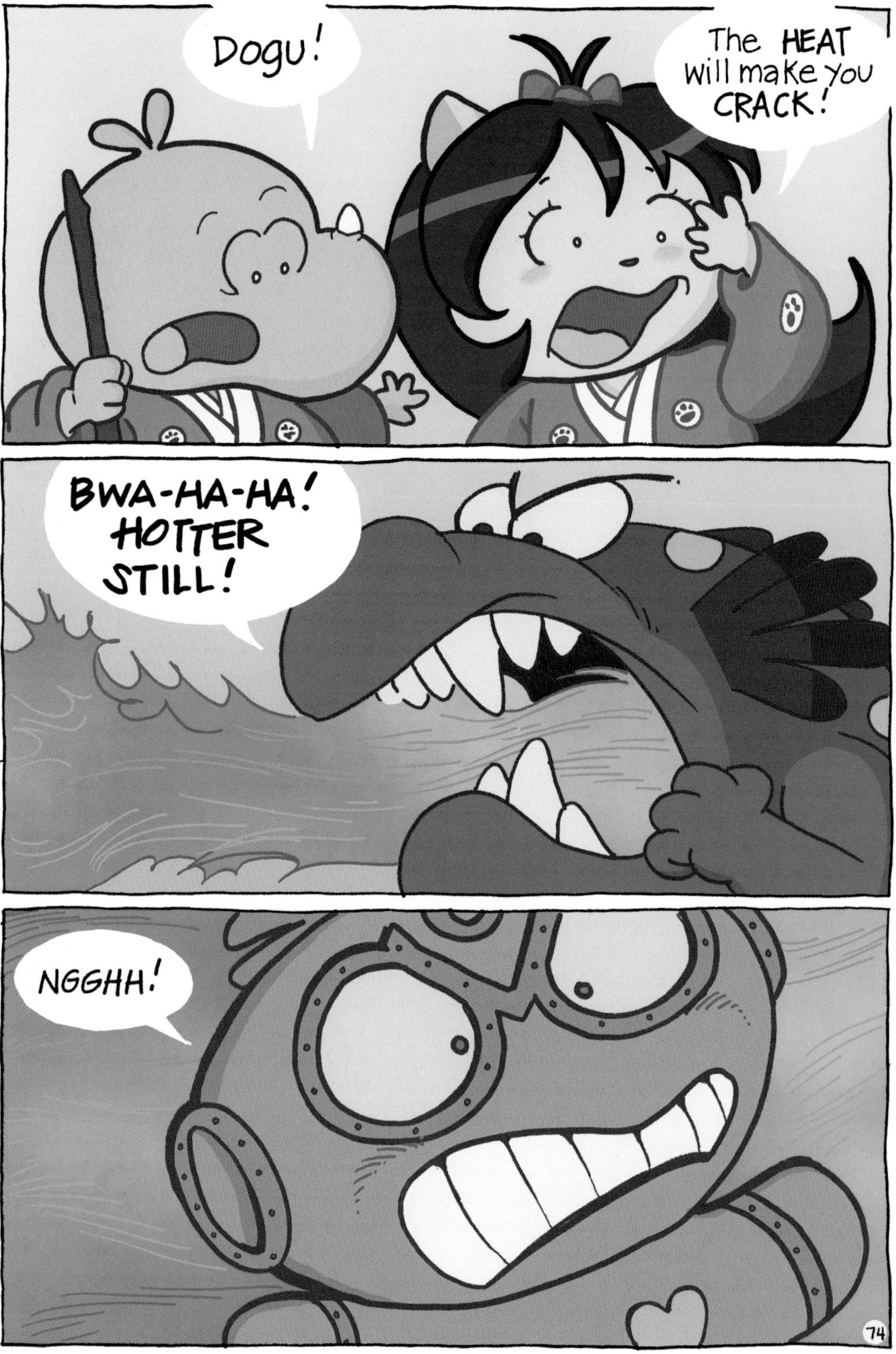

Dogu!
The HEAT will make you CRACK!
BWA-HA-HA! HOTTER STILL!
NGGHH!

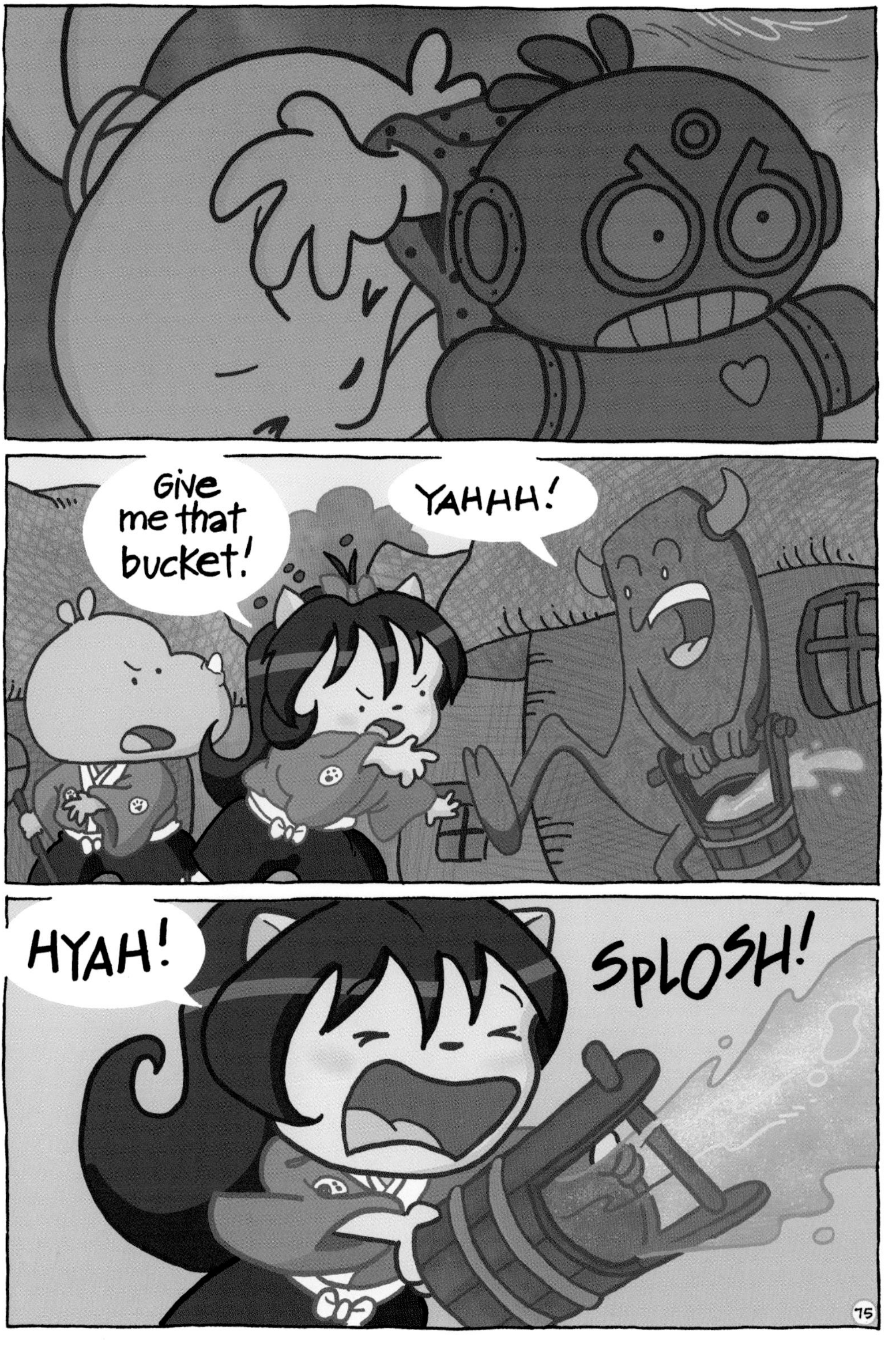
Give me that bucket!
YAHHH!
HYAH!
SPLOSH!

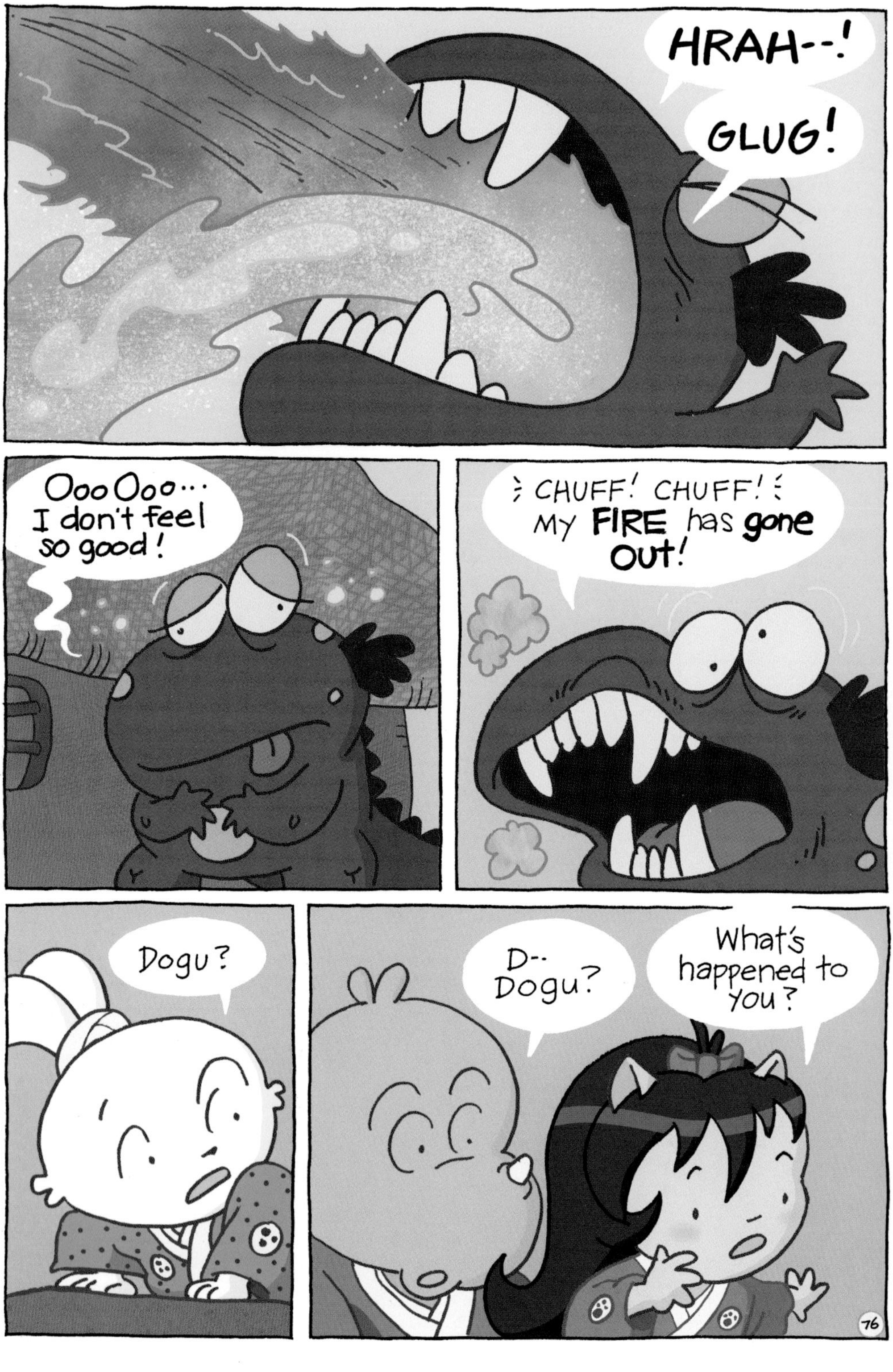
HRAH--!
GLUG!
OooOoo... I don't feel so good!
CHUFF! CHUFF! My FIRE has gone OUT!
Dogu?
D-- Dogu?
What's happened to you?

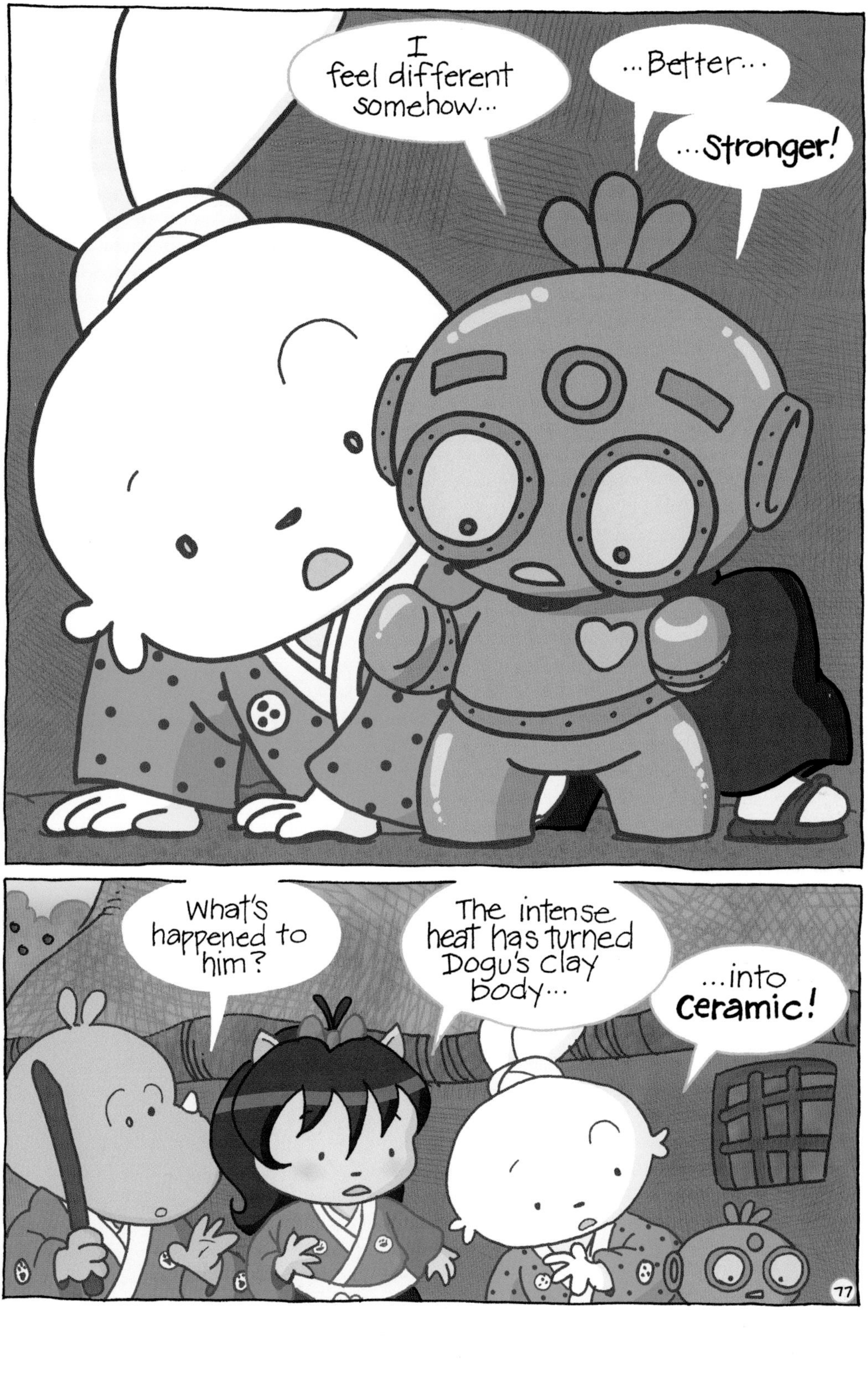
I feel different somehow...
...Better...
...Stronger!
What's happened to him?
The intense heat has turned Dogu's clay body...
...into ceramic!

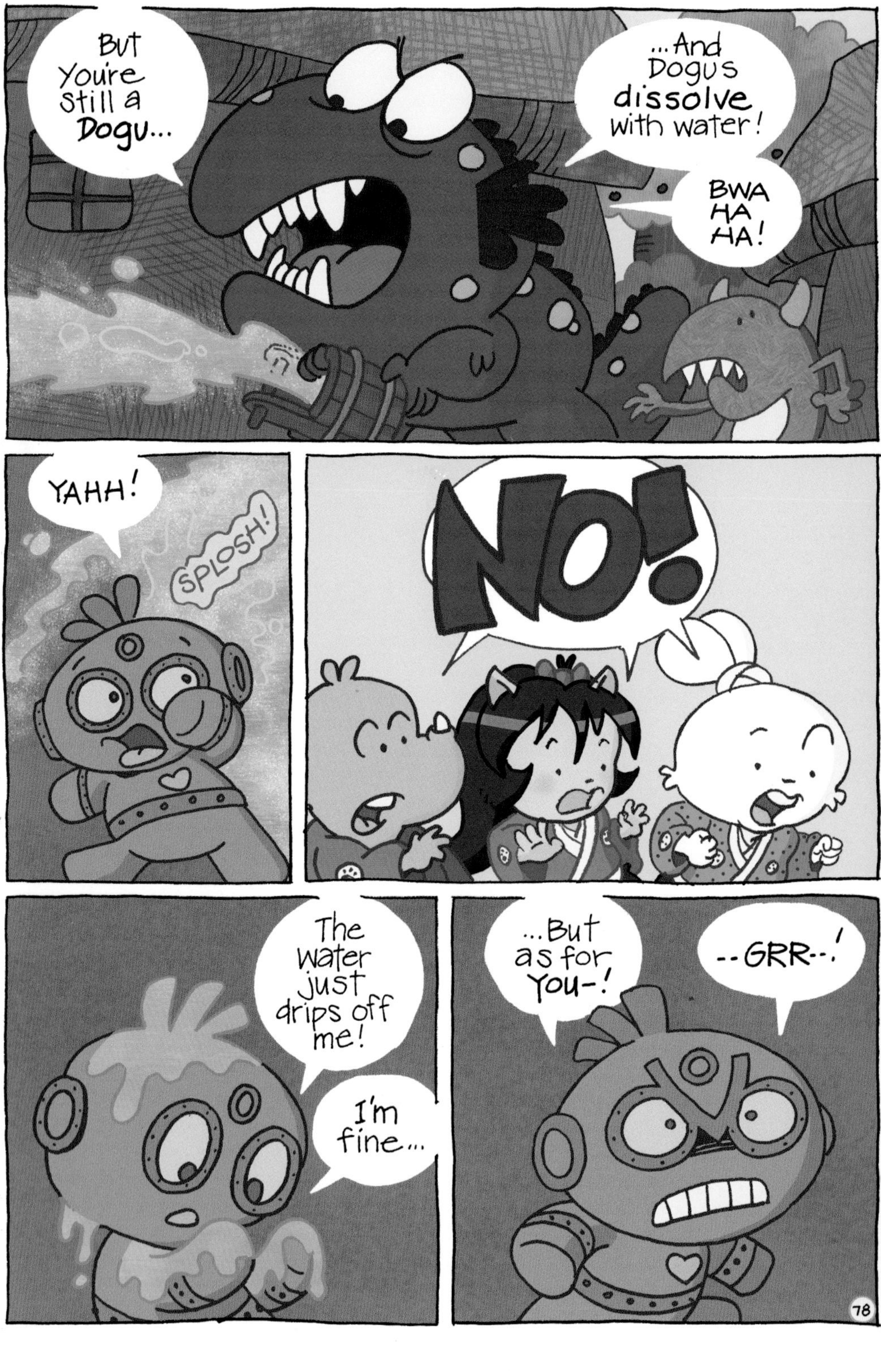
But You're still a Dogu...
...And Dogus dissolve with water!
BWA HA HA!
YAHH!
SPLOSH!
NO!
The water just drips off me!
I'm fine...
...But as for You-!
--GRR--!

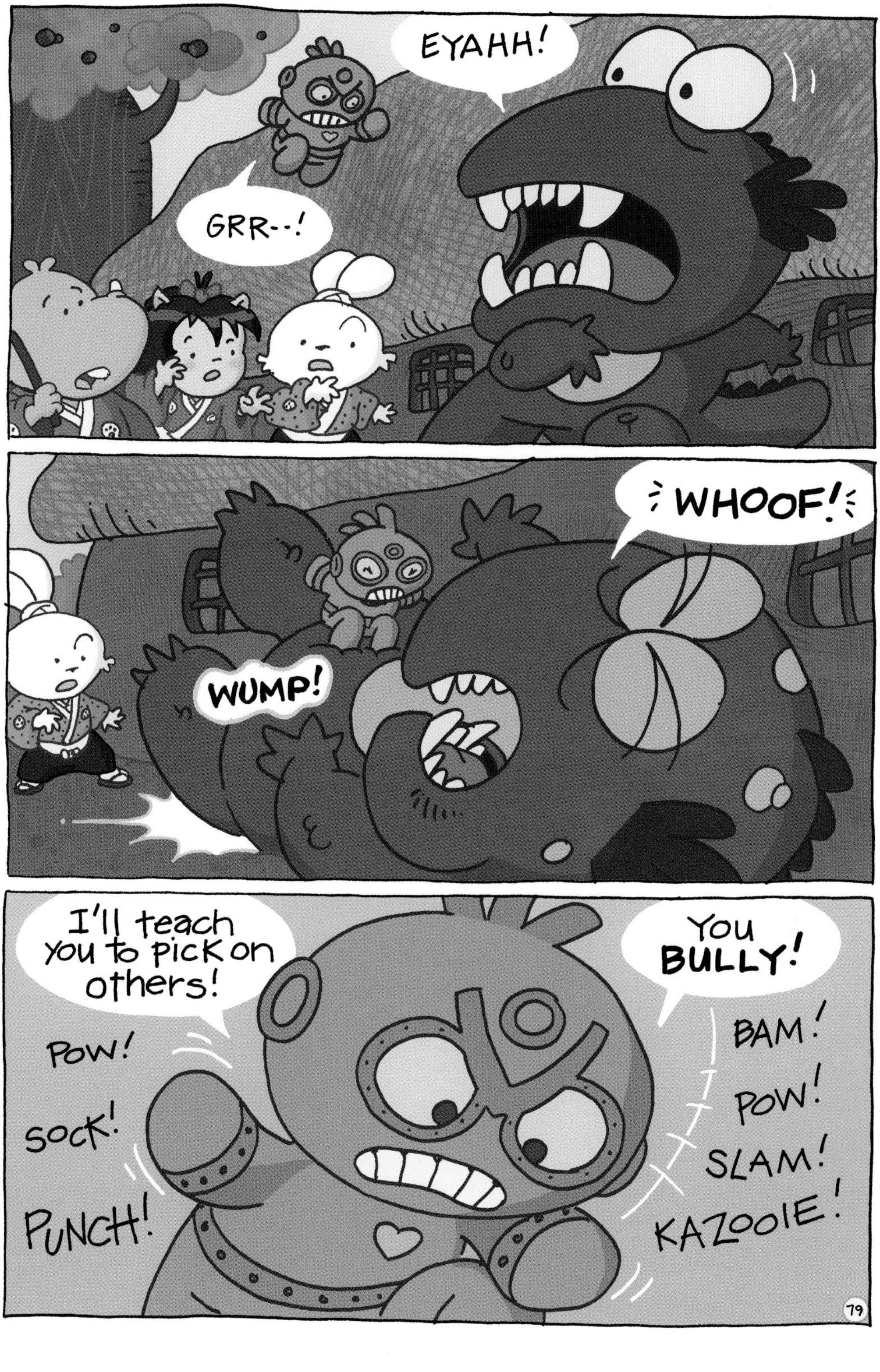
EYAHH!
GRR--!
WHOOF!
WUMP!
I'll teach you to pick on others!
You BULLY!
POW!
SOCK!
PUNCH!
BAM!
POW!
SLAM!
KAZOOIE!

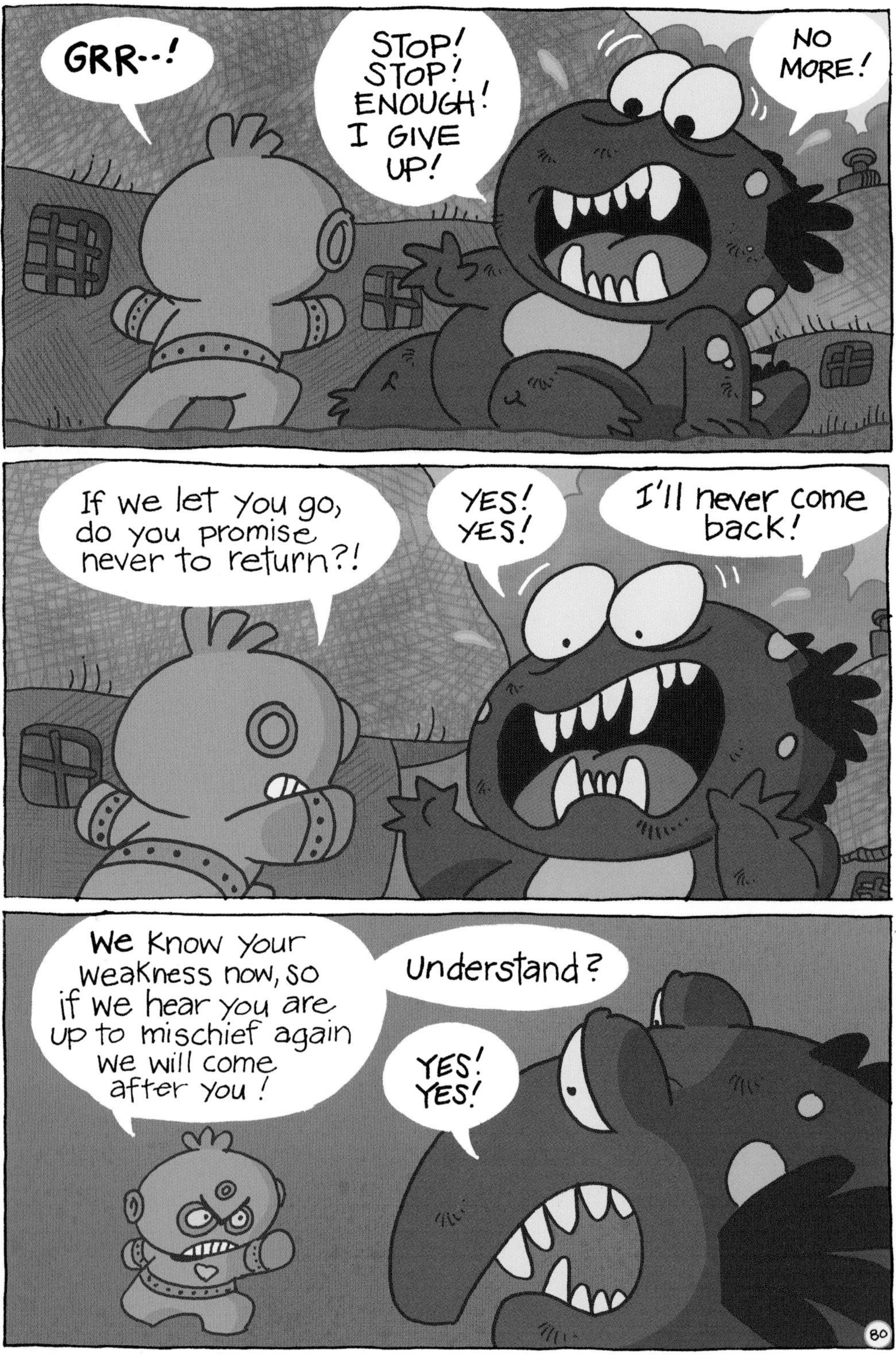
GRR--!
STOP! STOP! ENOUGH! I GIVE UP!
NO MORE!
If we let you go, do you promise never to return?!
YES! YES!
I'll never come back!
We know your weakness now, so if we hear you are up to mischief again we will come after you!
Understand?
YES! YES!

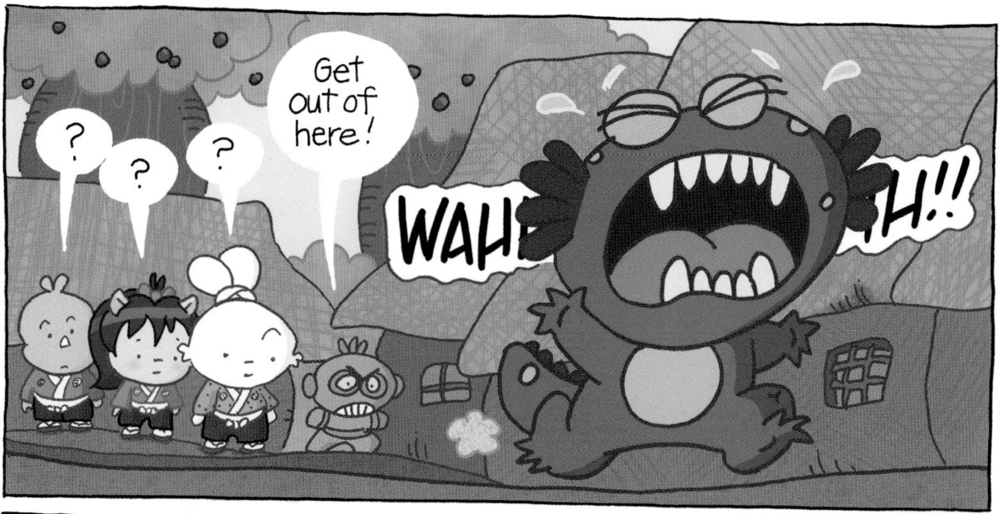
?
?
?
Get out of here!
WAH
H!!

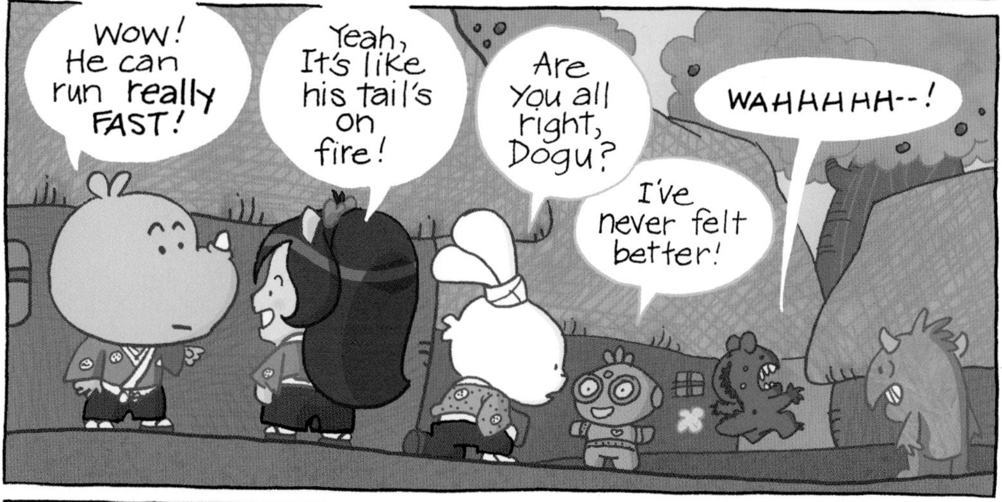
Wow! He can run really FAST!
Yeah, It's like his tail's on fire!
Are you all right, Dogu?
I've never felt better!
WAHHHHH--!

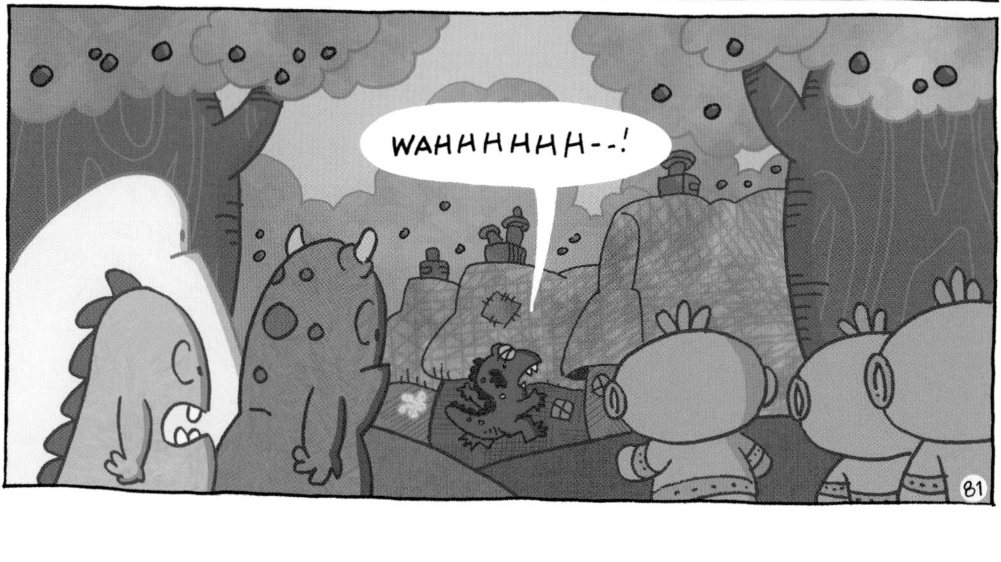
WAHHHHHH--!

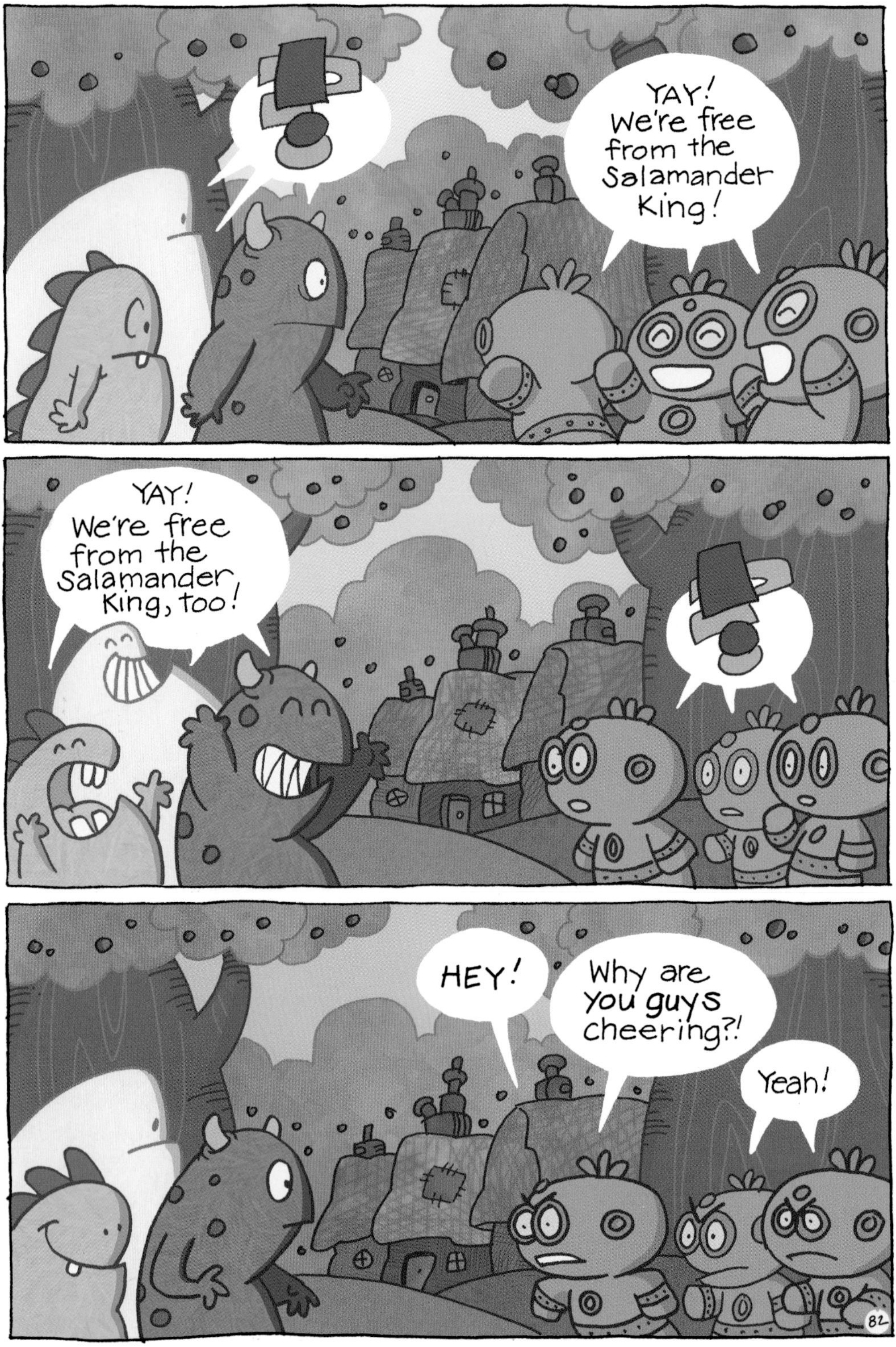
YAY! We're free from the Salamander King!
YAY! We're free from the Salamander King, too!
HEY!
Why are you guys cheering?!
Yeah!

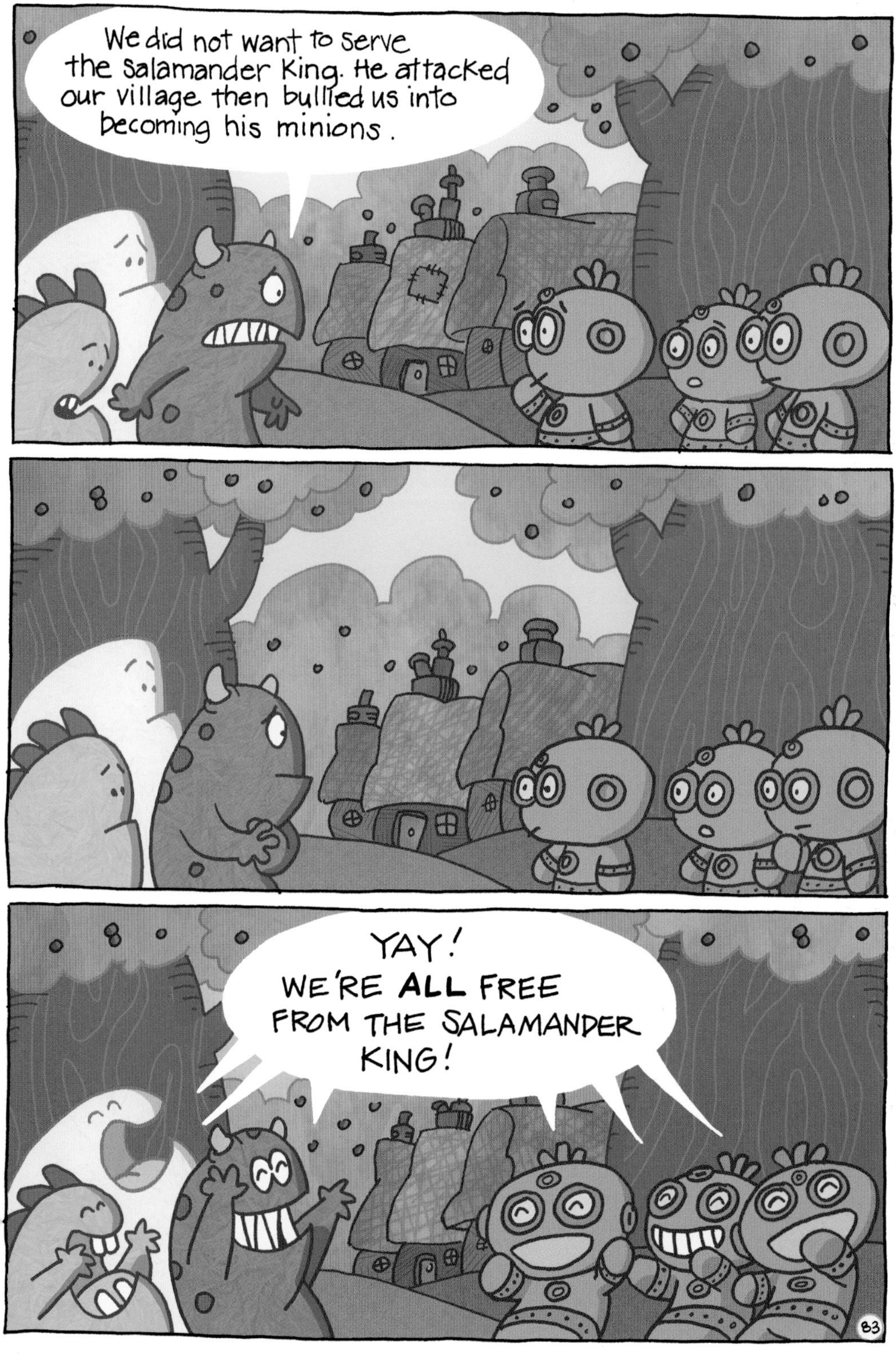
We did not want to serve the Salamander King. He attacked our village then bullied us into becoming his minions.
YAY! WE'RE **ALL** FREE FROM THE SALAMANDER KING!

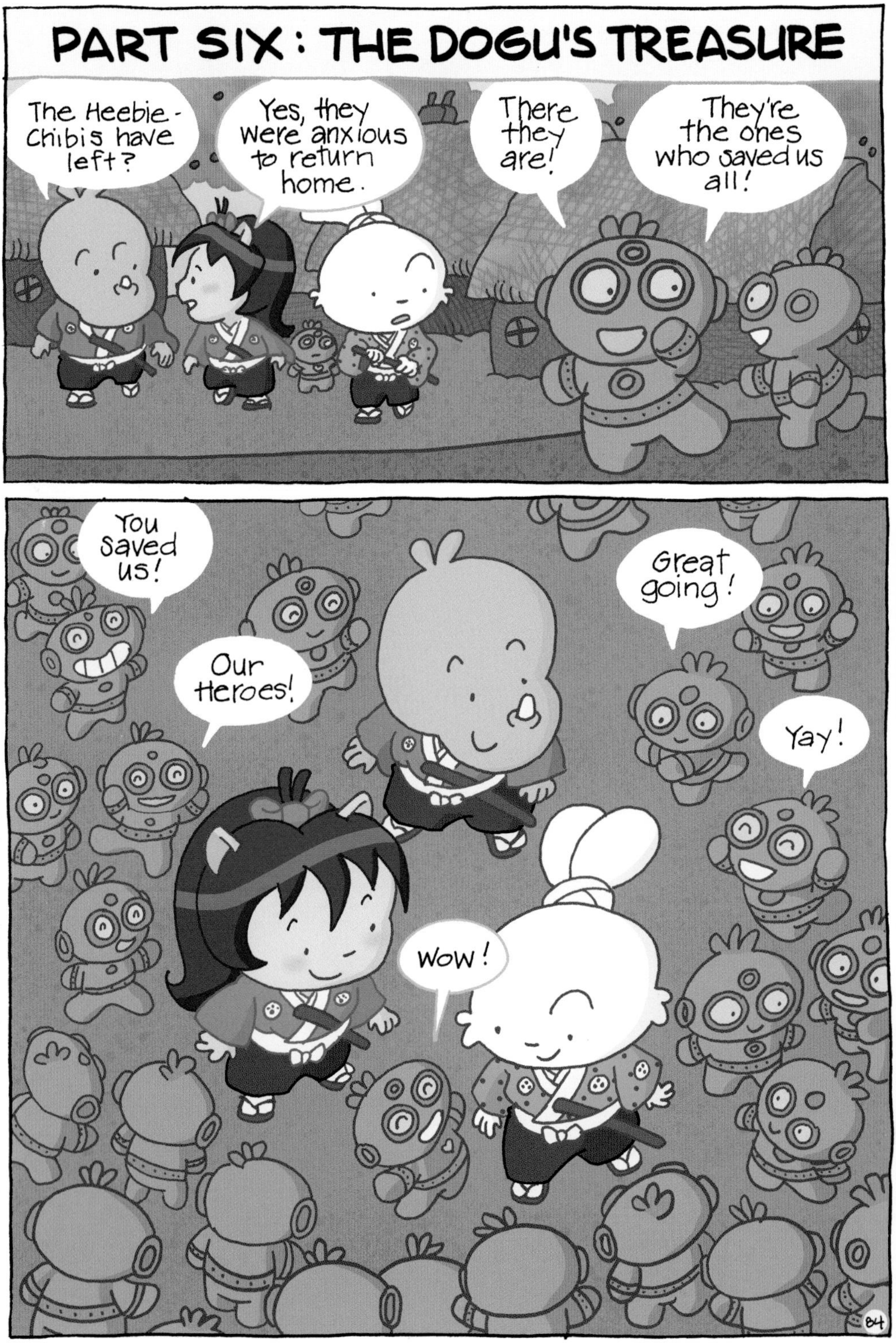
PART SIX : THE DOGU'S TREASURE
The Heebie-Chibis have left?
Yes, they were anxious to return home.
There they are!
They're the ones who saved us all!
You saved us!
Great going!
Our Heroes!
Yay!
Wow!

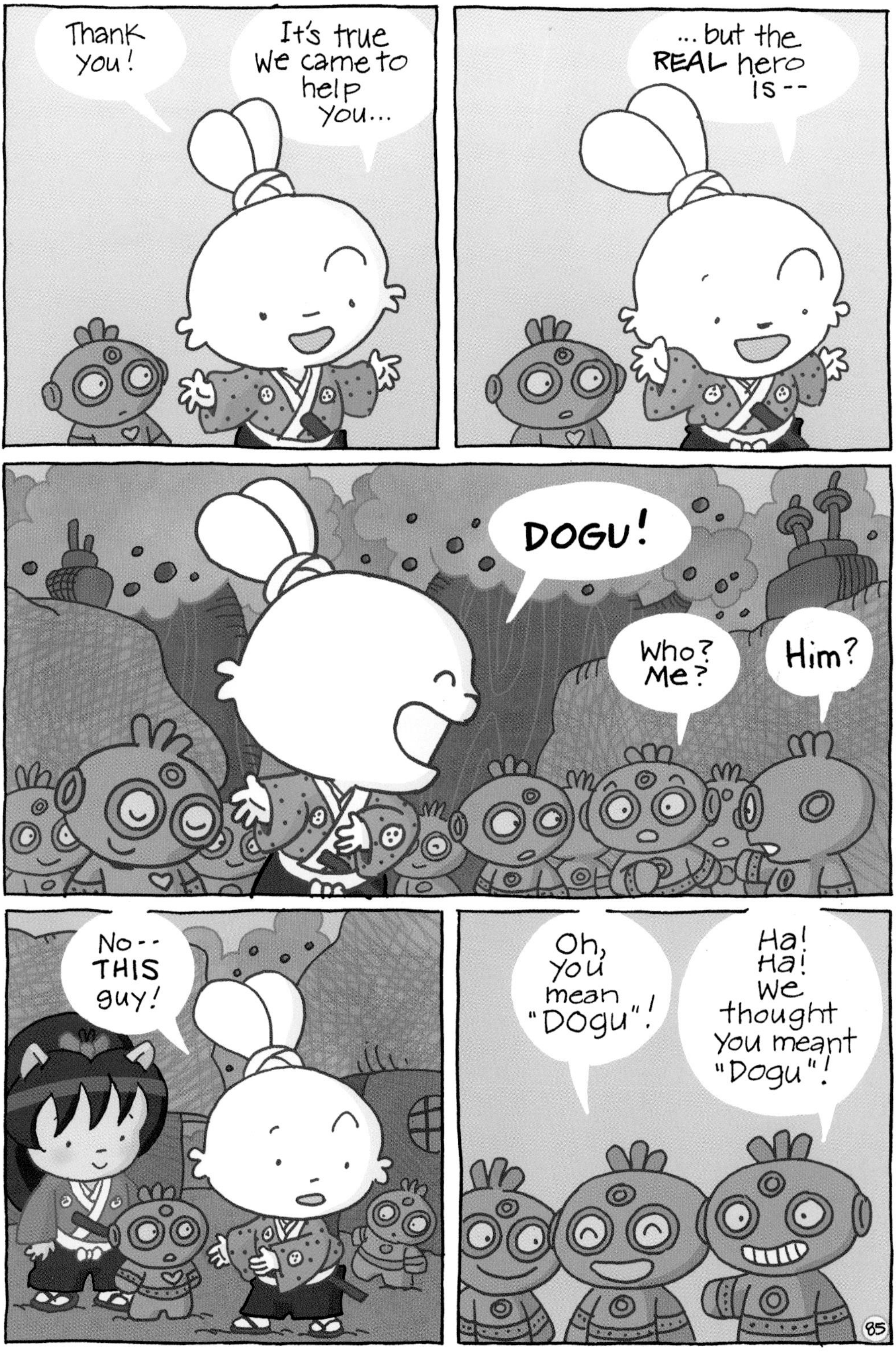
Thank you!
It's true we came to help you...
...but the REAL hero is--
DOGU!
Who? Me?
Him?
No--THIS guy!
Oh, you mean "DOGU"!
Ha! Ha! We thought you meant "Dogu"!

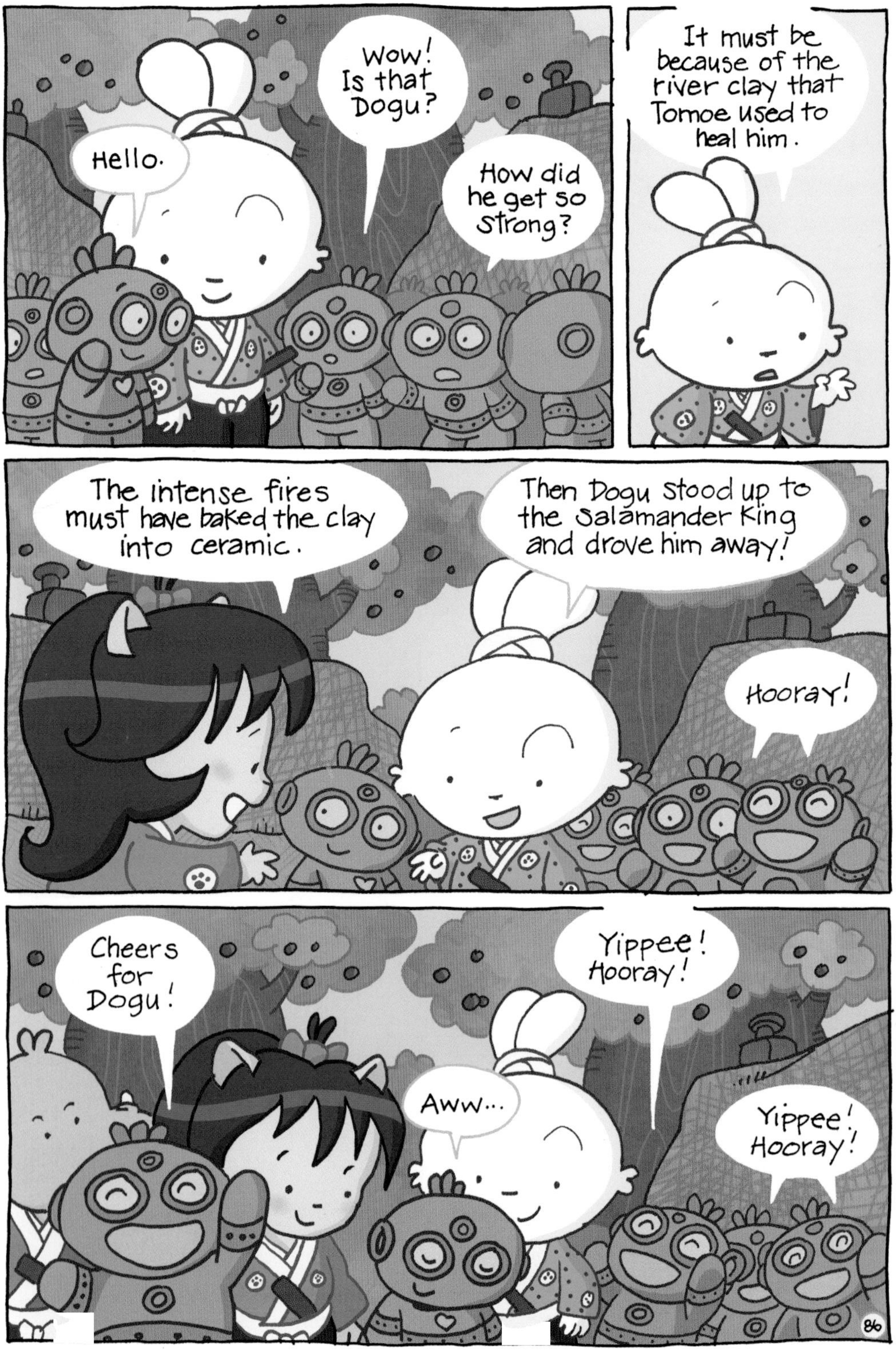

Hello.
Wow! Is that Dogu?
How did he get so strong?
It must be because of the river clay that Tomoe used to heal him.
The intense fires must have baked the clay into ceramic.
Then Dogu stood up to the Salamander King and drove him away!
Hooray!
Cheers for Dogu!
Yippee! Hooray!
Aww...
Yippee! Hooray!

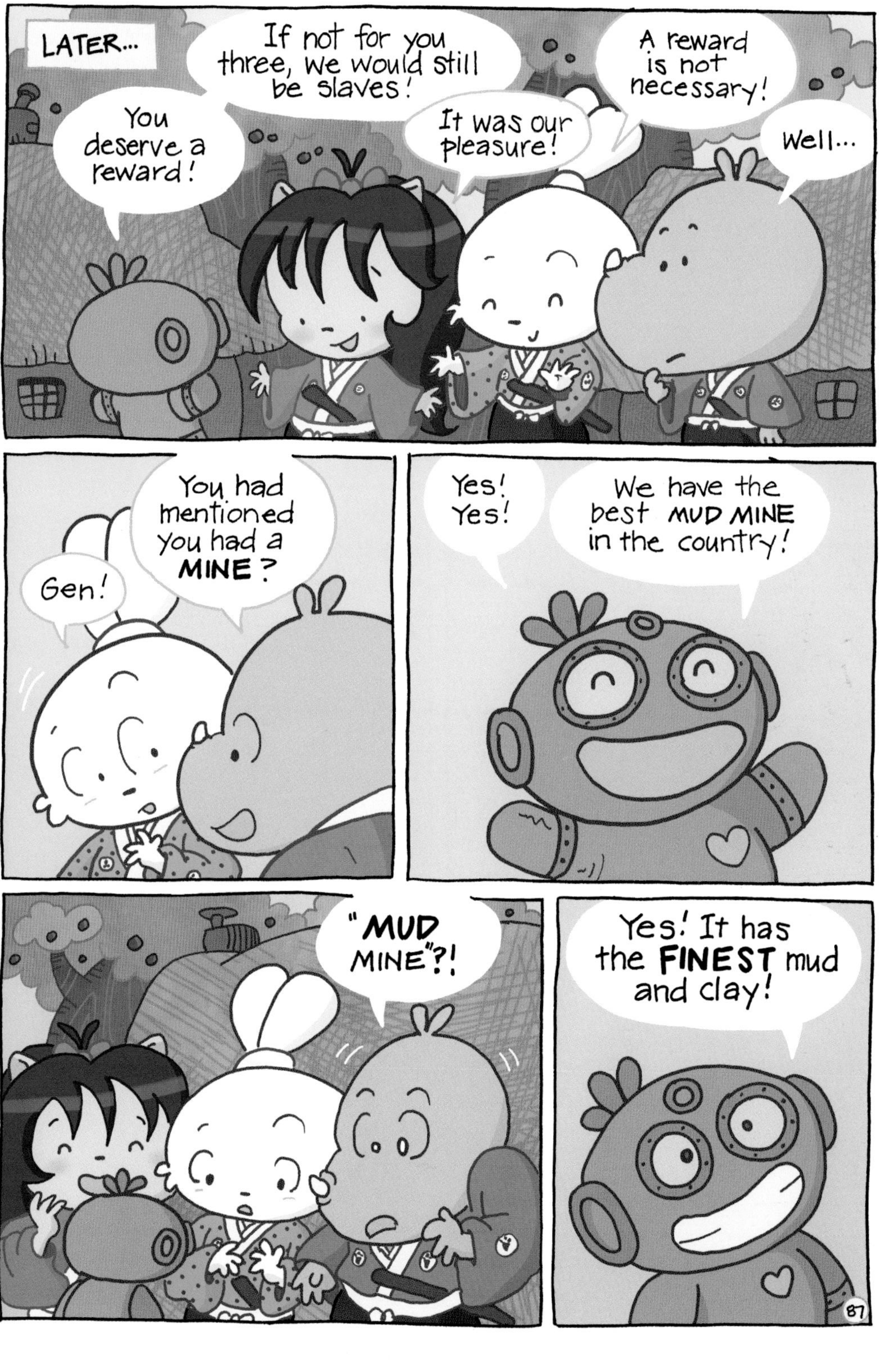
LATER...
You deserve a reward!
If not for you three, we would still be slaves!
It was our pleasure!
A reward is not necessary!
Well...
Gen!
You had mentioned you had a **MINE**?
Yes! Yes!
We have the best **MUD MINE** in the country!
"**MUD** MINE"?!
Yes! It has the **FINEST** mud and clay!

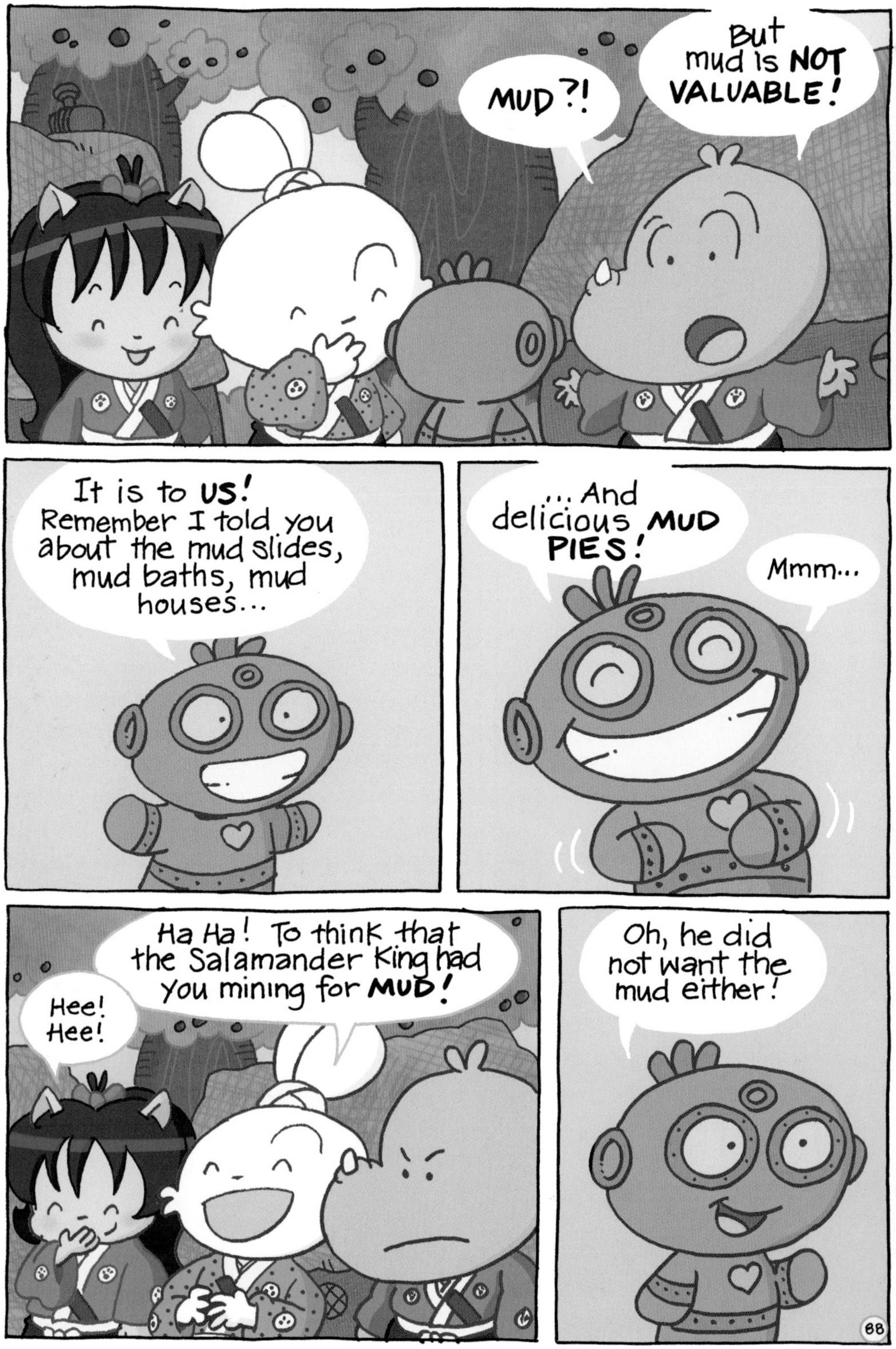
MUD?!
But mud is NOT VALUABLE!
It is to US! Remember I told you about the mud slides, mud baths, mud houses...
...And delicious MUD PIES!
Mmm...
Ha Ha! To think that the Salamander King had you mining for MUD!
Hee! Hee!
Oh, he did not want the mud either!
88

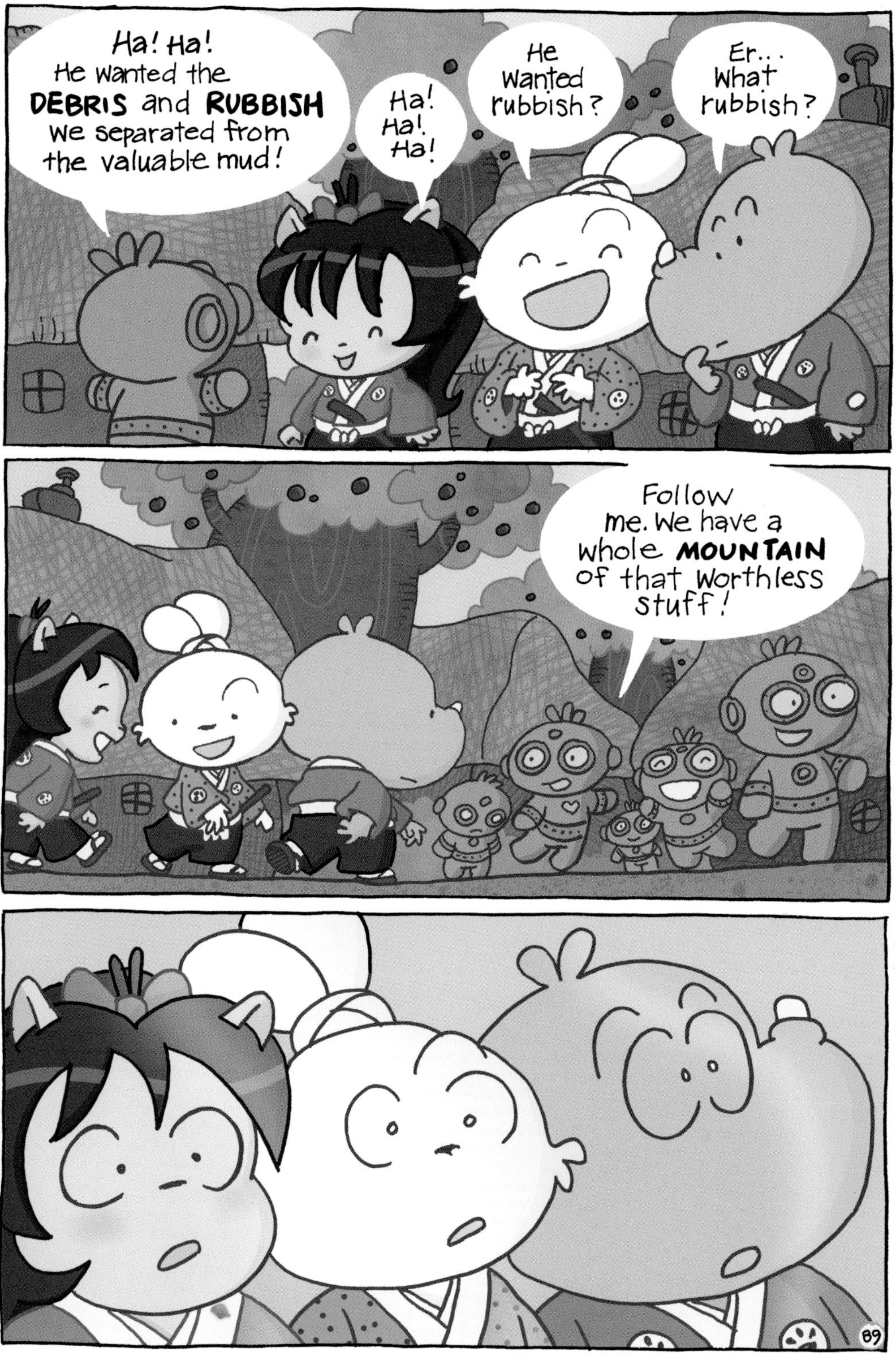
Ha! Ha!
He wanted the DEBRIS and RUBBISH we separated from the valuable mud!
Ha! Ha! Ha!
He wanted rubbish?
Er... What rubbish?
Follow me. We have a whole MOUNTAIN of that worthless stuff!

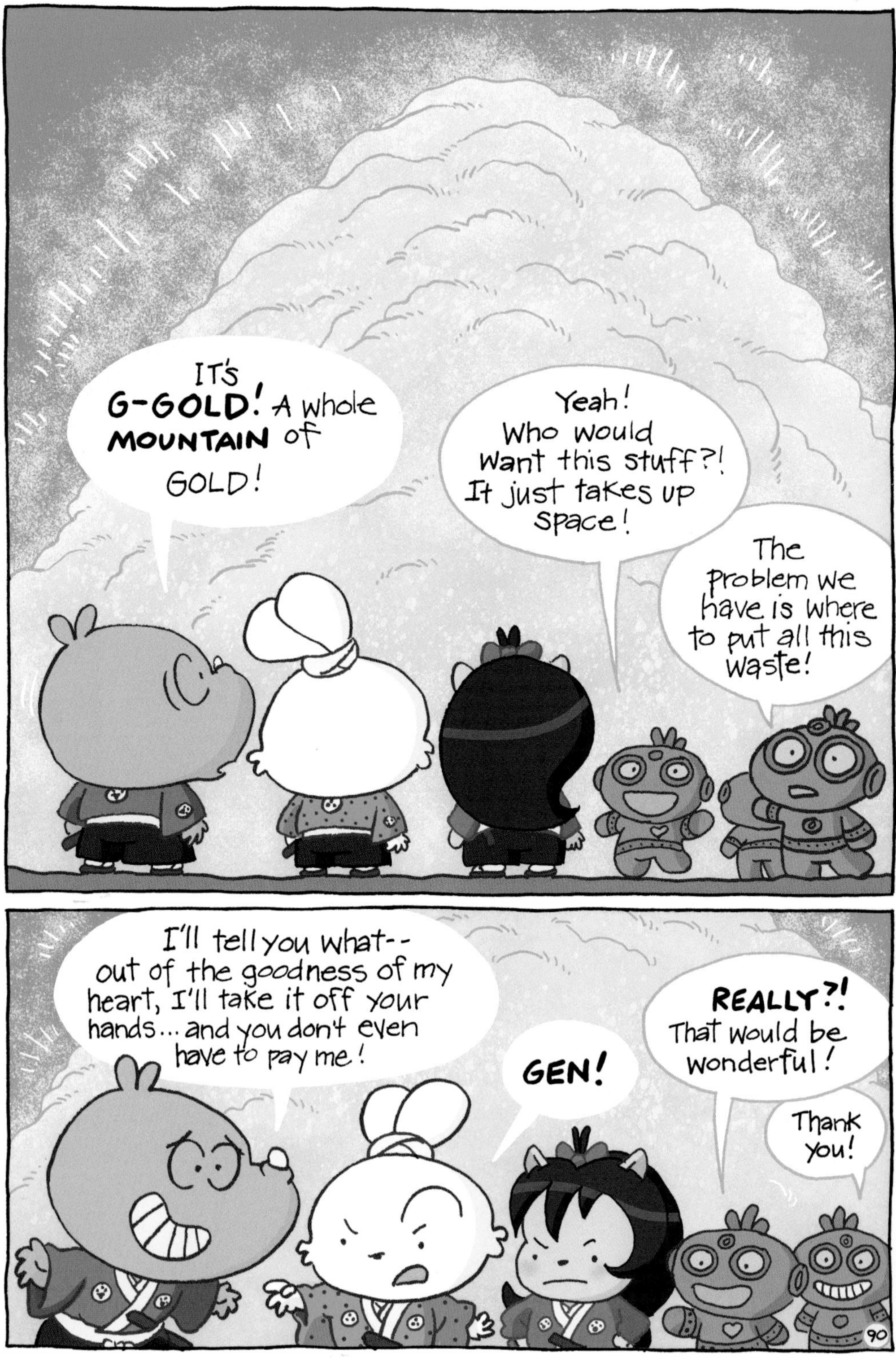
IT'S G-GOLD! A whole MOUNTAIN of GOLD!
Yeah! Who would want this stuff?! It just takes up space!
The problem we have is where to put all this waste!
I'll tell you what-- out of the goodness of my heart, I'll take it off your hands... and you don't even have to pay me!
GEN!
REALLY?! That would be wonderful!
Thank you!

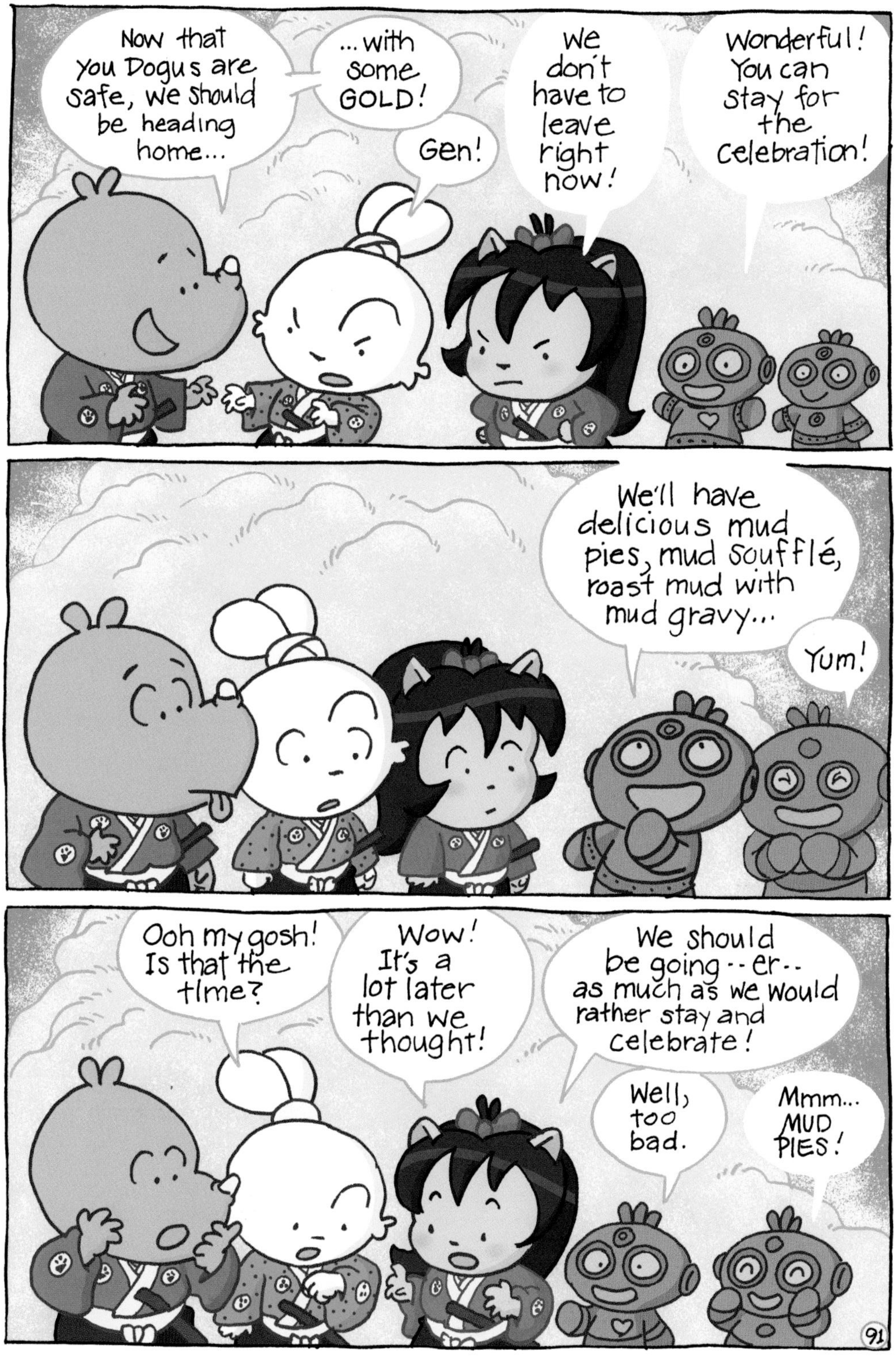
Now that you Dogus are safe, we should be heading home...
...with some GOLD!
Gen!
We don't have to leave right now!
Wonderful! You can stay for the celebration!
We'll have delicious mud pies, mud soufflé, roast mud with mud gravy...
Yum!
Ooh my gosh! Is that the time?
Wow! It's a lot later than we thought!
We should be going--er-- as much as we would rather stay and celebrate!
Well, too bad.
Mmm... MUD PIES!

PART SEVEN: THE ROAD HOME

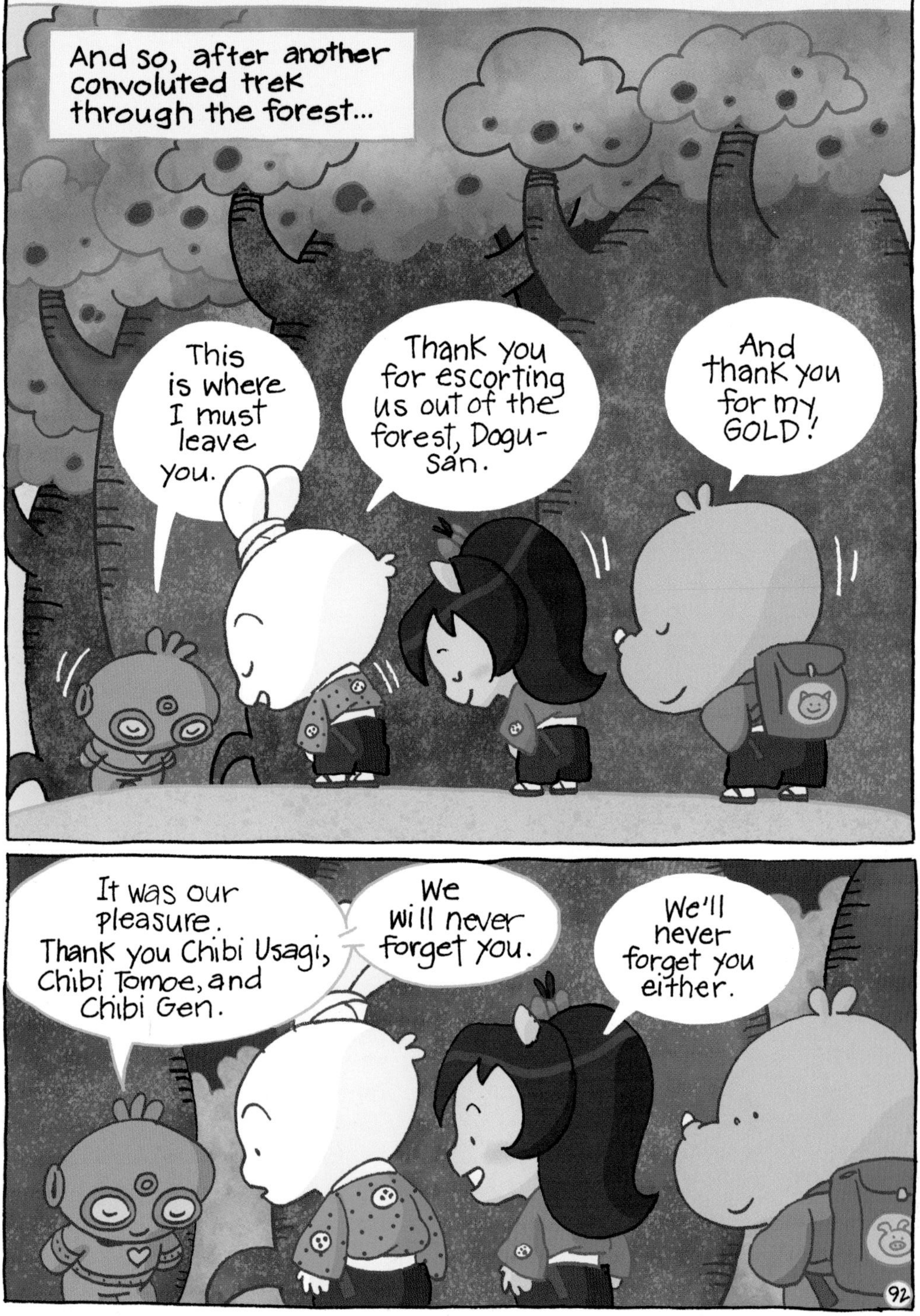
And so, after another convoluted trek through the forest...
This is where I must leave you.
Thank you for escorting us out of the forest, Dogu-san.
And thank you for my GOLD!
It was our pleasure. Thank you Chibi Usagi, Chibi Tomoe, and Chibi Gen.
We will never forget you.
We'll never forget you either.

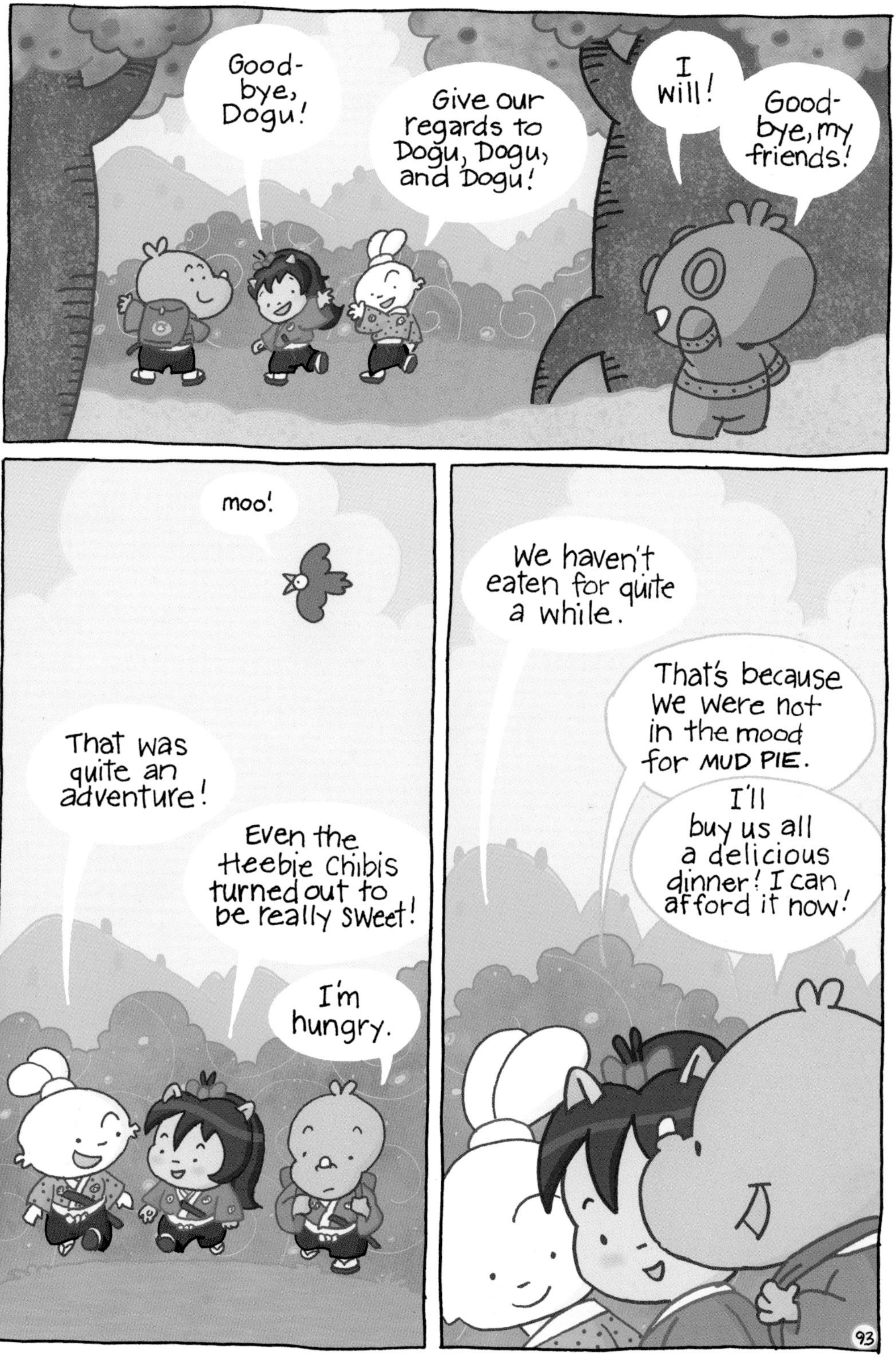

Good-bye, Dogu!
Give our regards to Dogu, Dogu, and Dogu!
I will!
Good-bye, my friends!
moo!
That was quite an adventure!
Even the Heebie Chibis turned out to be really sweet!
I'm hungry.
We haven't eaten for quite a while.
That's because we were not in the mood for MUD PIE.
I'll buy us all a delicious dinner! I can afford it now!

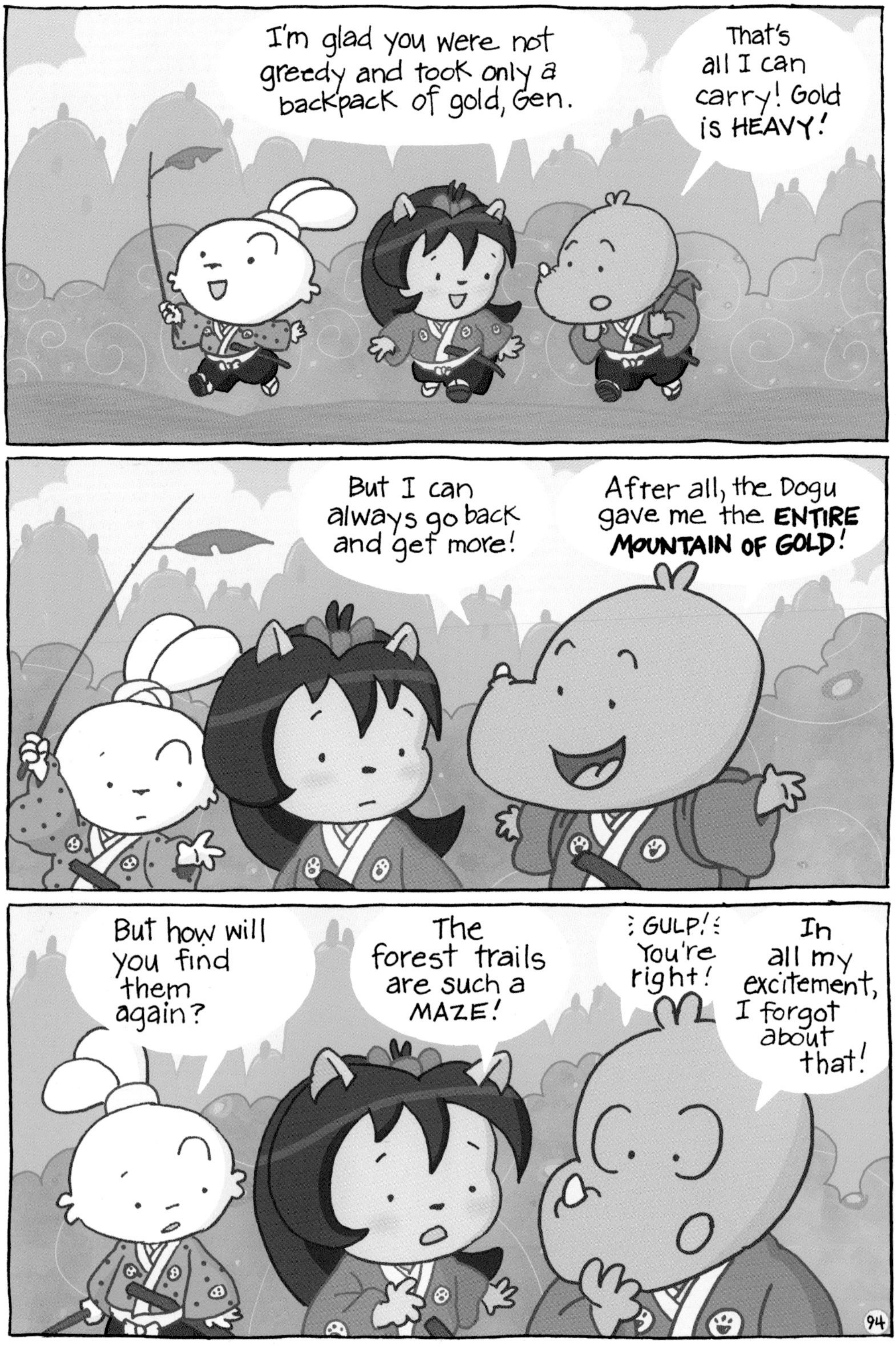

I'm glad you were not greedy and took only a backpack of gold, Gen.
That's all I can carry! Gold is HEAVY!
But I can always go back and get more!
After all, the Dogu gave me the ENTIRE MOUNTAIN OF GOLD!
But how will you find them again?
The forest trails are such a MAZE!
GULP! You're right!
In all my excitement, I forgot about that!

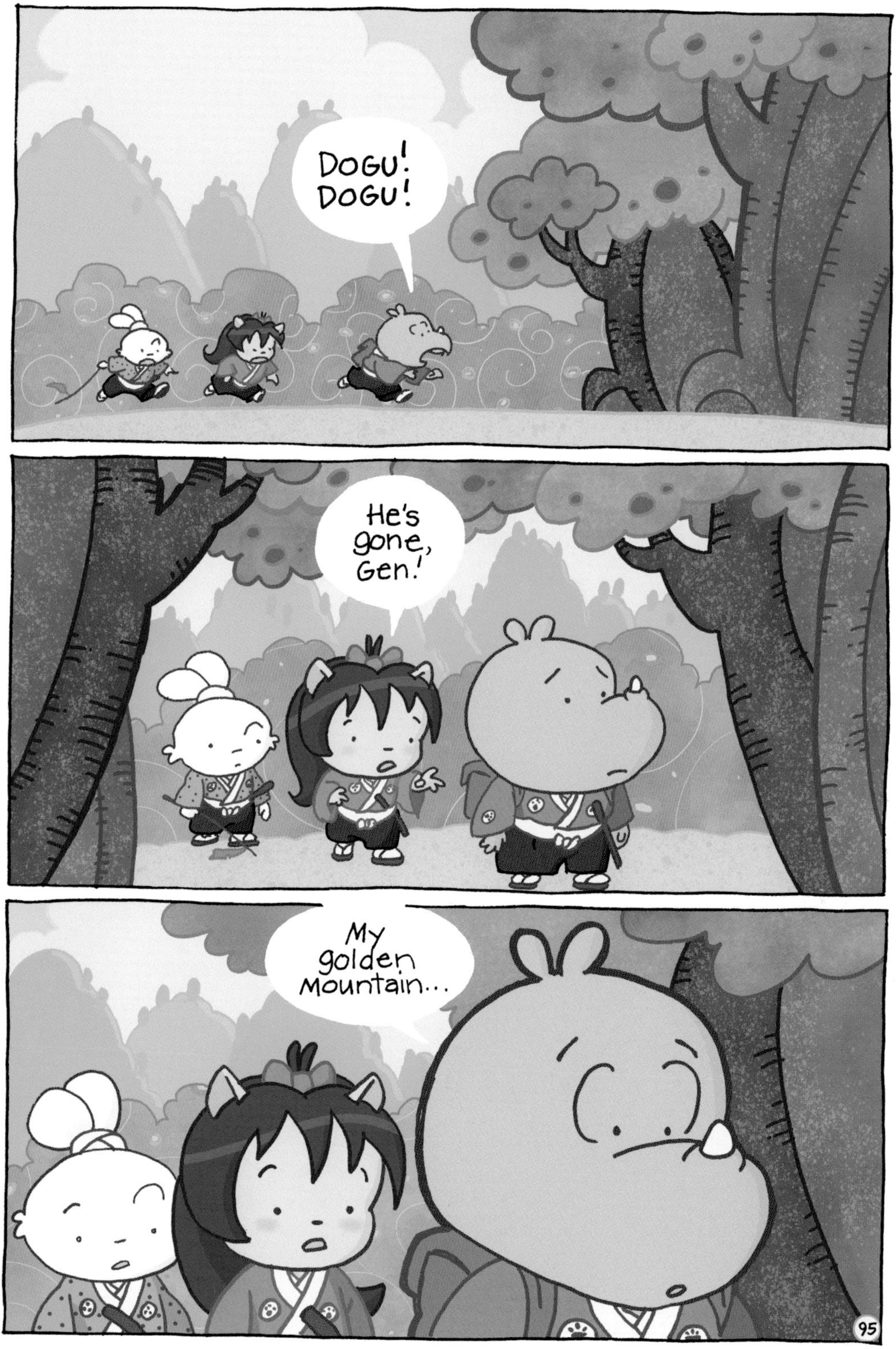
DOGU! DOGU!
He's gone, Gen!
My golden Mountain...

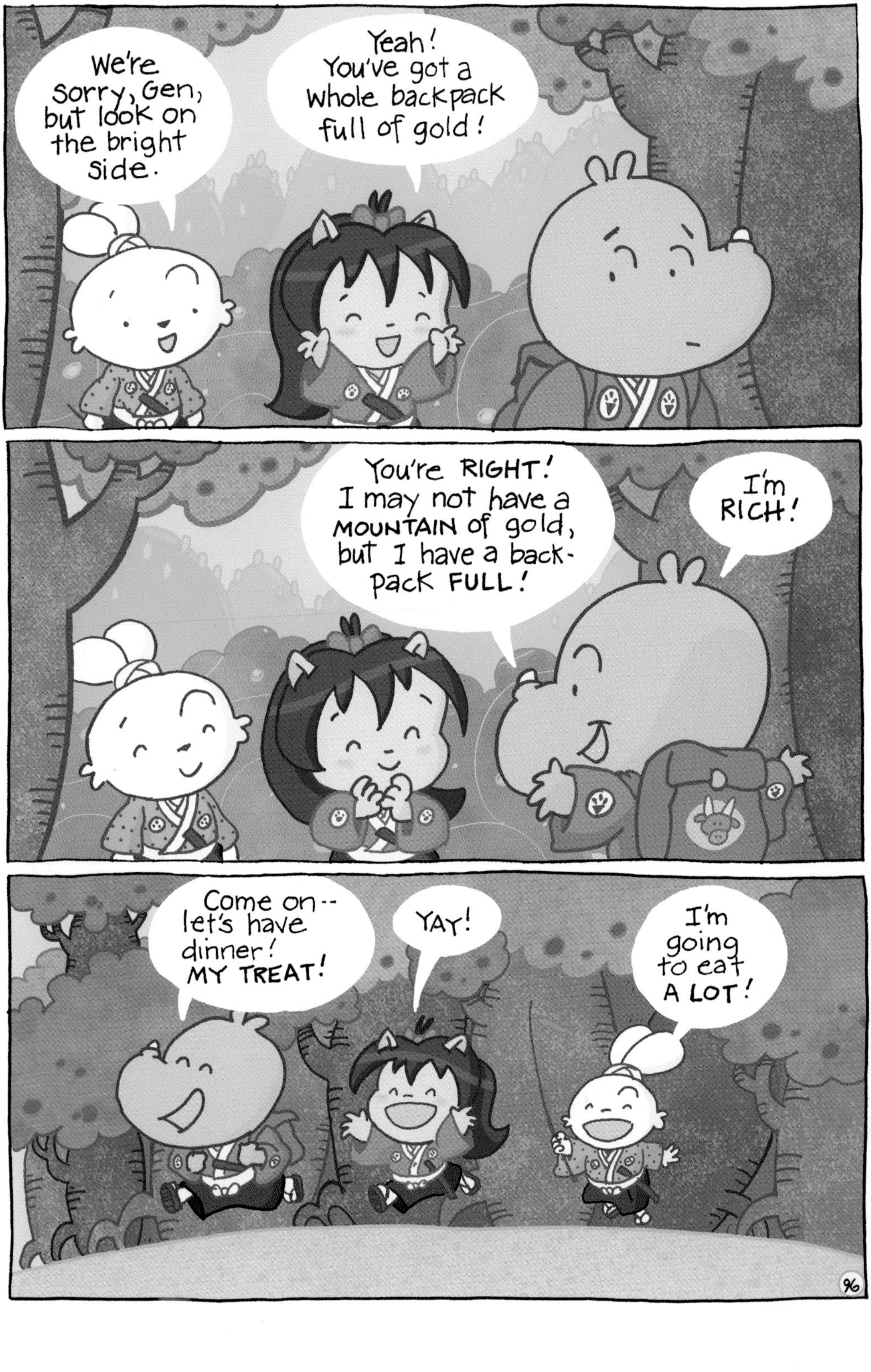
We're sorry, Gen, but look on the bright side.
Yeah! You've got a whole backpack full of gold!
You're RIGHT! I may not have a MOUNTAIN of gold, but I have a back-pack FULL!
I'm RICH!
Come on-- let's have dinner! MY TREAT!
YAY!
I'm going to eat A LOT!

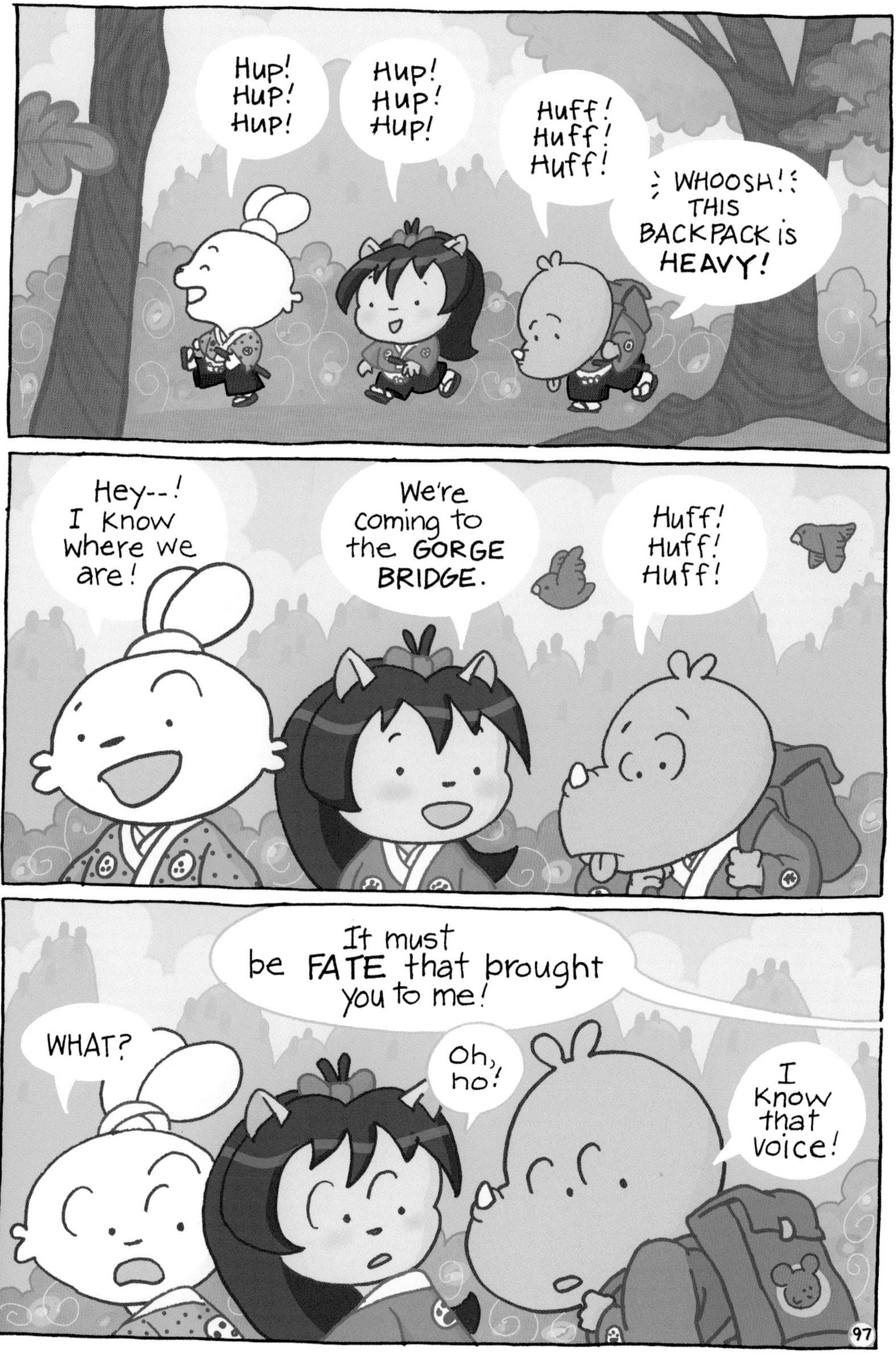
Hup! Hup! Hup!
Hup! Hup! Hup!
Huff! Huff! Huff!
WHOOSH! THIS BACKPACK is HEAVY!
Hey--! I Know where we are!
We're coming to the GORGE BRIDGE.
Huff! Huff! Huff!
It must be FATE that brought you to me!
WHAT?
Oh, ho!
I Know that voice!

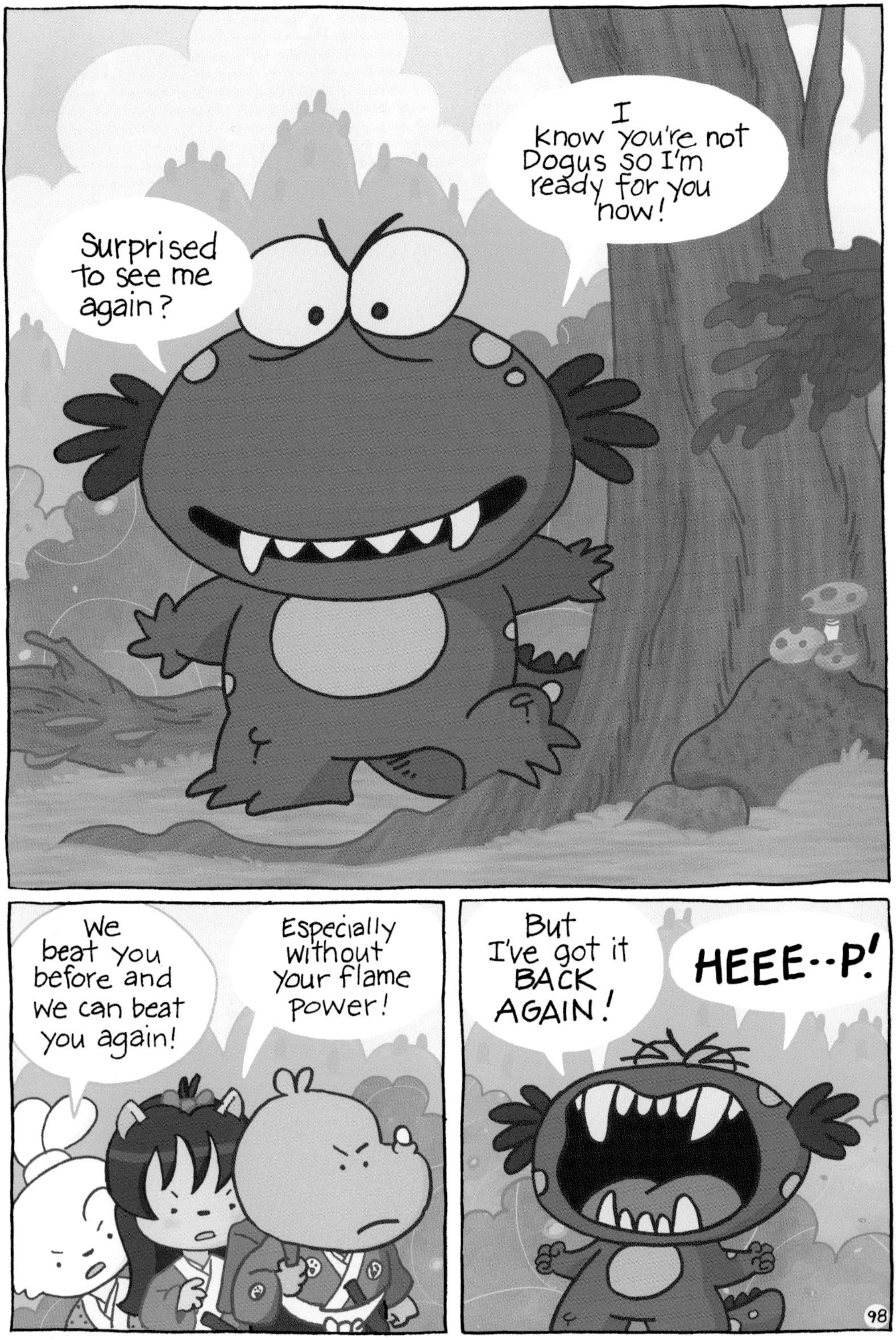
Surprised to see me again?
I know you're not Dogus so I'm ready for you now!
We beat you before and we can beat you again!
Especially without your flame power!
But I've got it BACK AGAIN!
HEEE--P!

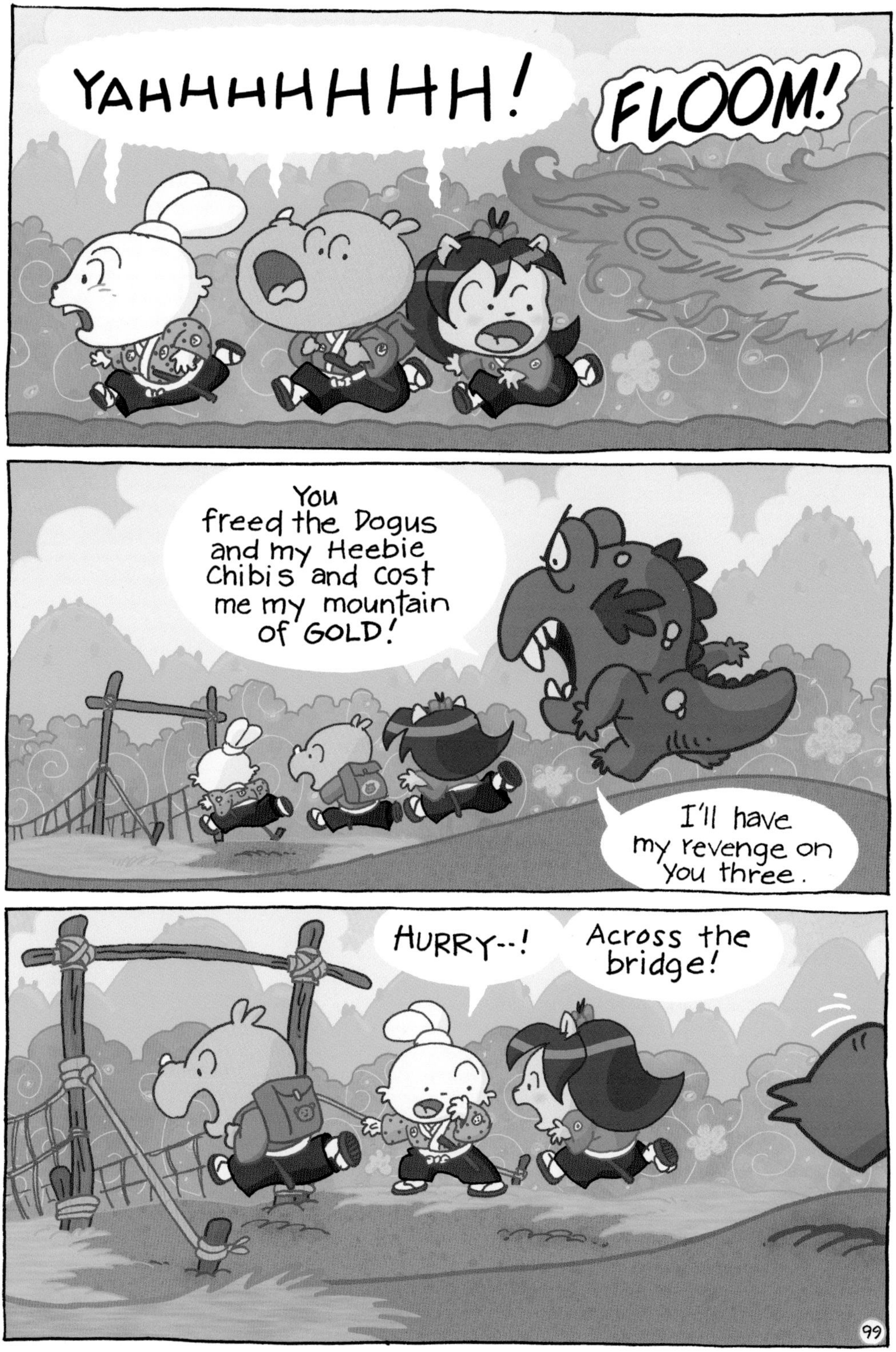
YAHHHHHHH!
FLOOM!
You freed the Dogus and my Heebie Chibis and cost me my mountain of GOLD!
I'll have my revenge on you three.
HURRY--!
Across the bridge!

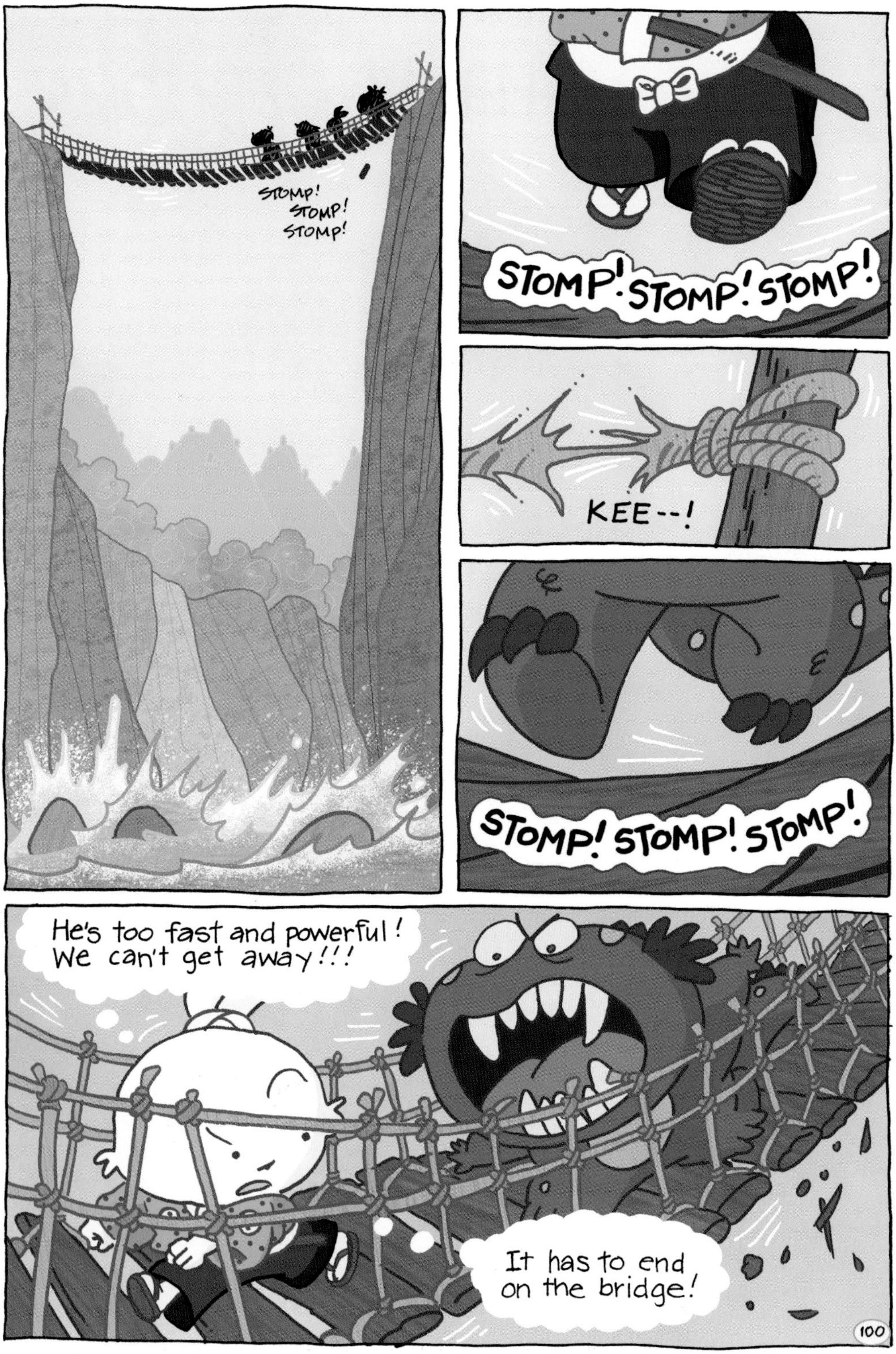
STOMP!
STOMP!
STOMP!
STOMP! STOMP! STOMP!
KEE--!
STOMP! STOMP! STOMP!
He's too fast and powerful! We can't get away!!!
It has to end on the bridge!

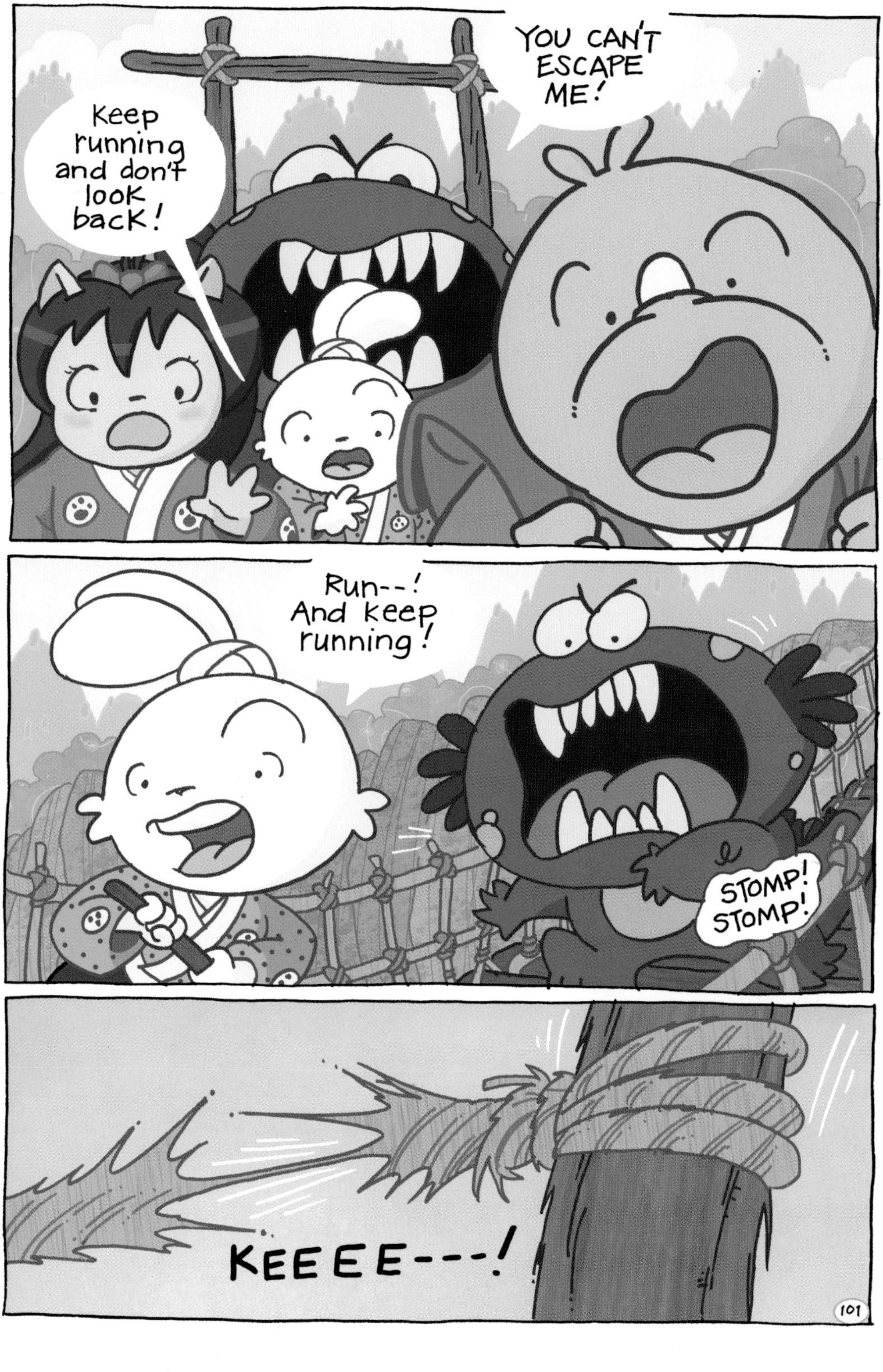
Keep running and don't look back!
YOU CAN'T ESCAPE ME!
Run--! And keep running!
STOMP! STOMP!
KEEEE---!

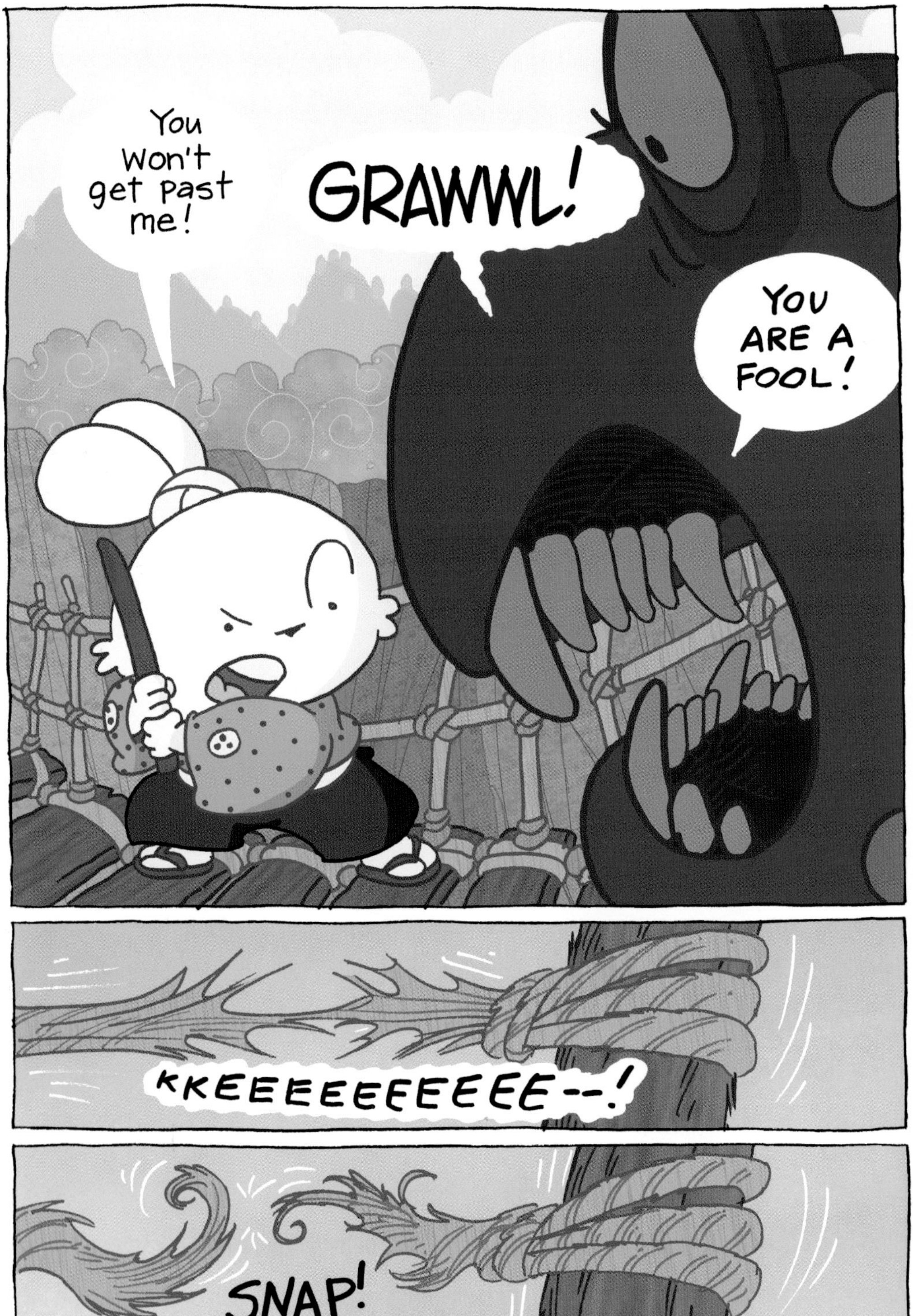
You won't get past me!
GRAWWL!
YOU ARE A FOOL!
KKEEEEEEEEEEE--!
SNAP!

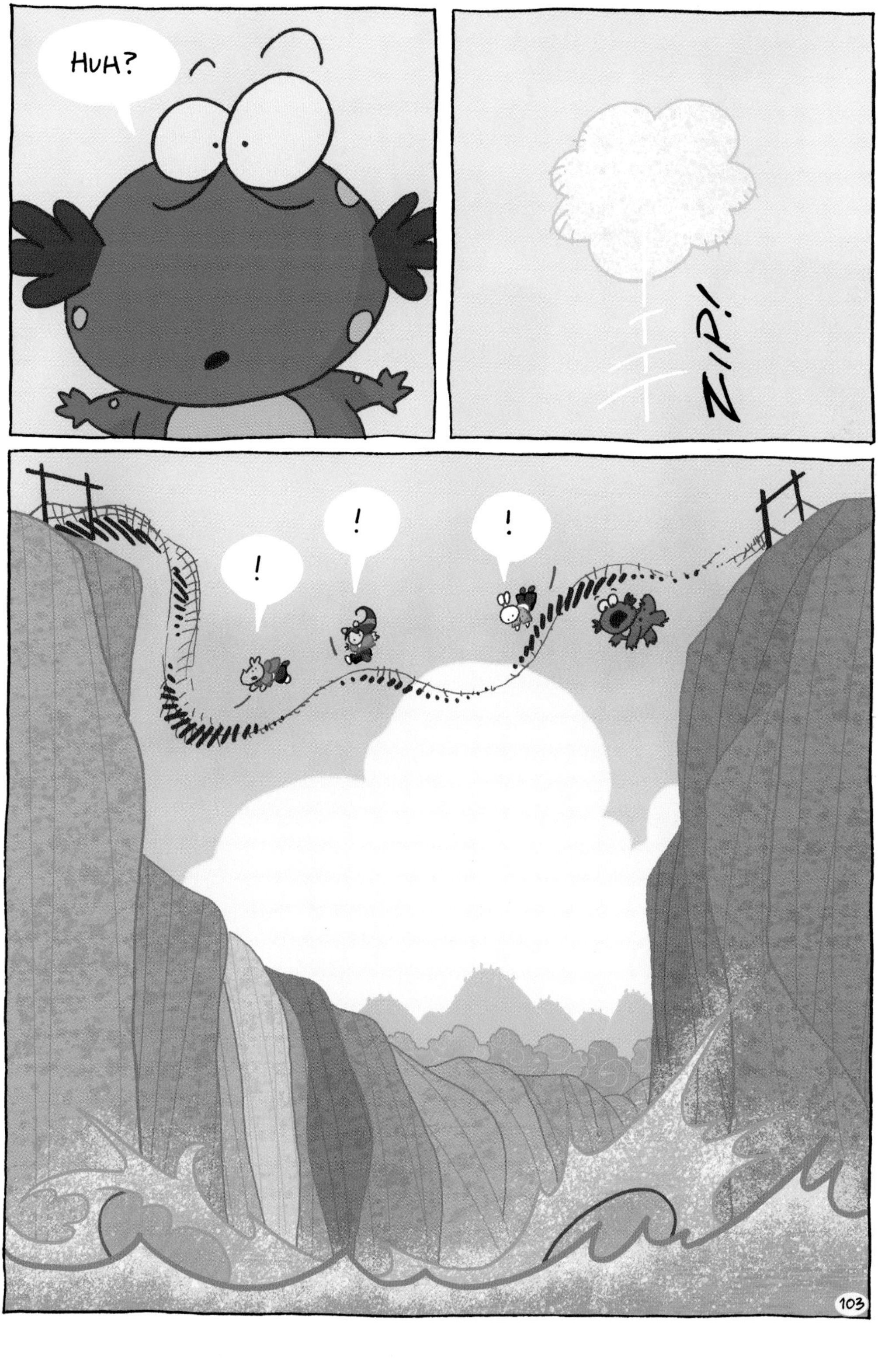
HUH?
ZIP!
!
!
!

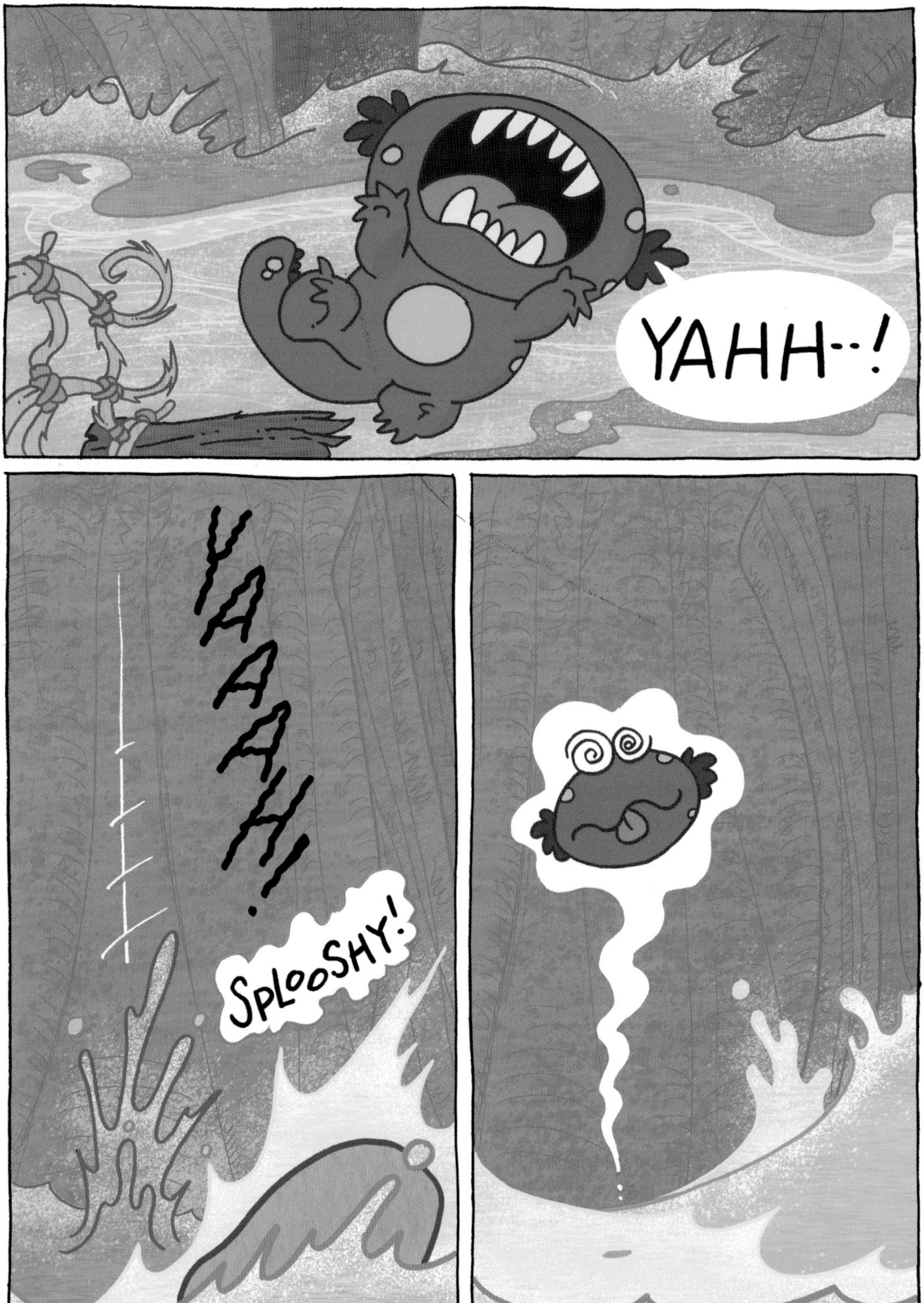
YAHH--!
YAAAH!
SPLOOSHY!

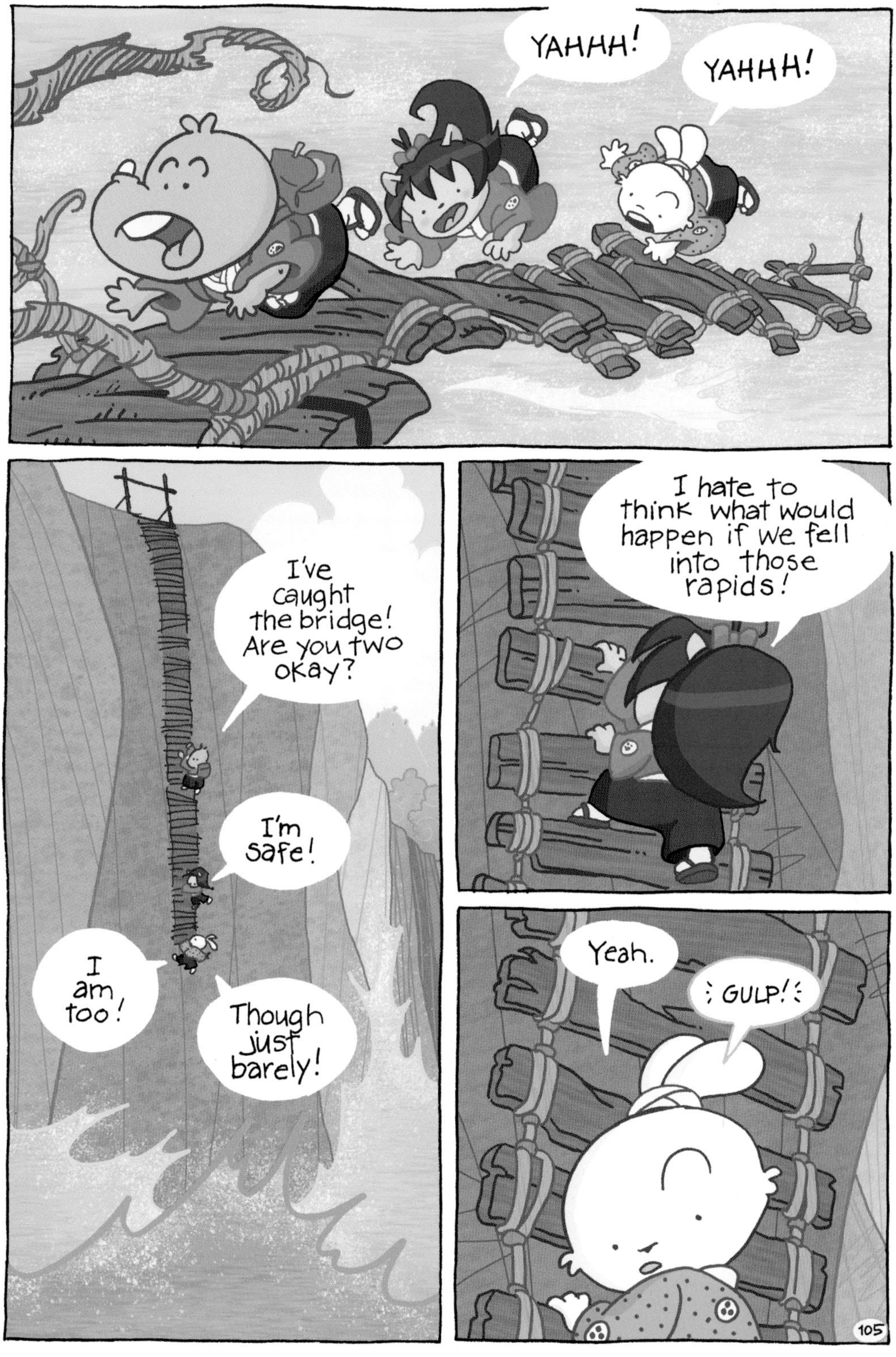
YAHHH!
YAHHH!
I've caught the bridge! Are you two okay?
I'm safe!
I am too!
Though just barely!
I hate to think what would happen if we fell into those rapids!
Yeah.
GULP!

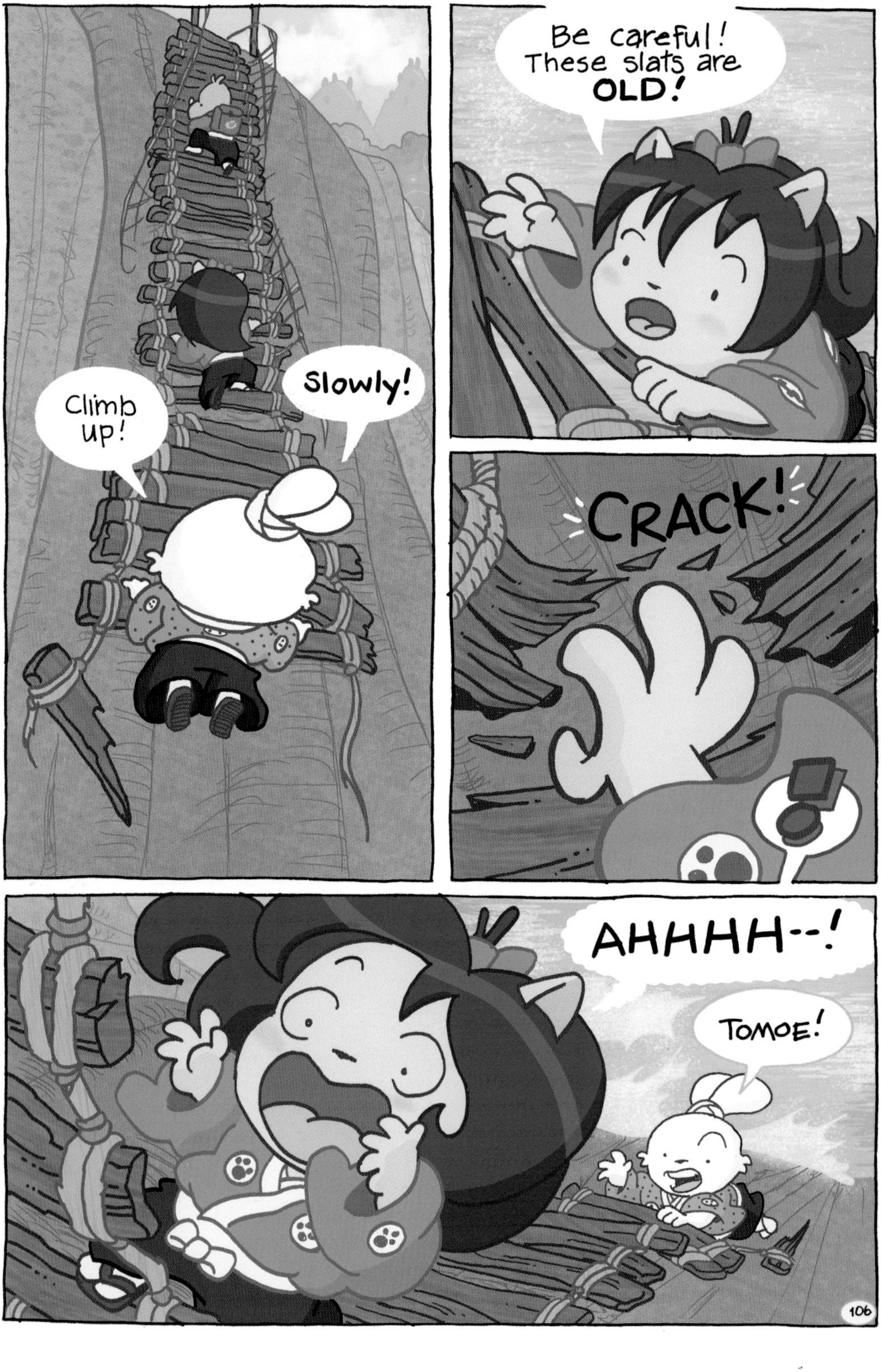
Climb up!
Slowly!
Be careful! These slats are OLD!
CRACK!
AHHHH--!
TOMOE!

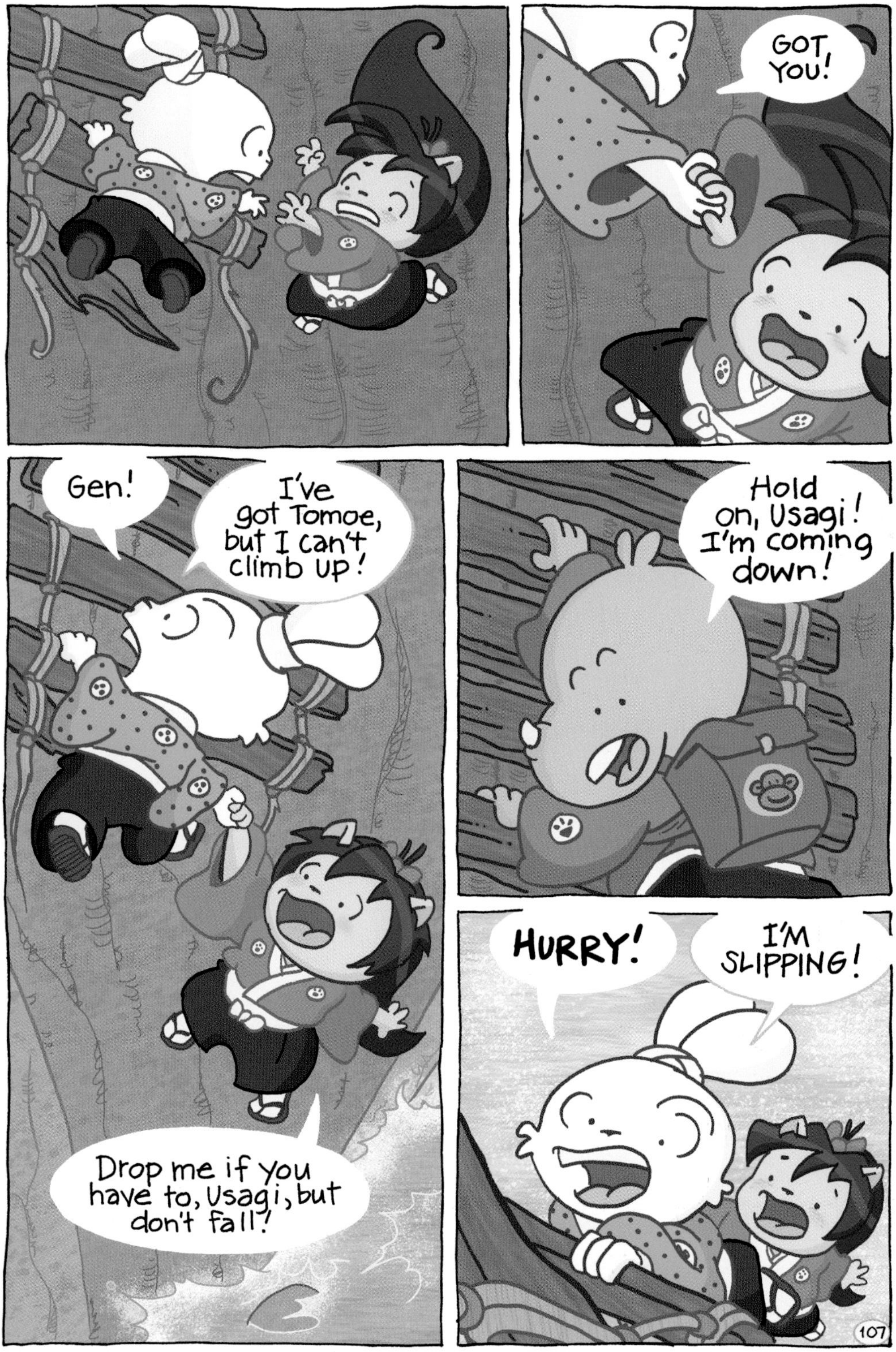
GOT YOU!
Gen!
I've got Tomoe, but I can't climb up!
Drop me if you have to, Usagi, but don't fall!
Hold on, Usagi! I'm coming down!
HURRY!
I'M SLIPPING!

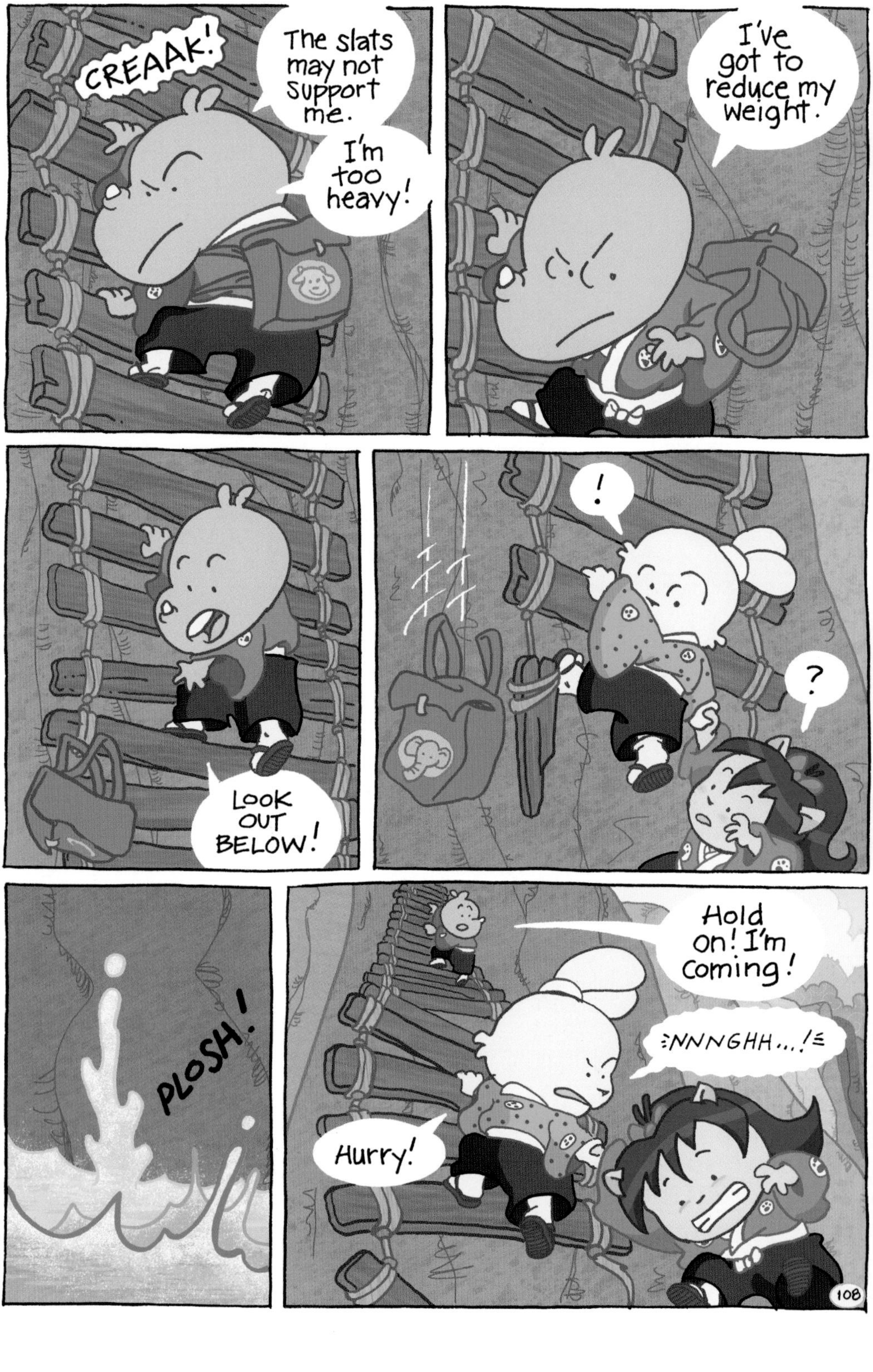
CREAAK!
The slats may not support me.
I'm too heavy!
I've got to reduce my weight.
LOOK OUT BELOW!
!
?
PLOSH!
Hold on! I'm coming!
NNNGHH...!
Hurry!

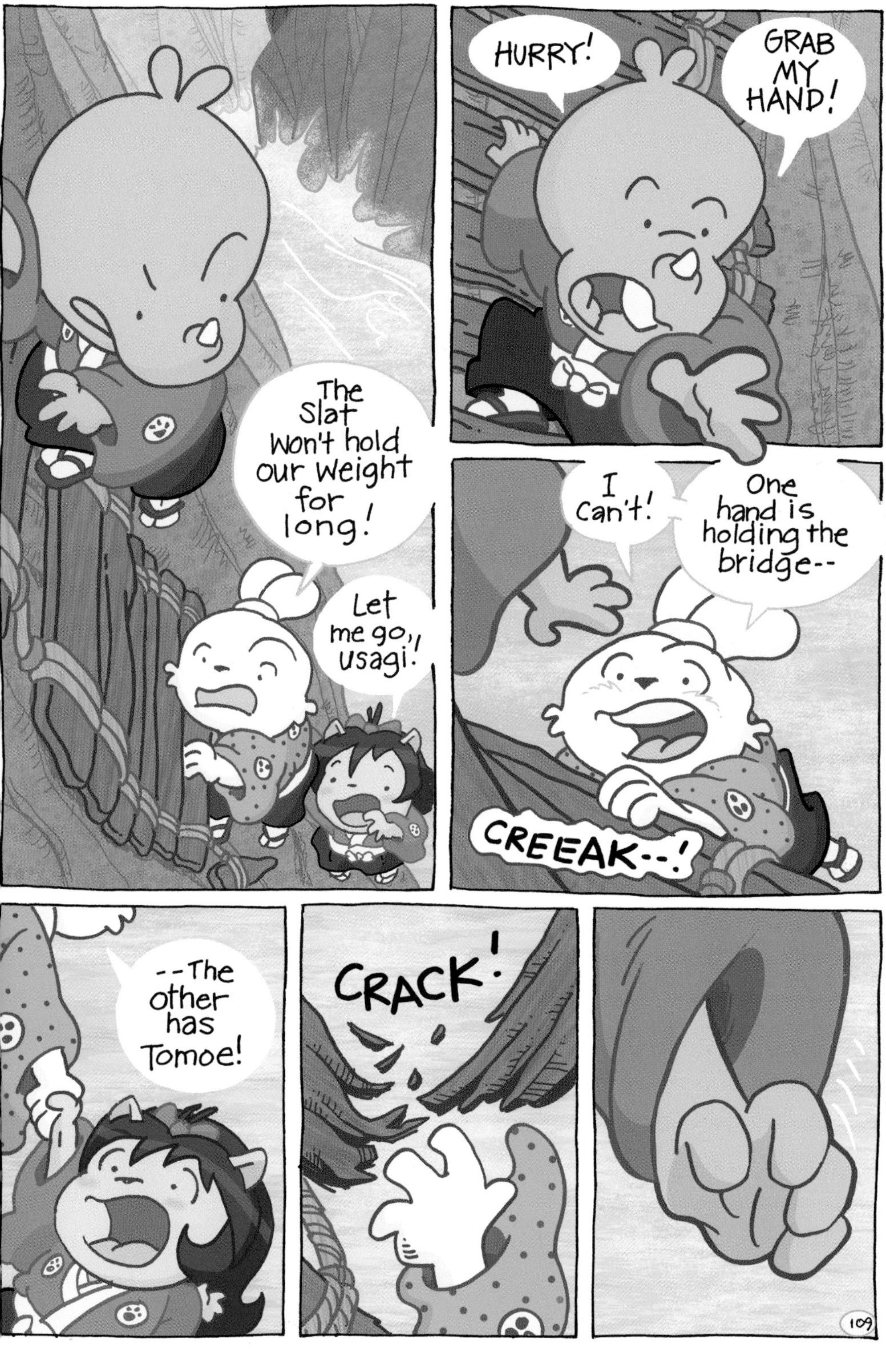
The Slat Won't hold our Weight for long!
Let me go,, usagi!
HURRY!
GRAB MY HAND!
I can't!
One hand is holding the bridge--
CREEAK--!
--The other has Tomoe!
CRACK!

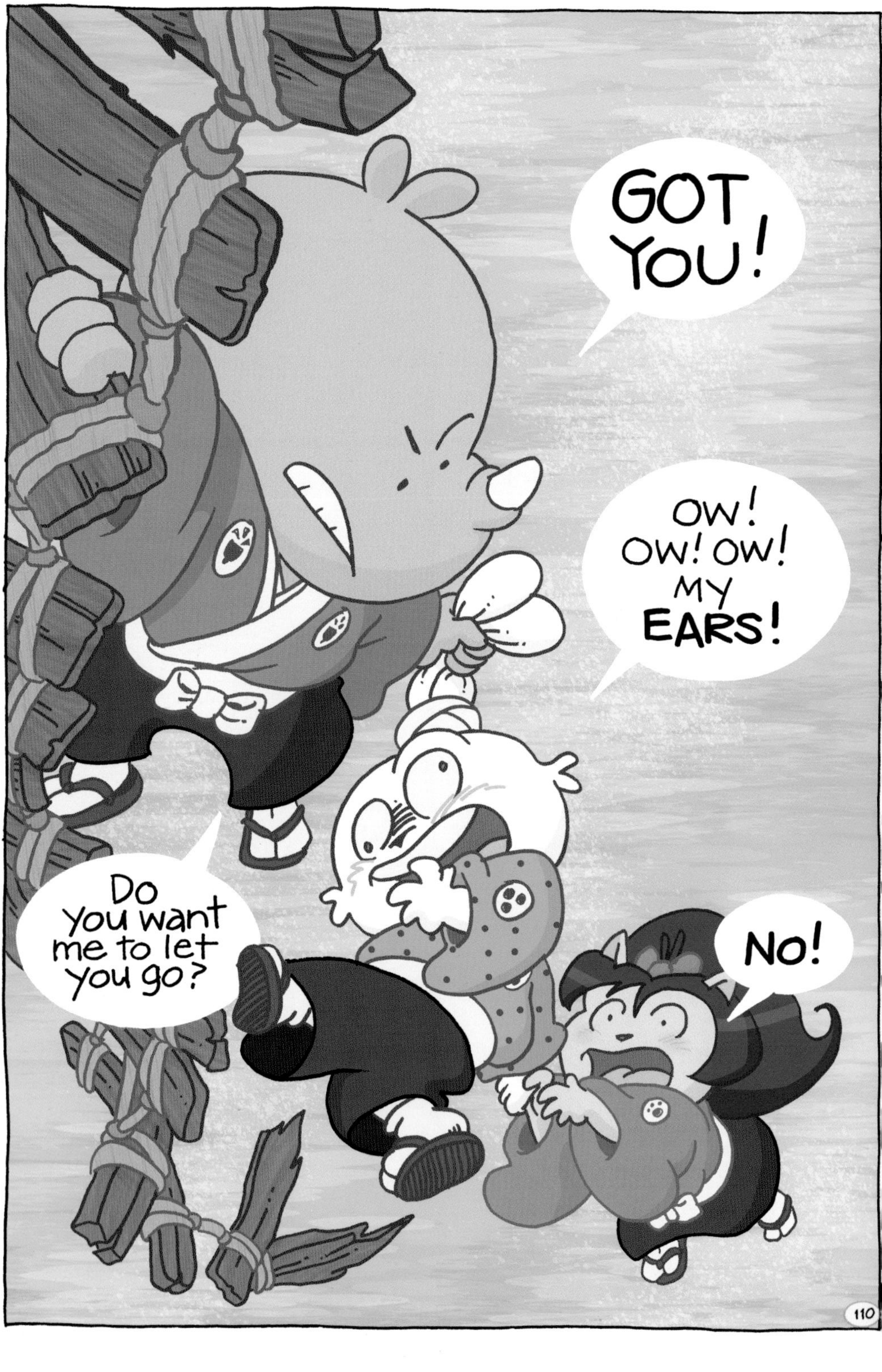
GOT YOU!
OW! OW! OW! MY EARS!
Do you want me to let you go?
No!

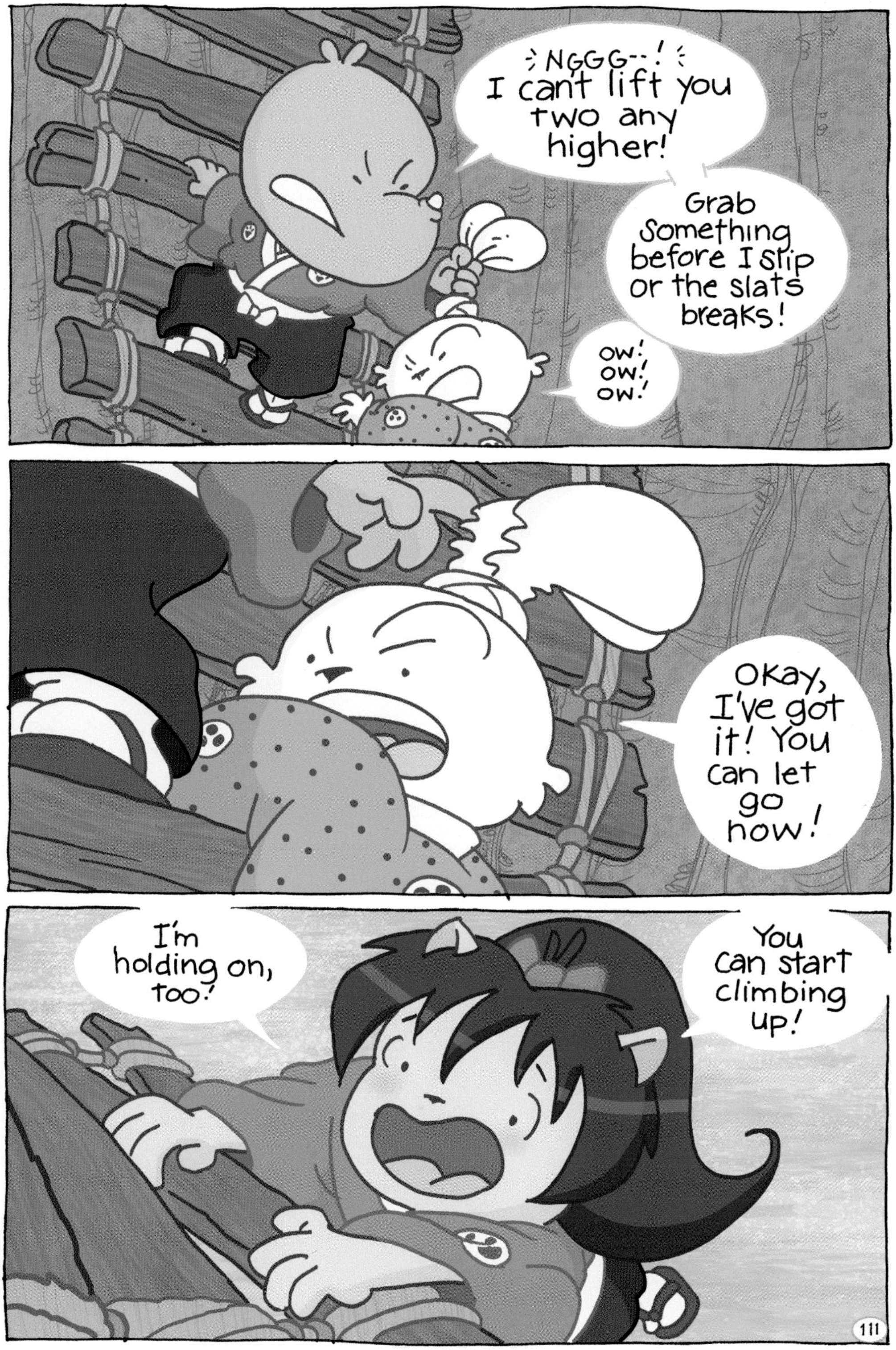
NGGG--!
I can't lift you two any higher!
Grab Something before I slip or the slats breaks!
Ow! Ow! Ow!
Okay, I've got it! You can let go now!
I'm holding on, too!
You can start climbing up!

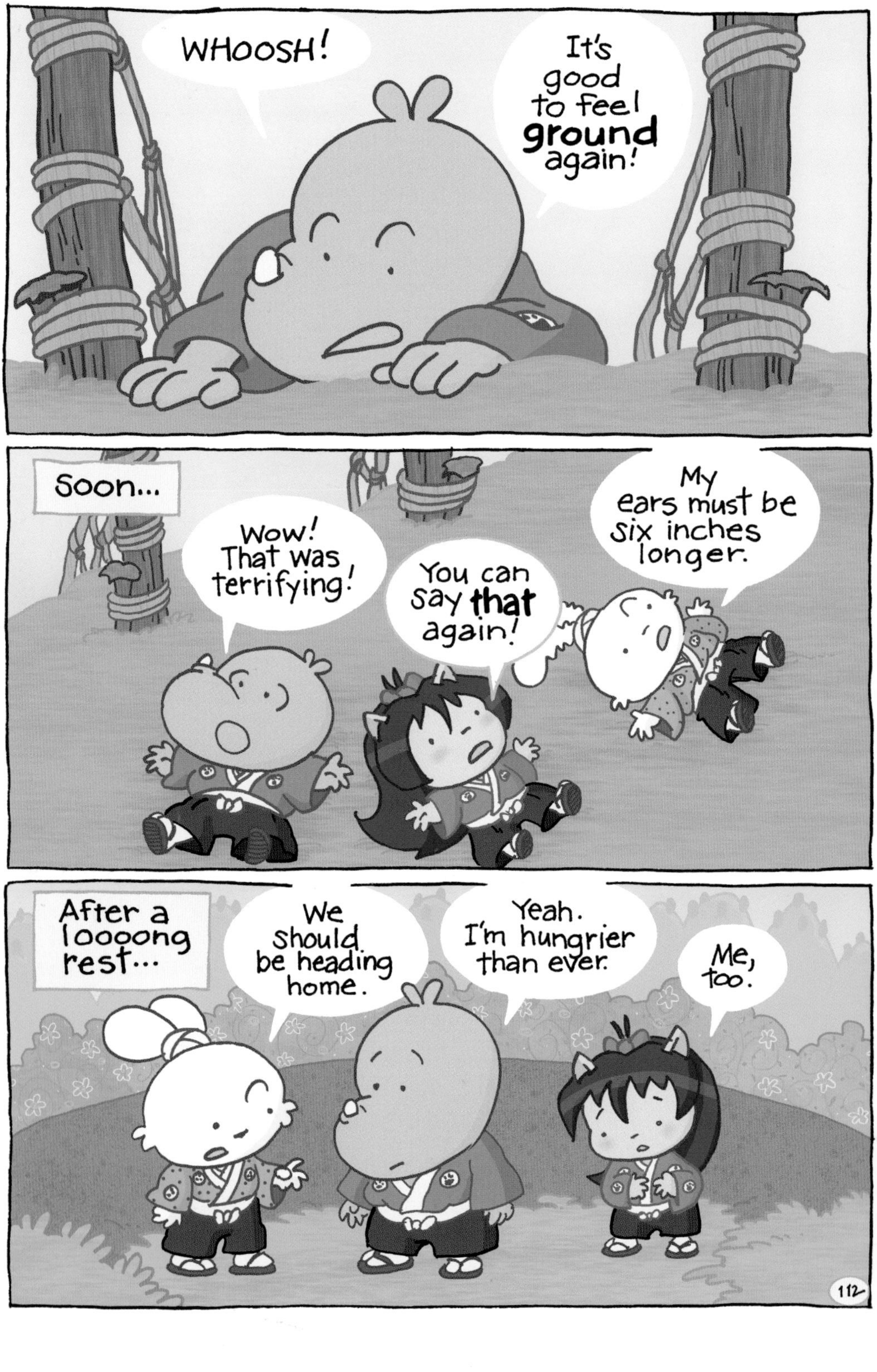
WHOOSH!
It's good to feel ground again!
Soon...
Wow! That was terrifying!
You can say that again!
My ears must be six inches longer.
After a loooong rest...
We should be heading home.
Yeah. I'm hungrier than ever.
Me, too.

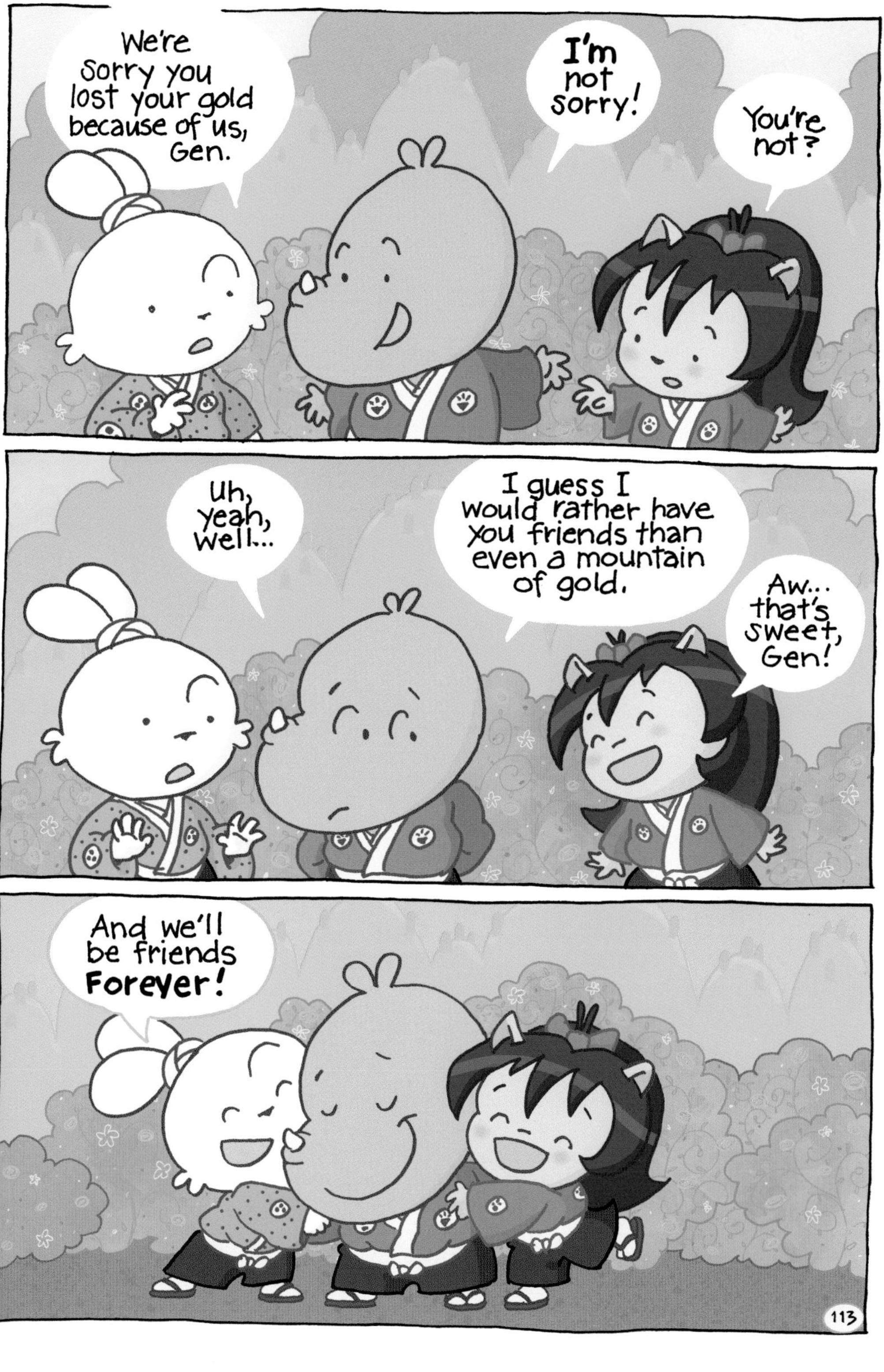
We're sorry you lost your gold because of us, Gen.
I'm not sorry!
You're not?
Uh, yeah, well...
I guess I would rather have you friends than even a mountain of gold.
Aw... that's sweet, Gen!
And we'll be friends **Forever**!

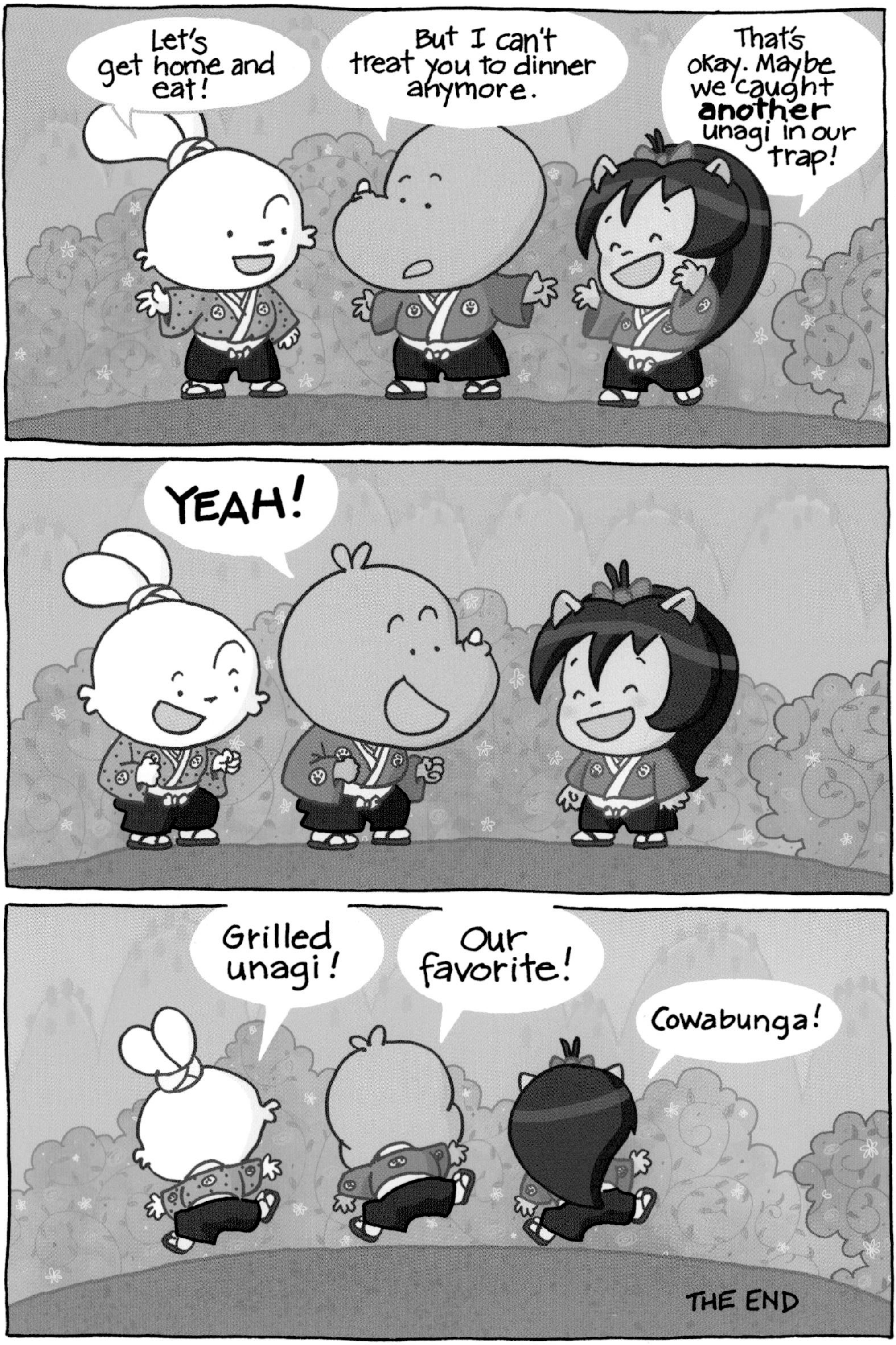
Let's get home and eat!
But I can't treat you to dinner anymore.
That's okay. Maybe we caught **another** unagi in our trap!
YEAH!
Grilled unagi!
Our favorite!
Cowabunga!
THE END

HOW TO DRAW

HEEBIE CHIBIS

1 Draw a squiggle

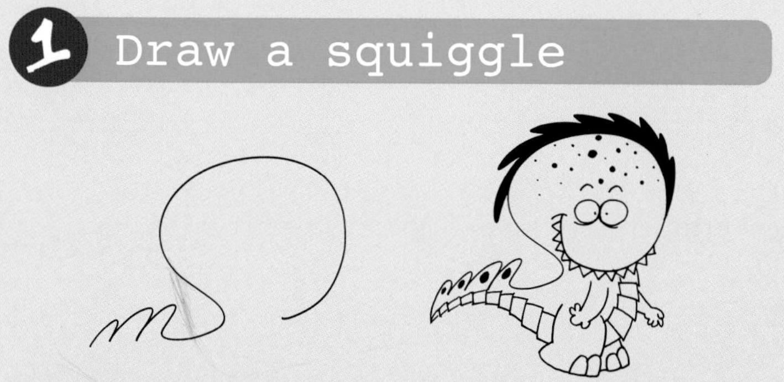

2 Use your imagination

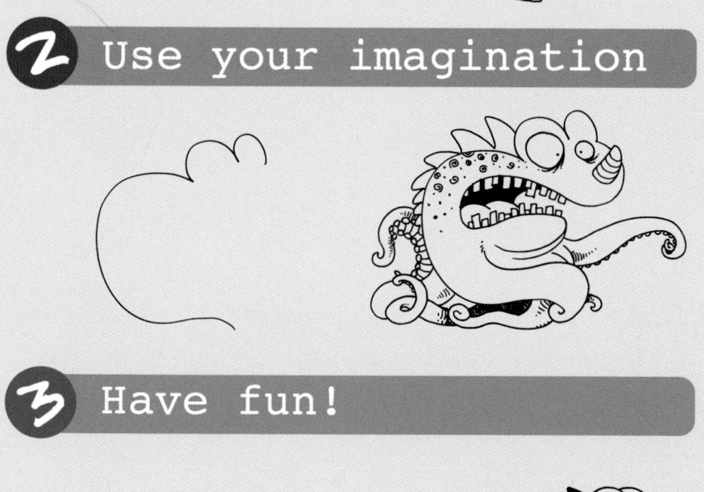

3 Have fun!

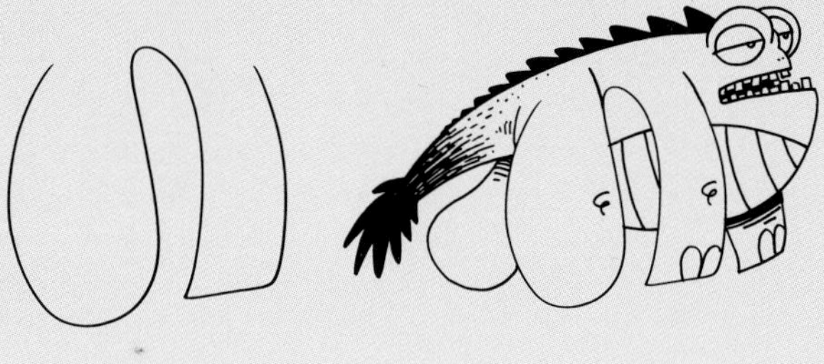

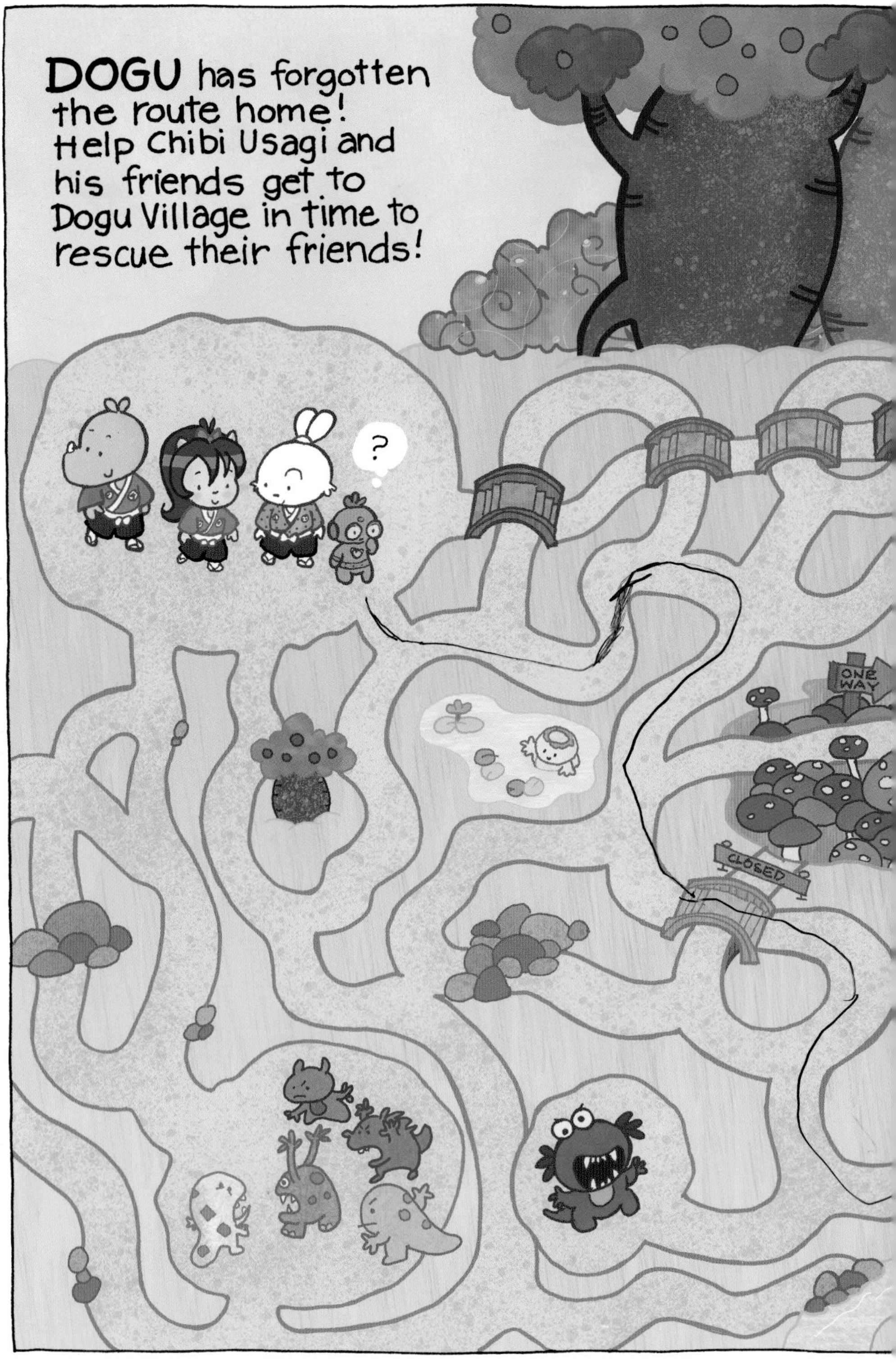
DOGU has forgotten the route home! Help Chibi Usagi and his friends get to Dogu Village in time to rescue their friends!
?
ONE WAY
CLOSED

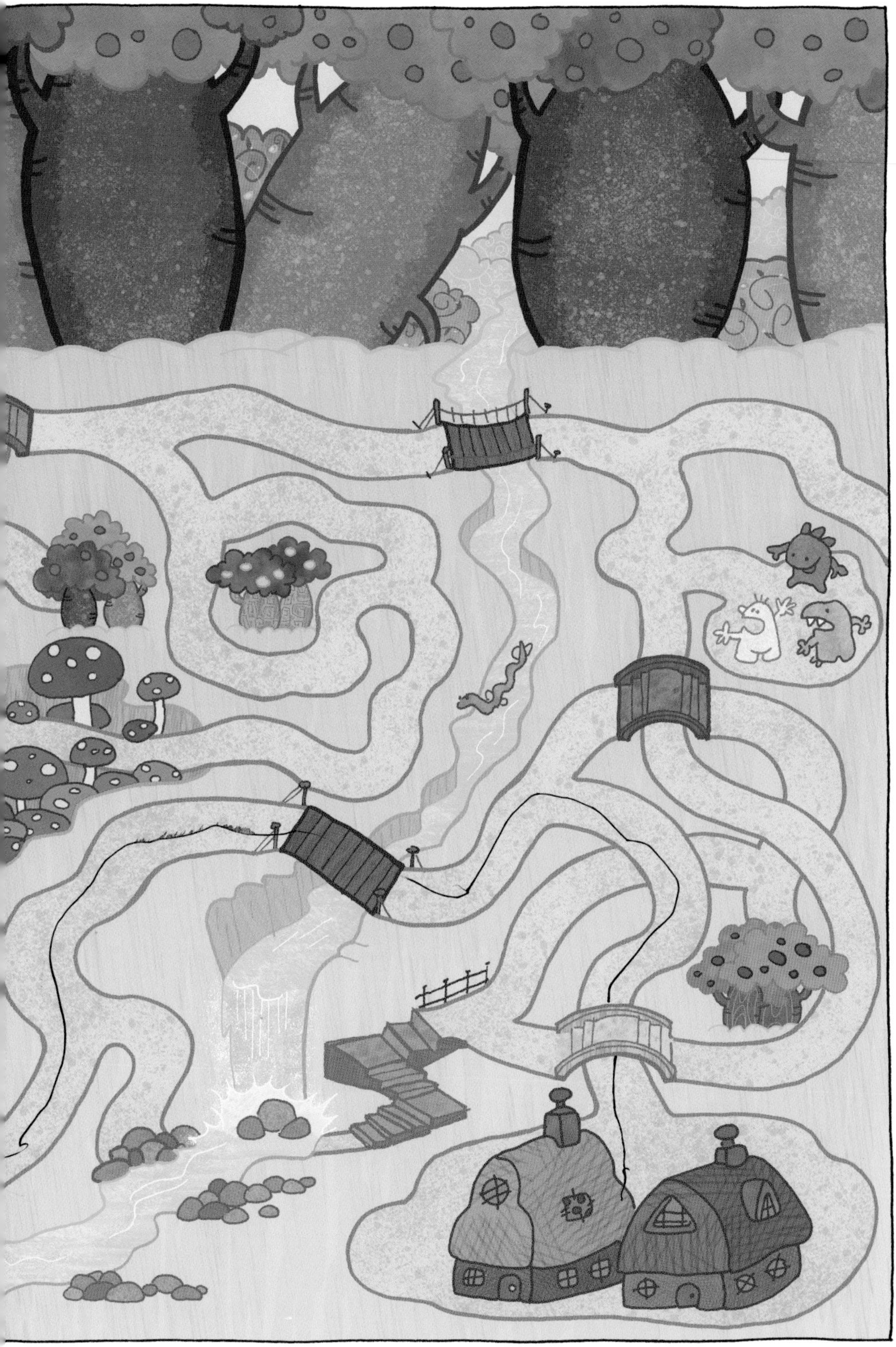

WHAT IS A CHIBI?

Chibi is short for the Japanese word "chibiru," which describes wearing out a tip of something to make it rounder or shorter and, in the case of cartooning, cuter. Much cuter. Chibi also means little one. Chibi art was made popular through Japanese animation (anime). It is also called "super deformed" because it changes the proportions of characters to an outrageous degree. A character's head could be gigantic and its body tiny, its eyes huge, but its mouth very small. It is often used to make cute or childlike versions of a character or to place that character in a humorous situation.

WHAT IS AN UNAGI?

An unagi is a Japanese freshwater eel. It is a common ingredient in Japanese cooking and is delicious. Unlike fish sashimi, unagi is never eaten raw but it can be smoked, broiled, grilled, sautéed, or made into soup. It is believed that eating it will give you energy and strength. Today, most unagi are farm-raised, but the best ones are caught in the wild using a trap like the one Chibi Usagi and his friends used.

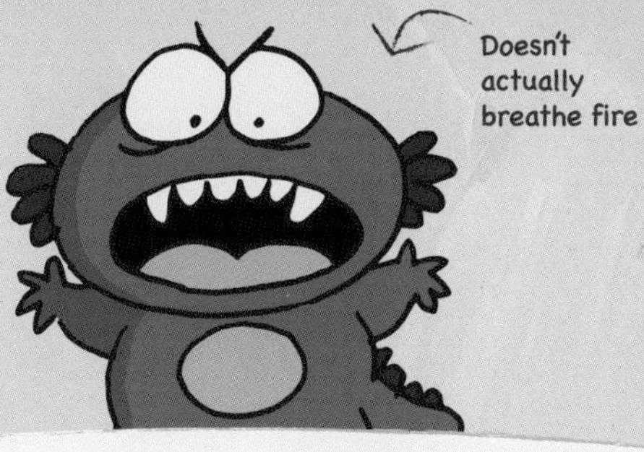
Doesn't actually breathe fire

WHAT IS A JAPANESE GIANT SALAMANDER?

The Japanese Giant Salamander is the second largest amphibian in the world and can grow up to five feet long and weigh as much as fifty-five pounds! It lives in the bottom of clear rivers and streams, and breathes through its skin. It has very small eyes and a huge mouth. It can give off an odor that smells like pepper so it is sometimes called the "big pepper fish." It eats mainly insects, frogs, and fish, and can live as long as 80 years!

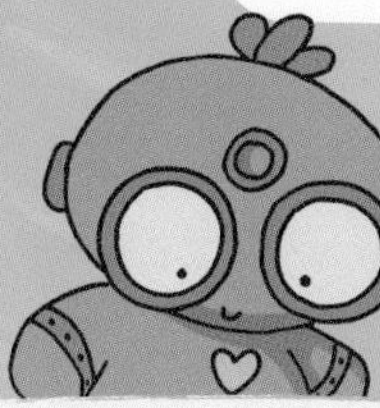

WHAT IS A DOGU?

A dogu is a small clay figure found in Japan. They were made during the Jomon Period a very, very, long time ago–about 3,000 years ago. They have been found all over Japan, so they were pretty common, but no one knows why they were made. Some scientists believe they may have been used as toys, like a doll. Others believe they look like astronauts or space people with their large helmet-like heads and goggles. What do you think they are?

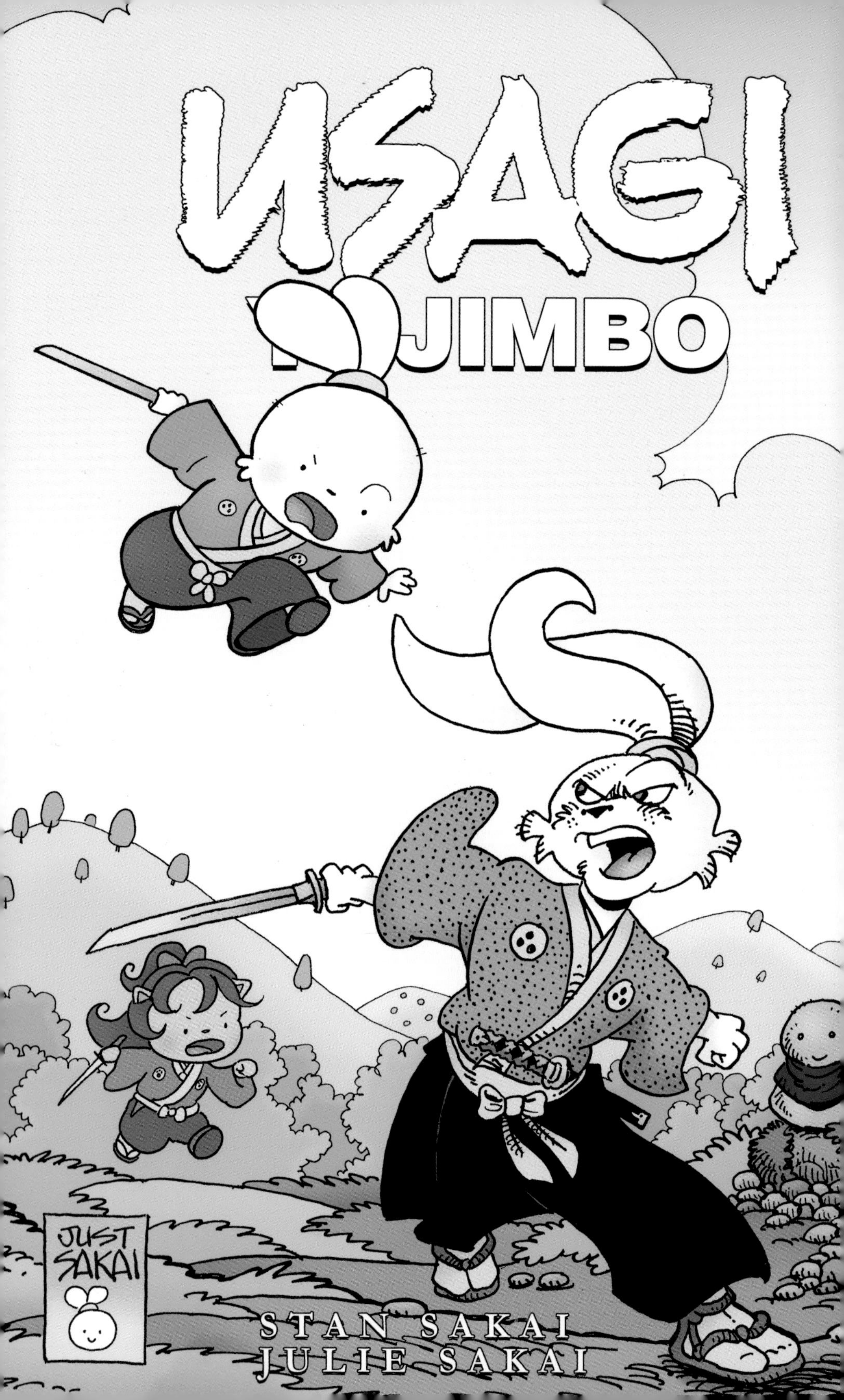
USAGI
YOJIMBO
JUST SAKAI
STAN SAKAI
JULIE SAKAI

ATTACK OF THE TEENIE TITANS

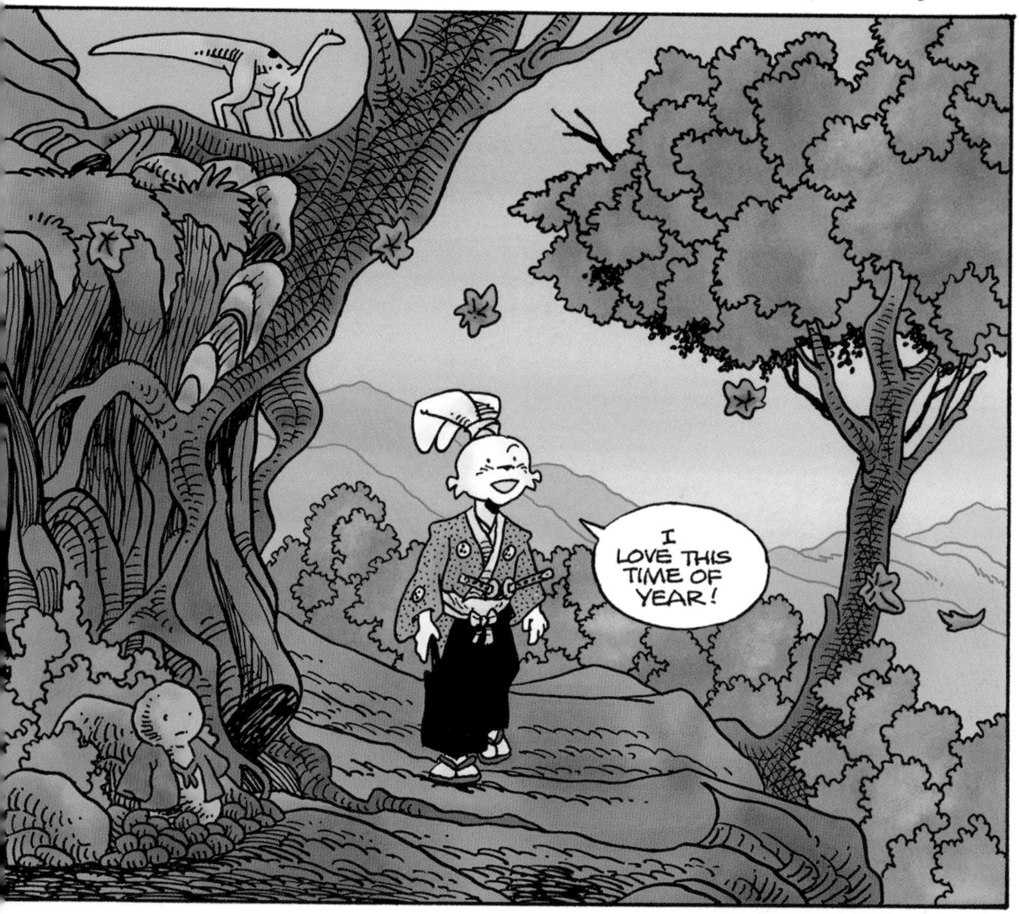
I LOVE THIS TIME OF YEAR!

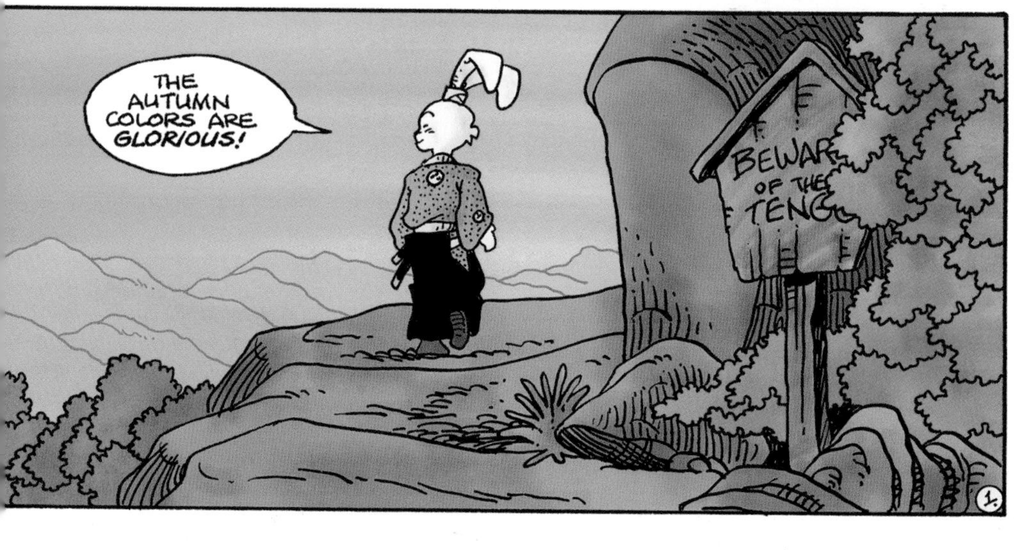
THE AUTUMN COLORS ARE GLORIOUS!
BEWAR
OF THE
TENG

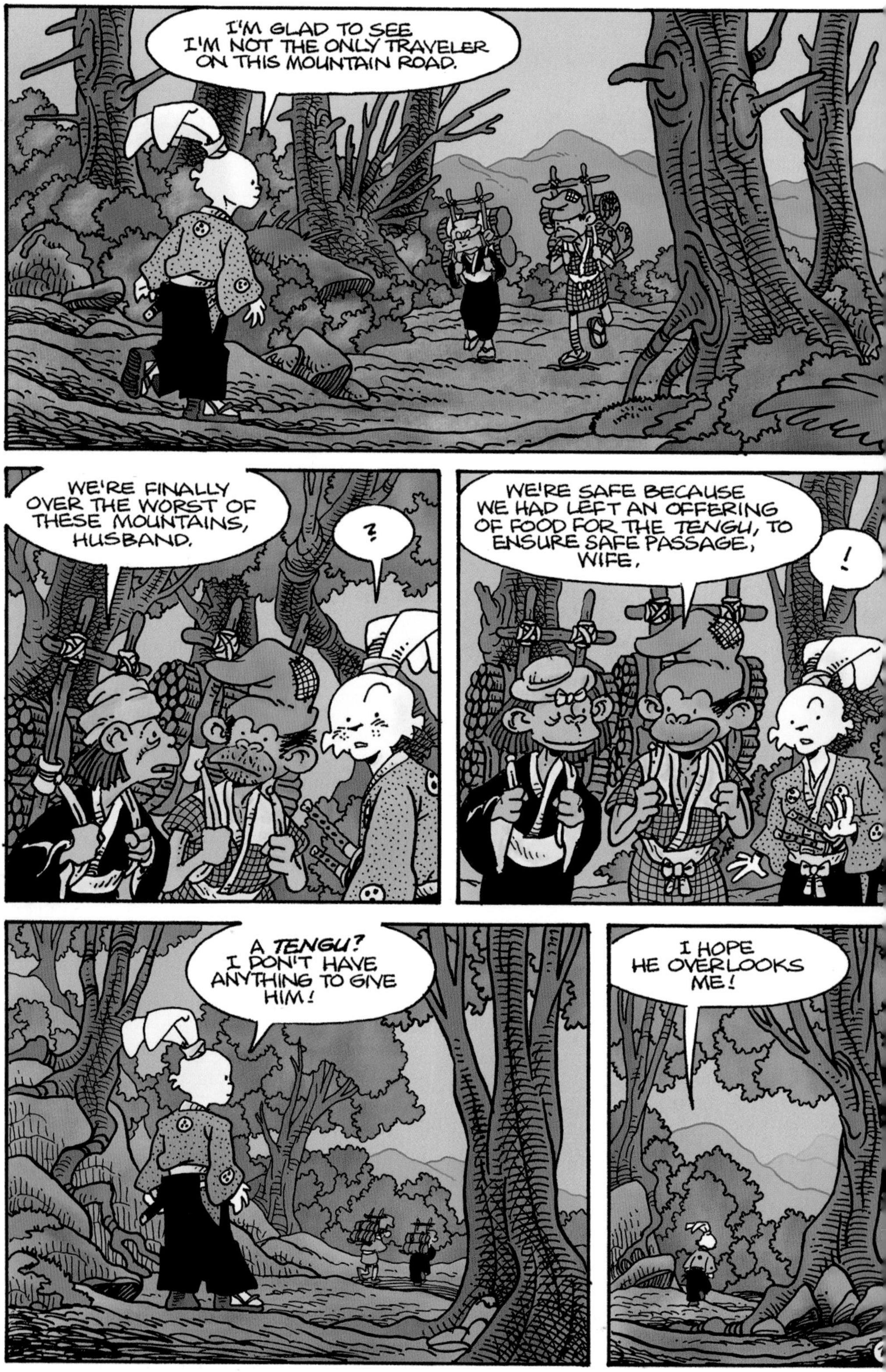
I'M GLAD TO SEE I'M NOT THE ONLY TRAVELER ON THIS MOUNTAIN ROAD.
WE'RE FINALLY OVER THE WORST OF THESE MOUNTAINS, HUSBAND.
?
WE'RE SAFE BECAUSE WE HAD LEFT AN OFFERING OF FOOD FOR THE *TENGU*, TO ENSURE SAFE PASSAGE, WIFE.
!
A *TENGU*? I DON'T HAVE ANYTHING TO GIVE HIM!
I HOPE HE OVERLOOKS ME!

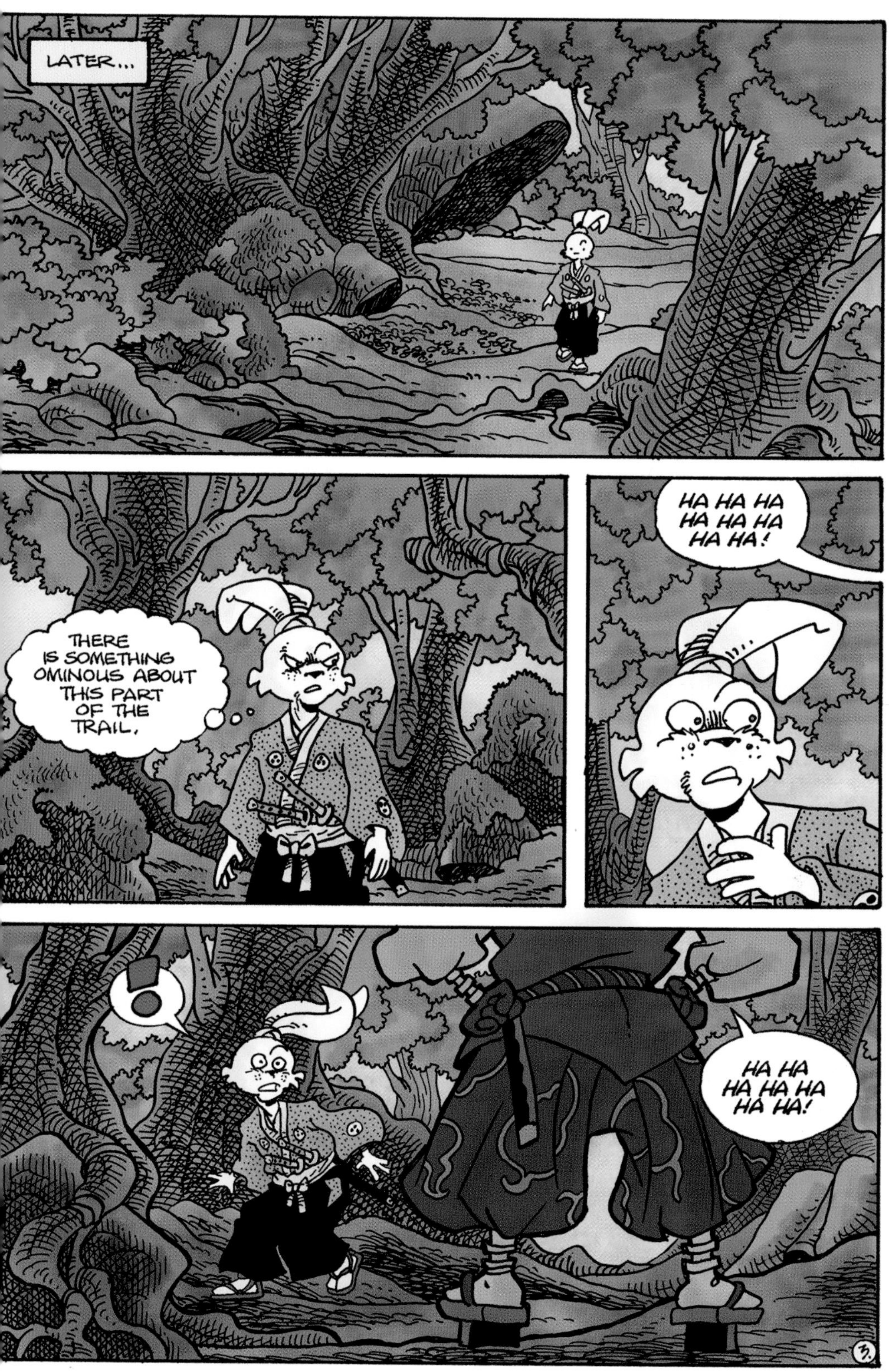
LATER...
THERE IS SOMETHING OMINOUS ABOUT THIS PART OF THE TRAIL.
HA HA HA HA HA HA HA HA!
!
HA HA HA HA HA HA HA!
3.

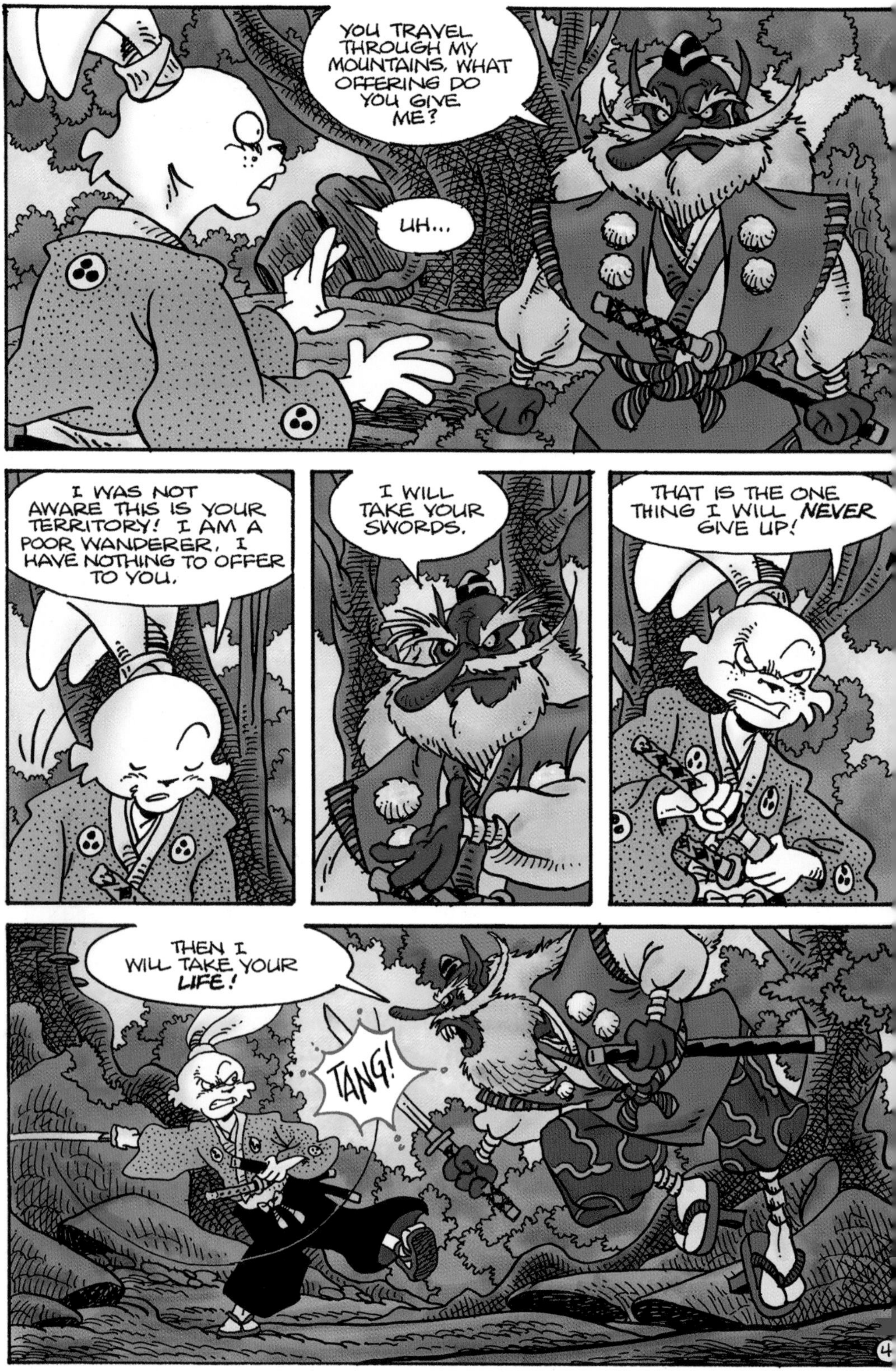
YOU TRAVEL THROUGH MY MOUNTAINS, WHAT OFFERING DO YOU GIVE ME?
UH...
I WAS NOT AWARE THIS IS YOUR TERRITORY! I AM A POOR WANDERER, I HAVE NOTHING TO OFFER TO YOU.
I WILL TAKE YOUR SWORDS.
THAT IS THE ONE THING I WILL NEVER GIVE UP!
THEN I WILL TAKE YOUR LIFE!
TANG!

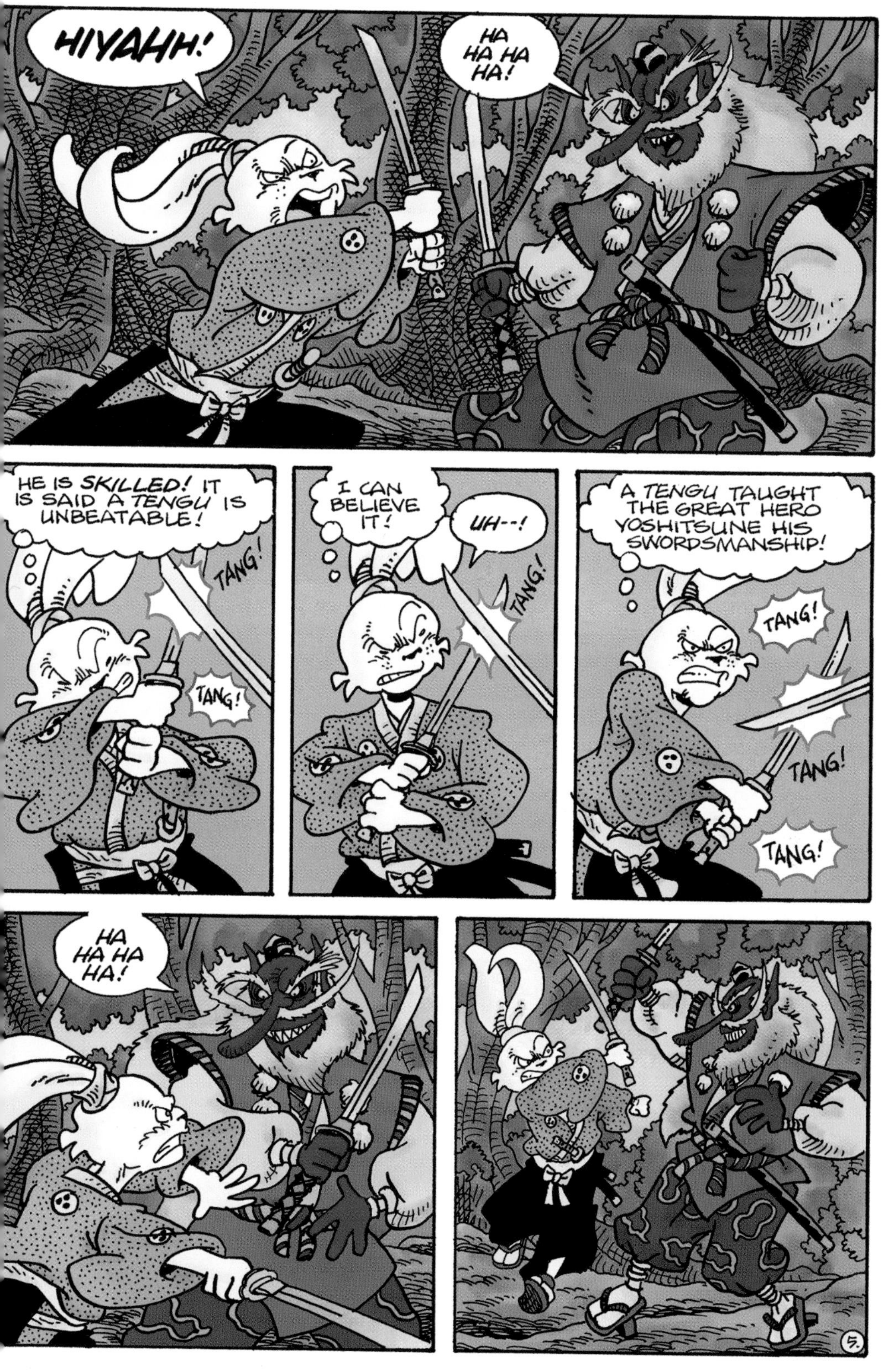
HIYAHH!
HA HA HA HA HA!
HE IS SKILLED! IT IS SAID A TENGU IS UNBEATABLE!
TANG!
TANG!
I CAN BELIEVE IT!
UH--!
TANG!
A TENGU TAUGHT THE GREAT HERO YOSHITSUNE HIS SWORDSMANSHIP!
TANG!
TANG!
TANG!
HA HA HA HA HA!
5.

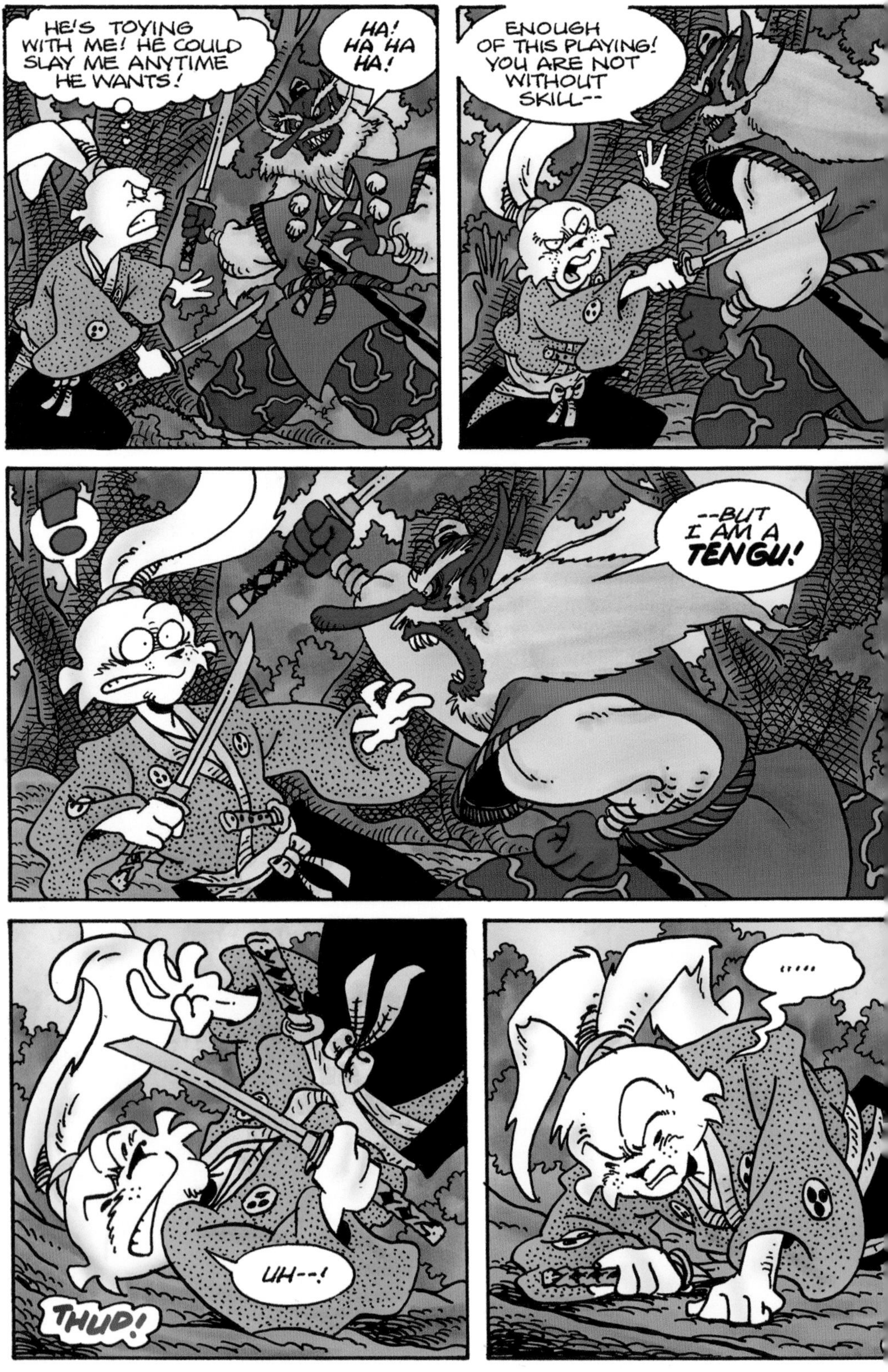
HE'S TOYING WITH ME! HE COULD SLAY ME ANYTIME HE WANTS!
HA! HA HA HA!
ENOUGH OF THIS PLAYING! YOU ARE NOT WITHOUT SKILL--
--BUT I AM A TENGU!
UH--!
THUD!
.....

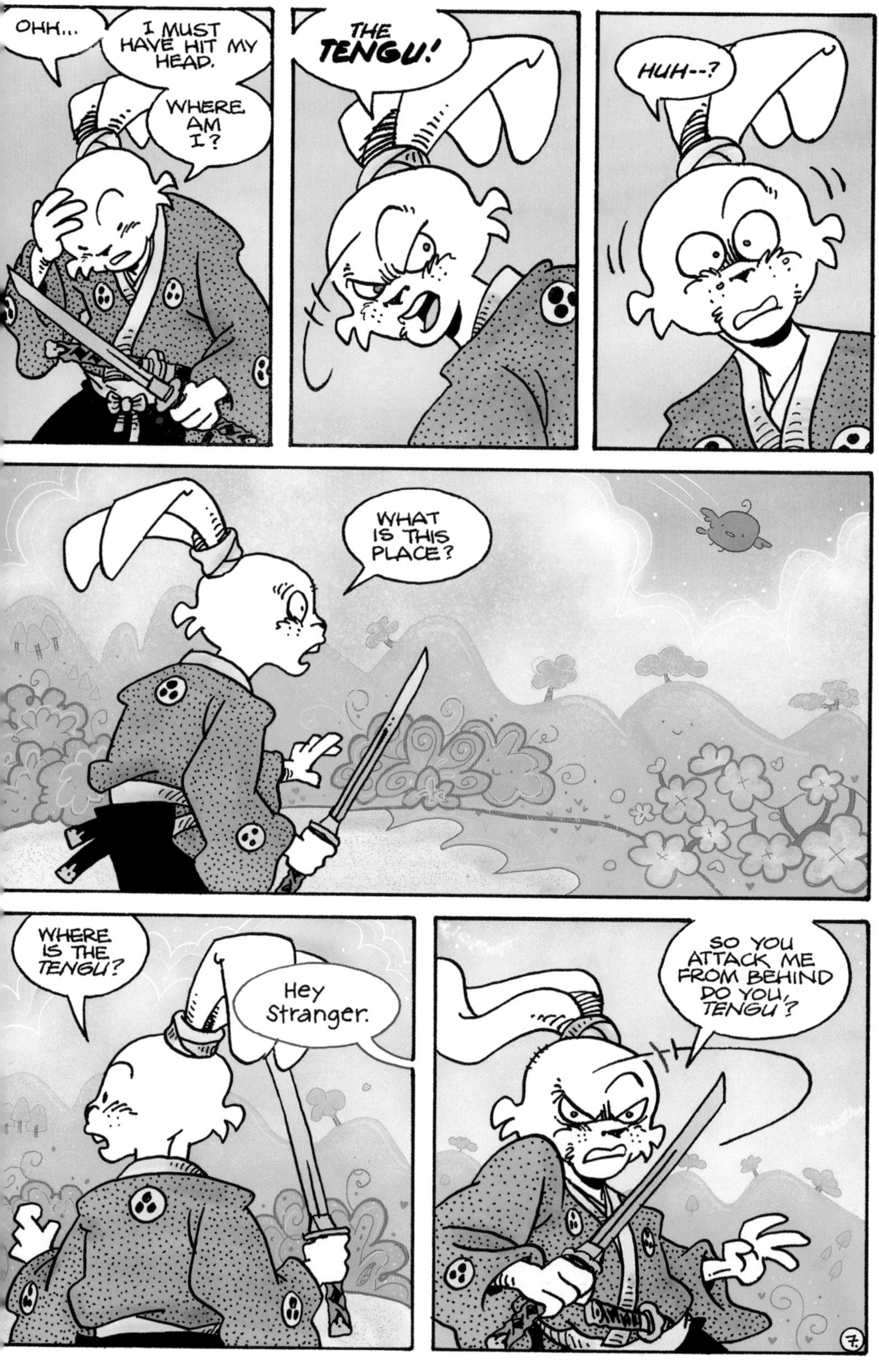
OHH...
I MUST HAVE HIT MY HEAD.
WHERE AM I?
THE TENGU!
HUH--?
WHAT IS THIS PLACE?
WHERE IS THE TENGU?
Hey Stranger.
SO YOU ATTACK ME FROM BEHIND DO YOU, TENGU?
7.

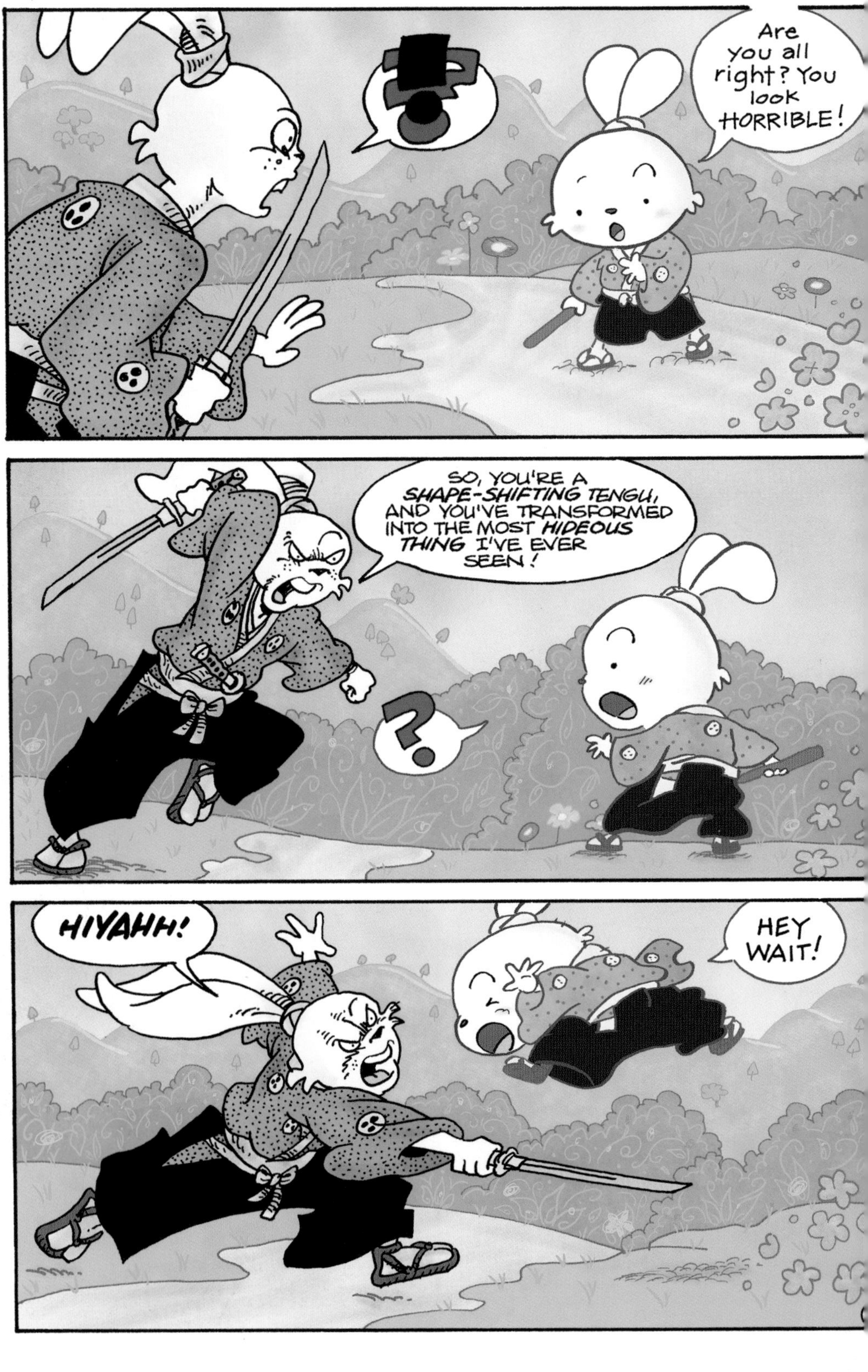
Are you all right? You look HORRIBLE!
SO, YOU'RE A SHAPE-SHIFTING TENGU, AND YOU'VE TRANSFORMED INTO THE MOST HIDEOUS THING I'VE EVER SEEN!
?
HIYAHH!
HEY WAIT!

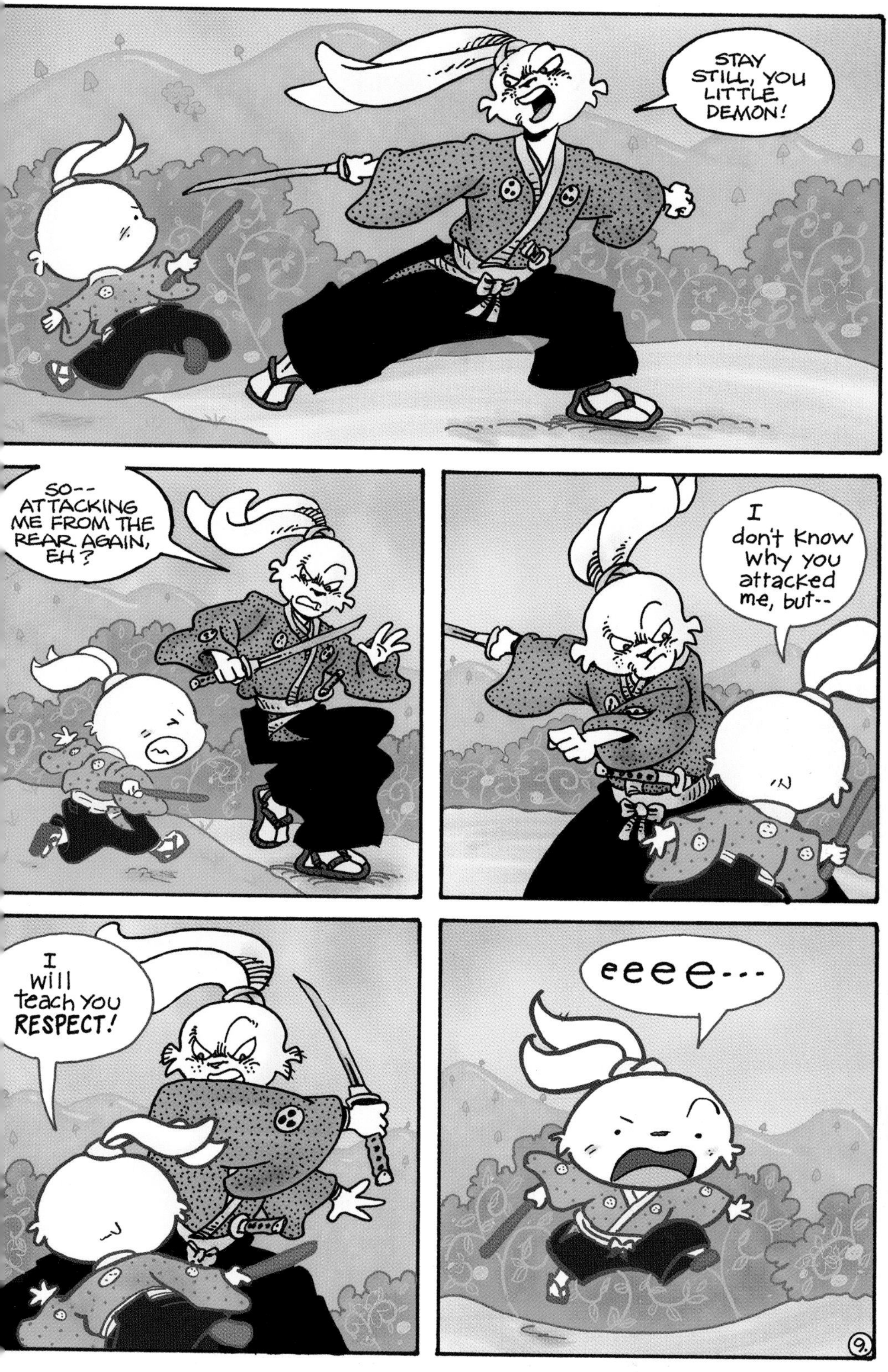
STAY STILL, YOU LITTLE DEMON!
SO-- ATTACKING ME FROM THE REAR AGAIN, EH?
I don't know why you attacked me, but--
I will teach you RESPECT!
eeee...

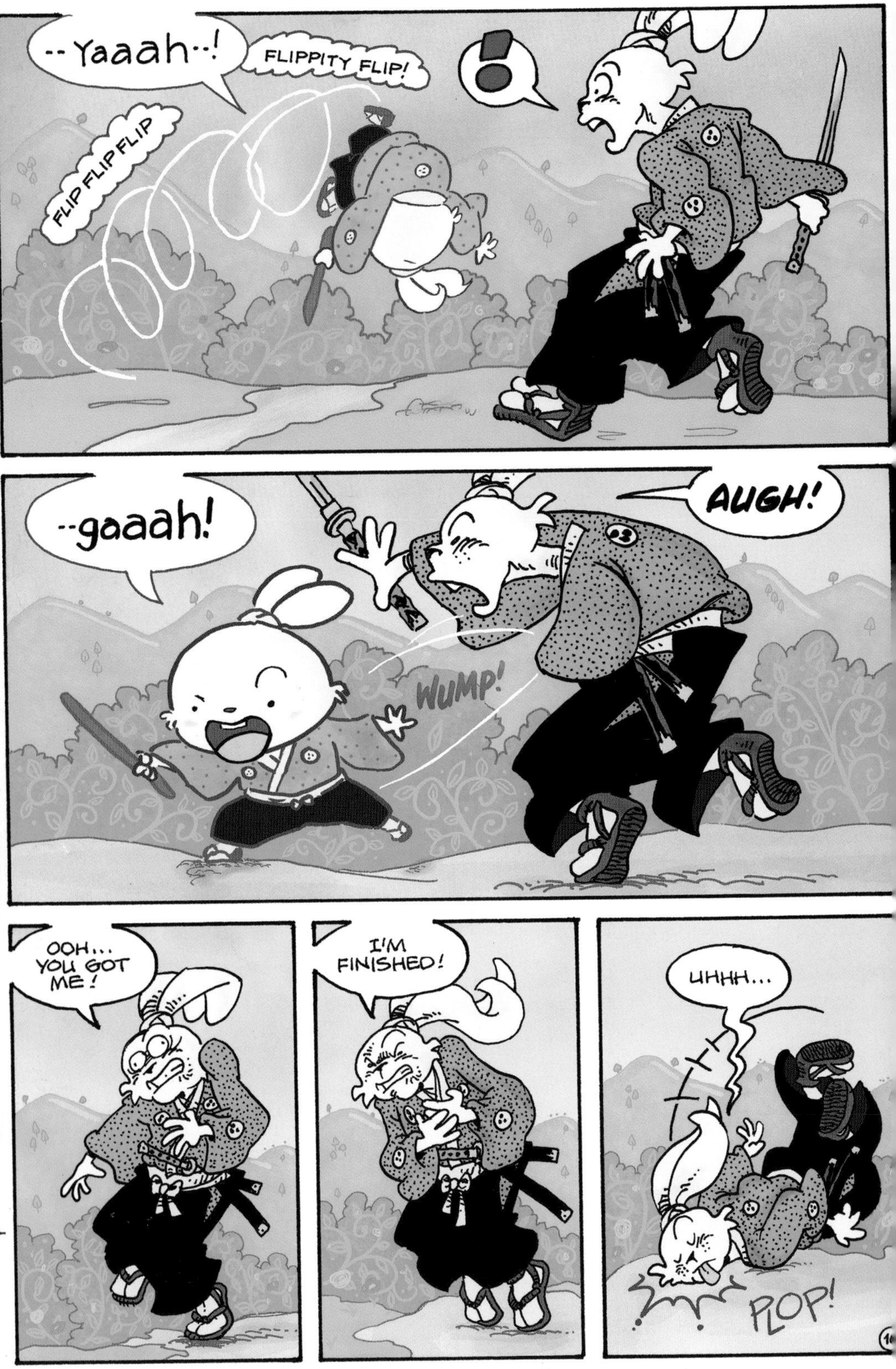
--Yaaah--!
FLIPPITY FLIP!
FLIPFLIPFLIP
!
--gaaah!
AUGH!
WUMP!
OOH... YOU GOT ME!
I'M FINISHED!
UHHH...
PLOP!

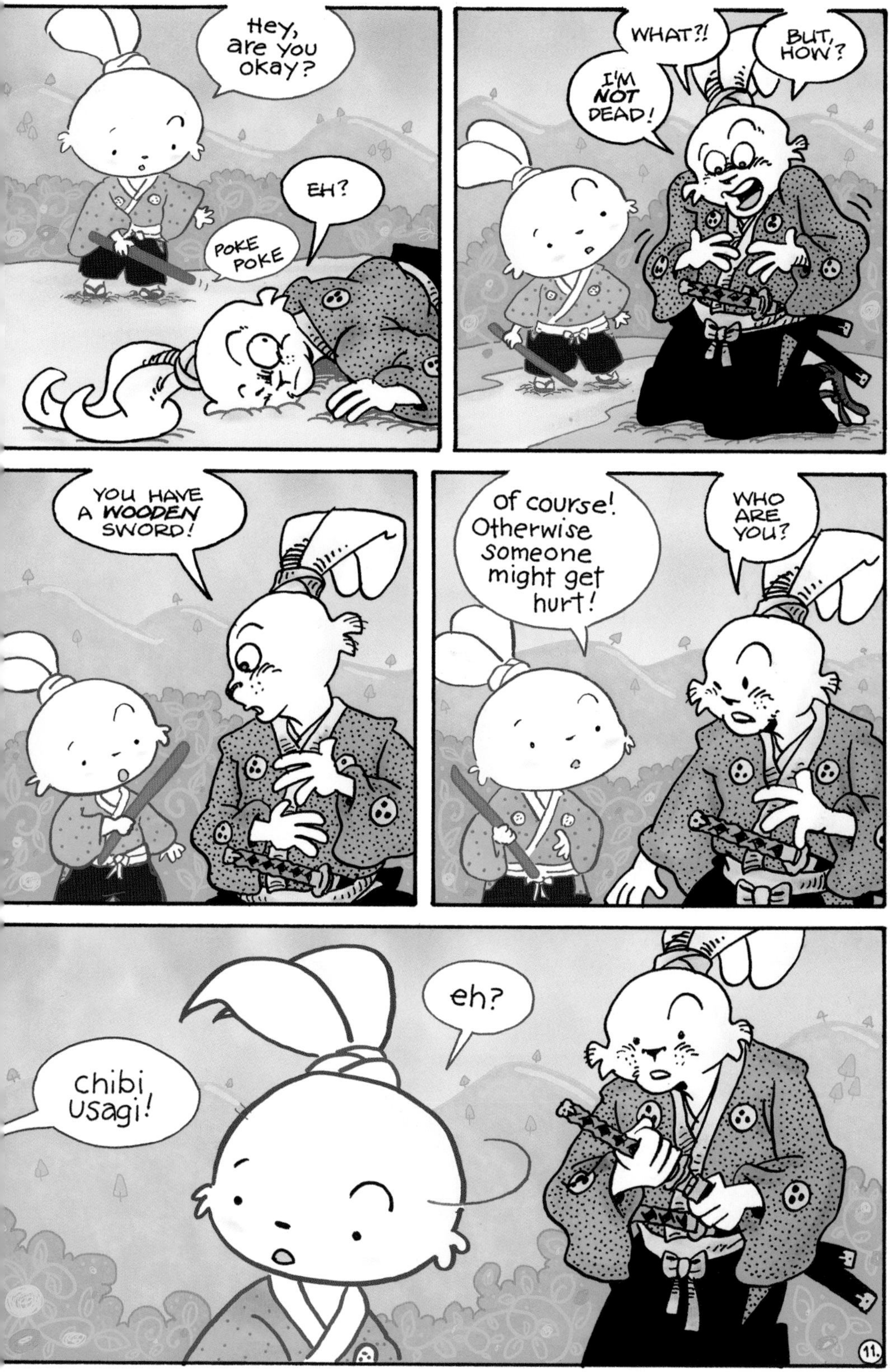
Hey, are you okay?
POKE POKE
EH?
WHAT?!
I'M NOT DEAD!
BUT, HOW?
YOU HAVE A WOODEN SWORD!
Of course! Otherwise someone might get hurt!
WHO ARE YOU?
chibi usagi!
eh?

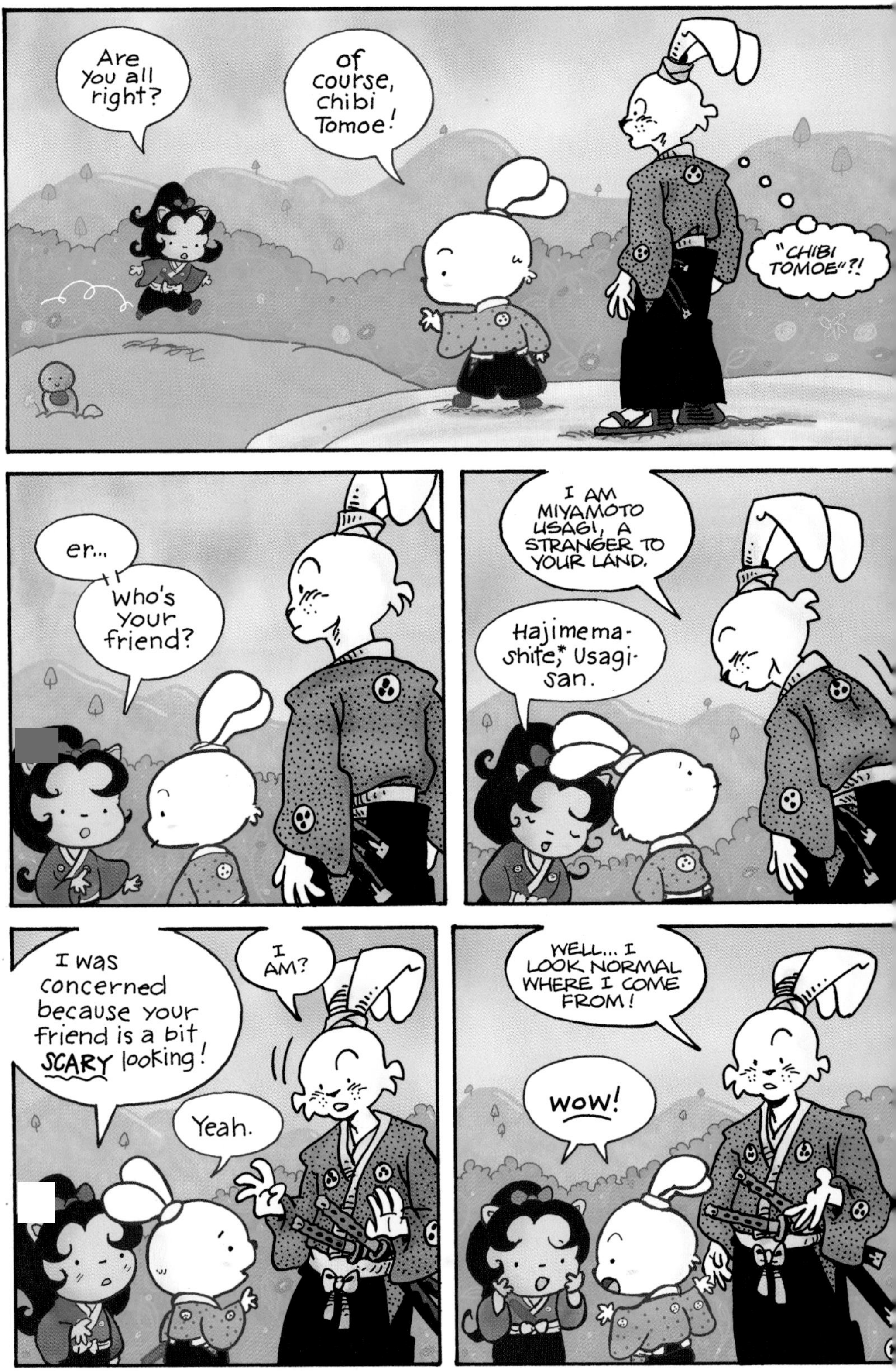
Are you all right?
of course, chibi Tomoe!
"CHIBI TOMOE"?!
er...
Who's your friend?
I AM MIYAMOTO USAGI, A STRANGER TO YOUR LAND.
Hajimemashite,* Usagi-san.
I was concerned because your friend is a bit SCARY looking!
I AM?
Yeah.
WELL... I LOOK NORMAL WHERE I COME FROM!
WOW!

*"IT IS A PLEASURE TO MEET YOU FOR THE FIRST TIME."

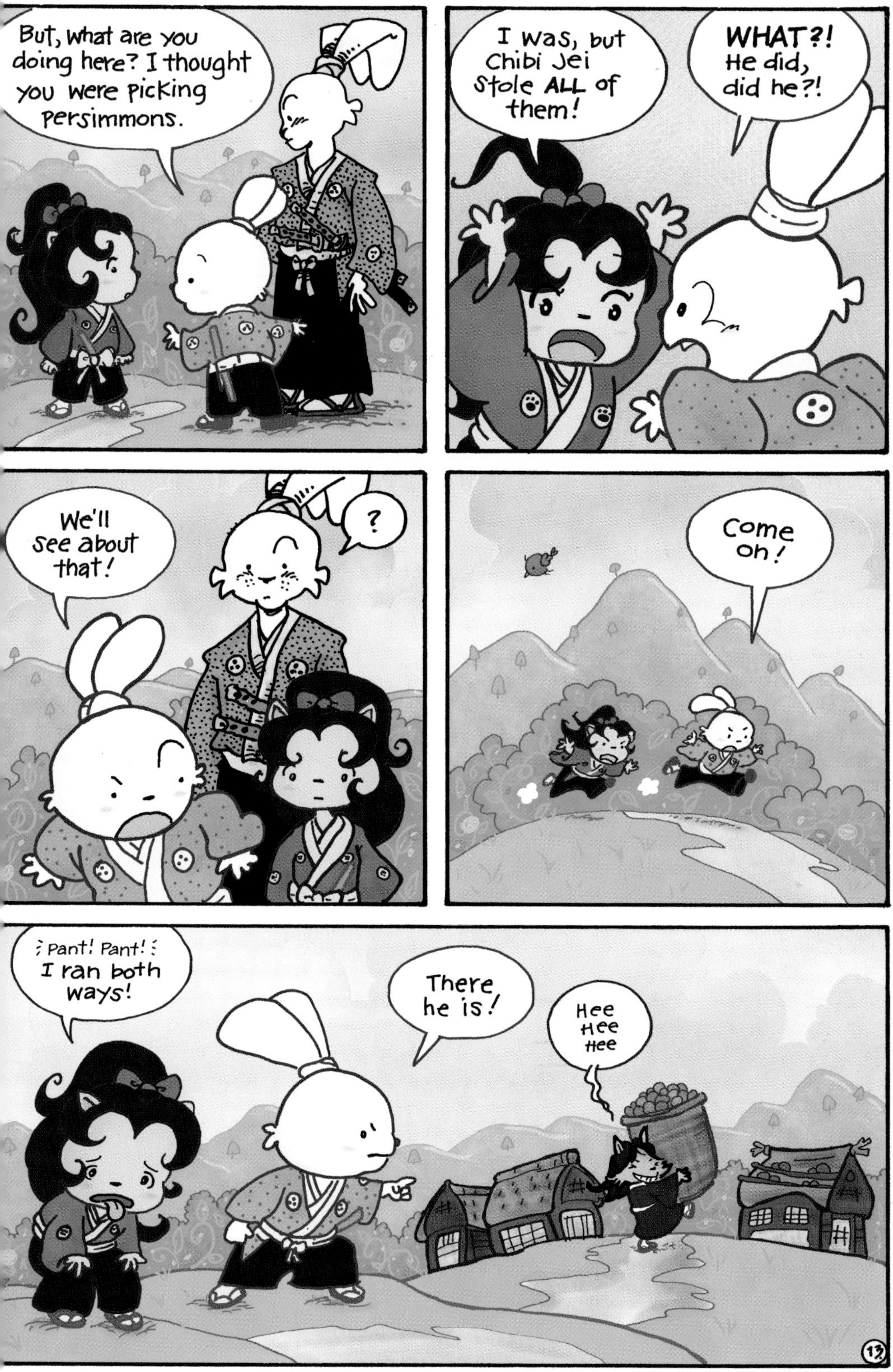
But, what are you doing here? I thought you were picking persimmons.
I was, but Chibi Jei stole ALL of them!
WHAT?! He did, did he?!
We'll see about that!
?
Come on!
; Pant! Pant! ;
I ran both ways!
There he is!
Hee Hee Hee

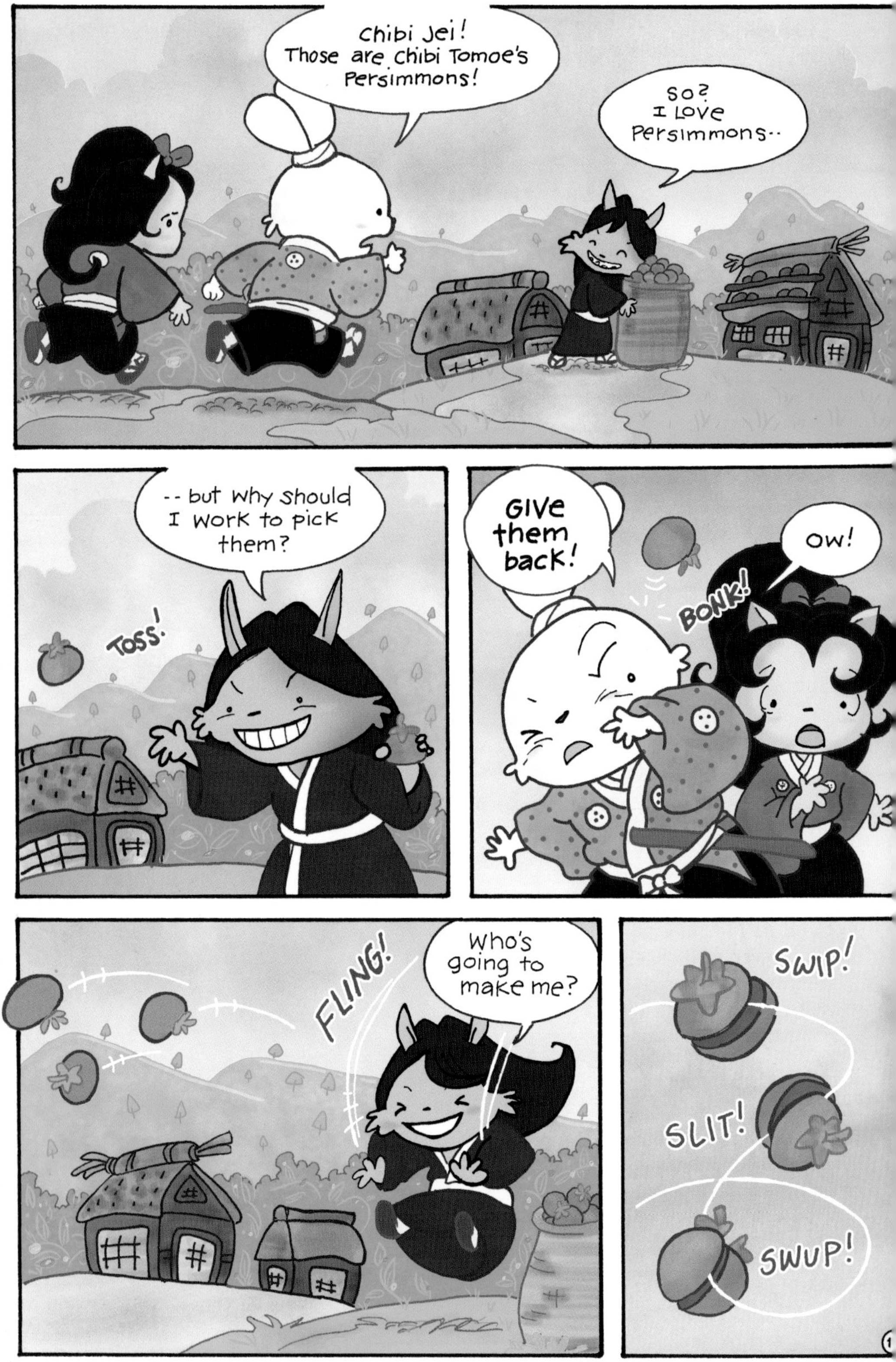
Chibi Jei! Those are Chibi Tomoe's Persimmons!
So? I Love Persimmons..
-- but Why should I work to pick them?
TOSS!
Give them back!
BONK!
OW!
FLING!
Who's going to make me?
SWIP!
SLIT!
SWUP!

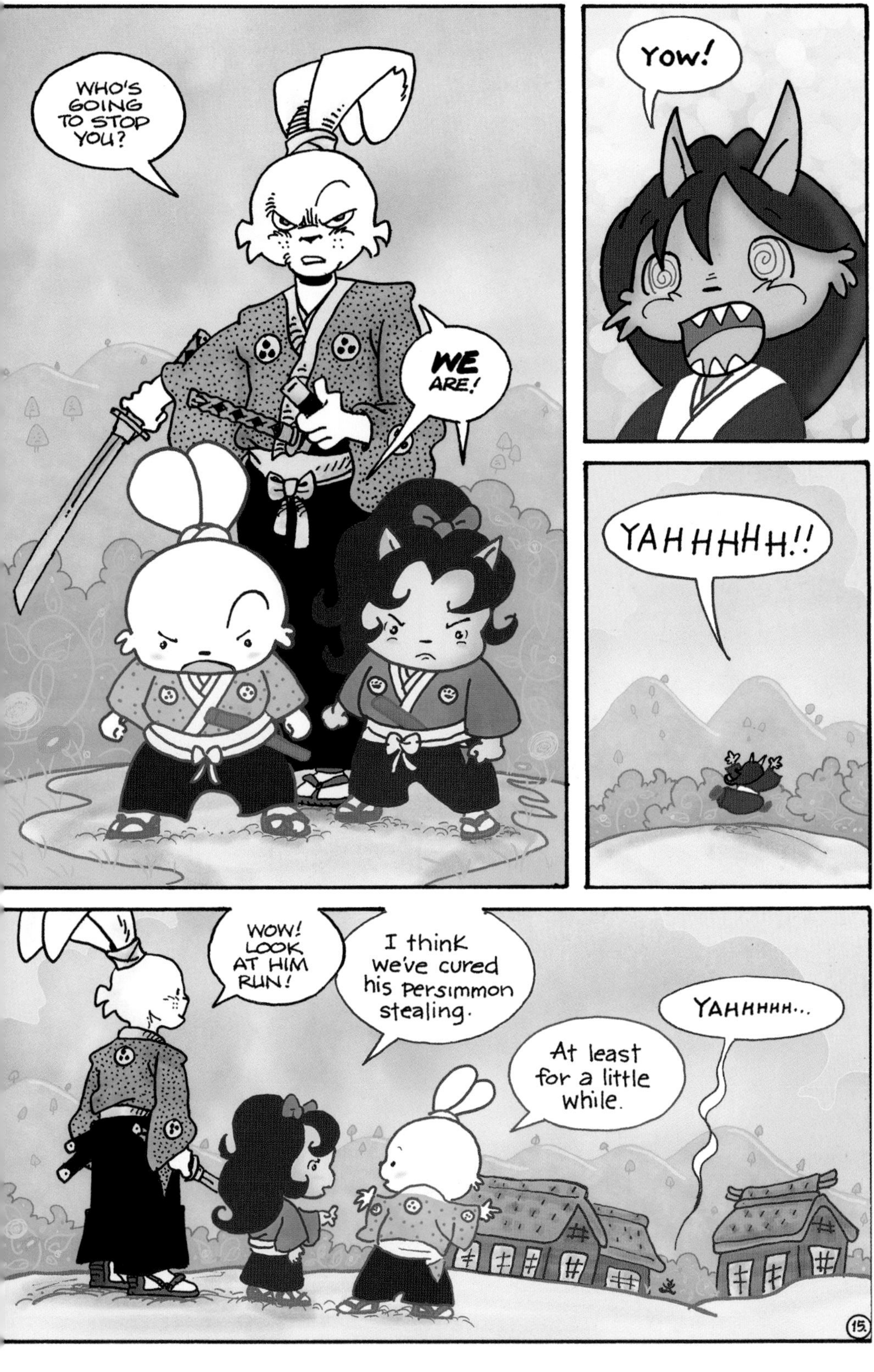
WHO'S GOING TO STOP YOU?
WE ARE!
YOW!
YAHHHHH!!
WOW! LOOK AT HIM RUN!
I think we've cured his persimmon stealing.
At least for a little while.
YAHHHHH...

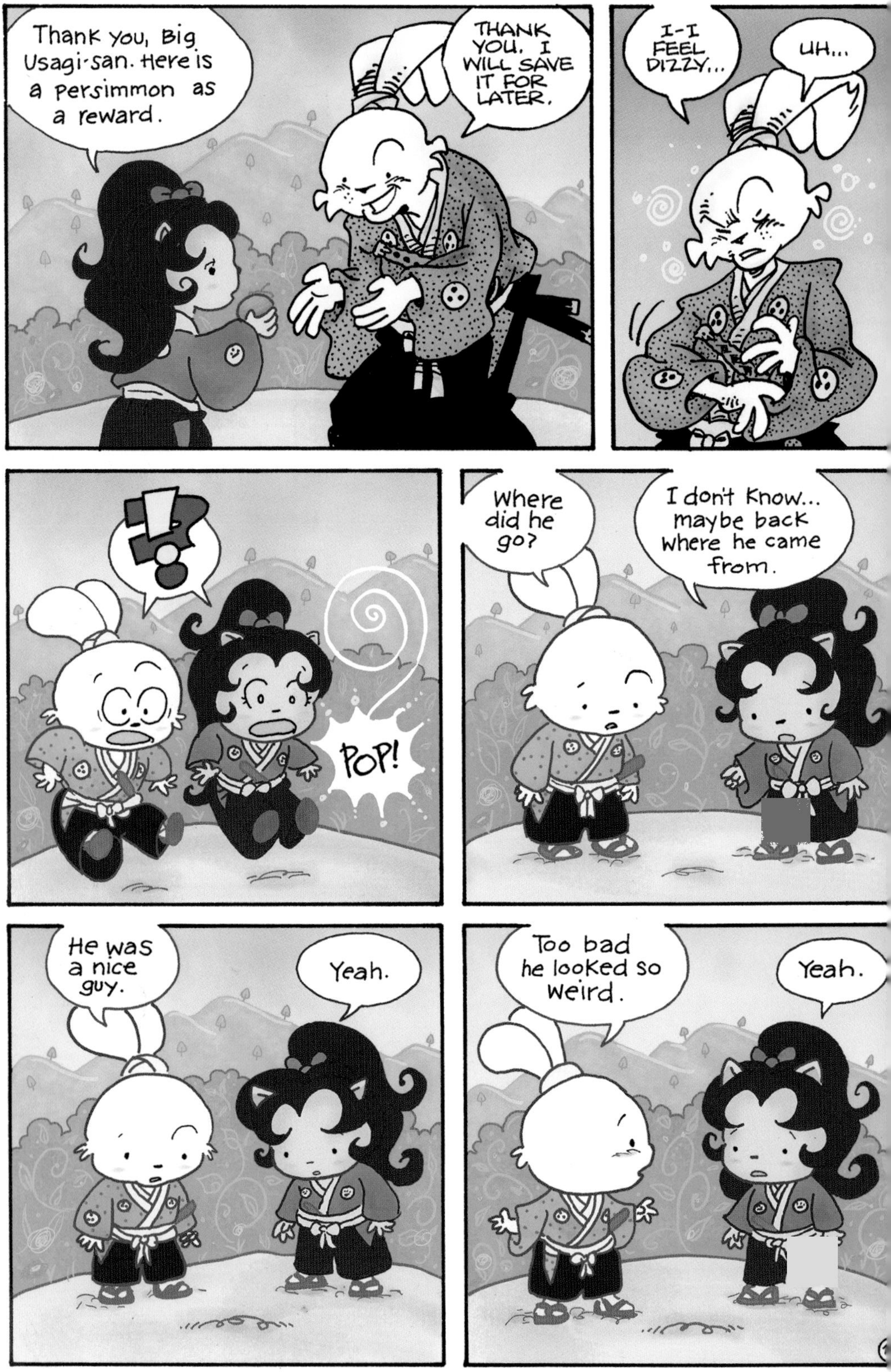
Thank you, Big Usagi-san. Here is a persimmon as a reward.
THANK YOU. I WILL SAVE IT FOR LATER.
I-I FEEL DIZZY...
UH...
!
POP!
Where did he go?
I don't know... maybe back where he came from.
He was a nice guy.
Yeah.
Too bad he looked so weird.
Yeah.

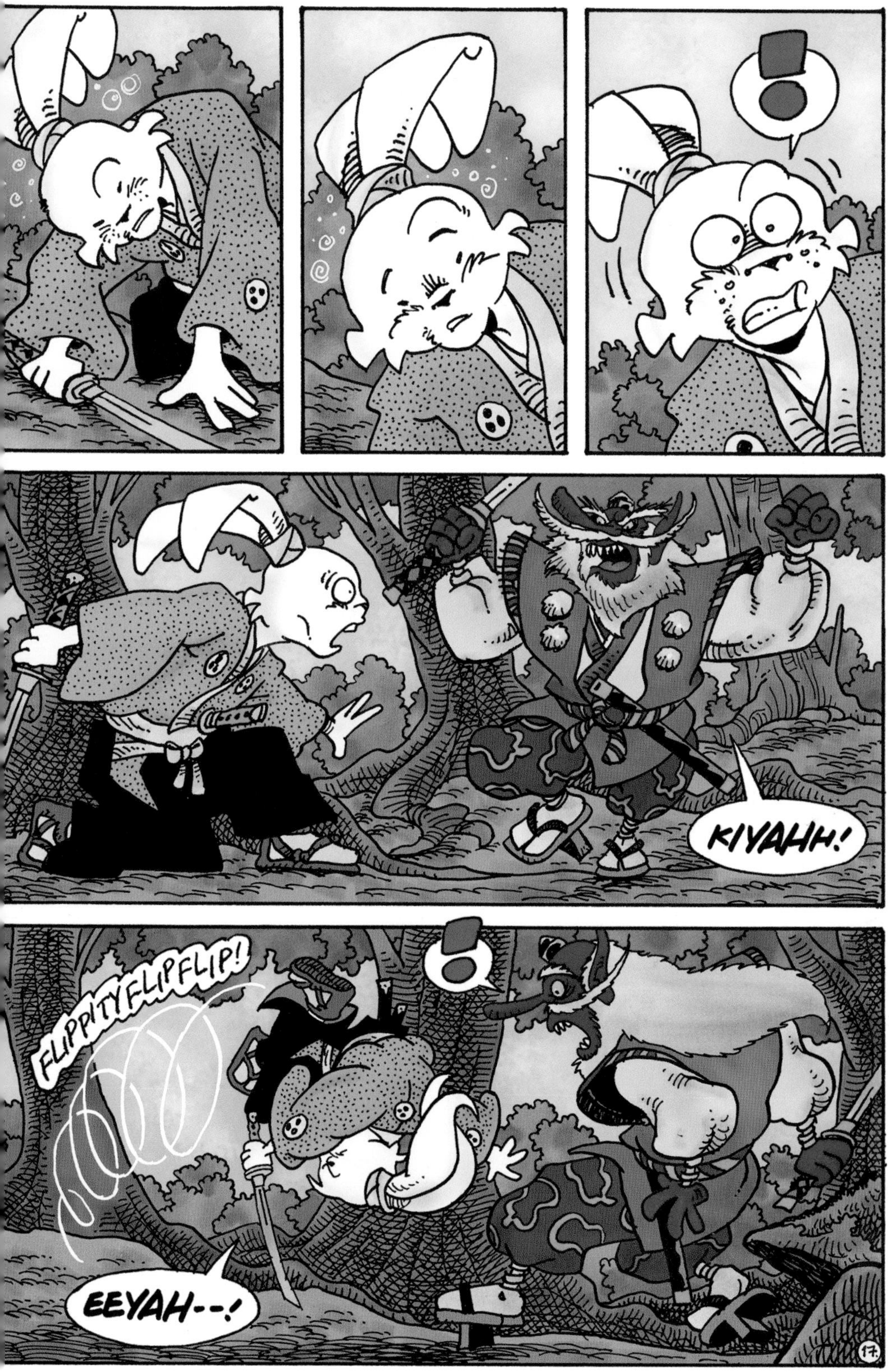
!
KIYAHH!
FLIPPITYFLIPFLIP!
!
EEYAH--!
17

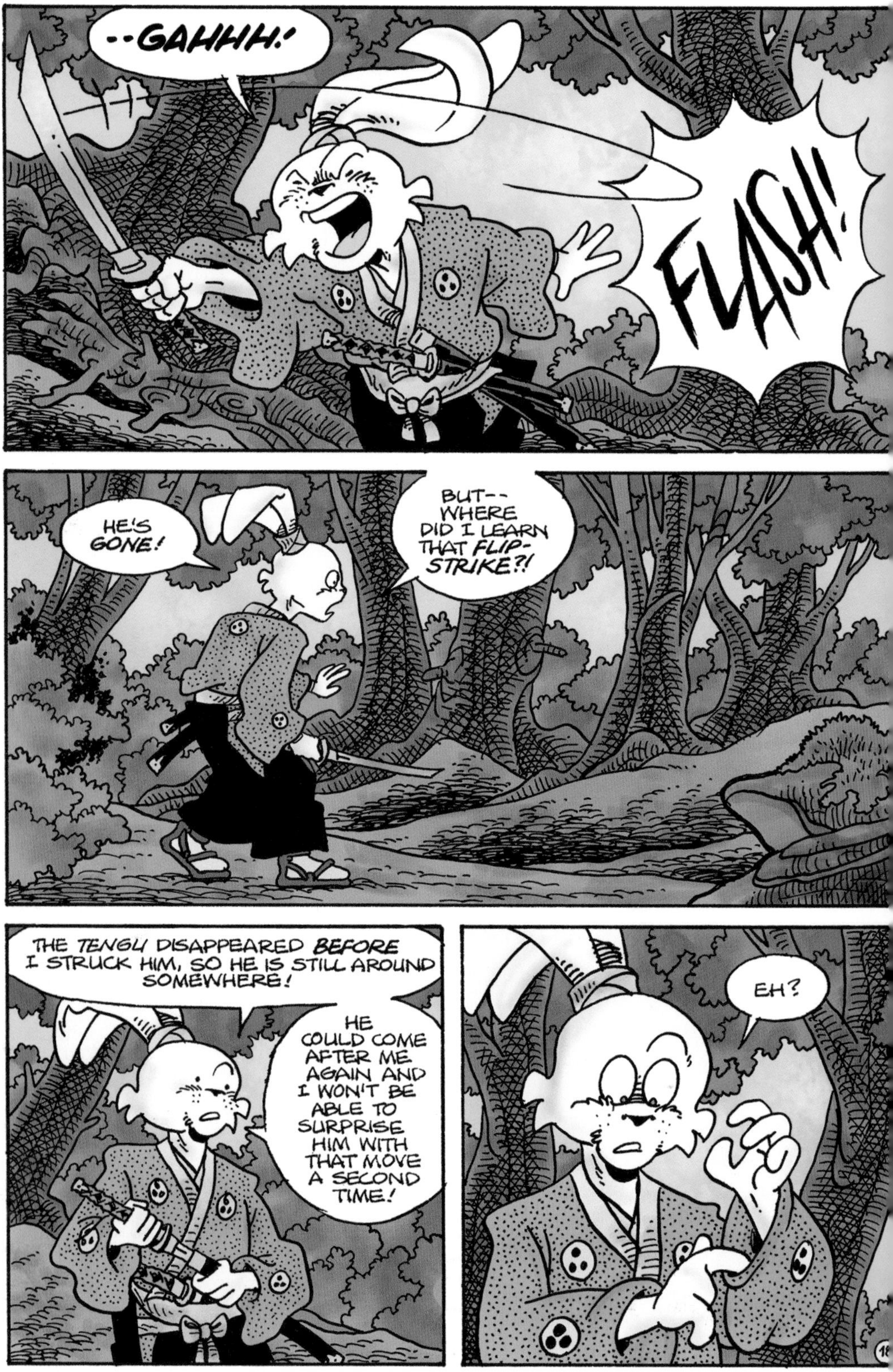
--GAHHH!
FLASH!
HE'S GONE!
BUT--WHERE DID I LEARN THAT FLIP-STRIKE?!
THE TENGU DISAPPEARED BEFORE I STRUCK HIM, SO HE IS STILL AROUND SOMEWHERE!
HE COULD COME AFTER ME AGAIN AND I WON'T BE ABLE TO SURPRISE HIM WITH THAT MOVE A SECOND TIME!
EH?

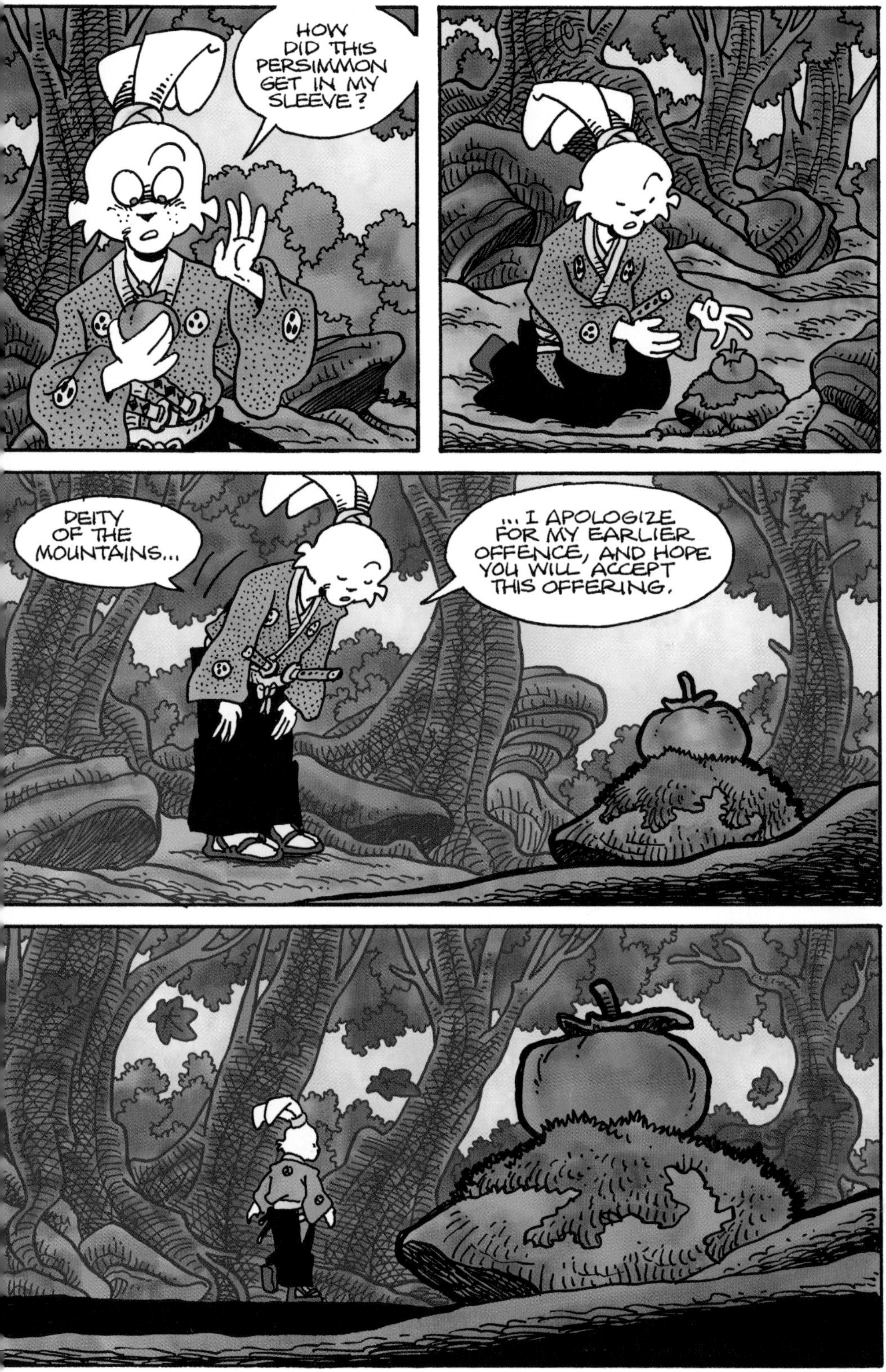
HOW DID THIS PERSIMMON GET IN MY SLEEVE?
DEITY OF THE MOUNTAINS...
...I APOLOGIZE FOR MY EARLIER OFFENCE, AND HOPE YOU WILL ACCEPT THIS OFFERING.

THE END.

MEET THE CREATORS

Photo by Emi Fujii Photography

Stan was born in Kyoto, Japan, and grew up in Hawaii. He began his comic book career by lettering Sergio Aragones' *Groo the Wanderer*. He also worked with Stan Lee, lettering the *Spider-Man* Sunday newspaper strips for 25 years. Stan is most famous for his original creation, *Usagi Yojimbo*, an epic graphic novel series that began in 1984 and now spans more than 35 volumes. It stars Miyamoto Usagi, a samurai rabbit living in early seventeenth century Japan.

Usagi has been published in 16 languages and Stan has been honored with a number of awards including eight Will Eisner Comic Industry Awards, two Harvey Awards including one for Best Cartoonist, the Japanese American National Museum's Cultural Ambassador Award, two National Cartoonists Society Silver Reubens, a Parents' Choice Award, the inaugural Joe Kubert Excellence in Storytelling Award, and an American Library Association Award. Because of his meticulous research into the history, culture, and folklore of Japan, *Usagi Yojimbo* is a favorite

among educators as a curriculum tool. Usagi has been a part of the Teenage Mutant Ninja Turtles in their TV series, comic book crossovers, and toy lines. In 2020 Stan was inducted into the Eisner Awards Hall of Fame. An *Usagi Yojimbo* animated series, produced by Stan, Gaumont Studios, James Wan's Atomic Monster, and Dark Horse Entertainment, is in development for Netflix.

While raising a family, Julie taught art in private schools, community classes, and at the Monart School of Art in Temecula, California. Julie has also been a designer and creator in the craft industry for over 30 years with her own line of T-shirts, rubber stamps, and whimsical illustrations. Her chibi-style work has been sold in museum gift shops, boutiques, and craft fairs throughout the United States.

JUST Sakai is the wife and husband team of JUlie and STan Sakai. JUST Sakai's first collaboration was a tribute to Charles M. Schulz, a 65th anniversary anthology published by Kaboom! in 2015.